To Michael

Contents

Augustus consists mostly of the transcripts, sequenced by date. But the story is explained in the Frontispiece and followed by important sections as shown below. This book is classified as historical fiction.

AUGUSTUS
Narrative of a Slave Woman

Robin Greene

Plain View Press
http://plainviewpress.net

3800 N. Lamar, Suite 730-260
Austin, TX 78756

ISBN: 978-1-935514-07-7
Library of Congress Number: 2010939024

Cover art: Library of Congress
Cover design by Susan Bright

Acknowledgments

I would like to acknowledge my deep gratitude to the following individuals and organizations:

Michael Colonnese, Barbara Presnell, Ruth Kravitz, Pat Roberts, Cristina Francescon, Emily Wright, Dan Greene Colonnese, Ben Greene-Colonnese, Jennifer Britton-Colonnese, Peter Murray, Rebecca Wendleken, Lori Brookman, Margaret Folsom, Laurice Mitchell, Jerry Hendricks, Elton Hendricks, Delmas Crisp, Katie Zybeck, Arleen Fields, Tracy Pearson, Helen Mathews, Kerry Jenkins, Writing Center consultants (current and past), Methodist University Department of English, friends at the Sandhills Dharma Group and Writing and Weymouth Center for the Arts and Humanities.

Frontispiece

Introduction

Even before I offer an introduction to the following manuscript, *Augustus*, a transcription of tapes first recorded in 1937, in Raleigh, North Carolina, I'd like readers to know that this project—just completed—has had a profound impact on my life. As I listened to and transcribed the coming-of-age story of Sarah Louise Augustus—a Fayetteville slave who lived from 1845 to 1939—my own life underwent a transformation. Whether this shift was the direct result of Ms. Augustus's words, I don't know. Suffice it say that as I listened to her unfolding story—spoken in her words, in her voice—my own life story unfolded in unexpected ways. As her life took turns, so did my own. In a sense, our stories became entangled, and this dead woman, who suffered so long ago, seemed to reach back her hand to guide me through my own difficulties to a place of forgiveness and reconciliation.

That said, my story is only *the story behind the story*—not the book's primary focus—so I will put it in its rightful place—behind Sarah Louise Augustus's story—in an addendum and short coda at the end.

For those readers who might be interested in learning how a transcriptionist, working alone on her computer, typing out the words of a stranger, might be so affected, I invite them to read this material. For those readers uninterested in my private woes, I invite them to skip both this introduction and the addendum; frankly, I'll never know.

How I Discovered the Tapes

Some years ago, as I was introducing myself to a new freshman English class at the beginning of a fall semester—I'm an English professor at a small liberal arts university in North Carolina—a young African American woman seated in a middle row raised her hand. I had just told my students that I was professionally interested in women's issues and had recently published a book of women's birthing narratives.

"Oh, oh, Professor Greene," the student blurted out. "If like, you're like interested in women's stories, well there's a bunch of old tapes in my grandmother's house—they're my great, great, great grandmother talking about slavery—the tapes are her story, her *narrative*—like you said. I don't remember much, but my grandmother knows all about them. Yeah, this ancestor was like a slave here in Fayetteville."

Immediately interested, I asked if she had ever listened to the tapes.

"No, maybe a little once," she said. "But my grandmother has. And my mother too, I think. Long time ago. They're on these huge reels. We don't have a machine to play them. My grandmother did. But it broke. I think she threw it out. I don't know. It was a long time ago. I could ask. Like if you're interested, you could come over to my grandmother's house and talk to her. I bet she'd let you borrow them. That might be cool. Like I said, they're something about slaves—my great great great grandmother talking."

I took a moment to look closely at the student—a diminutive young woman wearing jeans and a blue Bob Marley tee-shirt. She had her hair pulled back in a pony-tail, and an orange-colored knapsack lay open on the floor by her feet. A fairly typical student, perhaps a bit more animated than usual. And when she finished talking, she punctuated her invitation to me with an incredibly engaging smile. It lit up the room.

Yes, I told her. I was interested and asked that she see me after class. She nodded.

Then I proceeded to go over the syllabus and course expectations. But my mind was focused on the tapes, and I dismissed class early. Without knowing why, I felt my heart pound.

This student, who asked to be called Sam, short for Samantha, came to see me after class. We made a plan to meet next day and to drive together to her grandmother's home, located just north of Fayetteville. In the meantime, Sam would call and make the arrangement with her grandmother.

Mrs. Henderson, a quiet woman, probably in her late 70s, walked with the aid of a rubber-tipped wooden cane. When she met us at the door of her rather nondescript ranch home on an acre or so of land in a very rural area of Harnett County, she hugged Sam and extended her hand to me. The greeting was warm but formal.

"Samantha told me what you've come for," Mrs. Henderson said. And she walked us through the living room over to the narrow hallway that led to the bedrooms. I noticed that the house, with beige wall-to-wall carpet and well-placed, oversized furniture, was immaculate.

"Grandma, should we just go up?" Sam asked.

"Yes, you and the professor go on up. I'll get us some tea." Mrs. Henderson walked to the kitchen while Sam pulled the rope cord of the fold-down ladder to the attic. We straightened out the creaking stairs, which probably hadn't been used in many years, and proceeded to climb them. At the top, Sam pulled the chain of an exposed-bulb light fixture. However clean and organized the downstairs was, the attic looked in disarray, with piles of household items and dusty cardboard boxes. But Sam knew where the tapes were stored, and crouching low beneath the wide rafters, she made her way across the plywood floor to a wooden box that looked strangely like an infant's coffin. Gingerly, as if a real infant were inside, Sam picked up the box, moved carefully back across the attic to the ladder, and we both descended the stairs.

At the bottom, Sam took the box outside to dust it off, then promised to bring it in and meet us in the living room. When she joined us, Mrs. Henderson and I were already sipping tea—a strange herbal tea, homemade, Mrs. Henderson told us, from a family recipe handed down to her over the generations. I thought I detected some ginseng but, truthfully, couldn't be sure. It was strong, relaxing, and seemed to loosen my tongue.

"The tapes," I began. "What can you tell me?"

"Well, they were first made during the Depression, Professor…"

"Please call me Robin."

"Okay, Robin. It's a long story, and it used to be written down. But the paper got misplaced. I can tell you what I remember."

"Please do." I sipped my tea.

"Originally, they were made during the Works Progress Administration… you know about those oral histories taken from ex-slaves?"

"Yes. Recorded during the 1930s. I know a little about them. I've read…"

"Tell me about yourself first." Mrs. Henderson interjected. "Samantha says you're an English professor at the university."

"That's right. I've been there for over fifteen years. But I'm originally from New York City."

Mrs. Henderson nodded. As she bent to sip her tea, I noticed her thick gray hair was packed neatly into a circular bun.

"A few years ago, I published a book of women's birthing narratives, and I interviewed over two hundred women from around the country about their experiences during childbirth."

"You married? Children?"

"Yes, to another English professor at the university, for about thirty years. We have two boys—one twenty-five and living in Boston, the other seventeen, just graduated from Pine Forest High. Wants to study art, should be attending college in the fall."

"I have four children—all still living, thank God, but spread out across the country. One in San Francisco, the other in Arizona, one in Alaska—military, and one right here in Fayetteville. That's Samantha's mother, my middle child, only girl. We're all very proud of Samantha." Sam nodded from the maroon velveteen club chair where she sat, legs tucked beneath her, and offered us one of her award-winning smiles.

"Yes, Sam is a very bright young woman. Wants to be a history teacher, she tells me," I said.

Mrs. Henderson nodded, leaned forward, and tapped the wooden coffin, which Sam had placed on the coffee table. "History," she said, "very important. These tapes are the words of my great grandmother, Samantha's great, great, great grandmother. They've been up in the attic since 1955, a few years before Samantha's mother was born. We'd just moved here into this house. It was new then; we had it built."

When Mrs. Henderson said this, I felt an odd shiver, as if a ghost had suddenly walked into the room and the temperature had dropped.

"Where did you get them?" I asked.

"Long story. Again, Professor Greene—Robin, Miss Robin—it was all written down, but the paper got misplaced. I wrote down the story, but don't ask me where it is. Put it away for safe keeping. These, the tapes here, they aren't the originals." Mrs. Henderson tapped the coffin again. "No, these are copies made later." She paused, then turned to Sam. "Be a good girl, Samantha. I left some butter cookies on a plate on the kitchen counter. Get them for us."

Sam nodded and left the room.

"She's never really heard them," Mrs. Henderson said. "I'm surprised she even remembered them."

Sam returned in a flash and set a plate of sweet-smelling cookies down by the small coffin.

"Please help yourself, Miss Robin. They're homemade." And Mrs. Henderson looked at me until I picked one up and took a bite.

"Delicious," I said. "Excellent."

"Family recipe." Mrs. Henderson lifted a cookie and nibbled.

"The tapes," I said. "What do you remember about them?"
"The story goes that they were made in Raleigh on a recording machine. Not a tape recorder—wasn't tape back then. Some kind of discs they used. Acetate, I want to say. Presto acetate. Something like that."

"Can we look at what you have? Open the box?" I interrupted.

"Let me just finish. It's an interesting story. Not certain of all the details. I wrote some things down after this woman left. On paper. Probably turn up. I just can't—for the life of me—remember." Mrs. Henderson seemed distracted for a moment and looked up toward the ceiling as if trying to collect her thoughts. But she then gently shook her head. I helped myself to a second cookie.

"Let me see. Supposedly, they were made in 1937. Recorded, I mean. The woman who came by in '55 said I might want them. Told me she had worked for the WPA a long time ago. She was an older woman, but she seemed educated. Nicely dressed. Well spoken. Very polite—yet something about her. Odd. And I couldn't tell if she was white or a woman of color. Of course, I invited her in, though the house was a mess. We were just getting settled. The living room here was full of boxes. I had two children and a new baby. She didn't catch me at a good time. I couldn't tell if she didn't come in because she could see that, or if she never intended to visit. Sort of strange, struck me then."

"You say this woman just rang your doorbell? How did she find you?"

"She said something about being connected with the Library of Congress—this is the part I can't remember. She never did give me her name. But I wrote it all down—what she did tell me. That and other things. Wish I could find that paper. Our conversation must have lasted five minutes. Then she handed me these reel-to-reel tapes. We didn't own a machine to play them on. She brought them in a large paper bag from some New York department store. All she said was that they were interviews of my great grandmother, that they were recorded by a WPA worker in 1937, and that the original discs were stored in Congress, in the Library. Woman said she'd made a copy for our family because she thought we'd like to have them."

"I don't understand." I said.

"Wish I had that paper. What's strange is that the woman refused—politely, of course—to tell me her name. And she was so smooth that I didn't realize until I went to write it all down. I put the date, the time she came, other details. When the babies had their nap, I sat at the kitchen table, wrote down the whole thing, and put the paper in the bag, along with the tapes. But that's all I remember. And that she wouldn't come in, though she seemed tired and had come a long way to find me. She drove a big black Plymouth. Brand-new shiny car. I remember the way it looked in the driveway. Gravel back then. Wasn't paved until '60."

"Sam says you don't have a machine to play them on? But you've heard them. Yes?"

"Oh, yes. Like I've said. I've heard them. More than once." Mrs. Henderson stopped and sipped her tea. "Can't tell you how powerful it is to listen to her—my great grandmother—if that's really who she is. Her voice, her actual voice coming through the years.

I could feel my heart fluttering like the wings of a small bird.

"We bought a tape machine second-hand from our church," Mrs. Henderson continued. "Good machine, worked for years. Portable, with a long cord."

"Has anybody else heard them, the tapes?" I asked.

"I don't think anyone but me has listened to them entirely. They're long. Scratchy. And brittle, almost broken in parts. Need a lot of time to listen. Years ago, after hearing them a second time, I got a notion that they were important, real important, so I brought them to a local historian in Fayetteville and then up to Raleigh. Durham. To Chapel Hill. To the universities. To professors. No one seemed interested. After a time, I got discouraged and put them away. Then I forgot. Everybody's busy." Mrs. Henderson paused and looked at me. Then she shook her head. "Haven't thought about them for years. Till Samantha called the other day."

"But Sam said that they *couldn't* be authenticated. Isn't that right, Sam?"

Sam nodded but deferred to her grandmother.

"Yes," Mrs. Henderson said. "I was told that. One lady at the North Carolina Department of Archives seemed especially excited at first. But there's no record of them in Washington, in the Library of Congress, so she lost interest. I tried calling up there, too. To find that woman—the one who gave me the tapes—nobody ever could determine who she was. She told me that the original discs, on acetate, were stored in the Library of Congress, but no one could locate them. No one knew a thing about them. It's like that woman and those original discs never existed. And like I said, everyone's busy. Nobody wants to be bothered." Mrs. Henderson looked at me, a challenge in her eyes.

"Strange," I said and lowered my eyes, feeling as if I had already failed Mrs. Henderson.

"Like I said, Miss Robin, Professor Greene, I've done all I could. But you're right. It's *strange*. And the part that doesn't make a whole lot of sense is that the woman on the recording, Sarah Louise Augustus, who I'm sure is my great grandmother, *did do* a short interview, a WPA interview. Taken down on paper in 1937—same year as this long taped interview supposedly took place—but that's the only one they have. And that short narrative is the one that's official. Sarah Louise Augustus gave her story to a man in Raleigh, that same year. But this one—on the tapes—was recorded over about three months. It was as if the interviewer knew my great grandmother, lived in Raleigh, and saw her every day—August through October that year. So, we got the official version, the shorter story of her life, and this longer one—which, I believe, is the real story—covers her life right before and during the Civil War."

"And the stories aren't the same?" I asked. On some level, I understood why Mrs. Henderson had gotten the run-around. What she was telling me didn't seem entirely credible.

"That's what comes out on the tapes. You listen. You decide. And if they're fake, well, someone went through a whole lot of trouble." Mrs. Henderson's voice quivered.

"I think they're real, Grandma," Sam piped up. "I've heard some of what's on them, and I think they're real." Sam nodded her head, and this seemed to comfort Mrs. Henderson.

"And the other strange thing," Mrs. Henderson continued, "is that the person doing the interview seemed to want to keep her identity secret. She deleted all her questions, responses, anything that could identify her. She begins each recording session—like an oral diary—with the date. Never says who she is or why she's doing the interviews. Why she's spending so much time. Or who she's working for—what agency, organization. Hard to believe she was on her own—the recording machine must have cost a lot of money back then. This was the Depression. Where'd she get the machine?" Mrs. Henderson looked at me.

"Odd," I said. Then said it again. "Odd."

Mrs. Henderson nodded and sighed. "You want more tea? Samantha, go get the teapot, please."

Sam left the room. Mrs. Henderson and I sat without speaking. When Sam came back, she filled our cups, and Mrs. Henderson continued.

"I want you to hear them. I still have the machine somewhere, but it's been broken for years. But maybe it could be fixed—if I can find it."

Meanwhile, Sam had gotten up again and left the room. When she returned, she had a big claw hammer in her hand.

"I didn't know if you still had that old tape machine, Grandma," Sam said.

"Well, honey, I do somewhere."

"Let's open it up," Sam said. And she knelt by the box. For a moment, it looked as if she might pray.

"Carefully, Samantha," Mrs. Henderson warned. "I wrapped those tapes up in an old dress."

The room went silent but for the creaky sounds of dry nails being pried up through the old coffin wood.

As Sam began to pry, I noticed that the lid must have had forty nails in it—as if there were a dead child inside and nobody had ever intended the box to be opened again.

"This is a coffin," I remarked stupidly.

"That's right," Mrs. Henderson said. "Made for my first-born son, Willis, when he was an infant. Almost died of rheumatic fever—in the '50s—made and hand-carved by my brother, a carpenter. But Willy lived, thank God. I put the tapes there to keep them safe."

The lid squeaked opened, and I could see a number of old reel-to-reel tapes. Maybe ten or more. They were wrapped in an old red-and-white gingham dress. Mrs. Henderson lifted out one of the reels, removed a dried rubber band, and slowly unwrapped a strip of brittle tape.

"They're all here. Numbered in sequence. Nine of them. Like months in a pregnancy."

Nobody spoke for a few awkward moments. It was as if the tapes exerted some sad influence on us. Then, we made some small talk, but the visit was essentially over. When I got up and began to thank Mrs. Henderson for her time, she gently placed the lid back on the coffin and promised me that she'd look for the machine. I told her not to bother, that I could probably locate one.

"I want you to listen," Mrs. Henderson said. "Listen to the very end." And she looked up at me, then began to clean up.

"I'll be in touch," I replied. "And thank you. For everything."

Sam and I quietly transferred the coffin from the coffee table into the back of my old Saturn station wagon. We left the lid unnailed. On the way home, the coffin rattled, and a sort of thrill, coupled with grief, swept over me as we traveled the long stretch of Highway 401 back to school.

The next day, more easily than expected, I located a working tape machine at the university. The Department of Modern Languages had held onto some of their old audio equipment, and Cristina, the department chair and a good friend, had no trouble pulling out the machine from a storage closet in the very building where I teach. I plugged it in, and the reels began to turn. Then, Emily, the school dean and another good friend, gave me permission to borrow the machine for as long as I needed. But before I took the tapes and the machine home, I called Sam and left a message on her cell phone. I wanted her with me when I listened to the first reel.

Later that day, Sam and I sat together in my small office. It was overcast outside, the room was gray, and as I clicked on the machine, Sarah Louise Augustus's voice began to fill the space. Her dialect and accent were strong, her voice thin and high—an old woman's voice—but it had strength and integrity. Even through the distinctive Southern accent and African American dialect, I could hear confidence, clarity, intelligence—the voice of a person who had something to say.

Sam and I listened to about ten minutes of the first reel before she realized she was late for her afternoon class. I promised to wait for her before listening to any more. When she left, I picked up the phone and called the local history museum.

The woman I spoke with connected me to the county historian, an old-timer who remembered Mrs. Henderson. The historian explained that he had referred her to Raleigh and gave me the name and the number of an archivist there.

But I had much to do. The semester had begun, and my Reviewing Composition students already had turned in their writing samples. I had grading, committee work, emails, and phones calls to which to attend. Soon, I became busy with my professional responsibilities. Yet, always, the tapes were on my mind.

Over the next two months, Sam and I managed to listen to only one complete reel. In places it was scratchy, difficult to understand, and a couple of times the brittle tape snapped and had to be spliced. Then I had difficulty coordinating schedules, and Sam's initial enthusiasm for the project waned. At one point, Sam's academic advisor called to express concern about Sam's slipping grades. I checked my grade book and saw that Sam had received low Cs on her last two short essays. Right before midterm, I set up an appointment for Sam to see me, but she didn't show. In class she apologized and complained about being too busy, but I sensed our relationship had cooled. And even when Sam's grades improved, we remained cordial but distant.

All the while during that semester, I continued to email and call historians, professors, and archivists as I attempted to find some way to authenticate the tapes. And although Sam seemed very self-involved and I regretted that she had lost interest in the tapes and in my class, I chalked it all up to her need for autonomy; after all, Sam was a freshman and was adjusting to university life.

The Problem of Authenitcation, Candor, Provenance, and My Decision to Transcribe the Tapes

The authentication of slave narratives—especially those which are purportedly transcripts of oral accounts and come with no official documentation—is intrinsically problematic.

And even authenticated slave narratives that form the bulk of the WPA's Oral History Project exist primarily as transcripts recreated from the pen-and-paper interviews, edited and typed after the fact, and consequently reflect the biases and diction of the interviewers as well as those of the subject interviewed.

And in those rare instances where audio recordings exist (to which print transcription could be ostensibly compared) the question of "candor" arises. The subjects being interviewed were invariably black; the interviewers were mostly white, and the issue of trust between the races was certainly a factor.

It is also important to note that historians often question the truth of even the most canonized narratives because many slaves who told their stories had been children at the time of their enslavement, and their recollections were suspect.

Moreover, black parents would prevent their offspring from overhearing less-than-positive comments about slavery, and so kept these conversations private lest their children innocently blab and incriminate adult members of their family and community. Worse, some black children were recruited as unofficial spies and bribed with food and other treats to inform against adults.

Furthermore, because very young children were too little to be useful, they often escaped abuses their older siblings endured and did not have as many bad experiences about which to report.

Also noteworthy is the understanding that memory is fluid and vulnerable to the vagaries of inconsistent and changeable perceptions. The ex-slaves interviewed were old, and even under the best of circumstances, memories falter.

And then there was the question of the tapes' provenance. If, on many levels, *the material* on the tapes was problematic, *the origin* of these tapes was even more so. Where did they come from? Could I trust Mrs. Henderson's story about them? If the acetate originals were made during the 1930s, what had become of them? Were the tapes from the coffin accurate copies? If not, who might have altered them and to what purpose?

I am not an historian, however, so I only noted these problems. I had neither the background nor training to do more.

Early that fall I spoke to an historian, a colleague at my university. He was intrigued by the tapes and referred me to an African American scholar at another local university. This scholar then passed me along to another, a professor at a highly regarded university north of Fayetteville, who had heard about the Sarah Louise Augustus tapes but hadn't spoken directly to Mrs. Henderson. Although her specialty was the antebellum period of North Carolina and she had a special interest in local persons, she told me quite bluntly that the tapes were a forgery. She had accurate records of the more than 2,300 WPA interviews, and the Augustus interview was about seven pages and already part of the published collection. There was "no way," she assured me, that this lengthy interview could be "the real deal."

During the month of December, at the very end of the semester, I finally got to speak by telephone to a big-shot African American scholar associated with an ivy-league northern university, and he expressed an interest in "purchasing" the tapes. He offered me, or rather Mrs. Henderson, $5,000 so that he could use the material as the basis for a work of fiction. But in the end, he too assured me that the tapes could not possibly be authenticated, as there was no official record of them nor any existing interview of similar length. Knowing full well that Mrs. Henderson would not be interested in selling the tapes, I nonetheless extended the scholar's offer to her. She was clearly insulted, and I found myself apologizing on his behalf.

That January break between semesters was a difficult time for me. I was having marital, health, and sleep problems. In an effort to make peace, my husband suggested that he and our younger son would drive to Connecticut to his mother's house so that they and my older son, Dan, who was living in Boston, could all celebrate Christmas together. It was to be the first Christmas in more than twenty-five years that I would miss, but I was relieved not to have to make the long trip up and down I-95, and relieved to have snatched some free time I could call my own.

Delayed on their return trip by a heavy snow storm, my husband and son were gone for nine days. I used the time, especially the sleepless nights, to listen to the tapes. It was the first of three times that I would listen to them in their entirety. And it was during this first hearing that I felt my life begin to shift.

Suffice it to say that I had just completed a long and difficult semester, and I was no closer to authenticating the tapes than I had been that first week. I was tired and frustrated. No one with whom I had communicated about the Augustus tapes had offered me even a shred of hope that they could be authenticated. And strangely, I was being treated with something like disdain—which struck me as odd, very odd. On a deep visceral level, I believed—as did Mrs. Henderson and Sam—that the tapes were authentic. Yet on another level, I'd internalized the strange animosity directed at me, and I'd started to doubt myself—perhaps even to feel a little schizophrenic. On one hand, I was a professor engaged in a legitimate academic enterprise; on the other hand, I was a middle-aged woman in search of a ghost.

But perhaps I've said enough for now about the origins of the tapes. By the time my family came home from Connecticut, I had decided—bravely or stupidly—to begin transcribing them myself. Busy as my life was, I thought it a smarter use of what little free time I had. I'd become frustrated with dead-end emails, phone calls, and all the insulting insinuations about the authenticity of the tapes and my interest in them.

I worked a bit over my January break and decided on a Monday, Wednesday, Friday morning transcription schedule. Then, I planned to spend the next summer devoted to the project.

I contacted Mrs. Henderson with my plan, and she was thrilled to think that the tapes might one day be available to the public in book form. At first, we came to a verbal agreement that if I found a publisher—and I explained to her the process and possible difficulties involved—that we would split the advance and whatever small monies the book might generate. I told her that I myself was not interested in profiting from the sale of the book, and even felt some moral compunction about so doing. Mrs. Henderson understood, and, in fact, agreed. So she decided that her share of the book's proceeds would go to some charity or non-profit to help understand slavery's legacy in North Carolina. Sarah Louise Augustus would be credited as the book's author; I would be merely noted as its editor and transcriptionist. Mrs. Henderson and Sam would be generously recognized in an acknowledgment.

Community Reactions to My Project, The Process of Transcribing the Tapes, and My Own Background

As a natural result of my enthusiasm for the transcription project, I began to talk to others living in and around Fayetteville—students, colleagues, and friends whose personal histories were often connected with Fayetteville's past. In fact, even the local newspaper picked up the story, and the community of interested people grew. I began to receive snail mail, phone calls, and emails. Some friendly, some not.

People called my office at the university, but these were usually friendly calls. Hate mail—usually with no return address—arrived courtesy the postal service. One missive threatened that the KKK might come and pay me a visit. But the handwriting was shaky and the message so incoherent that I simply dismissed it. Essentially, the people who contacted me fell into three broad categories: the first group was composed of well-wishers, mostly African Americans who were genuinely interested in Sarah Louise Augustus's narrative and wanted to see it in print; the second group was composed of curious and occasionally suspicious locals who worried about how I, a northerner and white woman, had become interested in the project. They were predominately white Southerners who seemed driven by their discomfort. The third group was composed of those who seemed, frankly, hostile—not only toward my project but also toward me.

This group seemed to consist almost exclusively of white men who had family roots to the antebellum, slaveholding South. Their attitude can best be characterized as aggressive, possessive (as if they owned this piece of history that no "outsider" was entitled to discuss), and angry (though this emotion seemed cloaked and not particularly threatening). I was asked repeatedly what "right" had I to tell this story. They challenged the very idea that I might have the authority to take an unauthenticated manuscript and present it as "fact" to the public. And they all wanted to know what my *real* interest in Southern history might be. The insinuation was that I, a Northern interloper, had come down to stir up trouble.

Clearly, for some, I had intruded into a place I wasn't welcome. As a Northerner—connected by a long and eventful history to generations of other Northerners—I had accidentally—or not so accidentally— trespassed. Perhaps I hadn't bothered to read the warning signs, or more troubling, hadn't realized where these signs were posted, or if I had discovered them, didn't understand just how to decode them.

Although I have lived in North Carolina most all my adult life, I will always be an outsider, an intruder. Southern hospitality, I soon learned, extends just so far.

As many from both the North and South know, Southerners still call those who come from the North, "Yankees." It's a term of debated etymology. The *Oxford English Dictionary* cites a few possible contenders for its derivation: one coming from a pirate named "Yankee Dutch" (c.1683) and suggesting that perhaps New Englanders, "whose commercial enterprise outran their moral scruples" were much like pirates; the next coming from a Cherokee word "eankke," meaning "coward" (c.1789); and, of course, the last coming from the popular and still current song "Yankee Doodle" that dates from 1775, during the Revolutionary War, and was sung by the British to insult their North American enemies in battle.

Whatever its origins, the word "Yankee," used as it is by Southerners today, predates the Civil War and is most certainly a pejorative. What's more, if a Northerner comes to live permanently in the South, that individual is called a "damn Yankee"—a term Southerners use, often accompanied by a knowing smile and slight nod of the head, intended as both a sort of passive-aggressive welcome and a sign of contemporary truce—not forgiveness. In this way, a Northern transplant would feel the strike but could not challenge the blow.

So why do unwanted Northerners insist on coming to the South in such numbers and with such frequency? Does the presence of damn Yankees constitute another wave of Northern aggression? And if so, is it an unconscious assertion of some Northern sense of superiority? Another way to insist that we "won the war"? Or do Northerners move south like they move to Nebraska, New Mexico, or to California—because of jobs, living conditions, and a plethora of other reasons? Or, perhaps, as Southerners seem to suspect, we move down in droves not just to take advantage of employment opportunities and warmer weather but to interfere with the social machinery of southern living.

For there still exists an antagonism between North and South—begun before the Civil War and continuing today—and as much as I'd like to ignore it, I can't. This book won't let me; the community in which I live has reminded me that, in fact, this underlying tension makes Southerners *Southerners;* it is the force that makes them still want to identify themselves as distinct from their Northern neighbors. It is my belief that they don't want this tension resolved or—and perhaps I'm being a little unfair here—even examined. The tension to which I refer has become rooted in literary and social traditions, and to resolve it, some might argue, would be tantamount to admitting cultural defeat—a defeat worse than the one accepted almost one hundred and fifty years ago.

Also, perhaps more than any other Southern state, North Carolina was divided about secession. It didn't leave the Union officially until May 20, 1861, and was—according to many historians—the last of the eleven states to join the Confederacy. North Carolina had a rather large and vocal population of non-slave owners, anti-slavery Quakers, and free blacks.

When asked to express themselves by popular vote as to whether to convene a special session of the state General Assembly to discuss the matter of secession, voters chose the status quo—not to convene but rather to stay the course, which meant remaining part of the Union. Only when the Secretary of War under the newly-elected President Lincoln called for North Carolina to send 75,000 soldiers to fight their neighbor South Carolina during the military effort to defend Fort Sumter, did Governor John Ellis take action to secede from the United States. North Carolinians, I believe, have always been conflicted about this early lack of a clear popular mandate to join the Confederacy, and this ambivalence has been deeply embedded in the state's political psyche.

And then, of course, there's the issue of race. When I began this project, my first impulse was to blur the fact that I'm a white woman and Sarah Louise Augustus was an African American. I thought the tape would speak for itself; after all, I was just a transcriptionist—color was unimportant, for the words were *hers*, not mine. Like a medium, the words of the dead would simply flow through me.

But the community here in Fayetteville *reacted strongly* to the idea of a white woman presenting a black woman's story. And they reacted, not surprisingly, along what used to be euphemistically called "the color line." Many whites treated me suspiciously, as though I were about to accuse them once more of being slaveholders. Underneath their polite interest was an underlying hostility, a feeling that, because I was an outsider, I would misrepresent Southern culture and slander them. I spoke to descendants of slave owners, many of whom wished to remain anonymous. I spoke candidly and, I believe, they did as well—but only just so far. Every time I scratched beneath the surface, I encountered some layer of resistance too stubborn to penetrate.

Even the mention of slavery seems to provoke a kind of collective guilt among those whose ancestors participated in the slave-system, either directly by owning slaves or indirectly by simply being a member of a society that allowed slavery to become such an integral part of cultural and socio-economic life for over two hundred years. Also beneath the surface is the notion that to say anything against the past would be *bad manners* and constitute a dishonoring of history itself, along with the dishonoring of one's ancestors.

But these are sentiments I have only gleaned. And from time to time, there seems to be some government initiative afoot to deal with this guilt. Perhaps an initiative, such as officially apologizing for slavery, will be acted upon and legislation will result. It's hard to say; these public acknowledgments seem particularly difficult for North Carolinians. Although there has been real talk about them, apologies as recompense seem insufficient and perhaps suspect. But I could be wrong. It wouldn't be the first time.

In *Ordeal by Fire: The Civil War and Reconstruction*, historian James M. McPherson explains that antebellum Northerners were often thought to possess "a form of vulgar Yankee materialism," while the "South's ideal image of itself portrayed country gentlemen as practicing the arts of gracious living, hospitality, leisure…chivalry toward women, honor toward equals, and kindness toward inferiors" (33).

And though McPherson refers to the antebellum South, a more contemporary version of this stereotype, I believe, exists today—both in Fayetteville, and, I presume, in countless other Southern towns.

On the day-to-day level of social exchanges and commercial interactions, Southerners are very polite, smile often, are quick to say hello to strangers, hold doors open for one another, and wait patiently in check-out lines with a kind of chivalrousness that embodies moral superiority. No doubt, these attitudes and behaviors are kind, well-intended, and culturally bred into the native Southerner. In fact, these native behaviors do form a moral backbone that allows inhabitants to stand tall even when they carry within themselves a hidden legacy of defeat.

Personally, I am grateful for this politeness, though I confess that I am confused by it as well. Few people—neither native Southerners nor transplanted Northerners—have the time or inclination to sort through the muddle of often contradictory undercurrents of Southern culture. And these undercurrents, often swift and powerful, cause a vague but certain malaise. And just how much of this malaise is a result of the history of Southern race relations or the result of other factors unrelated to race I can't tell. Certainly, race in the South carries historical baggage so heavy that it's sometimes impossible to lift.

What I do know is that after the article about my project was published in the local newspaper, I was contacted by a number of residents from the black and white communities. The majority of whites with whom I talked were descendents of slave owners. And it is interesting to note a couple of similarities in what they said. I was often told upfront that their long-dead relatives were poor farmers who had worked in the fields alongside their slaves and had treated them like "brothers" and "sisters." Furthermore, some whites insisted that black and white were "always very close back then" and that poor white slave owners were in a better position to understand the essential experience of slavery in a way that their wealthier white neighbors could not.

North Carolina was a relatively poor state, and the experience of slavery was very different here than it was on the large plantations. I learned that poverty—at least white ancestral poverty—can be a badge of honor and that it can excuse behavior by suggesting that perpetrators are victims too. In essence, the subtextual message I received in these discussions went something like: 1) keep your nose out of our business—you can never understand, so don't judge; 2) we didn't do anything wrong—our ancestors were poor folks and therefore blameless; and 3) I don't see anyone else digging up this stuff—only a Yankee would be this arrogant and aggressive.

So I did a little homework and found that yes, most North Carolina slaveholders were relatively poor—only four families in the entire state of North Carolina owned big plantations with three hundred or more slaves. Most slave owners had holdings of fewer than twenty slaves. Owning twenty or more slaves entitled a person to be called a planter—and thus call the property he or she farmed a "plantation." A property with fewer than twenty slaves was simply called a "farm," and the owner of such a property, a "farmer." By 1860, according that year's census, blacks comprised 25 to 50% of the country's population. Many white families owned single individual slaves who—as their white descendants claimed—worked alongside their masters in the fields or as servants alongside their mistresses in the house. In 1860—when that important last pre-Civil War census was taken—there were 809 white families in Cumberland County, the county in which Fayetteville is located, that owned as many as a dozen but fewer than twenty slaves. Indeed, these farms were small.

What do these facts reveal? I guess the analysis depends on who you are and how you're invested. To the white descendants of slaveholders with whom I spoke—and perhaps I'm being presumptuous here—these facts support the notion that their ancestors treated their black slaves as individuals and as unique human beings because these numbers and the way they configure to create family groups and small social communities suggest close, continual contact between the two races. Blacks depended on whites and whites depended on blacks, and their exchanges suggest a mutual reliance that was substantive and profound—emotionally, psychologically, culturally. But that's not to say that close contact meant equality, because everyone knows it didn't. Interracial contact was governed by strict governmental laws, by social rules and conventions, and by deep racial prejudice—the ghosts of which can be easily felt today. In fact, perhaps the anger I aroused with this project came directly from stepping on the toes of those ghosts. So although I could further speculate about the meaning of these facts, instead I'll just back off. As I've said, I'm an English professor, not a historian.

And as I previously mentioned, when I talked to members of the black community, their reactions to my project were essentially very different—and, in fact, overwhelmingly positive. Although initially I worried that they would question my motives and react suspiciously to my desire to discuss slavery, I was wrong. Those in the black community to whom I spoke seemed gratified that some strange northern white woman, an English professor, would take on such a project. Unlike the subtext that stirred beneath my conversations with white Southerners, the subtext from black Southerners seemed to be: 1) pursue this subject; 2) be accurate; and 3) we know you can do it.

I have yet to account for this unexpected confidence. The African American community seemed to believe in my ability to complete this project, and without their support, I never could have succeeded.

At this point, I feel it is appropriate to say something about my own background. I was brought up in a Jewish home, first in a New York City apartment, then in a suburban house on Long Island. My mother is a diehard atheist, my father is a traditional believer with a strong agnostic streak, and my only sibling, an older brother, well, I'm not sure what he believes.

Growing up, I was close to both my maternal grandparents, who came to America from Bessarabia, a small country that no longer exists. In 1917, it was subsumed by Russia, and my grandparents spoke only Russian and Yiddish when they immigrated in 1921. Later, Bessarabia would become part of Romania and then Moldova. My paternal grandparents came from Russia and Germany, but I know very little about their histories—only that my paternal grandmother remembered seeing the Moscow ballet when she a young girl and that my paternal grandfather left Germany when he was an infant.

From my mother, I grew up hearing stories of Russian atrocities— stories that she passed down to me from her own mother because my grandmother refused to discuss these directly with me. My mother told me that her mother's family experienced the infamous 1905 pogrom of Kishinev and that my grandmother, a girl of four at the time, remembered that bloody pogrom her entire life. But these Jewish victims, like many American ex-slaves, felt somehow responsible for their victimization and therefore were reluctant to share their stories.

So mostly, I know about my heritage through my maternal line. I know that my grandparents left the city of Kishinev, Bessarabia, which is now called Chisinau, Moldova, and that by the time they landed in the U.S., they were virtually penniless. They arrived in New York with their only child, my Aunt Lee, but they left all other family behind as they escaped Kishinev for the proverbial "better life." My grandfather was nineteen when they arrived, and my grandmother was sixteen.

I also know that my maternal grandfather was descended from the Kohanim Levites, a branch of the Jewish tribe of Levi from which Moses and Aaron were supposedly descended. Although he was orphaned as a baby, his lineage was known, and he was adopted and raised by a rabbi. I don't know much more about my maternal grandfather and grandmother, other than that they were married very young—grandfather at seventeen, grandmother at fourteen—and soon had their first child, the above-mentioned daughter Lee, and that they lived rather comfortably inside the city of Kishinev, where my grandfather was a successful, self-employed tailor.

Soon after the family of three arrived in America, my grandparents lost contact with those family members they left behind. Some relatives "just disappeared" and other relatives immigrated to Austria, only to perish in the Nazi Holocaust. In short, no one else made it out of Europe, and both sides of my extended family evaporated into history. On a series of trips to Israel during the 1960s and 1970s, my maternal grandparents made attempts to locate survivors, but they never succeeded.

Although I don't practice the religion of my childhood, my early "Jewish training" has, to some degree, stuck with me. As a young girl, I walked alone to the local orthodox temple every Saturday. On holidays, my father came with me. Until the age of ten, I was a staunch believer in God and prayed every day. For many years my parents kept a strictly kosher household, but by the time I reached thirteen, they had abandoned any adherence to dietary restrictions and enjoyed eating bacon and shrimp.

So what was my early "Jewish training" and how has it stuck with me? Well, it exists as a series of contradictions—that God is central to Jewish consciousness but that many Jews, especially after the Holocaust, are inclined to be atheists; that Jews are God's chosen people but if history is any predictor of the future, I should expect to be the target of hatred; that in a group of non-Jews, it is normal to feel paranoid, but I should never discuss that feeling with a goy, a gentile. My training has left me feeling alienated, not part of the American mainstream, but feeling intrinsically connected to a persecuted people and to a way of life. Another contradiction—and one that I believe is very typical of many American Jews—is a love-hate relationship I have with "being Jewish," an inheritance that, according to Jewish law, is something neither I nor any Jew can ever disown. Regardless of what religion a Jew might adopt, if a person is born a Jew, that person will die a Jew. I think the same goes for being black.

It's interesting to note here as a sidebar that historically both Jews and blacks have been classified according to their maternal "blood lines"—an odd but still current term. Suffice it to say that Jewish "blood," like black "blood," runs through the mother's lineage. A black mother and a white father will produce an offspring that society will consider black. A Jewish mother and a Christian father produce an offspring that society (or at any rate, German society during the Holocaust) considers Jewish. Historically, many societies use this same matrilineal system.

As a young woman, I once tried to talk to my Russian-Bessarabian grandfather (who, by the way, only wished to be thought of an American) about my upcoming marriage to my Catholic-raised fiancé. He refused to discuss it and considered this "intermarriage" a crime and further implied that perhaps the real reason that I'd consider such a marriage is that I'd want to save my future children from the next Holocaust, which because of my own heritage and the system by which my children would be classified, I couldn't. But when I would try to reason with him about how there couldn't be a next war against Jews, he'd simply laugh, make a large cutting motion with his arm, and yell, "Fartik"—the Yiddish word he inevitably used to conclude any conversation he didn't wish to continue. The word literally means "finished," but is often used to express the notion that the subject under discussion is to be ended for now and for all time.

But unlike skin color that is immediately visible, my Jewishness is more hidden, less obvious—especially because, as so many Jews themselves have remarked, I don't look particularly Jewish. There's a kind of back-handed compliment that Jews give to such a girl who doesn't look typically Semitic; they call her a "shikse," which is a Yiddish word literally defined as "a girl who is gentile," but which has come to mean: a girl who is pretty in a typically non-Jewish way or a girl who could "pass" as a non-Jew. Growing up, I had strawberry-blond hair and nondescript features, and these traits were considered pluses in the Jewish community. It's the Jewish counterpart of being a light-skinned black. So, I have inadvertently "passed" as gentile for much of my life, and I have sometimes felt ashamed for doing so.

All this to say that my connection with this transcription project became personal. I felt drawn to the Augustus narrative because Sarah Louise's courage to meet her personal and social challenges gave me courage to face my own challenges. As she came of age, the world around her, the very fabric of her life, was being torn apart, and yet she found the strength to respond effectively. In a world that didn't encourage or teach young black women—girls really, for Sarah Louise's story begins when she is young—how to live, she found the wherewithal to persevere, to triumph. Although her life was so different than my own life has been, I recognized in her story our essential human condition. Of course, it is important to note that Sarah Louise's life was caught in the very dramatic shifts of national identity and civil war and that her struggles were particularly well suited to throw into high relief our own, perhaps less dramatic, struggles for meaning and identity.

Constrained by her skin color and gender, living within the narrow parameters of a racist society, Sarah Louise emerges from these pages as a living sister, a woman to whom—regardless of color, sex, or age—I hope, readers will feel connected.

Race, as we're now coming to realize, is an artificial cultural construct that has little grounding in biology. It's a rather superficial designation that historically has been used effectively to divide and exploit. The Nazis referred to the Jews as a "race" and published articles and drawings depicting them with dark, shifty eyes, bulbous or hooked noses, and blubbery lips. Sometimes we use the word "race" as a stand-in for a cultural or national identity. We call Native Americans or the Chinese "a race of people" in recognition of our need to see "the other" as not "one of us." Yet according to the American Anthropological Association:

> With the vast expansion of scientific knowledge in this century… it has become clear that human populations are not unambiguous, clearly demarcated, biologically distinct groups. Evidence from the analysis of genetics (e.g., DNA) indicates that most physical variation, about 94%, lies within so-called racial groups. Conventional geographic 'racial' groupings differ from one another only in about 6% of their genes. This means that there is greater variation within 'racial' groups than between them. (www. aaanet.org, "Statement on Race," May 17, 1998)

And so it is through multiple lenses that readers might look as they read the transcribed manuscript that follows. Through one lens, readers might find the Augustus narrative a complete fraud, a fiction—an interesting but implausible tale. Through another lens, readers might see the narrative as an historical text—American slavery uncensored. Or they may view the manuscript as a missing text of the oral slave narrative canon and either welcome or reject it—as some readers, I suspect, might not be too happy with its contents. Or perhaps readers might see the story as a feminist text, in which a young woman grapples with gender and oppression in a misogynist society.

Let me reiterate the fact that I am not an historian. Nevertheless, as I transcribed the tapes, my interest in all things related to the Civil War was piqued. I did much reading over the years it took me to complete this project.

Also, I feel I must apologize for any inaccuracies of names, dates, or facts that Ms. Augustus offers here. Memory, as I've mentioned earlier, is neither static nor completely trustworthy. At various points—and ironically my own memory fails me now because I can't remember at which points exactly—I wondered how Ms. Augustus's recollections could sometimes be so accurate and yet at other times so antithetical to the historical record. Yet, truth be told, I didn't—and still don't—really care. Her memories, I believe, were honest, and I feel privileged to present them.

In fact, at various points in my own reading of the antebellum and Civil War periods, I felt like I was watching Akira Kurosasawa's *Roshomon*. Even if readers haven't seen the movie, I'm sure they're familiar with its premise that the truth lies in the eyes of the witness. Indeed, as I read many of the Civil War accounts—written by scholars, historians, eye-witnesses, etc.—they began to weave themselves into a very post-modern story, with little objective truth upon which we all could agree, and a multiplicity of "valid-enough" interpretations and responses.

Robin Greene

Memoramdum from the Director of the Federal Writers' Project

One of the reasons that I was never able to authenticate these tapes lies in the fact that they don't clearly adhere to the guidelines established for the Federal Writers' Project by its director, Mr. Henry G. Alsberg. And nowhere has any historian or person discovered any similar tapes or interviews. While the interviewer follows certain WPA protocol, the Augustus tapes are clearly anomalous and therefore, I've been told, so suspect as to make them less than credible.

Readers, I hope, will draw their own conclusions. And to help them do so, I'd like to present here a memo from Mr. Alsberg, who writes in 1937, the year that our tapes were recorded, to state directors in order to offer suggestions and guidance about how best to conduct the ex-slave interviews. Below, I offer the complete memo of July 30, 1937, as published in George Rawick's *The American Slave: A Composite Autobiography, From Sundown to Sunup, The Making of the Black Community*, assembled originally in 1941 by The Library of Congress, and published by Greenwood Press in 1971.

```
    Memorandum
    July 30, 1937

    To: State Directors of the Federal Writers' Project
    From: Henry G. Alsberg, Director


    The following general suggestions are being sent to all
    the States where there are ex-slaves still living. They
    will not apply in toto to your State as they represent
    general conclusions reached after reading the mass of ex-
    slave material already submitted.
```
(Note: In 1936 some narratives were collected from ex-slaves in Florida, Georgia, and South Carolina.)
```
                                                       However,
    they will, I hope, prove helpful as an indication, along
    broad lines, of what we want.


    General Suggestions:
    1. Instead of attempting to interview a large number of
    ex-slaves the workers should now concentrate on one or two
    of the more interesting and intelligent people, revisiting
    them, establishing friendly relations, and drawing them out
    over a period of time.
```

2. The specific questions suggested to be asked of the slaves should be only a basis, a beginning. The talk should run to all subjects, and the interviewer should take care to seize upon the information already given, and stories already told, and from them derive other questions.

3. The interviewer should take the greatest care not to influence the point of view of the informant, and not to let his own opinion on the subject of slavery become obvious. Should the ex-slave, however, give only one side of the picture, the interviewer should suggest that there were other circumstances, and ask questions about them.

4. We suggest that each state choose one or two of their most successful ex-slave interviewers and have them take down some stories word for word. Some negro informants are marvelous in their ability to participate in this type of interview. All stories should be as nearly word-for-for as is possible. *(Note: Some stories were tape recorded, then transcribed, and some stories were recorded by hand on paper as the interviewee spoke. Actual recordings of recorded interviews can be heard at the Library of Congress in Washington, D. C., or on-line.)*

5. More emphasis should be laid on questions concerning the lives of the individual's *(Note: I think "individual's" is a typo, and the word "individuals" was intended.)* since they were freed.

Suggestions to Interviewers:

The interviewer should attempt to weave the following questions naturally into the conversation, in simple language. Many of the interviews show that the workers have simply sprung routine questions out of context, and received routine answers.

1. What did the ex-slaves expect from freedom? Forty acres and a mule? A distribution of the land of their masters' plantation?

2. What did the slaves get after freedom? Were any of the plantations actually divided up? Did their masters give them any money? Were they under any compulsion after the war to remain as servants?

3. What did the slaves do after the war? What did they receive generally? What do they think about the reconstruction period?

4. Did secret organizations such as the Ku Klux Klan exert or attempt to exert any influence over the lives of ex-slaves?

5. Did the ex-slaves ever vote? If so, under what circumstances? Did any of their friends ever hold political office? What do the ex-slaves think of the present restricted suffrage?

6. What have the ex-slaves been doing in the interim between 1864 and 1937? What jobs have they held (in detail)? How are they supported nowadays?

7. What do the ex-slaves think of the younger generation of negroes and of present conditions?

8. Were there any instances of slave uprisings?

9. Were any of the ex-slaves in your community living in Virginia at the time of the Nat Turner rebellion? Do they remember anything about it?

10. What songs were there of the period?

The above sent to: Alabama, Arkansas, Florida, Ga., Kentucky, La., Md., Mississippi, Mo., N. Car., Tenn., Texas, Virginia, W. Va., Ohio, Kansas, Indiana.

Stories from Ex-Slaves:

The main purpose of these detailed and homely questions is to get the negro interested in talking about the days of slavery. If he will talk freely, he should be encouraged to say what he pleases without reference to the questions. It should be remembered that the Federal Writers' Project is not interested in taking sides on any question. The worker should not censor any material collected regardless of its nature.

It will not be necessary, indeed it will probably be a mistake, to ask every person all of the questions. Any incidents or facts he can recall should be written down as nearly as possible just as he says them, but do not use dialect spelling so complicated that it may confuse the reader. *(Note: Most field interviews were written, and as noted above, a few were tape recorded.)*

A second visit, a few days after the first one, is important, so that the worker may gather all the worthwhile recollections that the first talk has aroused.

Questions:

1. Where and when were you born?

2. Give the names of your father and mother. Where did they come from? Give names of your brothers and sisters. Tell about your life with them and describe your home and the "quarters." Describe the beds and where you slept. Do you remember anything about your grandparents or any stories told you about them?

3. What work did you do in slavery days? Did you ever earn any money? How? What did you buy with this money?

4. What did you eat and how was it cooked? Any possums? Rabbits? Fish? What food did you like best? Did the slaves have their own gardens?

5. What clothing did you wear in hot weather? Cold weather? On Sundays? Any shoes? Describe your wedding clothes.

6. Tell about your master, mistress, their children, the house they lived in, the overseer or driver, poor white neighbors.

7. How many acres in the plantation? How many slave on it? How and at what time did the overseer wake up the slaves? Did they work hard and late at night? How and for what causes were the slaves punished? Tell what you saw. Tell some of the stories you heard.

8. Was there a jail for slaves? Did you ever see any slaves sold or auctioned off? How did groups of slaves travel? Did you ever see slaves in chains?

9. Did the white folks help you to learn to read and write?

10. Did the slaves have a church on your plantation? Did they read the Bible? Who was your favorite preacher? Your favorite spirituals? Tell about the baptizing; baptizing songs. Funerals and funeral songs.

11. Did the slaves ever run away to the North? Why? What did you hear about patrollers? How did slaves carry news from one plantation to another? Did you hear of trouble between the blacks and whites?

12. What did the slaves do when they went to their quarters after the day's work was done on the plantation? Did they work on Saturday afternoons? What did they do Saturday nights? Sundays? Christmas morning? New Year's Day? Any other holidays? Corn shucking? Cotton picking? Dancing? When some of the white master's family married or died? A wedding or death among the slaves?

13. What games did you play as a child? Can you give the words or sing any of the play songs or ring games of the children? Riddles? Charms? Stories about "Raw Head and Bloody Bones" or other "haints" of *(Note: "Of" is obviously a typo; the correct word is "or.")* ghosts? Stories about animals? What do you think of voodoo? Can you give the words or sing any lullabies? Work songs? Plantation hollers? Can you tell a funny story you have heard or something funny that happened to you? Tell about the ghosts you have seen.

14. When slaves became sick who looked after them? What medicines did the doctors give them? What medicine (herbs, leaves, or roots) did the slaves use for sickness? What charms did they wear to keep off what diseases?

15. What do you remember about the war that brought your freedom? What happened on the day news came to you that you were free? What did your master day and do? When the Yankees came what did they do and say?

16. Tell what work you did and how you lived the first year after the war and what you saw or heard about the Ku Klux Klan and the Nightriders. Any school then for negroes? Any land?

17. Whom did you marry? Describe the wedding. How many children and grandchildren have you and what are they doing?

18. What do you think of Abraham Lincoln? Jefferson Davis? Booker Washington? Any other prominent white man or negro you have known or heard of?

19. Now that slavery is ended, what do you think of it? Tell why you joined a church and why you think all people should be religious.

20. Was the overseer "poor white trash"? What were some of his rules?

The details of the interview should be reported as accurately as possible in the language of the original statements. An example of material collected through one of the interviews with ex-slaves is attached herewith. (Note: I will attach two WPA archival interviews, one of which will be the authenticated Augustus one.) Although this material was collected before the standard questionnaire had been prepared, it represents an excellent method of reporting an interview. *(Note: As I don't have access to the original interview Mr. Alsberg included in his memorandum, I will substitute for the second interview one that was taken after this note was made available.)* More information might have been obtained, however, if a comprehensive questionnaire had been used.

Notes by an Editor on Dialect Usage in Accounts
by Interviews with Ex-Slaves:

Simplicity in recording the dialect is to be desired in order to hold the interest and attention of the readers. It seems to me that readers are repelled by pages sprinkled with misspellings, commas and apostrophes. The value of exact phonetic transcription is, of course, a great one. But few artists attempt this completely. Thomas Nelson Page was meticulous in his dialect; Joel Chandler Harris less meticulous but in my opinion even more accurate. But the values they sought are different from the values that I believe this book of slave narratives should have. Present day readers are less ready for the overstress of phonetic spelling than in the days of local color. Authors realize this: Julia Peterkin uses a modified Gullah instead of Gonzales' carefully spelled out Gullah. Howard Odum has questioned the use of goin' for going since the "g" is seldom pronounced even by the educated.

Truth to idiom is more important, I believe, than truth to pronunciation. Erskine Caldwell in his stories of Georgia, Ruth Suckow in stories of Iowa, Zora Neale Hurston in stories of Florida negroes get a truth to the manner of speaking without excessive misspellings. In order to make this volume of slave narratives more appealing and less difficult for the average reader, I recommend that truth to idiom be paramount, and exact truth to pronunciation secondary.

I appreciate the fact that many of the writers have recorded sensitively. The writer who wrote "ret" for right is probably as accurate as the one who spelled it "right." But in a single publication, not devoted to a study of local speech, the reader may conceivably be puzzled by different spellings of the same word. The words "whafolks," "whufolks," "whi'folks," etc., can all be heard in the South. But "white-folks" is easier for the reader, and the word itself is suggestive of the setting and the attitude.

Words that definitely have a notably different pronunciation from the usual should be recorded as heard. More important is the recording of words with a different local meaning. Most important, however, are the turns of phrase that have flavor and vividness. Examples occurring in the copy I read are:

durin' the war

outman my daddy (good, but unnecessarily put
     into quotes)

piddled in de fields

skit of woods

kinder chillish

There are, of course questionable words, for which it may be hard to set up a single standard. Such words are:

Paddyrollers, padrollers, pattyrollers for patrollers

Missis, mistress for mistress

Marsa, massa, maussa, mastuh for master

Ter, tuh, the for to

I believe that there should be, for this book, a uniform word for each of these.

The following list is composed of words which I think should not be used. These are merely samples of certain faults:

1.	ah	for	I
2.	bawn	for	born
3.	capper	for	caper
4.	com'	for	come
5.	do	for	dough
6.	ebry, ev'ry	for	every
7.	hawd	for	hard
8.	muh	for	my
9.	naked	for	naked
10.	ole, old	for	old
11.	ret, right	for	right
12.	snaik	for	snake
13.	sowd	for	sword
14.	stor	for	store
15.	the	for	tell
16.	twon't	for	twan't
17.	useter, useta	for	used to
18.	uv	for	of
19.	waggin	for	wagon

```
20. whi'          for          white
21. wuz           for          was
```

I should like to recommend that the stories be told in the languages of the ex-slave, without excessive editorializing and "artistic" introductions on the part of the interviewer. The contrast between the directness of the ex-slave speech and the roundabout and at times pompous comments of the interviewer is frequently glaring. Care should be taken lest expressions such as the following creep in: "inflicting wounds from which he never fully recovered" (supposed to be spoken by an ex-slave).

Finally, I should like to recommend that the words "darky" and "nigger" and such expressions as "a comical little old black woman" be omitted from the editorial writing. Where the ex-slave himself uses these, they should be retained.

This material sent June 20 to states of: Ala., Ark., Fla., Ga., Ky., La., Md., Miss., Mo., N.C., Ohio, Okla., Tenn., Texas, Va., and S. Car.

Negro Dialect Suggestions
(Stories of Ex-Slaves)

Do not write:

Ah for I	Gwainter for gwineter (going to)
Po for por (poor)	Oman for woman
Hit for it	Ifn for iffen (if)
Tuh for to	Fituh or fiah for fire
Wuz for was	Uz or uv or or for of
Baid for bed	Poar for poor or por
Daid for dead	J'in for jine
Ouh for our	Coase for cose
Mah for my	Utha for other
Ovah for over	Yo' for you
Otuh for other	Gi' for give
Wha for whar (where)	Cot for caught
Undah for under	Kin' for kind
Fuh for for	Cose for 'cause
Yondah for yonder	Thort for thought
Moster for marster or massa	

Some Notes on the Above Memorandum

Two features of the memorandum jump out at me as being particularly relevant to authenticating the long Augustus narrative.

The first feature concerns Alsberg's suggestion that interviewers return to their subjects for a least a second time. My contention here is that Sarah Louise Augustus was told that part of the interview process involved a second interview. And because—as Alsberg predicted—this second interview established a more solid basis for a relationship, the interviewer was able thereby to come back again—then again—over a more extended period of time. After all, trust between strangers is difficult, especially between strangers of different races, emerging from such a charged history.

Following this point, I'd like to add that it is all together plausible that during the second interview Ms. Augustus herself became convinced of the importance of her own story and committed to its potential historical significance. If the interviewer is in fact *not* the same interviewer who recorded Ms. Augustus's archival seven-page manuscript, this makes perfect sense. And those interested not only in the manuscript but also in the authenticity of the manuscript will better understand my logic here by reading my addendum that follows it. Suffice it to say that there is no evidence that T. Pat Matthews, the WPA worker attributed as the interviewer of the archival text, ever conducted any lengthy interviews, and there is absolutely no evidence to suggest that he had his hand in this one. But I should also mention here that because some of the information in the very beginning of the long tape is almost identical to the shorter interview, I believe that the person who conducted the longer interview either had contact with Matthews or had read Matthews's shorter interview.

The second feature that links these tapes to Alsberg's memorandum deals with the similarity of topics that Alsberg suggests interviewers cover and the topics that this interviewer actually does cover. Perhaps these are coincidental, but I suspect not. Often in listening to the tapes I could hear harsh scratchy sounds in the background, and sometimes distinct noises that indicated the interviewer was turning off the tape recorder. I've noted these throughout the transcription. Also, at various points when Ms. Augustus departs from her personal story, we get background information about slavery and antebellum living conditions. We hear stories of punishment—again, one of Alsberg's suggested topics—and other descriptions that derail the storyline yet seem, perhaps on some subtextual level, encouraged.

Perhaps I should explain here that I only noted in brackets those breaks in the tapes in which the interviewer clearly intruded. Surely, this was an editorial decision, and one I made carefully and after much trial and error. There were so many small crackles and muffled sounds that I couldn't discern how many resulted from the primitive technology of the time, from the poor recording environment, from the transfer from wax to tape, or perhaps from the intentions of interviewer to remain anonymous. In fact, in the process of transcribing the tapes I began to think that the interviewer may have returned to the recordings and intentionally altered them so as to erase her own comments and questions—essentially removing any vocal evidence that might identify her. Although I obviously don't have the expertise to verify this suspicion, I do believe these erasures—depending on how one comes to see them—could, in fact, serve to strengthen the case for authenticity.

I believe the interviewer made a decision to conceal her identity. She wished to be anonymous. But for what reason, I am not sure. And this uncertainty was my nemesis in the process of trying to authenticate the tapes.

In an earlier section of this introduction, I wrote of pedigree or *provenance*. In art, when provenance is known, the value of a piece of artwork goes up because it has a history, a context, a birthright. When the provenance is unknown, the value of a piece is surmised, and we are told that it is best appreciated for itself, sans historical context, sans authentication.

So it is with this notion in mind that I bring readers this manuscript *sans provenance*. I ask my readers to decide for themselves not only if the manuscript is authentic but also how the manuscript should be appreciated and what, if any, value it might have.

Some Notes on Dialect Transcription

Some of the above suggestions on dialect transcription struck me as rather peculiar and inconsistent. So while I've tried to abide by the underlying philosophy behind these suggestions, I've not completely adhered to specific transcription advice. After listening to many hours of oral histories, I certainly wished that my transcription conveys the rich, distinctive dialect that gives the narrative such force and character. I came to admire and respect Sarah Louise Augustus for both *what she said* and *the way in which she said it.*

To convey Ms. Augustus's voice, I used my ear and my judgment. And I did consult with professionals about some of the transcription decisions I made. For the reader's sake, I tried to be consistent, though truth be told, Ms. Augustus herself was inconsistent with her grammar, usage, and pronunciation.

I had my teenage son, Ben, read over portions of the manuscript to tell me when he felt the dialect transcription became unreadable. I think my most egregious departure from the memorandum suggestions is my use of the word *wus* for *was*—surely one of the aberrant spellings that Alsberg warns against. Again, in my own defense, I would argue that the *us*-sound lingered in Sarah Louise Augustus's voice so powerfully and particularly that I felt the need to convey it.

Suffice it to say that I also found good reason to omit certain letters corresponding to certain sounds that Ms. Augustus didn't ordinarily pronounce, to include deviant spellings that suggested Sarah Louise Augustus's spoken dialect, to transcribe her sentences with incomplete and missing verbs, to allow sentence fragments to appear whenever I clearly heard them. As an English professor, however, I took care to punctuate correctly. But because punctuation can't be heard, I also made a point to keep my transcription free of comma splices or run-ons—nowadays generally referred to as "fused"—sentences. The problem with my approach is that it creates a sort of voice on the page that, I'm afraid, reads like a signature, a fingerprint, at once identifying and creating a bastard persona, a composite voice—part Sarah Louise Augustus's, part mine.

In an early version of *Real Birth, Women Share Their Stories,* my collection of transcribed birthing narratives, one editor insisted that I go back, re-listen to all the tapes with an ear toward hearing the speaker's punctuation, and then rework the written narrative transcriptions in order to "mix-up" punctuation ticks I had developed. This way, each story would, through its more idiosyncratic punctuation, have its own visual voice. I was told that the stories sounded too "academic," too correct. My hope is that I've not fallen prey to this problem here. I hope I've learned from this previous experience how to avoid falling into any bad "academic" groove of producing overly correct, too consistent punctuation. Yet, on the other hand, I hope that I've not overcompensated and become too loose or slovenly.

All I can say is that I've done my best. But as all writers know, "best" changes with every revision. No doubt, if I were to have the luxury of years of editing, I might make other decisions. But near the end of my semester-long sabbatical, I had a publisher interested in the narrative, and I had to move fast. For an unknown writer, finding a publisher can be an incredibly long and frustrating process, so this nibble coming at the end of a very difficult year of transcribing, prompted me to quickly ready my manuscript for publication.

Two WPA Archival Interviews—
Temple Herndon Durham and Sarah Louise Augustus

Before I present the unauthenticated Augustus transcription, I wish to make available two authenticated transcripts—Temple Herndon Durham's interview with Travis Jordan, and Sarah Louise Augustus's interview with T. Pat Matthews, which I earlier mentioned. I provide them unadulterated so that my more academic readers can see the dialect and transcription decisions that the interviewers made and get a feeling for the behind-the-scenes sorts of questions that interviewers might have asked. However, my less academic readers might want to skip over these, for they offer little in terms of adding to interest in the longer Augustus manuscript.

320271
Aug. 23, 1937
Temple Herndon Durham
Ex-Slave, 103 Years Old
1312 Pine St., Durham, N.C.

"I was thirty-one years ole when de surrender come. Dat makes me sho nuff old. Near about a hundred an' three years done passed over dis here white head of mine. I'se been here, I mean I'se been here. 'Spects I'se de olest nigger in Durham. I'se been here so long dat I done forgot near about as much as des here new generation niggers knows or ever gwine know.

"My white folks lived in Chatham County. Dey was Marse George an' Mis' Betsy Herndon. Mis' Betsy was a Snipes before she married Marse George. Dey had a big plantation an' raised cawn, wheat, cotton an' 'bacca. I don't know how many field niggers Marse George had, but he had a mess of dem, an' he had hosses too, an' cows, hogs an' sheeps. He raised sheeps an' sold de wool, an' dey used de wool at de big house too. Dey was a big weavin' room whare de blankets was wove, an' dey wove de cloth for de winter clothes too. Linda Hernton an' Milla Edwards was de head weavers, dey looked after de weavin' of de fancy blankets. Mis' Betsy was a good weaver too. She weave de same as de niggers. She say she love de clackin' soun' of de loom an' de way de shuttles run in an' out carryin' a long tail of bright colored thread. Some days she set at de loom all de mawnin' peddlin' wid her feets an' her white han's flittin' over de bobbins.

"De cardin' an' spinnin' room was full of niggers. I can hear dem spinnin' wheels now turnin' roun' and sayin' hum-m-m, hum-m-m-m, an' hear de slaves singin' while dey spin. Mammy Tarah stayed in de dye room. Dey wuzn' nothin' she didn' know about dyein'. She knew every kind of root, bark, leaf an' berry dat made red, blue, green, or whatever color she wanted. Dey had a big shelter whare de dye pots set over de coals. Mammy Tarah would fill de pots wid water, den she put in de roots, bark an' stuff an' boil de juice out, den she strain it an' put in de salt an' vinegar to set de color. After de wool an' cotton done been carded an' spun to thread, Mammy take de hanks an' drap dem in de pot of boilin' dye. She stir dem 'roun' an' lif' dem up an' down wid a stick, an' when she hang dem up on de line in de sun, dey was every color of de rainbow. When dey dripped dry dey was sent to de weavin' room whare dey was wove in blankets an' things.

"When I growed up I married Exter Durham. He belonged to Marse Snipes Durham who had de plantation 'cross de county line in Orange County. We had a big weddin'. We was married on de front porch of de big house. Marse George killed a shoat an' Mis' Betsy had Georgianna, de cook, to bake a big weddin' cake all iced up white as snow wid a bride an' groom standin' in de middle holdin' han's. De table was set out in de yard under de trees, an' you ain't never seed de like of eats. All de niggers come to de feas' an' Marse George had a dram for everybody. Dat was some weddin'. I had on a white dress, white shoes an' long white gloves dat come to my elbow, an' Mis' Betsy done made me a weddin' veil out of a white net window curtain. When she played de weddin march on de piano, me an' Exter marched down de walk an' up on de porch to de altar Mis' Betsy done fixed. Dat de pretties' altar I ever seed. Back 'gainst de rose vine dat was full or red roses, Mis' Betsy done put tables filled wid flowers an' white candles. She done spread down a bed sheet, a sho nuff linen sheet, for us to stan' on, an' dey was a white pillow to kneel down on. Exter done made me a weddin' ring. He made it out of a big red button wid his pocket knife. He done cut it so roun' an' polished it so smooth dat it looked like a red satin ribbon tide 'roun' my finger. Dat sho was a pretty ring. I wore it about fifty years, den it got so thin dat I lost it one day in de wash tub when I was washin' clothes.

"Uncle Edmond Kirby married us. He was de nigger preacher dat preached at de plantation church. After Uncle Edmond said de las' words over me an' Exter, Marse George got to have his little fun. He say, 'Come on, Exter, you an' Tempie got to jump over de broom stick backwards; you got to do dat to see which one wine be boss of your household.' Everybody come stan' 'round to watch. Marse George hold de broom about a foot high off de floor. De one dat jump over it backwards an' never touch de handle, gonna boss de house, an' if bof of dem jump over without touchin' it, dey won't gonna be no bossin', dey just gonna be 'genial. I jumped fus', an' you ought to seed me. I sailed right over dat broom stick same as a cricket, but when Exter jump he done had a big dram an' his feets was so big an' clumsy dat dey got all tangled up in dat broom an' he fell head long. Marse George he laugh an' laugh, an' tole Exter he gonna be bossed till he skeered to speak less'n I tole him to speak. After de weddin' we went down to de cabin Mis' Betsy done all dressed up, but Exter couldn't stay no longer den dat night 'cuz he belonged to Marse Snipes Durham an' he had to back home. He left de next day for his plantation, but he come back every Saturday night an' stay till Sunday night. We had eleven chillum. Nine was bawn before surrender an' two after we was set free. So I had two chillum dat wuzn' bawn in bondage. I was worth a heap to Marse George 'cause I had so many chillum. De mo' chillum a slave had de mo' dey was worth. Lucy Carter was de only nigger on de plantation dat had mo' chilln den I had. She had twelve, but her chillum was sickly an' mine was muley strong an' healthy. Dey never was sick.

"When de war come Marse George was too ole to go, but young Marse Bill went. He went an' took my brother Sim wid him. Marse Bill took Sim along to look after his hoss an' everything. Dey didn't neither one get shot, but Mis' Betsy was skeered near about to death all de time, skeered dey was gonna be brung home shot all to pieces like some of de sojers was.

"De Yankees wazn' so bad. De most dey wanted was sumpin' to eat. Dey was all de time hungry, de fus' thing dey ax for when dey come was sumpin' to put in dey stomach. An' chicken! I ain't never seed even a preacher eat chicken like dem Yankees. I believe to my soul dey ain't never seed no chicken till dey come down here. An' hot biscuit too. I seed a passel of dem eat up a whole sack of flour one night for supper. Georgianna sif' flour till she look white an' dusty as a miller. Dem sojers didn' turn down no ham neither. Dat de onlies' thing dey took from Marse George. Dey went in de smoke house an' toted off de hams an' shoulders. Marse George say he come off mighty light if dat all dey want, 'sides he got plenty of shoats anyhow.

"We had all de eats we wanted while de war was shootin' dem guns, 'cause Marse George was home an' he kep' de niggers workin'. We had chickens, gooses, meat, peas, flour, meal, potatoes an' things like dat all de time, an' milk an' butter too, but we didn' have no sugar an' coffee. We used groun' pa'ched cawn for coffee an' cane 'lasses for sweetnin'. Dat wuzn' so bad wid a heap of thick cream. Anyhow, we had enough to eat to 'vide wid de neighbors dat didn' have none when surrender come.

"I was glad when de war stopped 'cause den me an' Exter could be together all de time 'stead of Saturday an' Sunday. After we was free we lived right on at Marse George's plantation a long time. We rented de lan' for a forth of what we made, den after while we bought a farm. We paid three hundred dollars we done saved. We had a hoss, a steer, a cow an' two pigs, 'sides some chickens an' for geese. Mis' Betsy went up in de attic an' give us a bed an' tick; she give us enough goose feathers to make two pillows, den she give us a table an' some chairs. She give us some dishes too. Marse George give Exter a bushel of seed cawn an' some seed wheat, den he tole him to go down to de barn an' get a bag of cotton seed. We got all dis, den we hitched up de wagon an' throwed in de passel of chillum an' we moved to our new farm, an' de chillum was put to work in de fiel'; dey growed up in de fiel' 'cause dey was put to work time dey could walk good.

"Freedom is all right, but de niggers was better off before surrender, 'cause den dey was looked after an' dey didn't get in no trouble fightin' an' killin' like dey do dese days. If a nigger cut up an' got sassy in slavery times, his Ole Marse give him a good whippin' an' he went way back an' set down an' behaved hisself. If he was sick, Marse an' Missus looked after him, an' if he needed store medicine, it was bought an' give to him; he didn' have to pay nothin'. Dey didn' even have to think about clothes nor nothin' like dat, dey was wove an' made an' give to dem. Maybe everybody's Marse an' Missus wuzn' good as Marse George an' Mis' Betsy, but dey was de same as mammy an' pappy to us niggers."

320031
July 20, 1937
Sarah Louise Augustus
Ex-Slave, Age 92 Years
1424 Lane Street, Raleigh, North Carolina

"I wus born on a plantation near Fayetteville, N. C., an' I belonged to J. B. Smith. His wife wus named Henrietta. He owned about twenty slaves. When a slave wus no good he wus put on the auction block in Fayetteville and sold.

"My father wus named Romeo Harden an' my mother wus named Alice Smith. The little cabin where I wus born is still standing.

"There wus seven children in marster's family, four girls an' three boys. The girls wus named Ellen, Ida, Mary an' Elizabeth. The boys wus named Harry, Norman an' Marse George. Marse George went to the war. Mother had a family of four girls. Their names wus: Mary, Kate, Hannah an' myself Sarah Louise. I am the only one living an' I would not be living but I have spent most of my life in white folks' houses an' they have looked after me. I respected myself an' they respected me.

"My first days of slavery wus hard. I slept on a pallet on the floor of the cabin an' just as soon as I wus able to work any at all I wus put to milking cows.

"I seen the paterollers hunting men an' seen men they had whipped. The slave block stood in the center of the street, Fayetteville Street, where Ramsey an' Gillespie Street came in near Cool Springs Street. The silk mill stood just below the slave market. I saw the silkworms that made the silk an' saw them gather the cocoons an' spin the silk.

"They hung people in the middle of Ramsey Street. They put up a gallows an' hung the men exactly at 12 o'clock.

"I run from the plantation once to go with my youn' white folks to see a man hung. Sometime I run chores for missus, at the dock.

"The only boats I remember on the Cape Fear wus the Governor Worth, The Iser, The North State, an' The Hurt. That wus David's boat an' how we met. David wus the man I married. He a free negro man from Baltimore an' New York, travel down. We marry, an' I take his name, Augustus.

"Oh! Lord yes, I remember the stage coach come by the plantation. It carry the mail. Folks walk to it when they blew a horn. Blow it early so you'd know. Had to get there quick, on time, 'cause they could not wait. No. They stop but only a short time. There wus a stage each way, one up an' one down.

"Mr. George Lander had the first Tombstone Marble yard in Fayetteville on Hay Street on the point of Flat Iron Place. Lander was from Scotland. They gave me a pot, a scarf, an' his sister gave me some shells. I still got all the things they gave me. My missus, Henrietta Smith, wus Mr. Lander's sister. I waited on the Landers part of the time. They were hard working white folks, honest, God fearing people. The things they gave me were brought from over the sea.

"I can remember when there wus no hospital in Fayetteville. There wus a little place near the depot where there wus a board shanty where they operated on people. I stood outside once an' saw the doctors take a man' leg off. Dr. McDuffy wus the man who took the leg off — this before the war. He lived on Hay Street near the Silk Mill.

"When one of the white folks died they sent slaves around to the homes of their friends an' neighbors with a large sheet of paper with a piece of black crepe pinned to the top of it. The friends would sign or make a cross mark on it. The funerals were held at the homes an' friends an' neighbors stood on the porch an' in the house while the services were going on. The bodies wus carried to the grave after the services in a black hearse drawn by black horses. If they didn't have no black horses to draw the hearse, they went off an' borrowed them. The colored people washed an' shrouded the dead bodies. My grandmother wus one who did this. Her name wus Sarah McDonald. She belonged to Capt. George McDonald. She had fifteen children an' lived to be one hundred an' ten years old. She died in Fayetteville of pneumonia. She wus in Raleigh nursing the Briggs family, Mrs. F. H. Briggs' family. She wus going home to Fayetteville when she wus caught in a rain storm in Sanford, while changing trains. The train for Fayetteville had left as the train for Sanford wus late so she stayed wet all night. Next day she went home, took pneumonia an' died. She wus great on curing rheumatism; she did it with herbs. She grew hops an' other herbs an' cured many people of this disease.

"She wus called black mammy because she wet nursed so many white children. In slavery time she nursed all babies hatched on her master's plantation — kept it up for I don't know how long a time.

"Grandfather wus named Issac Fuller. Mrs. Mary Ann Fuller, Kate Fuller, Mr. Will Fuller, who wus a lawyer in Wall Street, New York, is some of their white folks. The Fullers wus born in Fayetteville. One of the slaves, Dick McAlister, worked, saved a small fortune an' left it to Mr. Will Fuller. People thought the slave ought to have left it to his sister but he left it to Mr. Will. Mr. Fuller gives part of it to the ex-slaves sister each year. Mr. Will always helped the negroes out when he could He wus good to Dick an' Dick McAlister gave him all his belongings when he died.

"The Yankees come through Fayetteville wearing large blue coats with capes on them. Lots of them were mounted, an' there wus thousands of foot soldiers. It took them several days to get through town. The Southern soldiers retreated an' then in a few hours the Yankees covered the town. They busted into the barn, the big house, missus' summer kitchen, broke things, took what they can — meal an' other provisions. White an' negro folks pled with the Yankees but it did no good. They took all they wanted. They said if they had to come again they would take the babies from the cradles. Soon we wus all free. The negroes begun visiting each other in the cabins an' became so excited that some began to shout an' pray. I thought they wuz all crazy.

"Some folks stayed right on with at the Smith place. Family soon bought a town house an' they has the big house on the plantation. A few eventually went to the town house to work, but mother an' some stayed on the plantation. Ma died there, an' the white folks buried her. There is lots of Smiths around Fayetteville today — some from that plantation. Some folks wus given little places nearby — shacks an' some plots. It wus a difficult time after the war.

"I remember weddings in them times. My sister Mary wus married in missus' graduating dress to James Henry Harris that lived nearby. We called her Mar — short for Mary. Miss Mary Smith give her away. Mar named after her. They jumped the broom, as that wus what negro slaves done back then. It happen some time before the war begun.

"My husband wus a stevedore on the Cape Fear River boats an' a white man's negro too, when he couldn't find no work right before the war. I met him when I just a girl. He came down on one of them boats, an' I met him at the dock.

"Later, I had one child, but I lost her in childbirth. My sister lost a child too. It wus real common for gals to lose babies. Sometimes the mother die theirselfs.

"My husband die. We never did get to spend much time together. He wus a good man. Things wus a mess after the war, an' many negroes formed Negro Lodges to help each other get theirselfs started in life afte' the war. It hard to go from bein' a slave to a free person. Before I get ole, I wus a member of several Negro Lodges an' wus on the Committee for the North Carolina Colored State Fair.

"There are only a few of the old white folks who have always been good to me living now, but I ain't in contact with them no mo'. I wus a youn' woman when Sherman's Army come through Fayetteville, but I remember it lak it wus yesterday. Guess I be about ninety-two years of age now."

Some Last Brief Notes

Before turning over this book to its main attraction—my transcription of the unauthenticated Sarah Louise Augustus tapes—I'd like to make some final remarks.

First, readers might take note of some regularizing of spelling. Although Sarah Louise Augustus often pronounces the same word differently, depending on its context, I decided to regularize the spelling in order to create a more readable text.

For instance, at one point the word "one" appears after the word "troublesome" and is pronounced: "troublesome un." I've transcribed the phrase as: "troublesome one." Later, however, when "one" appears sandwiched between other words as in the following phrase, "No one tell me nothing," Augustus's pronunciation of "one" sounds more like "one," not "un." Nonetheless, I decided not to represent that difference in pronunciation, and instead I focused on the more significant dropped final "g" sound in the word "nothing." Too many aberrant spellings, I believed, made the manuscript unreadable. And there were simply too many variants for me to accurately capture all of them.

In essence, I took to heart Alsberg's call for readability. I did not try to transcribe phonetically many differences in pronunciation that I clearly heard, although it is those differences, I believe, that contribute to the rich texture of Augustus's voice. It was a necessary sacrifice.

Another decision I made involved the word "ain't." When Augustus used this word before "never," the "t" sound slid away into the "n" sound, but I regularized the spelling, again for clarity's sake.

However, I have omitted the final "g" sound in the spelling of almost all words ending in "g" and have omitted the final "d" consistently in the word "and" because these adherences to her pronunciation did not compromise readability and were very consistently omitted in her pronunciation. I made the same choice with the word "was"; consistently pronounced as "wus," I spelled it accordingly: "wus."

Additionally, I decided to leave out the anonymous interviewer's responses and questions. The interviewer ordinarily turned off the tape recorder herself before she spoke as if she were trying to be as invisible as possible. I understand this impulse. When I worked on my earlier book, *Real Birth, Women Share Their Stories*, I chose to edit out my own voice in the transcription of the women's narratives. My voice, my occasional questions, my proddings were too intrusive, and I came to believe that Sarah Louise Augustus's interviewer believed this as well. The strength of the Augustus story rests in the story itself, and anything that detracts from that story should be omitted. Some readers might feel differently, and to them I apologize.

Moreover, I made another decision to refer occasionally to the *process* of the recording. And I do this by including a few italicized notations about the tape when I heard interruptions or vocal affects, such as pregnant pauses, sighs, changes in inflection, etc. I also noted when the "tape" is switched on and off, and I've left white space to indicate some pauses and or transitions. Part of the difficulty in accurately representing these oral signifiers, however, lies in the fact that the tapes I listened to were not the original recordings. Therefore, the possibility exists that the "switching on and off" might be handiwork either of the original interviewer or of the mysterious woman who copied the recording for Mrs. Henderson—unless, of course, they were one and same woman. And to that subject I will return in my addendum.

Finally, I'd simply like to say that what I present here is, no doubt, an imperfect, flawed text, transcribed from tapes that contained scratches and imperfections as well. I should note that these imperfections are most prevalent in both the beginning and the end.

But rather than apologizing ad nauseam for the book's many problems, I wish to simply express my gratitude to Samantha Henderson, to her grandmother Mrs. Iris Henderson, to our determined interviewer, and most of all to Sarah Louise Augustus, the woman who by speaking so honestly and courageously about her own difficult journey was able to illuminate and help me negotiate my own.

Disclaimers and Declarations

Let me state the obvious: Slavery was not a single unified institution. The various forms it took reflected the idiosyncrasies of individual families, individual slave owners, local and regional cultures, as well as a plethora of other influences. Slavery changed—over the years, decades, and centuries. And just as individuals and family dynamics change, so did individual slaves, slave owners, and the dynamics between them.

Many scholars have questioned the slave narratives' veracity and their ability to recollect an accurate version of collective memory. But perhaps no such "version" can exist.

Some scholars argue that because the stories were often collected and recorded by educated white interviewers for whom the ex-slaves had a history of deep mistrust, the ex-slaves were careful to censor their stories. Other scholars argue that the white interviewers "loaded" the questions they asked, and when the stories were recorded by hand, they perhaps inadvertently (or intentionally) changed the narratives so as to reflect better what they felt most comfortable hearing. Or simply, some argue that the slaves themselves chose not to remember what was painful about their early lives—or again, they were kept from the harsh realities of slavery because they were children. And much like many Jewish survivors of World War II's Holocaust, some experts believe that the ex-slaves colluded as a group to forget the painful past and to focus instead on a more hopeful future.

As a backdrop to the events that Sarah Louise Augustus describes, I think it might be useful to provide the briefest synopsis of the American Civil War. And to that end, I'm including below the first paragraph from the article about the Civil War found in the 1964 edition of the *Encyclopedia Britannica,* which I discovered on a bottom shelf in the Writers' Den at Weymouth Center for the Arts and Humanities, where I worked as a writer-in-residence on this project.

American Civil War, a conflict lasting four years between the United States federal government and eleven southern states that asserted their right to leave the Union. The total population (free and slave) of the southern states that seceded was slightly less than half the population of the northern states that remained in the Union. At the opening of the conflict, the seceding states set up an independent government named the Confederate States of America (q.v.). The Civil War began when the guns of the South fired on Federal Ft. Sumter on April 12, 1861; it ended with the surrender of Gen. Robert E. Lee at Appomattox Court House, Va., on April 9, 1865, and of Gen. Joseph E. Johnston at Durham Station, N.C., on April 26, 1865. (General Johnston had signed an armistice on April 18, but its terms were not acceptable to Gen. Ulysses S. Grant.) Approximately 4,000,000 troops took part in the war, which has been described as the first "modern" or "total" war—that is, a war in which the industrial potential of the victor determined the outcome. Total casualties exceeded 617,000 dead (North, 359,000; South, 100,000). The war resulted in the preservation of the Union and brought about important alteration in the U.S. constitution, the abolition of slavery and far-reaching social and economic changes. (730)

Augustus:
The Transcription

August 16, 1937

I just gonna sit down here while yo' hook up. My bones ache most time now. I can't see real good, an' my hands shake sometimes. I knowed yo' has questions for me about the ways things wus back then. When I wus raised up in slavery. Most don't wanna talk about it, 'cause it be such bad time. But not me.

I ain't ashamed—plenty of wrong done to me. An' the Lawd already forgive me for what wrong I done.

I wus born on a plantation near Fayett'ville, North Car'lina, in Cumberland County, an' I belong to J. B. Smith. His wife name Henrietta. They own about twenty slaves.

When a slave wus no good, they put on the auction block in Fayett'ville an' sold. Marster sell but two slaves all the time I around—Tibs an' li'l Sammy, who takes up together. He sell one gal, Sandy Beach, before I come along.

I about ninety-two, can't spell so good—especially now, when my eyes is bad. But I got mo' learnin' than most. Born in '45. My ma learn me my letters. An' I pick things up. All through my life, I be readin' somethin'. Durin' the war, I lives with a family in Baltimore, an' I reads me a whole big book by Mister Charles Dickens. After Surrender, I try to git mo' schoolin', but it never work out.

I remember slavery time, war time—the awful things that happen—an' the sad times after.

My pa wus name Romeo Harden, an' my ma wus name Alice Smith. They wus hard workin' folk. Not lak them today that don't wanna work, don't wanna do nothin'. I see'd them whar' I live today, in Raleigh. If yo' axe me, they ain't brung up right. When a man take up a wife from another plantation, they calls her a "broad wife." Ain't sure whar' the term come from—but that what she were, my ma.

The li'l cabin whar' I born still standin'. There wus seven children in Marster family—four gals, three boys. The gals name Ellen, Ida, Mary, an' Elizabeth. The boys name Harry, Norman, an' Marse George. Marse George. He go fight in the war an' get hisself killed—the only son that die. Marster gone first to fight in that very first regiment, an' he gone. Norman injured, an' Harry… he fight too, but he do his best to escape the whole darn thing. He get hisself conscripted. Later, he become a Quaker, move west, marry a Quaker gal. An' Marse Harry, he wus in school to becomes a lawyer, but I don't know he ever become one—or what become of him.

My ma had four gals. Their names Mary, Kate, Hannah, an' myself, Sarah Louise. I wus a middle child, second from the top, third from the last. Now, I the only one livin', an' I suspect that the Lawd have a plan for me still. Maybe me talkin' to yo' is part of it.

My first days of slavery wus hard. I sleep on a pallet on the cabin floor, an' just soon as I wus able to work, I wus put to totin', helpin' out, sometime in the big house. Our cabin stood with the other slave cabins in a li'l cluster by the field, near the cow barn. Slave cabins wus rude things, made of rough green lumber sawed right on the plantation. They be put up in a day or so, right after the wood wus cut. When the boards dry, yo'could see right through the walls. Chil'ren sleep on pallets on the floor. We got no blankets till we turn eight year ol'—before that, we'd take feed bags an' stuff ourself inside. It wus cold, I remember, in winter time. But we double up then, two in a bag, an' sometime we'd cut up an' has fun, kickin', squirmmin'.

Some nights, come evenin' time, we git a break around supper. Ma'd take us in the cabin, an' in the hard dirt, draw our letters an' numbers. It wus against the law then, but Ma knowed it important, so she done it. She wus learned herself by some white children when she wus comin' up.

Once—in August—same time about now, Ma wus sick with a summer cold an' laid up for a week. Pneumonia common. Fact is, my maw-maw die of pneumonia—it always a scare. But they had herbs back then for everythin'. Yo'd find a granny or someone that knowed these things, an' she treat yo' better than them docs today. Granny gather hoarhound, slippery elm for poultices, barks that make bitter tea, an' yo'd just has to drink.

Marster see Ma pretty bad off, an' he didn't wanna lose her. She work hard, an' she valuable—Marster done knowed that, so she gits his permission to stay in her cabin on her pallet for a whole week.

But soon, sure enough, she feel a li'l better, so she take me an' Hannah—the two younges'—behind the cabin to learn us a bit. Older gals knowed how to read real good—we all read an' write. Except my pa. He never knowed how.

By the end of that week, Hannah an' me, we knowed all our letters an' the sounds they makes. Alls we has to do after that wus practice. Ma'd make us fetch sticks to write in the dirt. Then she'd take her foot an' erase what she done wrote. We do the same. The sandy dirt be our board. Nobody had no paper, an' there be just a few books around. We had some—a Bible, whar' we keep dates for births an' weddin's an' such, an' we had some other books too, one big one about history, another slim li'l book, a primer—that Marster gals done give us on the sly. I don't remember when or why.

We'd hide them books beneath our pallets an' loose floorboards. A slave'd git whipped if white folk catched them with anythin' lak that. My first word wus "dog." I remember it clear 'cause Ma turned it around an' made "God." Them letters stay with me—that link between a lowly creature an' the Lawd.

That thing on? I guessin' it is. [*Ms. Augustus sighs.*]

All this happen before the war. Most slaves never thought there'd be no fightin'. We thought it just talk. An' even after the war, some colored don't believe they free.

Must been 1860—seem so long ago, another lifetime—when we first got the news from David— sweet David. He the man my story mostly about.

He be workin' on the Hurt—the A. P. Hurt steamboat. At the time, it were a new steamboat. That wus the boat that first brung David to me, an' it be the same boat that carry me home at the end of the war.

The day I met David—for the first time—well, that stand out real good. David, he be the one true love of my life—the man that give me my name.

I wus sent down from the big house to pick up fabric Missus order from Va'ginia. I be walkin'. Deep summer—July. I remember my ol' sack dress hangin' down, an' how I scoop it up to cross the wet patches. It a rainy afternoon, but no one complain 'cause the crops be needin' rain. There swamp Jasmine bloomin', sweet lak honeysuckle. An' crape myrtles comin' on—colored blooms hanging lak clusters of stars. I uset'ta walk on a dirt path along the river woods. Not the main road whar' I be seen. It weren't dangerous. Not if yo' know the way. I even had a li'l bounce to my walk back then, lak my soul bubblin' to the surface—couldn't keep it down. Didn't know no better. I also had on a white head scarf that us gals mostly wears.

An' when I go to the tradin' spot at the Hurt, there be David. Folk calls us *Niggas* then; even black folk say *Nigga*. There weren't no shame in it. *Nigga* this, an' *Nigga* that. But not these days, ain't respectful. No.

Well, David come off the Hurt. I see'd him, noticed him right 'way. He wus tall an' lanky, an' he come off the dock, lookin' for a place to eat. Hungry. But there weren't no place near the docks for colored. There wus a tavern nearby, only for white folk. When I see'd him, I stood there. Had me two big peaches an' some cold grits in a pail I brung with me for dinner. So I offer him what I has. Sound real forward, but God only know what I thinkin'—I about fifteen—a youn' fifteen, innocent. Just becomin' interested in boys, but Ma'd slap me silly if I be tellin' her.

David wus only about seventeen hisself then, so naturally, we be attracted. He say, "Howdy," an' when I tells him I got extra grub if he be hungry, David nod, an' we go down to a big willow oak that growed nearby an' sit together on some hard roots pokin' up from the sandy dirt. He has real nice manners—see that right off—an' we has dinner. David et both the peaches, which I gives him 'cause he won't et grits. Call them slop. "Cold corn slop." Ain't fit for mules.

David, lak I says, he be the boy I marry. My one true love. But I gettin' ahead of myself.

This be our first meetin', an' we only talk a short time, 'cause David, he leavin' south with the Hurt—back down the Cape Fear to the sea.

But our love begun that day, right at the very moment we sets eyes on one another—don't axe me how it happen, but it did.

David talk to me 'bout war, 'bout the North. I remember that, an' how there gonna be bloodshed soon; he swear his life on it, especially if Lincoln git elected. South, he say, gonna pull out of the Union—state by state, leafs droppin' off a tree. I hear war talk too—down near Fayett'ville, but we figure it all just talk. Lots of big talk. But comin' from David, it different somehow. It wus July, lak I say, the growin' season. There be David, an' he plant his war seed in my mind whar' it growed big as a watermelon.

'Cause right after I meets him, all a sudden, there be talk about war everywhar'—how the North wus plannin' on war if the South done pull away. David say the South ain't a good place, what with slavery. I say that the North weren't much better.

David, he been all over. An' he be the first person talk to me lak I ain't a child. Strange, 'cause suddenly I feels all growed up. Lak some magic wand waved over me an' turn me into a woman. I weren't, but David had a way 'bout him. He think somethin' an' it come true.

He wus mulatto—coppery skin, fine green eyes. From New York an' Baltimore. I ain't never knowed nobody from New York, but I heared of it. David, he free an' work as a stevedore. Been all up an' down the Cape Fear, an' even been to other countries too—Mexico an' across the ocean.

That wus the first time I actually thought 'bout war. I couldn't stay with David mo' than one-half hour, maybe less, 'cause I'd be missed. So I left him there beneath the shade of that ol' tree, sittin' on them roots. He so handsome. Green eyes, copper skin, an' thin as a bean—yas, he wus, skinny but all hard muscle from haulin' an' workin' barges on the river. Though he always had somethin' soft 'bout him. Somethin' gentle that attract me right off. All the ways home that day, there be a extra bounce an' skip to my walk. Lak my heart find its own tune.

When evenin' come, I still thinkin' 'bout David an' what he say, so I axe Ma 'bout war. But she busy an' tell me to hush. War talk fine for white folk, but us colored has work to do. Ma hand me a bucket to carry kindlin' an' send me out haulin'. But I knowed she heared me good. An' most colored folk did talk, but not in front of no chil'ren. I still a child accordin' to most. [*The interviewer's garbled voice is heard, and then clicks are heard, and something garbled again before Ms. Augustus resumes.*]

So, I gonna tell yo'. That evenin', the day I meets David—the very same day—I go down to the creek, get me the kindlin' Ma tell me to. I still thinkin' 'bout him, 'bout the war, the Hurt. North an' South. I take the trail an' skip off a ways from the shack.

Sun wus gettin' low, ain't quite dark yet, still could see—an' my heart still singin' its tune, when this young white man—tall, well-dressed—appear from nowhar'. He just come up on me when I is in the brush, gatherin' twigs.

Right away, he start up with axin' what I be doin' way out here. If I from the Smith place, which he must know I is. So quick, I answer him, "Yes, Sir, I a Smith, same as my ma. We be J. B. Smith slaves. Then he axe me, "Yo' ever been with a man, Nigga?" An' he glare at me, take a step forward.

I take a step back an' say, "Yo' ever heared a Nigga gal scream?" An' he grab a'hold of my arm. I squirm away, droppin' my bucket, an' the twigs spill out.

"Yo' yell, Nigga, an' I gits yo' whipped." His eyes burn into me.

We near the creek, near the piney woods thick with hawthorn, holly, pokeberry, wild magnolias—with big white flowers.

Again, I still young' an' sassy, always real sassy. But Missus an' Marster never whip me. Done some other slaves that way. An' there be one time, I almost whipped. Another time, I see'd a man whipped in Virg'nia, beat almost till he dead.

This white man…his name wus…wus Potter— Mister Potter. An' he be wearin' a fancy suit ain't wore in these parts. He around twenty year of age. I just a slip of a gal. He take me by the arm again, an' he throw me down hard. Then he come at me. I knowed what he about…

But jus' as he ready to pounce—I down on the ground with the empty bucket by—when Ma, with her second sense, she call out. Potter jus' about on me, when we hear her yellin' from near the cabin 'cause I just suppose to git kindlin' an' return quick. So Mister Potter, he let me go, but before he do, he say in a nasty ol' whisper, "Yo' gonna git yours, Nigga gal. Yo' knows what I means."

I picks myself up, tremblin', an' dust the pine straw off my dress. I real shaky. Ma still callin' from a ways, so I come, forgittin' my load of kindlin', just with that empty bucket bangin' an' clammerin' as I run. When I gits near the cabin, there be Mister Potter standin' by Ma. He don't look lak nothin' wrong—nothin' in the wide world could ever be wrong with him. He look shiny an' new, standin' there.

They both stare up at me—an' Ma axe what goin' on an' whar' the kindlin' be, 'cause I seem so fluster. Mister Potter laugh an' say he just come from them creek woods an' see'd a big snake, maybe I see'd it too an' gits me scared. I nod. Don't look Ma in the eye. Didn't look at that Mister Potter none neither. Ma slap me on the bottom, just for show. I say to her, "Sorry, Ma. I done git scare off an' dumped my load. I go back an' retrieve it quick."

That night, Ma axe me if there be anythin' I needs to tell her. But I shake my head an' go 'bout my chores.

Mister Potter wus company—I comes to find out—he be down from somewhar' up north to visit the white folk—from Pennsylvania, I wanna say. He travel by hisself, an' he leave the next day. I never see'd that Mister Potter again. But he give me a bad feelin' about Northerners.

After that day, I cling tight to Ma an' forget about boys, even David for a time.

Nowadays, Southern folk still don't much lak them Northerners. An' this here one reason why. Them folk come down, think they own the world. Before the war an' now. They cocky an' struttin'. Lots of money, no manners. Even them Negroes up north is uppity. Talk fast, act fast. Can't trust some. Not all, 'course. Can't judge everyone by some.

Anyways, that Mister Potter, he come right before Uncle Cicero die. But I all talk out now. Gotta rest. I saves Uncle Cicero for tomorrow. I a ol' woman. Gotta rest.

August 17, 1937

All right, now. Whar' wus I? Uncle Cicero. Yas. Gonna talk about how he die. Well, we calls him uncle, Uncle Cicero. An' it summer time, when the weather steamy. Start out bright day—blue sky, sun-shiny, turn into rain by afternoon. Kind of unpredictable. Cicero ain't my real uncle, by blood, I mean. But we all call him that. Always aunt so an' so, uncle this or that. An' he real close to Ma an' Pa. Pa live on another plantation—lak I say. Uncle Cicero, he on the Smith place with us. Knew Pa somehow, an' I think they relations.

Cicero, he a smart man, an' about as nice as they come. He preach at our place. Read real good, talk real good. An' he knowed his Africa history—knowed the tribe that his grandpap took from in Africa. We chil'ren lak to gather around Uncle Cicero at Christmas time an' hear his stories. Seem his grandpap or great-grandpap—don't remember how far back—he come from the Ibos, an' he some kind of prince. Wus snatched when he young. Story go that he out huntin' when he a small chil'. He an' his sister with him. An' another tribe capture him an' take him back to be a family slave in a village. West Africa.

Then he snatched up again by another tribe, an' it be then he get sold. To whites. Slave traders that took him 'cross the ocean by boat. Cicero say that his gran'pappy think he gonna get et by the white folks on the boat. He so young that he don't knowed no better. Them slave traders the first white folk he ever see'd.

Uncle Cicero tell us how his gran'pap walk one mornin' with his sister down a path—he had her with him the day he get catched up. An' after that day, he never see her ever again.

He say they out huntin' near his village. When he snatched, he never knowed what happen to his sister. He live with the family that snatch him almost a whole year before he get taken by another tribe an' sold to white men that put iron chains on his neck. The boy get strung together with strangers, men mostly. Few children. There other women an' gals, kept separate. Not his sister, though. No. Never see'd her.

The men, they put in some kind of fort, made of stone. An' a big boat come with rough bearded white men. The boat, it the biggest one Cicero gran'pap ever see'd. Now, he just a boy—didn't know nothin'. They white men looks lak ghosts, an' there rumors goin' 'round that they hungry ghosts that et up people. So gran'pap wus scare. He done figure that he be someone tasty meal. He even think about jumpin' overboard when they set out to sea. But he chained.

When Uncle Cicero tell us his story, which he do often, changin' up some of the details, but it told pretty much the same. Us children would pretend we wus that boy, an' we'd shape us a boat out of pine straw. We go out in the woods, gather up the straw, build a ship, pine straw an' baling twine, an' make believe we sail away. Play out parts—both slave an' white. We even take that twine an' tie "our slaves" up tight with it. Then we pretend to whup them when we gits them in the pine-straw ship. Lak cowboys an' Indians these days. Children play what they knows.

Well, when Cicero die, he left many sad black folk an' white—everybody love Uncle Cicero.

What I remember is this: Cicero wus trainin' a pair of new mules Marster done purchase up river, in the next county. Harnett. Which wus new. It part of ol' Cumberland broke off into this new county, Harnett. Marster bought this mule pair hisself. So he brung them to Cicero. Uncle Cicero wus good with the animals—horses, mules—an' he could usually break them in a single day.

He'd take them down to the lower field, whar' there wus a small pen. I never watch him work. But I heared he'd come home after a day with any horse or mule, an' that animal be complete broke. Well, this time, he come on up without them mules, an' early lak, around dinner time. He come creepin' along the dirt trail, holdin' his head. There wus blood, lots of blood. Seem one of them spunky mules gone kick Uncle Cicero in the head. He left that mule penned up an' walk on home, lookin' for help. Ma see'd him first. She call out, an' us gals come runnin'. Uncle Cicero barely made it. He kind of swooped down at our cabin. Belinda, that work up at the big house, wus out pumpin' water when she see'd the trouble. She gone to call Marster, but he weren't there. Missus come out to the back veranda an' say, "Oh Lawd!" She order fresh rags brung down for Uncle Cicero. But he about dead by then. Eyes closed, breath puffin' out real slow, moanin' somethin' terrible. They done take rags to soak up the blood, get a block of wood beneath his head. He lay lak this for while, outside our cabin. I wus there—everybody there. It be a real pretty day, not hot yet. An' there be Uncle Cicero dyin'. Right there with a clear blue sky above. No clouds. God work his will, ain't interested in makin' the day fit the occasion—no. Birds chirpin', bees buzzin'. That the way of the Lawd. Give one thing, take another.

Uncle Cicero wife, Aunt Nancy, she come runnin' from I don't know whar'. She start sobbin' an' hollerin' by his side. Prayin'. But it done no good. He never open up his eyes again.

They brung him inside his own cabin, an' his family—what he had—be there with him that night when he finally die. He got a son we call Swell. Swell a angry man—always wus. An' Uncle Cicero, he got two other children that die from the scarlet fever sometime back. Aunt Nancy, Swell, an' everyone—all real sad. Them times, death come easy. Always peakin' round the corner, castin' about for someone.

Uncle Cicero wus real playful with the young 'uns. He'd make dolls for the gals out of corn husks. He even paint eyes an' faces. He make ridin' horses for the boys. From wood logs, an' the boys would climb on them an' ride them. When we real li'l, we had few chores an' spent time just playin' an' mindin' ourself.

Uncle Cicero, a good man. Marster an' Missus make him a real funeral an' done gits their own church preacher come… *[The tape is very scratchy and unclear for a brief moment. Part of a sentence is lost.]*

…next day. We follow him in a line down the same dirt trail Uncle Cicero took. We didn't has no black to wear. We only wear what we had—work clothes, children barefoot in the dirt.

I remember there be wailin', carryin' on. White an' colored comin' to give respects. Swell, he wearin' a top hat. Don't know whar' he get it. But that wus somethin' to remember.

The slave cemetery wus below the outside pasture, across the road. There wus a hole in the earth for Uncle Cicero, been dug in the mornin' by his kin, mostly Swell, I guess, an' they laid him in. He wus in a pine box coffin, plain but made right. They lowered the box down with rope. It made a creakin' sound as the rope stretch with the coffin weight. Creak, creak, stretchin' lak it might break. All the folk starts to sing. Oh, I still knows that song. Yas. Let me sing what I knows. *[Ms. Augustus clears her voice and sings. The quality of her voice is timorous and high, but very pleasant.]*

> *Rock, chariot, in the middle of the air.*
> *Judgment gonna find me.*
> *I wonder what chariot comin' after me.*
> *Judgment gonna find me....*
>
> *Just lower down the chariot right easy,*
> *Right easy, right easy,*
> *Just lower down the chariot right easy,*
> *Right easy, right easy,*
> *And bring God servant home....*

Make me sad to think of that day, even now. Swell wanna play his banjo—he make it by hand—but folk say banjo pickin' ain't right for this occasion.

That all. All I recall. *[Ms. Augustus seems to clear her throat.]* Gonna need a li'l break. Too much gabbin'. Too much for a ol' gal. Why don't yo' turn that thing off. *[A clicking is heard, and Ms. Augustus resumes the next day.]*

August 18, 1937

I knows we talk about Uncle Cicero last time. Today, I rested, in a better way, an' I wants to gab 'bout happier times. Maybe 'bout a plantation weddin' we has at the big house. Then yo' get a notion not all wus bad. 'Course I ain't suggestin' we go back to those times—I value my freedom, an' most Negroes does—though there be them talkin' lak those times wus best. But don't git me goin' about that. No.

An' as I says before, my Marster an' Missus wus good folk. Not all thems bad. After the war, I work for white folk. Stay with some. They take care of me an' treat me right. Best they could.

But 'bout this plantation weddin'. Now, I remember that good—that time wus real happy. Weren't no real official marriage lak today. No. Black folk then would do what they call "jump the broom." Which mean that a preacher'd come—if there wus any. Else a marster do the ceremony. He say a few words in front a group of witnesses. On this here occasion, the two young 'uns that jump the broom, one be from our plantation—Harriet, her name. An' Joe, Dusty Joe, we call him—he from another plantation, just down the ways a few mile.

Now there two weddin's I recall. Tell yo' the second later. But this first weddin' wus in late fall, after most the crops wus in. We grow 'bacco an' cotton, so there always work—except by Christmas an' New Year time when we off—but after harvest time, things wus slow, an' we could take the day for a weddin'. Now this happen the year before I meets David. Late fall, must'ta been a year.

Harriet wus 'bout sixteen, an' Dusty Joe 'bout twenty. Missus let Harriet have her graduatin' dress, all white an' clean. Joe wore his Marster ol' fancy suit. An' what a pair they make. Wish we had us a camera back then. They wus sure pretty. We kill a chicken that mornin', an' make some fresh corn pone an' a mess of greens. We has the ceremony on the back veranda. Must'ta been thirty folks lookin' on.

Words wus spoke by Marster—he married them. An' after the couple say "I do," they both gits to jump backward over a broomstick. It held by two folk of the weddin' party, a foot high off the floor at either end. The groom, he try to jump backward over it, an' then the bride. Everyone stand 'round to watch. The one that lands best without fallin', that the person git to be boss of the household. If the gal win out, the boy git whooped an' holler at, teased. 'Course, there ain't no real wisdom in this. But it somethin' passed on. Negroes done this—somethin' Uncle Cicero tell us get passed from Africa. But I heared others done it too. Uncle Cicero, he tell us so much—about everythin'. Yas, when he die, it real sad. A loss.

Now, don't know for sure. Maybe this here broom weddin' weren't right. I mean, maybe it weren't from Africa. Or maybe in Africa it weren't a broom but somethin' else that they has to jump backward over. Don't know if they had brooms in Africa, but in North Car'lina, slave weddin's had this broom jump. I heared since that the broom mean somethin' about death, jumpin' death. An' jumpin' over it backward, a good sign yo' gonna live long. Higher yo' jump, longer yo' live.

I heared that sometime they carry a bucket of water on their heads— bride an' groom. But I don't know how that go. I never seen no one do that.

This here weddin', we had us a fine time. Henry, from our place, wus a fiddler. He so good, Marster hire him out for white folk dances an' balls all across Car'lina, Virg'nia. But he back home this time, an' Henry come to play at this weddin'.

Henry play religious songs lak "Somebody Talkin' 'bout Jesus." Yo' wanna hear that one? I remember…let me see now…gots my singin' voice back…after yesterday. *[There is a pause in the tape, some throat clearing, and again, Ms. Augustus's singular voice is heard.]*

Everywhar' I go,
Everywhar' I go, my Lawd,
Everywhar' I go,
Somebody talkin' 'bout Jesus.

Well, my knees been acquainted with the hillside clay,
Somebody talkin' 'bout Jesus.
An' my head's been wet with the midnight dew,
Somebody talkin' about Jesus…

An' it go on with many verses—can't recall….

Then we had other songs we sing, not about Jesus or God. "Turkey in the Straw," it one. Most time Henry play tunes, without singin'. We dance a jig an' some other dances that wus pop'lar back in them times. Wish I could do one for yo' now! But I too ol'. *[Ms. Augustus laughs.]*

Weddin's usually takes place on Saturdays. That way the bride an' groom can stay together Saturday night. Negroes gits passes for Saturday, an' husbands light out to their wives an' children, stay for Sunday, home ready for Monday mornin' work. Now sometime we work on Sunday—

when that happen, we call Sunday, Blue Monday. But that only once in 'while.

That weddin' sure wus somethin'. Henry fiddlin', folks dancin', carryin' on. There wus whisky, corn liquor. Our white folk didn't mind no drinkin', long as nobody took to no fightin'.

In some plantations, especially way down South, I heared the white folk provoke colored to fight—lak we do roosters or dogs sometime. For sport. They liquor them up real good an' bet cash money on who win. Sometime black folk gets hurt real bad, even die.

But no one I knows do this. No. We all church folk—black an' white, though we separate. Back then, we allowed to go to meetin'. For 'while, we has our own church right across the dirt road, by the lower field—in a 'bacco barn. That our meeting house. Afer Uncle Cicero die, it weren't the same, and somehow never seem right again. In bad weather, storm, or somethin', it just too far to walk—even for the Lawd. So we meet in one of them tool sheds near the big house them times.

In Fayett'ville now, there be big Negro churches: Evans Metropolitan AME, an' St. Joseph's Episcopal. Might be others, don't know, don't keep up.

Back in my time, we be keep ignorant—better lak that, white folk say. Learnin' be the tool of the debil. Readin', writin' make us uppity, an' we be wantin' somethin' we can't have. White folk come preach to us sometime, tellin' us about how the Bible say some born to be slave, others born to be free. That what they sayin', preachin'. We keeps our business to ourself—white folk didn't appreciate Negroes with too much learnin'. We wus taught that God want us all be content with our lot an' obeyin'. Some does an' some don't. There be stupid folk an' smart folk—black an' white. All sorts…good natured an' ornery, mean an' good.

Now, I wus young durin' slavery time—so I might feel different if I spend my whole life a slave. It be tiring—wear a person down. But there some colored speakin' now, say thems better times for us back then.

But ain't no one goin' back. Them times gone forever. Though there plenty of problems now. No, no shortage of trials now. Folks can't find no work. Some don't wanna work…some, if yo' axe me is lazy. But most wanna work. Just ain't no work to be had.

This slave weddin' wus special. One child—don't remember who— came an' did a cake walk dance on top of a table we piece together from some ol' slab boards. He the cutest thing. White folk laugh an' laugh.

One gal, a youn' miss from another plantation, flip coins on the table, an' this child dance an' pick 'em up, without losin' a step. That fiddlin' so dern good, I can hear it now.

Not all them weddin's be so fancy. No. On some plantations, a gal git to be hardly growed, an' they done pick her out a husband—not marry 'em, but throwed them together, expectin' chil'ren—increase a marster property. A man be brung out an' shoved on some li'l gal, an' she be ordered to stay with him—even if she didn't knowed or liked him. No, some marsters ain't ever allow Negroes to find their own sweethearts, so he go an' put 'em together. Take a bull man, sometimes a mean fellow, but strong, put him together with a nice youn' gal whether she agree or not. It lak mating dogs, expect them to gets plenty of babies—an' them babies were marster property, so he always be wantin' mo'. A gal would be plucked up at fifteen—sometime younger—force to git with some boy, barely a man. Sometime ol' marster show himself up at a ol' cabin an' say, "Frank an' Betty—or whatever them names is—I pronounce yo' man an' wife." An' that be it.

Ain't right. Give a slave a bad feelin' all 'round to see that. An' them feelin's ain't never die, not never.

Even whar' we wus, when a young gal or fella want to gits married, it need to be right with Marster first. But Marster always let our young 'uns to finds they own sweethearts. The young 'uns comes to their ma or pa, an' says, "We wants to gits married." Then theys go to Marster an' he would say if it be all right. Marster never put his colored folk together. No. Some white folk talk about God this an' God that, only when it suit 'em. Theys quotes scripture an' says, "Obey yo' marster" an' such. Make folk come together—no better than mules. Whip colored till they ain't got no will left. I'll tell yo' about whippin'—see'd it, but lak I say, I wus never whipped myself, no. Come close one time. *[There is a brief pause in the tape.]*

This a big wedding, but some folk comes together with just a few words—preacher or marster quote a bit scripture an' say, "I pronounce yo' man an' wife." Then they jumps the broom.

Now, the woman didn't never take the name of her husband. He have his marster name, an' she keep the name of the family that own her. Sometime the marriage don't last; sometime it do. Sometime husband or wife sold away, an' that be the end, right there. Sometime husband, wife can't see each other 'cause they live too far apart. An' there's them that cheat an' carry on.

After Surrender, northern preacher come around with a li'l book he keep for names, official, an' he marry slaves by law. Some young folks today laugh about slave love. Say it weren't real love back then. What they know? [*Ms. Augustus sighs and pauses.*]

Mar, my oldest sister, she be the jealous type. That right. She didn't have no sweetheart yet, an' she be standin' off to the side when this Harriet gal marry. We all gather 'round the board table, exceptin' Mar. She stand by the big magnolia, off to one side. I comes over to her an' axe her why she standin' away.

"I ain't got no beau," she say. An' I older than that Harriet gal."

Now, yo' ain't gonna believe this—but I just looks up an' says, "What's about that there young feller?" I points to a boy I don't even knows.

An' that boy, he become Mar feller before that party half done. His name be James Henry, an' he belong to the Harris McNeils from Cumberland County. Other McNeils from other counties, north an' south. But this one belong to the Cumbland ones. James Henry Harris McNeil.

Well, he lookin' on, not mindin' us at first. His wooly hair cropped close, an' he have a sweet smile—for no reason—just a natural smile. We take to gigglin', coverin' our mouths. But James Henry must have heared us, or maybe God whisperin' to him, 'cause he done lift his eyes lak he know somethin' up. He smilin', an' Lawd, it a nice day. Weddin' an' now James Henry comin' on over, before we knows it, to Mar an' me, whar' we standin'. Mar seem to glow, lak the heaven shine a light down on her. I just slip away back to the celebration.

There be fresh cooked chicken, pot-fried, an' corn pone, an' greens. An' plenty chores to keep me scurrin' around. But I looked back on them every once in while, an' there they be, smilin' at each there, with their heads bowed, lak at church. Then I knows this God work. Yas. He help me brung these two together. From that day forward, they a couple of peas in a pod. Weren't much later till Mar an' James Henry gits married theirselfs. But that weddin' I don't remember so well 'cause it come sudden, right before the war, an' I laid up with the croup. I has the fever bad, so the weddin' go by in a daze, an' I ain't remember much. But this

Harriet weddin' I knows it lak it yesterday—the whole weddin' lak a movin' picture in my mind—an' I can plays it again an' again.

The weddin' that day just brung 'em together. That an' God. Some folks, when they heared I'd spotted James Henry, thinks I gots some kind'a power. An' not just for match-makin'…

Nows I a ol' woman—mo' than ninety. Ain't the kind'a person that need glory brung to her. No. Never wus. But theys right. The Lawd done pick me out for somethin'. Made it through plenty hard times—I here, ain't I? [*Ms. Augustus sighs, and there are some garbled background noises, then silence, and a click.*]

August 19, 1937

This here's a hotter day than it been. Rain comin' an' my bones achin'. Arthritis. I gonna sits here [*There is a scraping noise and a brief pause.*] Gonna tells yo' 'bout childhood in slavery time. What I first recalls.

Must'ta been about four, four year ol'. It winter time, near Christmas. Cold outside an' in, too. Our cabin just boards what yo' could see through, but we had us a fireplace, big, one side of the cabin, an' we keep it goin' through the night, kindlin'—from the piney woods near the field—an' stoke it up good.

One cold Saturday night, I weren't but about four, an' Pa be with us 'cause he spend the night, lak he sometime do. Pa wus tellin' us gals to come over to the fire. Us chil'ren wus huddle up in a feed sack thrown over with a blanket made from weavin'. So we gather our sacks by the hot blazin' fire, an' Pa come close an' tell us this story that scare me half to death.

Pa begin by axin' us about the debil. We says, "Yas, sir, we knows all about the debil—how he have horns an' cloven feet. Then, he say that the debil always be travelin' around—see what folk up to—black an' white. An' when he travelin' around, he need shoes, 'cause his feet hurt. Well, one day, the debil be here—in these parts, right near the Ellicott place—that the next plantation north—an' he makin' his mischief 'cause that what he do. But he workin' so hard this one time, he takes lame an' need some new shoes.

It be cold an' dark, kind of wet, nasty weather outside, an' I warm an' toasty, imaginin' the debil slippin' in an' out of darkness…right outside. Wind howlin', rain blowin'.

Well, Pa, go on—"Not too long that debil travel, checkin' up on folks, see what they up to…if they be good or bad, when his feets gits too lame to walk."

Pa take his hand an' motion us to gits even closer—we squiggling 'round lak li'l piglets.

"The debil now," he go on with big eyes an' a deep, whispery voice, "wus a white man."

Debil always a white man—dress in trousers an' a coarse home-spun shirt. Yo' never knowed it the debil, but for his cloven feet an' horns he keep under his cap.

Pa say, "He go to a blacksmith shop an' axe the ol' smithy to gits him shod. Which the smith do, but only to avoids gittin' bad luck on hisself."

The flame from the fire flare up, spit on us lak the debil hisself.

Don't know if it be Pa trickery, but I thought the debil wus watchin' us for sure.

"The debil gits his feet right, then he out travelin' again," Pa say. But before yo' knows it, his feet done ache him some mo'. Pa say that the debil git angry at that ol' smith that done shod him poorly, an' he go back an' tell him, "Take off them shoes my feets, an' puts some on that fit properly. These ones they hurts too much!"

Now Ma wus listenin' off to the sides, the way she always do—listenin' but not lettin' on. Doin' some handiwork—darnin' or sewin' somethin'. Us gals wus gathered up in the sack, real close, kickin' each other, all wiggly.

"The smithy, he be wary of the debil anger an' afraid what a debil might do, so he agree to take 'em shoes off an' git him new ones—under one condition, that from now on, the debil leave him alone. Ain't come this way no mo'. An' the debil be in such pain that he agree to the smithy demand. So the debil git his shoes off an' new ones hammered on. They be lak horse shoes, just smaller to fit over his cloven feet. An' when the debil satisfied, he leave—but just before he do, he take his ol' shoe an' nail it up on blacksmith door. He make it into a upright 'U' and say 'long as he see this sign above folk door, he'd not gonna bother them that live there. That debil shoe, a sign, *Keep Out*."

Pa go on, "The debil knowed that he gits the raw bargain in this. But he promise hisself that he gonna make up for it with other smithies. There plenty 'round that don't know the sign." Pa say that any small horseshoe do fine, an' that why so many folks puts them on their barn doors—ward off the evil.

Now the wind pick up lak it agree with all Pa sayin'. We gals press together, lookin' lak a four-headed monster with a bunch of scraggly legs twitchin' about in the sack.

It just some silly ol' story, but I so scared, thinkin' that the debil be tryin' to locate a blacksmith that don't has no sign hung outside so that he could gits his feets shod. I thinkin' 'bout the blacksmith shops around, an' I checkin' them off in my head—thems that have the sign posted. Then, I axe Pa if we has a horseshoe over our blacksmith door. He say we done had one, but it fall down just last week. I tells him I gonna go right now an' hang it up again. Pa say to just forgits it—it can wait another day. Ain't good enough weather for the debil to be 'bout. But I shoot up out the warm sack, lak I done gits the spirit in church, an' barefoot, I unhitch the door an' runs out. All way to the blacksmith shop. Lak lighten' in a storm.

I makes my way out in the cold, ain't dress proper in my shift. An' when I gits there, sure enough, there ain't no horseshoe hangin', an' the shop all shut tight, spooky an' dark. I shiverin' out in the cold, an' hears Pa callin' me from ways off. But I stubborn an' won't comes till I finds myself a ol' shoe an' nail an' hammer, an', I tells yo', I stands there freezin', but quick I finds me a ol' horseshoe an' bent nails, an' I pummels it up with a rock by the door, high as I can reach. Not up high as it suppose' to be, but high enough. *Gotta do this thing*, I tells myself, feelin' real proud, an' runs all the way back to my cabin. Shiverin' an' cold.

When I done git there, Ma, real upset with Pa—"Why yo' let her go?"

"Couldn't stop her none," wus what Pa tell her. An' I guess he right. Ma punish me next mornin' an' didn't gives me no corn grit 'cause I cut out. But Pa save me some of his, an' I et while Ma wus out with some early mornin' chore.

To this day, I think of that story an' sometime wonder how the debil travel nowadays, when there ain't so many blacksmith anymo'. Silly—I knowed it just a story to scare children. But it done stay with me. *[There is a short pause, followed by some scratching sounds, and then Ms. Augustus continues.]*

Christmas, that wus the best time for us slaves. We gits a new pair of shoes an' some clothin' at Christmas—once a year. We'd has to makes good with them all year 'cause we weren't gittin' no mo'. Young 'uns would git a long shirt—a dress. Boy or gal, didn't matter. They wears the same. When they turn 'bout eight, boys gits regular pants, an' they be proud to look so growed up. The gals git real dresses around same time. Marster make a big deal over us gittin' these. An' the shoes, especially them shoes. He come out on the front veranda Christmas mornin' an' have us Negroes line up before him. Shoes wus made from wood or cow hide. Right there on the property. We come up to the steps, an' he hand us our rations. We be grateful. Say, *Thank ye, Marster.* Shiverin' an' cold, waitin' our turn to go up the veranda steps. We has blankets an' shawls over us. Pitiful how li'l we has. How grateful we wus.

Tell yo', I look back on them days an' wonder how we made do. Ma sew us some things an' done all the mendin'. But Christmas wus a big occasion. Sometime it be so cold or even snow. Sometime freezin' rain. We march up there an' keep our eyes low, couldn't look at Marster direct. Never allowed. The gals would curtsey almost to the ground, an' boys would bow low too—all sayin': *Thank ye, Marster*—real formal. An' *Merry Christmas to ye.*

Some slaves stole chickens an' make off with them to cook in the woods. Or sometime they steal from other plantations. That way they blame the chicken hawks an' don't git catched. Sometime—not just Christmas—if we gits hungry enough, we steal. Ain't right, but hunger have a mind of its own.

After Christmas, we dress up in our new clothes, come around to the meetin' house, strut about, an' show off. Everybody feelin' good, lessin' there wus winter sickness.

With time off, chil'ren play games lak base, cat, rolly hole, an' around town—ol' games. Don't know if they still play them these days.

Young chil'ren back then not expect to do much chores, only milkin', totin', gatherin' kindlin', goin' down with their elders to fetch mail or other goods from the stage that come in, or down to the river. The post office wus located in someone livery barn. Didn't have no official post. Stage come to the road with the mail, or it drop off a bundle, an' white folks git paid to keep it. Everyone have to come gits their own mail. Ain't no delivery lak today.

Chil'ren didn't have much sense. Slavery wus the only thing they knowed. If they real li'l…. Fact is, it just the life they knowed. Some has themselfs good memories of them times. Especially if they ain't treat bad. Some slave chil'ren wus lak pets to their white folks. They too li'l to understand. An', 'course, yo' sees how bad most things is now—bad for us Negroes. White folks too.

Lak I say, chil'ren work, but not too hard. They tote water an' food to them field slaves too. Totin' start at about five or six. Then, when they around nine or ten, they gits mo' chores, lak milkin' an' sloppin'. The gals sometime work 'round the big house, helpin' colored women with them house chores. But the grown folk never wanna say much in front us young 'uns—no. What I means—is that if a child of six overhear somethin' unfriendly a grown Negro say, she might repeat it to her marster or missus. Sometime, marsters use the li'l chil'ren as snitches. Chil'ren don't know no better. They just blabbin' what they hears. An' that git folks in trouble. Lak that li'l Sammy boy….

Happen after I meets David an' that Mr. Potter by the creek. I still a gal really, fifteen. Just had my change.

Well, that day, I come by the big house to help Missus with some chore. Everyone buzzin' about war. Don't remember what they sayin', but it a odd day with everybody out of sorts. Even the sky overcast. An' there a kind'a bustling—everyone whisperin' about how the nation gonna have its war.

Shift in the wind that day. Lak some big ol' storm brewin'. [*Ms. Augustus clears her throat.*] Things beginnin' to change. An' it ain't good. Folk ain't in a good way. Nobody really want that war, but white folk be talkin' lak they do.

I wus at the big house. An' walkin' by, I seen Missus raise her hand to li'l Sammy. Don't know what go on before I comes. Seem Sammy say somethin' he shouldn't. Sammy, he be a difficult chil', but I can't blame him. An' Missus, well she out of sorts—don't know who to blame.

Ma always tell us gals, "Yo's don't see nothin', no time. Yo' just mind yo' own business." But this time I curious, so I slip up close to watch, listen—just make sure to stay out of sight.

They in the parlor, an' I in the hall when I hear Sammy talkin' sass to Missus. He raise his voice—no colored allow to do to that. An' he a small chil'.

I see Missus slap Sammy upside the head, then stop. She walk across the room to the desk, pick up somethin'—ain't sure what. Paperweight maybe, some hard object from the desk she standin' by. She throw it at Sammy, who slink off to a corner an' be cowering lak a kicked pup. Crouchin' there, hands over his li'l self. Sammy squeal when Missus throw the object at him, an' Missus shout. I wus in the hall, keepin' myself hid. Next thing, Sammy crawlin' out on all fours. Though he be around seven year ol', he be crawlin' lak a baby that don't know how to walk.

I see'd most this from the foyer hall. Nobody know I there, an' I never learn what set Missus off—weren't lak her. She very upset an' go upstairs. So I take my chance an' creep out the house to the horse barn, whar' I think Sammy might be. An' there he is. I heared him wailin' an' carryin' on, cowerin' in a empty stall whar' there be new hay forked in. Never tell me what he done. But long as he live at the Smith place, Sammy hate Missus.

Don't know if there be other times lak this here one, with Sammy, I mean, gittin' somethin' throwed at him or if he get whupped. But Sammy get this mean look behind his eyes. See'd it in other colored too—as if the hate beat into them. A cur pup kicked too many times. Plenty tales from down south, way down. Louisiana, Miss'ippi. Negro slaves burned, irons put on them. Branded. Whippings. Bad stories. The Lawd work in strange ways…. [*A sigh is heard, and a brief pause follows.*]

Well, I 'bout ready to quit. Tired. I be back tomorrow. Needs myself some rest. [*The machine is quickly clicked off.*]

August 20, 1937

Nows, I ain't finish yet what I begin the other day … what I told yo' 'bout. Last night after we gits done, I remember somethin'. When he about four year ol', I hear li'l Sammy say to Missus, "Yo' a mean ol' bitch!" —barely talkin', but that what come out his mouth. 'Course he didn't understand what he sayin'. Just must'ta been repeatin' what he heared somewhar'. Don't think Sammy git no beatin' that time. Just run out the house.

He an' the stable boy he take up with—they get sold later. But I wants yo' to understand there some history between Sammy an' Missus. Not just that one time.

I goes to the store here in Raleigh—after yo' left yesterday. An' I runs into some folks I know, here in Raleigh.

This here one gal, ol' woman, live but a few streets over—she the one I meets at the store. "Howdy-do,"—we say an' somehow gits to gabbin' about ol' times, an' then she go on about how nice her marster wus back in slavery times. He lak her pa, she say.

I tell her she crazy. I ain't talk bad 'bout my white folk, lak I say before. But slavery, no, we ain't goin' back to that.

Take this here ol' gal. She says she'd be thinkin' slavery times wus better than times now. She tell her stories about how nice her white folk treat her—yo' ought'ta go speak with her. She go by name Grady. Mary Grady. Say her white folk same as her pappy an' ma. They take care of her, an' she swear she'd go back an' be slave again, if she have the chance. I tell her she crazy, ain't in her right mind. She axe me if I has enough to et now. I tell her that ain't the point.

I goes stay on at the Smith place for a time after the war over. But I ain't no slave. Things different. My white folk ain't never treat me bad. But I ain't foolin' myself 'bout them bein' my ma an' pappy—no, I has a real pa an' a ma that born me.

Some colored folk full of hate. Sammy, if he around, he be that way. A chil' treated bad ain't never gonna forget. Some Negroes treated lak mules, cattle. Even worse.

Now, as I gabbin' on about chil'ren, they often put out as playmates for the white folk chil'ren. That what we done. Play house—the colored gals pretendin' they house slaves, an' the boys, they pretend they livery slaves. White children gits to be the marster an' missus. Order us around. All in fun—they just doin' what they'd see'd them kin folk do. All according to the color line. That ain't surprisin', but I tell yo' they doin' the exact same today.

Here I is, an' I watchin' the neighbor children playin' out in the dirt street. They take on them roles lak they done before. Till things change an' colored come up from what they wus, we Negroes has a long road to hoe. We come a ways, but not far enough. Take near a hundred year before colored folk pull themselves up whar' they need be…. *[There is a brief pause in the tape, and then Ms. Augustus resumes.]*

We chil'ren has ourselfs corn shuckin's, candy pullin's, even dances an' prayer meetin's at the meetin' house. In August, there be what we call "camp meetin' days" when we lay by canned goods. We play games of high jump—jumpin' over the pole what be held by two folk on either side—wrestlin', an' leap frog. We sings "Go Tell Aunt Betsy." Somethin' lak this [*Ms. Augustus clears her throat*]:

> *Some folks says a Nigga won't steal,*
> *I caught six of them in my corn fiel'*
> *Run, Nigga, run,*
> *The patteroller catch yo',*
> *Run, Nigga, run, lak yo' did the other day!*

I remember hopscotch too. There in the dirt, we'd draw out the boxes with a stick an' find some pebble to throw down. We'd sing a song—don't remember that one. It'd be somethin' lak: *Penny down, I go 'round....*

Now, I gonna tell yo' somethin'—recalls it when I speakin' 'bout Mar, an' hows I links her up with James Henry, an' folks say I gots powers. Well, this here day, it wus the first time.

It fall, an' all the leave floatin' off the sycamore tree near our cabin. I look up while we wus all playin' hopscotch. Us gals, all Negro gals that day. We drawin' our board in the dirt by quarters. Must be evenin', after chores. There weren't no boys 'cause it weren't a boy game. We out behind the cabins. An' there these leafs sailin' across the sky, caught in a strong wind. They flutterin', an' when I look up, see angels among them. I just stare, though it my turn to throw down the pebble.

Now this before I turn ten. Maybe eight. I just a child. Plaited, nappy hair. Ma would braid us all so tight we gits headaches. "She skinny in her bones"—Ma would say. She ain't never git a dress to fit me right.

Yo' believes in angels? 'Cause I sure see'd them an' heared music too. Heavenly music, not fiddle playin'. Harps, lovely.

Sally—she Aunt Patsy chil'—give me a shove when she see me stop. I got the pebble in my hand, but it lak I far away. So Sally shove me, an' I wakes up an' says to her, "Yo' see them angels, Sally?" But she laugh, an' say, "Ain't no angels, Sarah Louise—them be leafs caught in sun as they tumble down."

She be tryin' to hand me a pebble for the game. But I ain't be in the mood no mo'. I says, "I gonna go on home, Sally. Gotta tell Ma about them here angels." I see'd them all right. Sure as day.

It weren't no leafs comin' down nor no wind makin' that harp music. That the first time, but them angels appear again an' again. All through my life. Come to warn me, save me, who know what else. With me all my life—appearin'… *[Some scratchiness in the tape here makes it difficult to discern how Ms. Augustus completes this sentence.]*

…some folk believe in guardian angels, but that ain't my religion. But what do Jesus care about rules? He make us free with His love, an' I believe He send them angels here for a reason. That why I growed to such an ol' woman—them angels takin' care. Not all the times, no. An' the debil hisself come too. Yas, he do. Yo'll see that. An' when he come, nowhar' wus them angels.

That there game of hopscotch wus the first time I see'd them—two of them. An' when they speaks, it be in one voice—without sound. I mean their thoughts travel to me, an' I hears them loud an' clear together, as if they practice what they gonna say. No matter how bad what they tells me is—about war, death—they never scares me. Somethin' 'bout their voices. Calming, soothing, lak a poulice applied just right. They could come today—right now. Tell me I gonna die tomorrow—an' that be all right.

I sees them most when I awake—not in dreams. An' I've stared at them, rubbin' my eyes, an' they still there. I knows them real. They come to predict the future, warn, or comfort.

An' they never ol', never young. Always the same. Not quite chil'ren, but lak small grown gals. When Surrender come, I see'd them. They come after I meets David one time an' tells me 'bout the war—confirm what I already knows. When there be rumors flyin', these here angels sometime come an' dispel any iffy business. Lak after David come, an' I axe Ma about the war—they come again soon after that.… *[Ms. Augustus's voice trails off here for a moment, and then she continues.]*

…I wus about sixteen year ol', considered a growed woman. Nowaday, sixteen still a child. Back then yo' growed up quicker. I wus pluckin' up ears of corn an' puttin' them in a big sack I uset'ta carry. Had a big shoulder strap that we sew on, but it lak a feed sack. I walkin' my usual way, hummin' somethin', alone, 'cause it past harvest time—an' these ears of corn wus the late, stumpy kind. I heared somethin' in the distance, somethin' lak…can't describe it, really. Somethin' lak the rustlin' of a scamperin' squirrel. I look up an' see my angels. They warn me in that silent single voice that the war gonna come an' the South gonna lose. Lose bad. I didn't tell no one at the time. What the point? But it stay with me. An' 'course, it come true. *[The interviewer can be heard indistinctly in the background, and then the tape is turned off.]*

August 23, 1937

Monday again. Still rainin'. *[Some static and scraping noises are heard.]*

I gonna start today before the war. Back to the time right after I meets David—fall, 1860. Met David in July. Now it be September, before the war—War Between the States.

It go different by some. Northern folk say *War of the Rebellion*. Southern say *War of Northern Aggression*. Don't matter. War is war—this one ain't no exception.

Let me see…year now '37. We talk about '60 'cause the war start in '61. Lincoln git elected in '60. Folk git stir up from that election. Say if Lincoln git elected, they ain't stay in the Union. Others say we should stay, no matter. We wus divided—a mess. North Car'lina take awhile to secede from the Union. Before that war, it wus a fearful time.

Today I gonna recollect a hangin' I see'd. It be what they calls Southern justice. I see'd a man hung from his neck till the life go out of him.

They hung men in downtown Fayett'ville, in the middle of Ramsey Street. Put up a gallows an' hang a man exactly 12 'clock noon. Yo' too young to know such things. Folks today don't know nothin' about hangin's.

This here time, it wus early fall—'tween crop harvest. There wus a lull in work an' li'l for us chil'ren to do. There a hub-bub 'bout our plantation about a white man gonna get hisself hung for horse thievin'. Story go he a stranger. A horse trader. Gamblin', drinkin' man. Don't remember his name. But he a cheatin' man an' a thief. Convicted an' sentence to hang till he dead. Ida, one of Marster elder gals, tell Kate, my older sister. Then the word spread out lak lightnin'. One of Marster boys says we can all go watch, an' he gonna make a plan.

Marse George—he be the one killed in the war—done come up with it. Say we gonna go to town, white an' Negro both in the ol' mule wagon—nobody won't be missed. He could drive it, an' load up the back with hay. We all could rides there. We be back before supper chores. So he axe his Pa, an' Marster say we chil'ren ain't needed much till evenin' chores. Do us good to see a man hang, see what happen to them that don't behave.

There be 'bout five or six us chil'ren that day. All excited. Not one of us never seen no hangin'. Heared about them.

Early that mornin'—cloudy but a nice day—we load into the wagon by the horse barn an' start out, bumpin' along the dirt road an' out the plantation. Bumpin' an' bumpin'. We laugh an' laugh, carryin' on. Hannah, start up singin'. We tell stories. Cut up. Even Marse George take on with us. He good, Marse George. About 17 year ol'—handsome—tall with black silk hair an' green eyes. I remember those eyes—'cause David eyes green. Feel bad when Marse George die'. Yas, I do. An' they never even send the body home. They has a service without it.

Well, the trip to town take 'bout a hour. Bump, bump, bump, over them dirt roads. Even Ramsey Street wus dirt back then. Though it be early fall, this day cool. The sun come poke out the clouds now an' then, warm us up. I lay back an' watched the sky. Dreamin' lak I do. Clouds magic—takin' shape, changin'—a message there, if yo' knowed how to read them.

When we gits to whar' the gallows wus, there must'ta been a hundred people, colored an' white, all mix up in a large crowd. Women an' chil'ren, mens an' boys. The man to be hung weren't there yet. But there a scaffold built of pine logs, an' there wood stairs up to it. There weren't no commotion till the Fayett'ville Independent Light Infantry come with the prisoner. They all costumed up, might as well be a parade for the Fourth of July. But no music—no band. It a somber occasion. There wus mounted deputies along with the sheriff. An' the prisoner, he wearin' dark clothin' an' don't look at no one. When he walk up the steps an' git to the top, everyone hush, lak folks git in church. Could hear a bird fly across the sky, it so quiet. Fact is, a big ol' crow fly right above. Make a black V as he sail by. Marse George had left the wagon with the mules tie up to a post. Us chil'ren wus in the crowd, keepin' close to Marse George, an' a li'l behind him. But we could all see.

The arms an' legs of the condemned man wus bound. A reverend come out an' read a scripture from the Holy Book. Some verse about repentin'. Then sheriff step forward an' axe the man if he have anythin' to say before these friends an' neighbors. But the man say that these folks ain't be no friends nor neighbors of his, an' he don't deserve the punishment he 'bout to gits. Then that man look up—an' there that big crow circlin'. The prisoner smile at it as if he recognize somethin'. Then he clear his throat lak he gots mo' to say. The sheriff wait a few minutes but then axe if that it. The man drop his head an' nod.

Out of nowhar' come a black hood to cover his head. A black sack with no eye holes, mouth hole, nothin'. That man didn't look lak a man no mo'. He look lak the crow just winging overhead. He be a large, strange bird with his wings clipped, standin' in heavy black boots, legs tied. Seem already dead.

Bang! A trap done spring, an' there he go, flappin' an' swingin' free. Yo' could hear the rope around his neck creakin' as he swing. Folks start talkin' again, but in whispers, out of respect. Marse George look at me. I look at Hannah. No one got nothin' to say.

After about twenty minutes, the hanged man wus pronounced dead. His immortal soul launched into eternity. Everybody there that day feel bad. Even if that man deserve to die. Somethin' soberin' 'bout a man bein' hanged.

We all walk to the mule buggy. Nobody say a word. Just kind of shuffle back. All the way home, no one say nothin' neither. No cuttin' up, no singin'. Just the bumpin' along, an' the lonesome sound of the wagon wheels turnin'—they uneven. One of 'em wheels always out of true.

I remember that day good 'cause no sooner does we gits back after the hangin' that we hears the news about a run'way slave from another plantation. Mister John Ellicott hisself come ridin' up our dirt path to tell us. Mister John Ellicott, he the marster from Ellicott plantation, just north of the Smith place—north Fayett'ville. Come on horseback, real gallant, on a black stallion, just a few minutes after we gets back ourself. We just unloadin' our mule cart when he ride up.

Mister Ellicott shout, "Yo Niggas be on the lookout!" An' before he even introduce hisself, he pull out a paper. Marster approach on foot from the big house, an' Mister Ellicott seein' him, spur up to greet him. They nod at each other, shake hands.

Mister Ellicott then come ridin' back, shoutin' for us to gather. Marster don't ring no bell, so it just be 'bout seven us gather around. Marster walkin' to us too. Missus wus still somewhar' inside.

"Tell my Niggars what your man name is, John," Marster say.

"Johnny." Mister Ellicott speak out loud, an' he gaze out at us, a challenge.

"Got a description?" Marster axe.

An' Mister John Ellicott fumble with a paper from out in his coat pocket. It be a announcement he gonna put in the newspaper so as to catch up his man. That be whar' he off to—newspaper office down Fayett'ville. He gonna post his notice. Ellicott hand it over to Marster an' nod to him.

"All yo' Niggas be on the look out for this here Johnny fella," Marster begin. He read from the notice. Johnny around six feet tall an' lank. His wooly hair short cropped. An' he has lash marks on his back, been in trouble before. He got shifty eyes an' can't be trusted. "Yo' hear that?" Marster axe. Both men look around at us.

"He wanted for murderin' one of his own. Get drunk an' kill another Nigga," Mister Ellicott add. "Yo' can't never trust this man, this Johnny— no matter what he say."

Everyone silent. We keep our eyes low. Few of us just seen the hangin', an' we ain't feelin' so good.

"Ya'll hear me now? Hear what Mister Ellicott say?" Marster axe. By this time, a few mo' us together on the dirt path fork that lead to the big house. We mumble low, "Yas, Sir," but that ain't good enough.

"I axin' yo'," Marster shout out. "Mister Ellicott deserve some response." The sky still a mixture of cloud an' sun. A mockin' bird call from a tree.

We all nod an' murmur again—a li'l mo' loud.

Marster nod now, turn to Mister Ellicott, then back to us. "If this Johnny show up here," Marster say, "the mens needs to catch him up, or someone come to the big house straight away. He ain't to leave."

"He dangerous, may be armed with a kitchen knife," Ellicott shout.

"Yo' tell everyone what I say. Spread the word. "Escapee, Nigga Johnny. Lash marks on his back. Shifty. Dangerous."

Mister John Ellicott nod to Marster, say he gotta be goin'. Then he tip his hat, spur his stallion, an' take off in the dust, raisin' his hand as he leave. Dirt cloud kicked up all along as he flyin' off in a gallop. Marster tell us, it over now—go back to work.

I help with the chores—feed the cart mule, check the chickens that been cooped—some problems we'd been havin' with hawks. It near supper time when I go back to the cabin an' find Ma fixin' corn pone in them ashes. We also has some canned beans from last year harvest. Smell good around the cabin. I just need to rest a bit.

"Whar' yo' been, child?" Mama axe. "All cover with dust? Yo' been ridin' in that ol' mule buggy?" Ma busy, stirrin', back toward me.

I sit on the stoop by the front door. "Yo' heared about that Mister Ellicott Negro man, Ma? Name Johnny. They say he a murderer. Might got him a kitchen knife. Run from Mister Ellicott plantation."

"No," Ma say. "I out with Mammy Rae by the dye shack; then I in the field. Ain't know nothin' 'bout it. I seen them gather, but I got chores. Ain't no supper unless somebody cook it." Ma turn around to me. "Marster there? Tell me what gone on. What they say."

"Marster there. An' that Mister Ellicott come gallopin' down from the big house. Hannah with me. Marse George an' Norman, an' …Aunt Patsy there. Mister Ellicott got hisself a notice. His boy Johnny run'way. Now we got to watch for him."

Ma shake her head. Then she stir the pot. "Yo' mind yo'self gal. Ain't no Negro man gonna come bother yo' skinny bones none. All foolishness. That what it is." Ma look at me, shake her head again, tiskin' lak I makin' up the whole story. "Go wash yo' hands for supper. Whar' yo' sisters? Ain't yo' has enough to do? Go brush that nasty dust off yo' dress. Git me some wood outside. Wash, an' call them gals!"

Accordin' to Ma, we never give her no rest. We a handful to look after. I stands there a moment, an' watch her gits the rag an' take the pone from the ashes. Smell real good. When she turn her big broad back to me again, I thinks, well, she my ma. She know.

I goes out into the evenin'. First touch of dark, air tinged with cool. Rain maybe. Can't quite tell. I gits the wood from the bin behind the cabin an' yell for my sisters.

Then quick, here they come. Mar, so graceful, an' Kate an' li'l Hannah. "Whar' ya'll be?" I axe. No answer, just laughin' an' scamperin' behind the cabin to wash.

I takes a deep breath an' catch a picture of the man with the black hood. In my mind. He stayin' with me. The rope creaks. I see the crow circle above.

In another minute, we all around outside. Ma there with food. But there bugs too, so we take up to et in the cabin. It warm inside, but that feel good. An' the hot, steamy corn pone, umm, good too. Them wus good times. Quiet an' safe, no harm in the whole wide world ever gonna come to me. No—not in that there li'l cabin. *[There is a pause in the tape. Then Ms. Augustus asks to take a break, and the tape machine is turned off. When the machine begins again, it seems to be later that same day.]*

Lak I says we et our supper meal inside that night. All us. It be gittin' dark earlier each day. Then, we has evenin' chores to do. Gittin' wood in for the night—some heavy logs. Season changin'. It gettin' chill at night, but with warm days still. I suppose to sweep off the back porch at the big house an' also axe if there be anythin' mo' I needed for. But there weren't, so I go on home.

That night, we bed down. Our cabin—don't know if I say this before— but this cabin I live in so long, it come to me in dreams sometime even these days. I can smell the wood, the ol' musty ol' table, the way the sacks we chil'ren sleep in feel scratchy but good. Not that long ago, somebody tell me that the shack still stands in Fayett'ville. Hard to believe, after all this time. Chinks must'ta fallen out, the cut logs, rough, probably all split by now. They sort of squared off, with notches an' mud plaster in between. One door, two windows. Fireplace at one end, an' a table… straw filled pallets for beds. Flour or grain sacks. We pulls 'em out to sleep an' pulls 'em back for day, unless someone sick. Ma have the nicest quilt, stitched together out'ta white folks' rags. She always savin' scraps too tore up to be much use. Ol' tablecloths from the big house, or we gets some ripped curtains. Or maybe if we'd outgrowed some no-use garment, she savin' scraps for a quilt.

We didn't have no carpet, not even a rag one. No slave did. We had a solid table nailed together good, an' three chairs an' a bench to go with it. Ma had a shelf she'd do her cookin' an' fixin' on. Some days, she cook outside in a big iron pot over a flame, away from the cabin. Too hot to cook inside in summer. She also boil lye outside for cleanin' clothes. The windows wus open holes with boards propped up by twigs for shutters. At night, we close them most times—to keep out bugs, critters. But when it summer, we just leave them.

But I gittin' away from my story.

That night, after I sweep an' check for chores, I come back. It dark then. We all there—gettin' ready for sleep, pullin' out pallets, fluffin' sacks. Someone in another cabin—maybe it be Henry—git his fiddle out an' begins playin' some tune. Nice to lie down—even in them rough sacks—an' listen to fiddlin'—safe in that ol' shack.

When fiddlin' stopped, I already asleep. There be hootin' owls sometime, an' wild critters makin' noise. If yo' had to git up in the night—yo' know—yo'd go outside to the privy. We has one two-holer shared by all. But that weren't uncommon back then.

Well, that night I *did* has to go, so I wakes up. Darkness all around me, an' quiet. But for the hoot owl an' cicadas makin' noise. So I slips from my pallet.

The cabin door make its creak as I go out. Now, I weren't really afeared of nothin'—I do this my whole life. But middle of night I be half 'sleep, not real alert, an' I in my shift an' barefoot, 'course. I be sort of stumblin'. Well, I goes to the privy, do what I has to do, finish up, an' begins to walk back when I feels somethin' in the wind.

Well, I whip wide awake with that. An' call out, "Who there?" No one answer, an' I think I dreamin'. The moon weren't real bright. It cloudy lak rain comin'. No stars out neither. Just some dull half moon pokin' through the clouds. I looks all around, alert, but nothin' happen, so I starts back.

Then, all sudden, someone grab me from behind. Cup his hand over my mouth. Yas, just lak that! I feels my heart poundin' lak an Indian drum—boom, boom, boom, boom.

Then there someone warm breath in my ear, "Don't be afeared, gal. I just a Nigga from up the road. I ain't gonna harm yo'. Don't call out. Yo' gotta promise. I lets go of yo' mouth, but yo' gots to promise now. Don't say nothin', an' I won't hurt yo', won't hurt no one. But yo' gotta promise."

I real scared. I think back to the dead man hangin' from his rope. How he look lak a crow with that big ol' black hood. But I know I gots to control myself. I gots to gits back to my cabin, an' I gots to gits this here man hand off me. So I nods.

He axe again: "Yo' be quiet now. Yo' knows I ain't gonna hurt yo', gal."

I nod again, an' real gentle, slow, he uncover my mouth an' release me. I turns around careful, an' I sees a big black man standin' there. He look scared an' nervous, lak it him, not me, been grabbed.

"What yo' name, gal?" he axe.

"Sarah," I says. "Sarah Louise." An' suddenly, I ain't scared no mo'. He just a skinny, raggedy man. Not much to him. An' he be young. Standin' there in ol' ripped trousers an' tattered, dirty shirt.

He take me by the hand, an' off I go with him a small way to the edge of the woods. He speak to me in whispers, an' all a sudden, I knows that he be run'way slave Mister John Ellicott tell us 'bout. But he don't look lak no murderer. No, he sure don't.

"Sarah," he begin. "I runs away. Yo' ol' enough to know what that mean?"

I nod. Then, I says boldly, "I know who yo' is. Yo' Mister John Ellicott Negro."

"How yo' knowed that?" An' I see that he look nervous, stare at me.

"Well, Mister John Ellicott hisself come gallop up this way to tell us. He say that yo' a no-good slave run'way—wanted for murderin' another of his slaves. Say yo' stole a kitchen knife."

"Masser Ellicott say that?"

"Yas, he did." Then I say—even surprise myself—"But I don't believes him. No." Then I think: here I is, just standin' here in my shift, talkin' so boldly in the night to a stranger. God know what I thinkin', 'cause I sure don't.

"Good, chil'. Good. 'Cause I never do nothin' bad. No. Masser Ellicott make up that story, gal; I swear he do. I ain't got no kitchen knife." John pat hisself down to show me; then he get this woeful look, an' sigh. There a log by the path. He sit on it. Johnny look at the ground, lak there some great sadness in the dirt, an' he got his eye on it. Then he pat the log, an' I sit down beside him.

This be his turn to nod.

"What yo' gonna do?" I axe. An' I see Johnny exhausted, all tuckered out, sittin' pitiful in his ragged shirt, torn pants. So I axe if he want me to wake Ma so he could stay the night with us. But he say no. No! That the sure way he gits caught an' end up whipped or dead. He just want some food.

So I tells him to set right there, an' I goes off to the big house, thinkin' I can snatch some victuals out of the summer kitchen near the back of the big house. Now, it the middle of night, an' I walkin' barefoot. But I finds my way an' manage to steals some food—cooked ham an' corn cakes left over from Marster an' Missus supper. I carry them an' stop by the well to fills one of them empty tins always hangin' there.

When I comes back, John still settin' whar' I leaves him. He scared, an' he look at me lak I up to no good, maybe. But I smile an' hands him the food, slip in beside him on the log. "This all I could gits."

He take the ham an' cakes begins to chomp into them lak he never done et nothin' before. Gobble down all I brung.

Meanwhiles, we don't speak.

Then I hands Johnny the tin. An' he drinks it down in one gulp. Finishes off by wiping his dirty arm across his mouth. Then he look at me, nod, git up, turn his back to me, an' lift up his raggedy shirt.

"This the reason I leave Masser Ellicott. He done this." I stand up an' see these raised purple streaks —lak a family of snakes crawlin'—beneath his skin. There be ol' purple an' deep fresh red ones. I see them in the dim moonlight. I touch Johnny back. But he quickly lower his shirt an' sit down.

"I gotta go," Johnny say, an' he take my hand in his, look at me. "An' yo' gots to promise to say nothin'. Word spread worse than wildfire among Niggas." Johnny look at me. "That Ellicott place, ain't what yo' think—anybody thinks. It be strange what goin' on there…. Yo' hears anythin'?"

"Nothin'," I say. "Know nothin' about that place. An' Marster don't do nobody lak that." I thinkin' of the snakes. We standin' up in the dark night, moon peekin' in an' out of the clouds.

"I knows yo' ain't no killer, Johnny." I say.

"I ain't. That right." Then Johnny tells me a story about his gal. Mulatto, youn' an' pretty he wanna marry. Johnny come in from the field one day—he just a regular hand out there—an' he stop in on his gal who be in the summer kitchen. She one of the cooks—I think—an' she alone; that why he go. But she don't look at him. Keep her head down, won't look up. After some proddin', she tell him that Mister Ellicott there earlier that mornin'. An' it ain't the first time—he havin' his way.

"Don't know why I tellin' yo' this," Johnny say. Then, he say that he don't do nothin' that day. He just go back to the field, work. But soon he realize he feelin' so bad, helpless, not a man. Lak the wrong done to hisself—not his gal. Soon, Johnny go back to the kitchen an' tell her not to worry, that gots a plan; he gonna takes her out of there.

But before he can explain hisself, she order him to go. Mind his own business. Shouldn't worry 'bout her, she say, just worry about his own sorry self now. She too far gone for that, she say.

Johnny look at me, his face caught in moonlight. "Yo' knows what I mean?" he axe me. His eyes look strange. Hurt, but angry too, underneath.

Somethin' terrible inside that man—I think.

I nods at him, lak I understands, but truth is, I don't. I too youn' to really know what he talk about. I just has this bad feelin'. But I wants to be all growed up, so I nods lak I understand.

Johnny gal, she just shove him away. "Never come around no mo'!" she hiss at him. An' so he go. That the other reason John leave the Ellicott place—this here gal of his.

So Johnny runs. An' Mister Ellicott inventin' some tale so we gonna be against Johnny an' turn him in. But Johnny ain't bad. The way yo' knows things, I knows this.

Johnny leave me standin' there as he take off. Before he go, he warn me again not to tell no one he travelin' through.

"Gal," he say, "it the middle of the night, an' youn' gals dream strange dreams. Yo' don't know nothin'. Everyone be safe that way."

An' then, in a flash, Johnny gone. Just lak he say—a dream.

I needs to take a break now. Quit. Tired out with all this—Johnny, them snakes, his gal…. *[Some noise is heard, and the tape machine is turned off.]*

August 24, 1937

Wants to keep it short today. Have some doc comin' to make a call early noon time. Rheumatism again—them aches an' pains. Same fella come every now an' then, got his tonic he give me, no charge. Neighbor tell me at the grocery that he makin' rounds today. Gotta be ready. Well… go back….

Next day, very next—after Johnny come by, that is—I naturally kind'a sleepy, draggy. Ma keep axin' what the matter with me. I just says, "I all right. Just didn't sleep real good." Ma shake her head, tell me I better not be gittin' sick with the weather changin'. An' I better do my chores—all of them.

"Yas, ma'am," I says. An' she give me the look. The look when she think I up to no good. Sly. I never could figure out how she knowed when somethin' were up.

I be draggin' that mornin'. But I don't says nothin' 'bout Johnny comin' by. I helpin' Ma with the washin' early, before breakfast. I gits the cast iron pot steamin' for soakin' the clothes in, out back the cabin. The clothes in a wove basket, an' I dump them in. I got a big stick to stir up them up, give them a good turnin'. Then, after they soak, I takes the clothes out an' puts them into another tub—wet an' heavy. An' I pours mo' water into that tub to git most of the soap out. Wring them the best I can. Then I cart out that big ol' heavy tub to the creek for rinsin'. It a beautiful day, with a cool wind blowin' from the east. Sure don't feel lak rain. Clouds from yesterday night all gone. I doin' my chores, but I thinkin' 'bout Mister Ellicott, Johnny an' his gal. What she mean by tellin' him *it too late*. I nods my head when Johnny tell me, but I still tryin' to figure it out.

I start back from the creek, down the path. This time I put the tub on my head so as to haul it mo' easy. But soon I so caught up in my thinkin' that I stop there on the sandy path. My thoughts driftin' to Johnny an' the snakes on his back. Tub heavy now, so I puts it down. Alone there, I thinkin' about Johnny hand over my mouth, me takin' him food, not tellin' no one, an' how that too a heavy load.

Then, I hear Hannah callin', say Ma been hollerin' for me. I takin' too much time with my chore. Ma want me home now. There be mo' work to do. When Hannah walk up, we both lift the wash tub—even though she li'l—we each holdin' one end, an' we go bumpin' off.

Ma got some corn pone ready an' some milk still warm from Marster cow. Nothin' fancy. We never had nothin' fancy. But that plain stuffs mighty tasty. So, I sits on the door ledge outside the cabin an' ets. Ma axin' me all the time what git into me an' whar' I been an' why aren't the washin' hung up yet. She stand over me, shakin' her head, hands on her big hips.

I says again that I just tired. I be all right by an' by. Ma tells me I behind in all my chores an' has to hurry now. She losin' patience with the likes of me.

So, I spreads out the clothin' over the bushes lak we always do. Hannah help me gits the wash hung, then gots to clean up breakfast stuffs, an' Mar an' Kate already done gone to the big house for their chores. Mar work as a housemaid—she have the important job with Missus. An' Kate work in the kitchen with the cook. I suppose to train that year in the big house too. I learnin' hows to iron linen an' stitchery an' sewin'. I uset'ta milk the cows early in the mornin' an' then late afternoon again. But that chore now for them that young.

I do my chores, but I distracted. Head filled with that Run'way Johnny an' things he say. I wearin' my ol' muslin dress, an' when I gits to the big house, I puts on a starch linen apron—full body, cover most of it. That way I presentable.

So I walkin' out to the big house, lost in thought, wonderin' if Johnny make it out. Can't imagine whar' in the world he go. Down to the port of Wilmington? Ships there he might stow away on an' gits free. Would he go north directly? Through them swamps an' low land, with critters an' snakes? Maybe alligators—heared there some those, but never seen them myself.... I almost can't thinks 'bout runnin' away. But I do. An' I thinks back to David an' he bein' free....

Nobody I knowed ever talk 'bout freedom. Or maybe they do, but I still too young, an' I ain't heared nothin'. Most folk I know satisfied just to be treated right. But after Johnny come, my mind shift back to what he say. It slow me up. Should be thinkin' about my chores an' gittin' to the big house, 'cause I behind—Ma right about that. But my mind get to wanderin' bad—an' I occupied with David, Mister Ellicott, Johnny, an' his gal troubles.

That be the first time I really think 'bout my condition. Bein' owned. An' as I be thinkin', I come to know what Mister Ellicott done to Johnny gal. He done get her with his child.

These thoughts with me as I strollin' up to the big house, even before I gets my apron on. When I there, Marster havin' his breakfast an' the whole place smell good of coffee an' fresh ham. Missus is there with him, an' so is Marse Harry an' Marse Norman, Marse George, an' Miss Ellen, Miss Mar, an' Miss Elizabeth—alls there but Miss Ida. I stays in the kitchen fixin' my white my apron an' gittin' my iron an' board. Kate somewhar'—must be. Aunt Patsy cookin' an' hummin'. She always hummin'. She dark an' large, an' her face always shinin'. Even in winter. Lak she oil herself every mornin'. She be one of the holiest women I know. Couldn't swear in front of Aunt Patsy. No. Wouldn't tolerate no swearin'. Nor no laughin'. She always say to keep yo' thoughts sanctified. She know her Bible an' always callin' up verses. An' prayin'. Never git angry nor complain neither. An' Aunt Patsy always know what yo' up to. She could read yo' mind. Worse than Ma. Fact is, she had the power—mighty strong. She one of the only person, black or white, I knowed that could pray an' git results.

Miss Ida ain't at the table, lak I say. No, come to find out, she taken up with the pneumonia. It were fall, changin' weather. Some warm days but then chill ones. Missus wanna call Aunt Patsy to pray over her—that what they talkin' 'bout at the breakfast table. Marster call Missus a silly woman—forbid her to call on Aunt Patsy for help. Marster—now he a religious man—but he don't believe that God answer no Nigga prayer. "No white folk gonna gits well with the hocus-pocus," he say.

There were a argument that mornin' in the house. Pretty loud. Marster call Aunt Patsy "a superstitious ol' Voodoo gal from way down south." Aunt Patsy come from Louis'ana when she a youn' gal.

"I ain't bringin' no Nigga woman in to sit by our Ida now, Henrietta," Marster yell.

"I tells yo' J. B., Aunt Patsy got the gift, and she'll be summoned here for Ida." Missus raise her voice, gits up from the table.

"I won't have it!" an' Marster raise hisself up too, pound his fist on the table, leave the room, an' takes off out the house. Missus follow him. It the mornin' after a hard night with Miss Ida. He yell back that be goin' for the regular doctor some miles away. That doc, Doc McNair, he the white folk doc an' live in town, south Fayett'ville. Marster take his fancy buggy, so Doc McNair can ride with him in comfort. Missus on the front veranda, then come on back inside. We don't has no telephones, no nothin' back then. No cars, trams, no way to get somewhar' fast.

So, off he go. An' meanwhile, Missus inside the foyer, an' she gittin' crazy with worry, thought of losin' Miss Ida. She pace up an' down that hallway for a few minutes. Then she walk herself into the kitchen, whar' we all be. We heared the whole thing. Entire household. But we look busy when Missus come in, pretendin' we don't knows nothin'. I busy myself with reheatin' the iron, which git cold mighty fast—summer, fall, winter—no matter.

"Aunt Patsy," Missus say. "Now yo' understand how sick Miss Ida is, don't yo'?"

Aunt Patsy by the big stew pot, stirrin'. "Yas, ma'am, I knows Miss Ida gots the pneumonia."

"Now, Patsy, I want you to go upstairs with me. We had a very bad night, and Miss Ida is very sick. I want you to go and get whatever medicine you need—teas, balms—and then to come upstairs and do what you do. Make her well. Pray for her. I wants you to kneel by her bed, lay your hands on her—heal her." Missus start to cry, shake her head lak she knows it wrong to break down in front of us. She pull a handkerchief outs from her frilly sleeve an' dabs it around her eyes.

Aunt Patsy wipe her own hands on her big ol' apron, an' nod. She hand over the wood spoon to Kate an' walk out with Missus. First, she go to her cabin to gits her conjure kit. Then she go with Missus up to Miss Ida bedroom to work her magic.

Now, I doesn't know what happen upstair. When Aunt Patsy give Kate the spoon an' Missus leaves the kitchen, we looks at each other an' just goes on. Everyone real quiet. Yo' could hear the pot stirrin', the heat of the iron sizzlin' as I wet the cloth—but no one say nothin'. The room get silent.

I knowed Aunt Patsy got some kind of healin' gift. We all knowed it, an' we all feel that the Missus humble herself to axe for somethin' she powerless to do herself. Somethin' no white folk can do. *[There is a pause in the tape here, and then Ms. Augustus continues.]*

Don't remember much mo' 'bout that day. But when I comes back next mornin', Miss Ida feelin' better. Sure as the sun do shine. Aunt Patsy herself, though, she don't say much.

Doc McNair never do come. He be out of town up near Raleigh. An' by time Marster come home late that evenin', Miss Ida already feelin' better.

News travel fast in them days. That very night Aunt Patsy done her cure, we get word that Miss Ida well enough to be settin' up in bed an' axin' for somethin' to et. Someone from the big house—maid, housekeeper, don't remember—come give us the news. Seem lak when

Marster come home an' see'd Miss Ida, he just stand there with his mouth open. Don't even holler at Missus when he see'd Aunt Patsy still prayin' on the settee at the bottom of the stair. She moppin' her brow again, I suspect. Her face, I sure, be shinin' lak it always do. Shinin' so strong inside that she glow. Aunt Patsy got what we call "healin' hands." She a good Christian woman, yas. But she also practice conjure. Marster call it Voodoo, but we calls it conjure.

Nowadays it hard to find—conjure medicine. Back then, it common. Come mostly from Africa, but some slaves brung it up from the Caribbean—passin' along their knowledge of herbs, barks, roots, potions. Mostly through the women folk. We call them "grannies" when they got the power. It take many years of practice. If yo' axe me, them ol' grannies got mo' know-how than most of the doc these days, even today with all their medicines.

When Miss Ida git sick, Aunt Patsy probably give her tea made by boilin' them shoat hooves or bark. She keep a stock of everythin' in jars in her cabin. She also got a small garden whar' she growed some. But them shoat hooves is what they use when the fever git bad. Break it down. Or sometime they use ginseng tea—roots they has to dig. They beat them roots into a horrible tastin' brew. But it cure most folk. An' whatever Aunt Patsy give to Miss Ida, it sure done cure her. An' when Marster see'd Ida so perky, he couldn't brings himself to say nothin' against it.

Aunt Patsy cure me once too. Just a bad cold I caught, but Ma thought it turnin' into the pneumonia, an' she call her to me. She make dogwood bark tea—an' she boil it up with somethin' nasty. I cried an' cried 'cause I too li'l to understand what be good for me. Ma make me drink it all down. She hold my nose an' I keep swallowin' an' swallowin' 'till it all gone. Next day, I better.

I tells yo' that conjure medicine work good. An' most of what yo' need can be found in the woods, pasture, or growed, if yo' has the know-how. An' that pass from one generation to another. Aunt Patsy try to pass down her conjure to her two daughters—older gal, Sandy, an' the younger gal, Sally. But I don't think she did. I only knowed Sally—she had some learnin', I suppose. An' Sandy, she might'ta got some of it, but she so wild—especially with the men folks—Sandy gots herself sold on the auction block—don't know what become of her. *[Some scraping sounds are heard. Then Ms. Augustus clears her throat.]*

Now, that business with Johnny. Nobody except me know he come. Whole plantation wus taken up with Miss Ida, till she git well. But less than a week later, after Miss Ida recover—and we all think things is back to normal—all tarnation break loose. A whole load of trouble. For me an' everybody. *[There is a pause. Then the interviewer is heard asking if Ms. Augustus would like to take a break, and Ms. Augustus replies that she would prefer to end her session for the day and to resume the following day.]*

August 25, 1937

Whar' wus I? Ready to gab 'bout Johnny. Well, 'course I didn't tells no one, lak I promise him. But after Miss Ida recover from her sickness, lak I sayin', things gits back almost to whar' they been—then the trouble come.

In the meantime—maybe few days later—we gits word that Johnny be see'd down near Wilmington. There a road, the Wilmington Road, go to the coast. We heared some white folk catched him in the swamp, goin' south. News travel in peculiar ways—word of mouth, from white, black—gets heared, repeated. Everybody know everybody business. This news 'bout Johnny leaked from the big house, overheared from them that work there. Gossip. Lot of it in them days. It all get jumbled up—what be truth, what be lies. But Johnny do git caught up—I knows 'cause I see'd him comin' up our way again. This time in chains.

It be near night, dusk. I trailin' behind a bit, so there weren't many folk around. It must'ta been October by then. Not real cold yet, just Mother Nature givin' us bursts of what gonna come. I finishin' chores, takin' some canned goods down to the root cellar by the summer kitchen, when I hears a wagon comin' along the road. I wus curious—not many folk come this way. So I sets out to see. An' in the distance, I makes out a rough mule wagon goin' along with a black man chain up an' walkin' behind. He gots rough chains around his hands an' a iron collar around his neck. He lookin' mighty downcast. Right ways I see who it be. I come around the bend whar' the split rail fence begin an' look real hard. It gittin' dark earlier. I not quite finish with evenin' chores. I keeps lookin'—an' I though I know, I still hope it ain't Johnny.

When he an' the mule wagon get close enough, I feels my heart race. Quick, I pray, an' I be axin' God, "Don't let that man be Johnny."

Sometime God listen, an' sometime He don't. Has other plans. This time, God done heared me good 'cause that man trailin' behind the mule wagon turn his face in my direction. An' it wus Johnny, all right. But I ain't sure that he see me. I wants him to smile, wink, somethin'…but he done look lak he starin' at death hisself. I wave real small so no one but him can see.

Then, it hit me: *Johnny ain't lookin' 'cause he believe it were me that turn him in!* An' I gits this pain in my belly, lak I done swallow a stone. Never git hit so hard before. Johnny just go walkin' by—shufflin'. When he finally close, he look right up at me, an' it be as if I wusn't there; I be some haint, an' he peerin' through.

That moment—when Johnny walkin' hisself in his chain, same as a sad ol' shoat walkin' toward slaughter, look up—that stay with me. It burn itself into my mind lak God hisself want me to keep it.

The sun just about close up for the day, leave a trail of orange light set off behind the wagon, an' Run'way Johnny just a shadow, walkin' from nowhar' an' goin' back to it. Only thing left wus the sound of them jinglin' chains.

I tells yo' bout this 'cause, well, yo' hear mo' about him later. He the man become lak a brother, change my life. At the time here, I don't know nothin'. Only I taken up by what I see. With his lookin' through me. That the beginning. In some way, I guess I become the haint he see.

Such a big man, Johnny. An' there he be, turned into somethin' small an' shameful. I come away from the fence, an' walk over to the big house, settin' my mind against slavery an' my own situation. How my life weren't really mine. I had some pots to dry, an' I take up a clean linen towel an' rub them. I wus alone for a bit before I finish up, an' I walk home to the shack in the dark. Ma wanted to know whar' I been, why I so long in gettin' there.

Later, that night I heared from Sally that a young Nigra gal give Johnny up, turn him in. An' then I knowed I must'ta been dead right—Johnny thinkin' it be me that done it.

When he wus retuned to the Ellicott place, Johnny git whipped somethin' awful. Then, we heared, he git sold by Mister Ellicott at the market. Auctioned off with some household goods, an' he be bought up by speculators.

Why—I axe myself—*if he be the murderer Mister Ellicott say he is, why he gits sold?* If he be dangerous, why not hang him lak the horse thief?

An' that be the last I heared about Johnny—for a while. *[The tape is so scratchy here that it is hard to discern what Ms. Augustus says. I believe only a sentence or two is lost before the tape is clear again.]*

...knows much about them. No. But I see'd them with my own eyes one time. That be when I in Fayett'ville. It a bustlin' market day, an' I wus out with Missus. I wus a li'l gal, maybe four, five. We come upon a estate sale, an' there be a family on the block—mother, two youn' children, an' an infant that weren't mo' than six month ol'. We stop to watch. Folks gather around the market place, mostly out'ta curiosity. Man in some ol' tawdry suit come up to start the biddin', an' them speculators wus in the crowd. Yo' could tell them from the way they dress an' talk. An' act—lak they own the place. They wus in the back an' shove a path to the front. Shout out. They wearin' dark, wool suits, an' it summer, too hot. Misses weren't interested in watchin' much, so we leave soon. Must'ta come with Marse George too, 'cause I remember meetin' up with him. Come from the silk mill.

Anybody could see these men wus bad. Never see'd them again. Don't even has a clear memory. Too young. *[Some coughing and scratchiness are heard on the tape. The interviewer is faintly heard asking if Ms. Augustus would like to take a break. Ms. Augustus answers that she would, but only a short break to collect her thoughts. The tape machine is turned off. When Ms. Augustus resumes, it seems to be the same day.]*

Feels better after this here tea. But I gonna say mo' 'bout the speculator trade, 'cause it be somethin' in these parts. Not just here but all over North Car'lina. Speculators travel up from down south— Miss'ippi an' Louis'ana, come to North, South Car'lina to buy slaves cheap, especially men. But they often gits them gals, unruly ones— misbehave, run away, steal, thieve. Some people sellin' their slaves 'cause of debt. When a masser die an' leave his bills for the rest of the family, they sell off slaves.

Gettin' sold off wus somethin' we all feared—'cause there wus nothin' yo' could do. If a farm, plantation go bust, ain't nothin' gonna help. White folk sell what they has. Everything. Even babies got sold.

One time, I recalls this ol' trader from Raleigh by name of Bill Avery, that would ship out slaves to the Miss'ippi bottoms. They go south in a boxcar leavin' from Raleigh. Go to the big cotton country whar' there nothin' but hard, hard work. Them Miss'ippi plantations be big, with hundreds of slaves. We never have nothin' lak that in these parts around Fayett'ville. Mostly, we has small plantations—farms really.

But even here, slaves be lak mules. Hard work is hard work. If a mule pull a wagon, that mule don't care what be in it, who it be for—he just struggle with his load. An' if the driver mean, well, then, that mule git whupped. Ain't the mule fault, an' it can't choose the driver.

I once knowed a gal wus a slave down Miss'ippi way. She from Louis'ana originally, an' she…her name…I can't recall exactly. Hmm… Yesterday…. That it. It be Louise. Louise Yesterday. Some odd name lak that. [*Ms. Augustus is heard clearing her throat, and then she continues.*]

Well, this is what I recalls: that Yesterday gal come down from Raleigh to Fayett'ville some spring with her massa'. Some business take her to the Smith place. At some point, she git hungry an' sent to quarters for water an' food. She settin' down on a three-leg stool outside Uncle Cicero cabin. She gabbin' about the Miss'ippi plantation. Say how all the children there got to et out of a trough. Lak li'l shoats. Them chil'ren would line up, set on the dirt ground—sometime outside the cabin, if it warn't too cold—an' they et lak beasts. Scraps an' crumbs scraped off white folks plates, mostly. But sometime they allowed to gather mussels an' fish from the creek. They always hungry. Never gits enough to et. She say that they don't do it that way in Raleigh, an' she laks it here in North Car'lina much better. She shipped out away from her mother when she a young gal. Never knowed her pa. But she lak it here better than south—much better. An' she gab on about what it lak there, as she etin' the grits an' pone we gives her.

Her ol' masser had him a hundred slaves. The plantation lak a small town there. There be blacksmith shops, cobblers, loom shacks for weavin', a tannin' place for hides, a mill, an' even a liquor still. There a bell be rung to wake them up in the mornin' before sun up. An' rung so loud it have a echo. Lak a church bell. An' they use that bell to call them to dinner durin' the day an' after supper when it light out an' they has to return work.

In the big house there wus eighteen, maybe twenty room. An' outside, there be grand porches sweepin' this way an' that. Must'ta been nice for the white folk. Gals in them big swirlin', clean dresses, rustle when they walk. She say slave quarters wus lak a street in Raleigh—cabins arranged in rows on hard dirt streets. An' they be far off from the massa' an' missus' house. The house slaves, they uppity. Live in the big house with their white folk. Not in quarters. Think they way mo' better than them field hands, an'—fact is—must never see'd their massa' an' missus. Just see the overseer. An' he do the whuppin' if a slave don't work enough.

Some hands slack off, others work hard. That just be the way it is. Folks be folks. An' some, no matter how hard yo' whup a body, it ain't gonna pull no harder.

I gonna go back to Johnny. He brung trouble with him. Drug it down from the Ellicott place and then dragged it back out'ta the swamp near Wilmington when he get caught. *[The interviewer is heard in the distant background, encouraging Ms. Augustus, telling her that she is doing fine, but asking if she would like to take a short break. Ms. Augustus says she would rather continue.]*

I tells yo' what happen the day after Johnny go by in those chains. I hasn't yet told what I see'd. No. Not that night. So, I goes home late—lak I says. But not so late that Ma give me trouble 'bout what I up to.

When she axe me, I tell her, "I just doin' my chores an' gits ready for supper." An' that satisfy her. But, 'course, I thinkin' 'bout Johnny all the while, pretty taken up by what I see'd.

Next day, early mornin', sun up, all the Negroes whisperin' 'bout Johnny being caught. Everyone know by then.

Now folk say that Johnny must'ta come through our plantation. An' that when I hears 'bout the youn' gal that turn him in. Story go that Johnny be out in the marsh swamp toward Wilmington when some slave gal, younger than me, out in the field. See Johnny slinkin' around. So she tell her young miss, who tell the master.

Johnny survivin' on wild chestnuts, bark. They catch him up, put him in jail, an' the news go into the paper 'bout this youn' colored gal.

Well, yo' could just blow me over with a summer breeze when I heared this tale. I knowed then an' there that Johnny do believe I be the gal that turn him in. That why he look right through me.

The news make me feel awful again. Goin' around an' around in my head, I be worryin' even mo'. The story be burnin' through me 'cause I like Johnny right off, an' he trust me, an' now I can't gits to ever tell him the truth. I just alone with it. An' the mo' I think about it, the worse I feel. It cold out, but I starts to sweat an' gittin' so distracted that I scarcely remember whats I suppose to do.

Well, I wus on my way to the big house for mornin' chores when I runs into my sister Kate, who been lookin' at me kind a' strange since breakfast. Now she stop me—she be goin' one way, me another.

We alone on the path, an' Kate tug at my sleeve, fool with somethin' in her apron.

"Looky here," Kate say. "Look at this note I founds me, Sarah Louise." She gotta teasing way to her voice. An' she reach down into her apron pocket an' pull out some ol' crumpled piece of paper.

Lak I say, ain't no one is around; we private by ourself. I takes the note from her an' straightens it up so I can reads it, an' first I don't understand. Kate meanwhile is smirkin' at me as if expectin' some kind reaction. I only thinkin' 'bout Johnny, so I not fully takin' this in. But then I read the note:

My Dear Miss Sarah Louise—it say.

Then go on—somethin' lak this:

Forgive me for trying to write to you like this, but since we met just a few short months ago, I cannot get you out of my mind. I have no way of knowing if this here letter will reach you, but you say you can read real good, so I feel compelled to write because each word I write reminds me of you. I am giving this letter to a Negro man that says he knows who you are and can get this letter to you, though he is traveling the other way. I hope so.

I want you to know I will be passing your way on my return trip north, the third week October. We are scheduled to dock Thursday, 18 October. If you can meet me again by the A. P. Hurt, I will be forever in your gratitude. I would surely love to see you.

> *Yours Sincerely in the Lord, Ever More,*
> *Mister David Stephen Augustus*

Well, I shocked. Truly shocked. Cans yo' just imagine? Me, a fifteen-year-ol' slave gal, standin' on a dirt path, in some ol' hand-loom, ill-fittin' smock, gittin' such a love letter. I been thinkin' of Johnny all night, all mornin'. An' now this.

Kate there, as I look up, tryin' to take it all in. She just eyeballin' me, starin', smirkin'. There still a chill in the air, an' it set a shiver through me.

How she know it me? How she so certain I the Sarah Louise that the note be for? I think. Now, 'course, it seem plain. How many Sarah Louises there gonna be?

So, quick I says to her, "Kate, why yo' think this here letter be for me?" I figurin' I have enough to think about with this Johnny business. Ain't ready for no mo'.

"Don't yo' even wants to know how I come by it?" Kate say, lookin' at me with this sly grin.

"I don't cares nothin' 'bout it." I lie, 'cause my heart racin', an' I already feel drawn back to David, to our time by the landing when the Hurt come in.

"I bet yo' do too! An' she grab hold of my arm. "How many Miss Sarah Louise there gonna be near here? Yo' think me a fool? This ain't no white gal beau! An' I comes by it crumple in the road after folks see that Run'way Johnny come past." Kate look at me with her smile an' give me a li'l shove. "I gonna tell Ma."

"Tell anyone yo' want," I says. But I ain't know what to think.

"I gonna. But first, yo' gonna tells me the truth."

This all happen in about ten minute. An' I know it just a matter of time before we missed or others come up the path. So I says to her, "If yo' swear to Jesus Christ that yo' won't breathe a word to anyone, Kate, I tells yo' the whole story. But not now. Later."

Fast as a jack rabbit, Kate snatch the note from my hand.

"Tells me now!" she complain. An' she begin to make faces an' do a dance around me.

"Gives it back!" I say. An' I goes to grab the note from her.

But Kate too quick an' sly. She swing her arm around an' block me off.

"I gonna hold on to this here ol' L-O-V-E note till yo' tells me all about it." She crack a wide smile an' kick up some dirt lak she dare me to cross her.

I tries to snatch that ol' crumple' paper but can't catch holds of it, so I swears on the Holy Bible, an' on Ma an' Pa an' the whole family that I tells her the story later. But Kate ain't satisfied. No. She git me to swears on the white folk too—runs me through Missus an' Marster an' all the chil'ren.

So we each be on our ways. I distracted with thoughts of David an' thoughts of Run'way Johnny swimmin' all around my head, lak hungry fish in a shallow pool. I keeps tryin' to remember what exactly that ol' crumpled note say—I reads it so fast. Fact is, I can't believes that li'l ol' Sarah Louise done git a love letter good as any white gal. Wish I had hold of that note today. 'Course, as time march on, I gits others from David. But that first one wus somethin' special. *[Ms. Augustus is heard laughing, chuckling really. The interviewer asks if she would like to take a short break, and Ms. Augustus says that she would; in fact, she would like to stop for the day.]*

August 26, 1937

...I remember whar' we leaves off yesterday. Yas, I do 'cause I be dreamin' an' dreamin' all night about this time before the war. I recall things—yas I do—that I hadn't thinks about for years an' years. Things that happen seem they be from another world. I done live too long. *[Ms. Augustus sighs, pauses, then continues.]*

Well, that day Kate tell me 'bout the letter—that day move pokey slow—till the trouble. Then everythin' pick up lak leafs carry in a storm.

I suppose to help Mammy Rae with the dyin' of some homespun. She have a shelter outside, down from the big house. Use one of them big cast iron pots—fit a gaggle of geese inside. She knowed every kind of root, bark, leaf, an' berry that turn yarn or thread red, blue, green, brown, black—whatever she want. She fill a pot with water, boil it over wood an' coals; then she take them roots, bark an' plant an' boil the juice out. Next, she strain the chaff an' puts in the salt an' vinegar to set the color. After the cotton been carded an' spun to thread, Mammy take the hanks an' puts them into the boilin' dye.

They do the spinnin' an' cardin' other places. Sometime in quarters they sets up a loom, or gals might card in a evening before the sun go down. At cardin', we has some good times. Stories be told. Gals settin' around, cardin', spinnin' in front of quarters on a cool evening.

This time Mammy Rae see'd me comin', an' she axe me to stir the pot for her whiles she tends to somethin' else. There be a mess of cotton thread wound up in loose skeins an' throwed inside the kettle pot.

"Yo' puts on that apron first." An' Mammy point to a peg inside the shelter. It be ol' an' splashed with' color lak some crazy trout.

"Yas, ma'am," I says, pullin' on the big apron so I wouldn't get splash.

Mammy give me the long, thick wooden turnin' spoon, tell me she be back, an' I begin stirrin'. It easy work, an' I be stirrin' an' turnin' an' turnin' so, that soon my mind gits to turnin' too. I still thinking of Run'way Johnny an' my David. Still can't believe how that crumple ol' letter find its way to me.

Folks say that the debil take advantage of folks who minds ain't occupied right. An' that what happen to me. I thinkin' too much about myself. Too caught up in my own small life, mistakin' it for some great, big ol' thing. An' 'course, that when the debil come.

It a beautiful October day. Oak trees turnin' orange an' red, lak some soft fire lit up—not a flashy one, but mute an' hazy. There be some birds around chirpin'—an' mostly I can tells which one makin' which sound. I know a mockin' bird from a robin from a pesky ol' blue jay—by the way they call. So for a moment, I gets caught up listenin'. Then I recognize the low, chill wind comin' in from the east—gentle, shake the tree branches an' rattle the brittle leafs.

Sudden, a crow appear—from nowhar'. Usually, a crow announce hisself. But this time, Mister Crow swoop down almost on top of me. That get my attention. Then he disappear. I stop turnin', wipes my hands on my apron, an' peeks out of the dye shed. But ain't no crow to be see'd. I goes back to turnin' when, swoop again! Now Mister Crow standin' on a shelf inside the shed.

An' this the strange part—he speak to me. Ol' Mister Crow speak just as clear as I speakin' now. "Bad gal," he say. "Bad gal." Then he squawk an' flutter his shiny black wings. "Caw, caw, caw," he call out.

"What yo' mean—*bad*? I say to him. What's I ever done to yo'? An' I stands there in my mottled apron, with the dye ladle still in my hand.

"Bad gal! Bad gal!" Mister Crow call again. "Bad gal, bad gal—caw, caw, caw!" Flappin' his big wings!

Then I understand. Mister Crow ain't tellin' me I bad now. No. I ain't bad yet. He predictin' the future. Just lak them blank-face angels. Only this time, there ain't no floatin' angels. Only a big, shiny crow that come to give me the news. Mister Crow tellin' me that I bound to be bad. An' there ain't nothin' I can do about it.

I about to object, when I look at Mister Crow, an' see that big ol' bird raise his wings till they looks like horns on his head.

Well, my mouth just 'bout fall open. But then Mister Crow call out again, "Caw, caw, caw," an' he flap his big ol' wings an' he gone. I blink an' don't even see him fly.

I stands there a minute, an' just starts to turnin' my pot again—knowin' now I just see'd the debil hisself. Here I is one minute, a fifteen-year-ol' gal, helpin' a run'way slave that thinks I betray him an' gets him whipped; then I a gal thinkin' she got a beau an' she is mad in love—with a love note circulatin'—thanks to Kate. Next minute, I a gal that been conversin' with the debil, who be tellin' me I about to step in a mess of trouble.

An' yet—it be the brightest fall day. No chill wind now, just sun in the blue sky—an' those trees, gold an' red. Nature know not to gits caught up in our human tribulations. No. It just a beautiful day.

When Mammy Rae git back, I must'ta seem lak a gal possessed. I stirrin' that ol' iron kettle pot lak my life depend on it. My mind sweepin' over my thoughts lak wind through a storm.

"Easy now. Dye gotta cover good. Or else it be gettin' streaks. Slow." Mammy Rae say as she come in with some baskets of berries an' bark, look at me. "Why yo' be stirrin' so hard, gal?"

"Mammy…" I begin to say, then think better of it. Fear is—some folk think Mammy Rae a witch…

So I stops myself. *Witch*, I thinkin'. Maybe Mammy Rae herself is up to no good, leavin' me here with this ol' pot—this ol' witch brew. Maybe she in cahoots with the debil.

Mammy Rae put down her baskets, take a step back, hands on her fat, wide ol' hips, tryin' to look me in the eye. "Gal, yo' gots somethin' on yo' mind. I knows yo' has." I gone back to stirrin', but she come toward me an' say, "Stops that now, an' look at me."

I stops my stirrin' again, but the cat git my tongue, an' I can't say nothin'. Suddenly, I feel dizzy, lak I just swallowed the wind, an' it done make me faint. Or maybe it be the smell risin' off them dyes.

"I ain't feelin' too good," I mutter, an' I ain't foolin' now, 'cause I begin to lose my balance, sway a bit.

Mammy Rae swoop in, catch me up an' help me to the side, to the log bench. I sets there but can't make much sense of anythin'.

"Maybe I take yo' back to yo' cabin, gal. To yo' ma. Or maybe yo' come home with me, an' I fix some soothin' tea."

My head fall over, restin' on Mammy's big bosom. An' it feel good, calmin'. So, I say, "Yas, ma'am."

Mammy lift my head, take off her apron, which she make a pillow, an' she put me to lie down on the log while she git the dye an' thread out.

We walk together along the path back to Mammy Rae cabin. I done tired out with all that goin' on. Mammy take me to her li'l cabin—she live alone. Could never have no chil'ren. Some say she cursed.

It dark an' soothin' inside. Didn't knows it, but that bright mornin' sun must'ta been botherin' me. So restful here. Mammy lay me on her bed—she have a raised bed made from spindles. An' a pretty quilt with lots of colors—patchwork in long, thin strips lak a rainbow.

Mammy still has her li'l black kettle warm from breakfast, stove still burnin' embers. So she gits me some tea.

An' as I sips the tea, Mammy go an' stroke my back, lak I a small kitten been out wanderin' an' finally have the sense to come home.

"What I do, Mammy Rae?" the words just rise right out of me. An' I begins to cry. Slow tears at first, then the cryin' turn to weepin'. An' suddenly the dam done burst 'cause I weepin' a big ol' river full of tears. Enough to fill the Cape Fear.

Then I begins to tells Mammy everythin'. Ain't no use hidin' nothin' from her now—I don't care if she be the debil or a witch—I needs to talk, an' there she be. *[There is a short pause and some throat clearing.]*

Oh my. Thinkin' back. I already tired out with this here tale…. So long ago, but I feels I could lay my head down again on Mammy Rae big soft bosom right now, an' go to sleep. *[There is a long pause, and the interviewer asks Ms. Augustus if she would like to take a break. Ms. Augustus admits that she is very tired and would like to stop for the day.]*

August 27, 1937

Now I back. Ready for another day. We left off just as I about to tell Mammy Rae my woes. They growed too big for my youn' heart.

Well, I weepin' in Mammy Rae arms, an' she strokin' me, lettin' me be all sad an' sorrowful—till I done tell her everythin'. Everythin'. I tells her about David an' our meetin' at the Hurt. I tells her about Run'way Johnny an' sneakin' out victuals for him. I tells about how he be catched up an' likely thinkin' it be me that turn him in…an' I tells her about my love note give to me by Kate an' snatched away by the same.

Mammy Rae listen to me chatter on—never interruptin' or commentin' other than to say, "Um, hum…um, hum…yo' go on, gal, um, hum…"

Finally, I says "…an' there be mo', one terrible piece of news mo'." I lift my head an' turn to Mammy Rae on the bed. She look at me, with her big eyes an' her open heart.

"Go on, gal. Yo' can tells Mammy Rae." She nod her head encouragin' lak I be a toddlin' child, about to take my first step.

"Well," I begins…. "Yo' know how yo' leaves me just now to turn the dye pot?"

"'Course I remember—weren't but a hour past."

"Well, I be out there, stirrin' an' stirrin' when this ol' big crow swoop down an' land on the high shelf whar' yo' keeps them dye jars. An' this ain't no regular crow." I shakes my head an' look at Mammy for a sign. But she just nod, tell me to continue.

"That big ol' crow speak to me…clear words, no mumbo-jumbo. He say—an' keep on sayin': 'bad gal, bad, gal….' Then he lift his great shiny black wings till they look lak horns atop his head. An' I knows it be the debil hisself." My eyes fills back up with tears, an' before yo' knows it, I sobbin' again.

"I ain't no bad gal, Mammy. I swears I ain't."

"No, honey child, yo' ain't bad, yo' ain't bad." An' she stroke me again lak I that li'l wayward kitten. "But that crow wus sent to warn yo', an' this here the bad part."

So I pulls away, brace myself.

"That crow be the debil—yo' right about that. An' the bad news is that when he come in the form of a crow, he come tell the truth. Somethin' yo' done bad about to catch up with yo'—an' there ain't nothin' yo' can do stop it. Only be strong. No woman can fly away from trouble. Yo' ain't got no wings, an' yo' ain't got no powers." Mammy shake her head, an' I knows she right. She be tellin' the truth—somethin' bad set in motion lak a loosed cart unhitched.

By this time, mo' than a hour gone by. We still gots our chores to do, an' we be missed if we stays out too long. So we walk back to the cast iron dye pot to finish up. Missus want some fancy dress goods made 'cause there some big ol' gala ball she plannin' for Christmas.

We gits back to the pot. I help Mammy Rae, an' we don't talk. The heavy weight I been carryin' done fall away, even though I now knows somethin' bad gonna happen.

An' it do. That very night before supper. Aunt Patsy begin to holler for everyone to come. Hurry. She ring the iron bell that hang outside the summer kitchen. She ring it loud.

Usually, no one ring that bell. That bell gone rusted a long time ago. No bell needed, except when there trouble. Which there were now.

The summer kitchen wus near the back of the big house whar' we gather. That ringin' draw in all the slaves—about twenty of us. An' after we all together, Marster hisself come to out to the piazza. He dressed up for supper an' lookin' stately. An' in his loud, boomin' voice he tell us there be a big problem, an' he want the honest truth about the situation.

We all quiet. I standin in the back 'cause I knowed that Mister Crow prediction 'bout to come to pass. I see'd Kate off to the side, an' she look at me, eyes poppin', thinkin' this here *situation* be 'bout the note.

"The other day," Marster begin. "We had a visitor to our farm, a Mister Ellicott, who owns the Ellicott Plantation up a short way north from here. Mister Ellicott came to tell us that his slave Johnny had run away, and Mister Ellicott wants each and every one of us to watch out for this here runaway—for he is a dangerous and murderous sort." Marster pause, an' he got his hands clasp together in back of him. He strut back an' forth a couple of times.

"Now, cook here," he begin again, "just report that we missing a half slab of ham—missing out of the storehouse cabinet in the summer kitchen, right where we are standing now."

Marster stop, pause again. "I know one of you took it. I know one of you saw that runaway Nigger passing through and helped him. I know one of you went against my specific order to turn that scoundrel in. He's a murderer! And he could have killed any one of you—or us! Could have robbed us blind. A dangerous Nigger! And ya'll knew that but went against this family just the same…." Marster shoutin' now, worked up an' turnin' red as a full-grown rooster, struttin' up an' down.

"Who amongst you is the traitor? Who has done this deed?" Silence fall. Absolute silence. Never heared it so quiet.

"I ask you again. I want the culprit to come forward. If he does, he'll get forty lashes. Forty lashes delivered by me, personally. And in front of all you Niggers so you can see justice. No more, no less. Forty." And there Marster stand, expecting one brave Negro man or woman to come forward an' confess.

But no one do, a'course. I standin' there, shiftin' my weight, sweatin', feelin' guilty, but not havin' the courage to come forward. Kate don't even look at me now, 'cause she don't know nothin' 'bout this business. Only one that know is Mammy Rae, an' she not lookin' at me neither.

"Well," Marster go on. "I'll give you Niggers until tomorrow morning to confess. Until morning. That's all. If no one comes forward, then each of you will suffer. No meat rations until someone confesses. And if so much as a chicken gets gone, or one egg—here on this farm or on any neighboring place—the one that done the stealing—when I catch him—will be sold from this place.

"I hate to do it. You're my Niggers…and I treat you well—I take you into my house when you get sick. I gives you food and clothing. No one can say I work you overmuch. I don't sell you away from kin nor the good life you know. Now, all I ask for is honesty. Come forward and tell me who betrayed me." Silence. Marster stop his struttin' an' look at us.

It be 'bout all I can stand. I feel so guilty that I sweatin' lak I has the yella' fever. An' all the time that Marster been walkin' back an' forth, down on our level, near the veranda, we all can see how bad it is. None never see'd Marster so hateful.

"Once more…" Marster voice boom out. "Once more—who did this?" Marster look across the crowd. He wear his dark suit, put his hands up, lak he a preacher.

Silence still. Then Marster sweep his hands across the sky, shake his head, as if tellin' us that we standin' in front of the eyes of God. Then, exhausted, he just shake his head. He tell us we dismiss.

We all scatter slow, walkin' away—everyone mutterin' with heads low, lak we just buried the dead. Mammy Rae an' I sort of find each other an' gits into step. She don't say nothin', don't even look at me. I looks at her though—her wooly hair tied back in a bun, her large moon face an' wide flat nose. Black skin, almost ebony. An' she barefoot, paddin' with dark, heavy steps.

When we gits mo' alone, Mammy turn to me. "Well, yo' gonna say somethin' or not?

The sky wus gettin' toward evenin', the sun shinin' bright but low in the east, an' there a coolness in the air. The chill of it wash me clean. I know what I has to do. Mammy Rae know it, an' I knows it, without no one tellin' me. I just can't muster the strength. I thinks 'bout them lashes smackin' an' slashin' at my skin. I remember Runaway Johnny an' the family of snakes crawlin' all over his back An' I thinks 'bout my dress bein' torn or it bein' down in front of all my folks—my nakedness. An' Ma ashamed of me, an' how, she just the other day, wus thinkin' I up to no good.

Mammy Rae must'ta been readin' my thoughts, 'cause she don't say nothin', just take her hand an' gently stroke my back—exactly whar' them whip lashes would cut. I still that wayward kitten need to come home. An' this simple thing, these here soft strokes, they begins to gives me the encouragement I needs. Each stroke measured to protect me from them lashes that is sure to come. She must'ta stroke me forty times.

Somehow with our walkin', we end up at Mammy Rae cabin, an' I give Mammy a big hug, turns around without a good-bye, an' I takes off slow to home. *[Some throat clearing is heard, and Ms. Augustus says that she wants to take a break. There is a pause, and then the interviewer says that they can resume tomorrow.]*

August 28, 1937

Today Saturday—gonna take tomorrow off. Always mo' to say, but I tired at the end of the week. *[Ms. Augustus lets out a deep, long sigh.]* Let's just begin before the day turn too hot.

After that business with Marster, I draggin' myself home. It gettin' cool an' dark out, an' I feelin' so confused that I takes a minute to set awhile on the side of the dirt path. There a fallen tree, an' I sits on it. Sits an' sits, tryin' to finds the courage to turns myself in.

As I settin' there awhile—so long that the darkness come on—in the distance, I hears a ol' barn owl hootin'—*who, who, who*—askin' its question.

Me, me, me, I answer.

An' then David come to mind—I see his face as he set beside me on them tree roots—an' it make my heart pound. This be the evenin' I suppose to tell Kate about him. Kate probably lookin' for me now. She don't knows I mixed up with this here Run'way Johnny.

So I gits up an' begins to walks home. My heart still beatin' hard, but I can't makes myself hurry none. I feels my bare feet in the cool sand as I walk the path. Moonlight peekin' out the clouds, good enough to see. I pass the big house—some of the windows lit up—an' meets Mar. She walkin' toward me, holdin' a small lantern, swayin' gently, castin' its glow right, then left.

"Ma lookin' for yo'," she say. "She sent me to fetch yo'."

So we fall in walkin' together.

"Mar, yo' ever thinks about slavery?" I axe.

"Some. They don't got it up North. I thinks 'bout that sometimes. Maybe South pull out of the Union—maybe we has war, lak they say. Who know what happen if Lincoln git elected. Mess of stuff goin' on in the world, Sarah Louise. Big ol' world out there...."

"What yo' knows about this run'way slave?" I axe her.

"No mo' than yo'."

"What yo' say if I knows somethin' about it. Somethin' I ain't sayin'?"

Mar stop in her tracks. Turn to me. "What yo' knows?"

"Well, I ain't sayin' I knows nothin'. Only what if...."

"Sarah Louise!" Mar hold up the lantern an' look me in the eye. "Yo' gotta tells me what yo' knows!"

"I be the one that help that run'way," I blurts right out, lookin' Mar straight back. As soon it out my mouth, I regret it. But it too late. "He come to me when I out goin' to the privy. He take his hand over my mouth an' swears me not to yell. So I don't. Mar, when I looks at him, I knows he ain't no murderer."

"Yo' helps him? Did yo' do the stealin'? Steals for him! Sarah Louise!"

"Mar, he wus hungry," I begins. "Mighty hungry." My eyes downcast as I speak, an' I tries to lift them, but it ain't no use. Guilt an' shame got me good. But I go on. "An' he pitiful, sad an' pitiful. All in rags, so skinny yo' could see his bones."

"Yo' done look at his bones!" Mar gaspin' at me.

"Mar, his shirt ripped. In tatters," I explain. "He show me his back whar' he wus whipped. Some strokes still fresh. They lak snakes crawlin'…."

Mar put the lantern down on the path. She stand there an' I can see her mouth wide open, ready to catch some late October flies.

"Go on," she say. "Tell me the rest."

"Well, lak I says… Run'way Johnny come to me, an' I gets some food to feeds him. Just some ol' ham an' pone from the summer kitchen, thinkin' it weren't gonna be missed. Johnny gobble it down, an' axe me not to tell no one. He say folks here better off not knowin' nothin'."

"He got that right!"

"Mar…there be mo'…. 'bout Johnny gal—Mister John Ellicott done take her for his own. Now she with child—Mister John Ellicott child!

So he done run away—'tween his gal get taken an' him gettin' whipped, he ain't got nothin' mo' to lose. That why he run. Ain't no murderer. Mister Ellicott make that up to gits him catched."

Mar seem over the shock, just shakin' her head. "Yo' gonna tell, Sarah Louise? Yo' gonna confess?" By this time, Mar pick up the lantern, an' we slowly walkin' again down the dirt path.

"Anyone else know about this? Yo' tells anyone?"

I nod my head. "I tells Mammy Rae. She know."

"What she say?"

"She don't say nothin', but she know what I gotta do. All us Negroes gonna suffer if I don't."

"She right about that." Mar make some noise. "Uh, uh, uh."

By this time, we at the cabin door—home. We done stall enough. Then I thinks 'bout the other part—with David. But it too late now to start in with all that. I in enough trouble already.

Mar say, "I ain't gonna tell Ma. This yo' business. Least till tomorrow. Yo' gots to think 'bout what yo' gonna do. Ma gonna be real disappointed when she hear, Sarah Louise. I think facin' her gonna be harder than facin' Marster," an' she look at me one last time before she go in the cabin, door open then shut behind.

For a minute, I stands there in the crisp, dark air—back so Ma can't see me by the open window—but I sees her: she lit up by lantern light, an' I sees the wood flickerin' in the fireplace. I hears Ma axe 'bout me, an' Mar just say I outside, be in soon. She tell Ma that she find me on the path toward home, an' we walk together. Hannah there too—with some li'l wood laundry pins painted up lak dolls, she play with. Sittin' by the fire, hummin' an' playin'. Kate here too, but when she hear that I outside, she look up through the window hole but turn away when she don't see me.

Well, by now, I just tired. Plum tired out. I takes my chances an' goes in.

Ma look up, tell me I late, but she go about her business. "Yeah, Ma," I say. "Sorry." Kate look at me, question in her eyes; I just look away an' puts on a apron to helps Ma takin' taters out the fire. She has some smoked ham left over from yesterday, an' that need gits sliced up. Also Ma got a mess of late wild greens cookin' in a pot.

"Ain't be havin' this again for awhile," Ma say as she puts a plate of sliced ham on the table.

We all sits down to et. An' this whar' I thinks it right to say what on my mind. I in turmoil, an' this here my family—too many secrets. Too much goin' on that need come out. Mar an' Kate each know half the story. Ma need to hear it all from me, I thinkin'—or else word travel so, she sure to hear it from somewhar'.

"I gots somethin' I wants to tell ya'll," I begin an' put the plate of ham on the table. I waits till I gits some attention, clears my throat 'cause there some lump there all a sudden, a big dry hard lump catchin' me up. Ma, Kate, Mar, Hannah, they stop for a minute, look at me.

"I the one that done it," I say. "I the one that help the run'way an' feeds him."

Ma let out a gasp—lak someone get up from the table and slap her across the face. That the only sound in the cabin.

I goes on: "That night, after Mister Ellicott an' Marster tell us about the run'way, I goin' to the privy, an' there I stumble on him."

"Yo' meets a murderer, Sarah Louise, an' yo' doesn't say nothin' to yo' family…" Ma begin. Her voice raise already.

"Ma, that man ain't no murderer," I cut her off. "That just a story Mister Ellicott make up…"

"Yo' don't knows nothin', gal! Nothin'. How yo' gonna tells who is an' ain't a murderer? Yo' ain't no judge? How I raise' yo' up? How I learns yo' to behave? Ain't no murderer."

"Ma, let me explain….I ain't finish my story…"

"Yo' done, child. Yo' done through!" An' Ma pull herself away from the table an' begin pacin' the floor.

Kate an' Mar an' Hannah still at the table. Kate an' Mar look at me. They on my side—I can tell from they eyes. They lookin' from Ma to me an' back again, till Mar say, "Ma, I knowed she done wrong, but least lets her explain…."

"Ain't no explainin' to do, Mar. No. I done hears enough! My child, my own child. My own flesh an' blood…" Ma carryin' on lak I be the one that kill somebody. Never see'd her so worked up. She always the cool member of the family. Now Pa, he gits hisself excited sometime. When he git angry, he lak a fire cracker on the Fourth of July. But Ma, this the most worked up I ever see'd her.

This scene go on for a few long minutes—silence, then Ma pacin' an' scoldin' me, explainin', then silent an' pacin' again.

But she must'ta walk off some of her shock, 'cause in a calm voice, she finally say, "Hannah, if yo' done, go play with yo' pin dolls by the fireplace. Me an' yo' sisters, we needs to talk."

Hannah say she don't have much appetite. Her li'l face downcast, an' she just foolin' with her greens after she et her ham. "I done," she announce, an' bring her plate to the basin. Then she go off to do as she told—sit by the fire with her pins.

Ma throw a small log off the pile into the fire, an' come back to join us gals—we still at the table. "I ready to hear, Sarah Louise. Tell me what yo' gots to say for yo'self." She pull her chair in up to the table.

My heart beatin' hard now, an' I feel regretful an' confused. But I recognize that this be the time to speak.

"Ma," I begins. "That day—the day all this happen—we all gone to town to see the hangin'. Yo' remember? I goes down Ramsey with Marse George, Mar, Kate, an' some of them others? We takes the mule cart to town? We in high spirits 'cause of the public hangin'? Remember that day, Ma?"

"I remember, I do," Ma urgin' me on.

"Well, it were awful, Ma. Real awful to see a man hang. No matter what he done. They puts the rope around his neck, black hood over his head, then drop out the floor beneath his feet. Hands tied behind his back, can't struggle none. Yo' could almost hears his neck break lak a chicken neck bein' snapped. Our high spirits done left us after that. We rides back home, feelin' low, and then Mister Ellicott come tearin' through. He be all wild, lak a mad dog lookin' for someone to bite. An' Marster be all whipped into a fury—they talkin' about this here run'way, how dangerous he be. Ma. Yo' remember hows I flies in here an' tells yo' all 'bout this? I scared, worked up. An' how yo' say ain't no murderer comin' into our parts? See, Ma, I didn't expects to meets no murderer.

"But that night, after I forgets 'bout the hangin', the run'way, settle down, goes to bed, I has to git up come night to use the privy. So I goes. An' what happen? No sooner I gits outside, I feels one hand grabs me, an' another cover my mouth. I hears a deep voice say that he let me go if I don't holler. So I nods, an' he lets go. Now, quick, I figure out who he supposed to be. But when I looks at him, I can tell right away he ain't no murderer."

Ma eyes is wide, an' she puts her hands together lak she need to pray. "Lawd," she mutter.

"Ma, this man, he young an' in tatters. He gots a gentle face—kind eyes. An' he show me his back, striped with whippin' marks. Some still fresh. Others lak purple rope buried beneath his skin."

"Sarah Louise! Yo' lets some strange man lift his shirt, show yo' his naked flesh…" an' Ma raise her voice again, start in with them tiskin' noises lak she always do, shakin' her head side to side.

"Ma, his shirt in tatters. He half starved an' bony. Shirt ripped an' hangin'. I knows he ain't no murderer, Ma! I just knows it!"

"Yas, child—yo' knows everythin'. Everythin'. 'Course yo' do! Fifteen-year-ol' gal with not a lick of sense, but yo' size up a growed man real good, go stealin' food in darkness an' keep secrets from yo' kin…"

"Ma, it weren't lak that. I just takes some pity on him. That what I done. Show kindness for this human bein'! Lak yo' always say we should."

Then somethin' go wrong with all my talkin', my explainin', 'cause suddenly I burst out in big sobs. Puts my head down on the supper table an' begins my blabberin' again. Just lak I do with Mammy Rae.

But that don't soften Ma none. Ma don't stroke my back. No. She just up from the table again, pacin' an' sayin' that we needs ourself a plan. Somethin' to gits us right before mo' trouble come. "An' it's a'comin'," she say.

"My fault," I sobbin'. I'll tell Marster what happen—the truth. If I gits whipped, I gits whipped. An' I picks my head off the table, wipin' my eyes with my sleeve. "If I done wrong…"

"Oh, yo' done wrong, gal!" Ma start shakin' her head again. "Yo' ain't thinkin' 'bout nothin' but what catches yo' up in the moment. An' that ain't good enough. Not here, not now. What goin' on in yo' mind? Trustin' some strange man. Sarah Louise, what that man could of done to yo'… well, it make me sick. Yo' just lucky. That all. Dumb luck carry yo' through. Oh Lawd, have mercy on this here child. She think she know it all!"

Mar chime in. "We could say that Sarah Louise wus held by this run'way an' she had to steal the ham 'cause he held her with a knife to her throat."

"How about that she saw the run'way, but that he stole the ham hisself. Sarah Louise done see'd the whole thing but were too afraid to talk," wus Kate idea.

So we concoct a plan. We decide to tell Marster that Ma heared somethin' strange that night but don't think nothin' of it. Then the next day, she seen remnants of this run'way supper meal. She could see there be a ham bone an' a tin cup from the well by the big stone step near the privy. Didn't know whar' the ham from, so she didn't say nothin'. But that all she knowed. Ma wus ready to swears on the Bible before God, Marster, an' all her own chil'ren, us three gals.

Ma join us at the table, an' we all sits for a bit to lets Ma story settle in. "What if Marster don't believe yo'? What if he think yo' hidin' somethin' from him? What if he think yo' guilty an' whip yo' anyways?" Kate axe.

"I prepared. I gits right with my maker before I confess. God will just has to forgives me for this lie that I makes to protect my child. God mercy be infinite. I knows that."

Ma stand up again an' begin to pace. I sittin' there, goin' along with the plan, but all the time thinkin', I ain't happy about it. Then, we hears a knock on the cabin door. [*There is a long, scratchy sound on the tape, and Ms. Augustus says that she needs to take a break. The interviewer can be heard asking if Ms. Augustus wants to continue later today, meet tomorrow, Saturday, or break for the weekend and resume on Monday. Ms. Augustus says that she needs the time off so she would like to wait until Monday to finish this part of the story.]*

August 30, 1937

I remember how I leaves off on Friday. Ma come up with a lie to protect me. An' there a knock on the door.

An' who is it? Pa. Pitch black, night outside, but he slip over our place 'cause he hears 'bout trouble at the Smith farm.

Now when Pa come, he don't know nothin' but there trouble of some kind. The run'way slave gone through here an' someone help him, victuals gits stolen, an' there a heap of mess. Don't know nothin' 'bout me, what I done. No. Just come to see if we all right. Which we is. He done a whole day work an' walk these miles out'ta concern.

Li'l Hannah, playin' with her pins, run straight into Pa arms—right away, lak she always do. She fly to him lak metal to a magnet, the second she see'd him. Wrap her li'l self around him.

Ma come over an' give him a hug too. But we all quiet, subdued.

"Ro, yo' takes a seat," Ma tell him. "Have some supper—we gots lots left over." An' Ma pull Hannah off him an' slide a chair over.

"Chill outside. Long way to come…" Ma stallin' an' we dumbfounded, lookin' at each other for what to say.

"Well," Ma begin, an' serve Pa victuals what we have… piece of ham, taters, cold greens. Pa hungry an' begin to et. Silence for a moment, then Ma begin. Tell Pa the story—not the real one, but the one she make up. The lie. How she see'd the crumbs an' ham bone from the run'way slave supper, didn't think much of it, an' now she know she has to tell Marster. Which she gonna do in the mornin'. Should'a done it before. She know that now. What Marster gonna do when he hear 'bout it… can't say. But she do say she gonna do her duty an' tells the truth. Takes whatever punishment he give out, an' life gonna be right again. She ain't afeared of the truth—before no man, no how. She ain't feared of her maker neither. He know everythin', see everything. Ma say that her faith will see her through. Then she end on, "Glory, hallelujah, amen!" An' she take her seat on the empty chair next to Pa. *[There is a brief pause in the tape, and background noise and shuffling sounds are heard. Then Ms. Augustus resumes.]*

Well, it don't take Pa long to understand Ma ain't tellin' the truth. Pa knowed right away somethin' up, but he don't say nothin'. He know Ma good enough to tell when she fibbin'. But all he do is nod lak he understand.

Pa don't even axe Ma no questions. Don't need Ma to explain herself or to tell mo' about the run'way story. No. He just nod. All the while us gals gathered around, an' the room turn quiet again—unnatural almost. The only sound is Pa scrapin' his plate with a fork.

Then Pa axe about the crops, if everythin' in. If we gits any of the runty corn. Any mold there? Some in his fields, he say. But that don't stop the hands from pickin'. So we tell him that us gals got some good corn that wus missed durin' harvest. Pa nod, say he ain't surprised. Say that women folk got better sense—they gots smarter hands than men folk does. An' they stronger, last longer.

Pa never say another word about the run'way business, nothin' about Ma story. It strike us as odd, but we all happy not to have to lie mo'.

Just small talk. After about a hour, Pa say he glad we all right an' he have to go. Pa give Ma a hug, a tight squeeze, say he love her. Kiss her one mo' time, then come give us each a kiss on the forehead, an' he take his leave.

Our ol' wood door bang shut after him, an' we all know that the conversation be over. Lies been told. Things set in motion.

It lak the air gone from the room. This empty feelin' left. Nothin' to talk 'bout now. Kate take Pa plate, his bowl from the table. Put it in a bin outside. "I get it wash up in the mornin'," she say.

We do our evenin' chores an' gits to bed. All us thinkin' about next day, 'course, but we keepin' the thoughts to ourself.

Later though, when I almost asleep, Kate sneak over an' she nudge me. I open my eyes, see her face in the weak moonlight, peakin' though the clouds an' the window. But I just whisper, "Tomorrow."

Next day, after chores an' breakfast, Ma go down to the big house. It be a pretty day—clouds gone, but it feel lak fall. Nip in the air, an' the breeze crisp as a sheet on the line. I already at the big house, helpin' with somethin' when I see'd Ma comin'. Immediately, my heart start poundin' lak it want to leap from my chest—it be some kind of criminal, about to break free from jail. But Ma, she go right past me, don't say a word.

Ma always had this way of floatin' when she walk. Lak she glidin' on a soft carpet or a cushion of air. She never walk hard. No. Never plod lak some big women do. An' Ma a large woman—an' solid. But she graceful. An' that mornin', she do her glidin' so smooth that she float right on past me. An' I let her go. Even up them stairs at the big house. She comin' up the back stair an' into the winter kitchen. That be the entrance us slave use. An' inside the house, the winter kitchen lead to the dinin' room an' on to the parlor.

Meanwhile, I beatin' a small rug on a line. I wus in a full-length house apron—it one that kept on the back door of the rag closet, an' everybody use it. It the one that stay dusty.

After Ma float up the stairs, I start beatin' that rug real hard an' fast. She float in an' seem to stay for a long time. Seem that the faster my heart race, the slower the time go, an' the worse I get to feelin'—about everything.

Then I see Ma face glide over the rug on the line. Her coppery face. She got no expression. Just her round moon face, the color of the Cape Fear River, sailin' along. She wear her hair tie up in a bun with a kerchief tight around her head. Ma hair smooth too, not so natty lak mine. Everything about Ma smooth. Skin, the way she talk, walk, even do her chores. She got big work-woman hands an' broad flat feet—but they too is somethin' fine. She gots a natural-born grace—an' it ain't just me that say so.

Well, Ma sail on past, an' I see'd her from the rug, which hung on the line by the empty wash tub. We alone together out there, an' I thinks Ma wanna say something. She look at me for a moment, an' I try to read the expression on her face. But nothin'. An' for some reason, I can't seem to axe what happen.

I smack the rug one mo' time, try to break the silence. But Ma walkin' back to the winter kitchen now. So I drops my rug paddle an' run up to her.

"Ma," I says, catchin' up when she just about on the path that go to the kitchen or split to the horse barn. "Ma, tells me what happened? Did yo' speak to Marster? Did yo' gits to see him? Maybe Missus…" I lak a lamb nudgin' up to its ewe. But Ma on her way up to the big house.

"We talks about it later. Everythin' be all right now, Sarah Louise. Everythin' all right." Ma look at me.

I still tuggin' at her. "Sure, Ma? Everythin' all right? Sure?" I tries to stop her, holdin' on to her dress.

Ma just brush away my hand, an' walk away. I stand there, an' when she gits up the stairs, she call back without even turnin'. "Sarah Louise, mind yo' Mama! Go on now back to yo' chores. Everythin' fine." An' she make a shooin' motion lak I a pesky mosquito. Off into the house she go. Door open, shut.

Now, Ma right—I gots chores to do. So I only stands there a short time before I walk on back, pick up my paddles to finish the rug. Weren't till supper time that I learns what happen. It take me by surprise. *[There is a long, scratchy-sounding pause in the tape; then Ms. Augustus continues.]*

Supper time, lak I say, arrive. An' when it do, I hear that four other colored folk confess to helpin' Run'way Johnny. My Pa be one of them. By the time Ma get to the big house in the mornin', there already be others that tell their story before her. Mammy Rae be one, Pa another, an' two others I never knowed.

Ma tell us that she go to Missus 'cause Marster were on the road to town already. An' after Ma tell her sad tale about seeing the remnants of the ham from the run'way, an' such other evidence, Missus just shakes her head an' axe Ma what she ought'ta do with such Niggas? They all comes forward an' there no tellin' what is an' ain't the truth'. Pa be the first—the night he come see us. He go to the big house straight after. Then in the mornin' there be the three others. All with different stories. Missus say that Niggas don't knows how to lie real good, but they all seems to want to do it. She shake her head an' say she gonna talk to Marster about the situation. Missus say it a conspiracy an' just keep shakin' her head. Tell Ma to return to her chores.

Ma say that the whole quarter done git the same notion all at once. She think that be the end of it. No whippin' for anyone. She think Marster gonna let the whole Run'way-Johnny-thievin'-ham incident go. But then she say that Pa shouldn't a'tried to protect her. End up makin' mo' trouble. She take care of her own business. An' she gonna tell him so. An' if he gits hisself whipped, it be his own darn fault. She talk hard, but the look in Ma eyes tell me she worry about him, nonetheless.

Well, as Ma predict, Marster, all spit-an'-vinegar, don't do nothin'—no whippin', no rationin'. He be a good man, lak I tells yo'. Make a show of somethin' different, but he all right.

At supper time—again, someone ring the big ol' rusted bell. Lak the day before. This time, when we all together, Marster back home by then, an' he prance up an' down the piazza—same as before—sayin' that the culprit has come forward, an' justice been served. He say that the Nigga responsible for aidin' an' abettin' the run'way wus from another plantation, an' he be punished by his own master. But he warn us good that he hisself ain't above takin' out the lash an' servin' justice. An' he don't wants his Niggas ever catched up in this sort of business—ever. He say he not above selling a no-good Nigga south. An' he look all around to make his point. Say he glad that none of his Niggas wus responsible—an' he remind us to keep to our chores an' stay out'ta trouble. Marster, he look lak some big ol' rooster—strut back an' forth again, voice raised, makin' hisself clear. An' we all act shameful an' downcast accordingly. He tell us we back on meat. Then he let us go.

When we starts to walk to our cabin for some supper, I catched up with Ma, an' she begin to fret right away. She thinkin' 'bout Pa, 'course. If he be the one Marster say gonna gets whipped by Mister Hardin for somethin' he didn't do. No. Ma shakin' her head an' worryin'. An' there nothin' none of us could do but wait. [*Ms. Augustus says she is ready to stop, although she understands that they haven't been talking for long. It is Monday, and because it rained on Saturday, she explains, she has many chores to do. She asks the interviewer if they can resume early on Tuesday, as she has another doctor's appointment later that afternoon and plans on walking the mile to his office. Her bones are still aching. The interviewer agrees to meet early on Tuesday morning, around 10:00 a.m.*]

August 31, 1937

[*Some clicks are heard, and Ms. Augustus's voice begins mid-sentence.*]

…says my bones are bad, brittle an' thin. Doc ain't gonna tell me nothin' I don't knows. Rheumatism, arthritis. Both knees. But I gonna go anyways, for the medicine. The doc got this new stuff. Pills. Gonna give me some. Worth the trip.

Ain't about to give up on myself yet. Done lived too long to give up. No. Everyone I talk 'bout is gone: Marster, Missus, Kate, Mar, Ma, Pa, Hannah…an' David. He gone too.

Begins whar' I leaves off. We walkin' back from the piazza after Marster say how glad he be that it ain't his Negro that aid an' abet Johnny.

Ma upset, thinkin' Pa get in trouble. An' we go to the cabin to has our supper, then disperse to be at our regular chores for the evenin'. An' it weren't till after evenin' chores that I tells Kate about David an', then even later, before I learns about Pa.

Can't remember what chores I doin' that night or whar' I wus, but Kate come along the path to finds me by the lower field, whar' I walkin'. I see she gots her hand in her apron, an' she smilin', with that twinkle in her eye.

"Knows what I gots?" An' she smooth the dirt in a half circle with her foot. "Yo' do, don't yo'? Right here." Kate jump aside me an' do a li'l jig; then she fish a folded piece of paper from her pocket an' dangle it lak a worm on a hook. Seem lak ol' Miss Kate couldn't wait for this mess of trouble to be over with so that she cans gits back to the juicy business of the note. Ain't too troubled about Pa an' what happen to him. No. She just anxious to move along an' gits her fun.

"Kate," I says," I sworn off fellas. I tell yo' the story, but after this all mess with the run'way an' now Pa, I through."

"Oh yeah? Then I just rip up this li'l ol' note lak it never been. That all right with yo'?" Kate make lak she gonna unfold the note an' tear it up.

"Yo' does what yo' want, Kate Lilly Smith?" I axe her. "I ain't interested in this mess no mo.'"

"Ma would be, Sarah Louise. Ma be very intersted. Maybe Pa too. After this here run'way thing, he might wanna know what you up to. Other folks too. Great entertainment—gonna gets awful slow an' tiresome around here. Pa gonna be all right. He always all right. An' that Run'way Johnny done get hisself caught up."

I know she tauntin' me. That I shouldn't falls for her teasin' ways. But I can't stands it, so I snatch the letter from her hand, an' runs! Fast as I can, across the pasture an' down toward the piney woods.

Kate up behind me in no time. She catch me by my skirt an' we tumble down onto the cool, damp grass, wrestlin', tuggin' till the note git tore in two, an' we stop—all at once, layin' there, each with our ragged, crumpled-up half.

"Tell me, Sarah Louise, tell me the truth now."

All heat gone, an' so I tells her the story of how David an' I meets. Not so long ago, but seem I done lots of growin' between that day an' now.

"Yo' love him, Sarah Louise? Yo' gonna marry him?" Kate turn toward me an' almost whisper the questions in my ear.

"Yas," I says. "I gonna marry him some day." Though it be news to me.

Kate quiet. She hand me her sorry half of the letter, an' we dust ourself off to go home. On the way back, I makes Kate promise to keep David our secret. 'Course, she don't know that Mammy Rae know. I tells her we needs concern ourself with Pa an' his trouble.

"Oh, Pa…" she say. "He gonna be fine."

The mood at quarters wus quiet. By then, almost everyone knowed some piece of the truth. Everyone love to gab about what they know, or think they know.

An' sure enough, the very next mornin', Ma get word that Pa weren't gonna be whipped. He fine, just lak Kate say. No one believe him when he confess. Master has him walk back to the Hardin place with a note to Mister Hardin, who penned him up till mornin', then let him go.

Ma relieved but still mad at Pa for interferin'. An' if some other poor slave got hisself whipped for somethin' he never do, well, we never knowed who.

Next day, after all this business die down, wus Thursday. An' the Thursday next wus the day David want me to meet him by the A. P. Hurt. So I has the week to think.

Now I needs to interrupt myself. Yo' never interrupts me—but I needs to interrupt msyelf, tell yo' mo' than this here about me an' David. 'Cause there this other story, happenin' alongside.

Just as this thing 'tween me an' David heat up, the war be heatin' up too. Fall turnin' to winter, peace to strife.

Yo' wasn't born then, but everyone know 'bout Mister Abraham Lincoln—though most folks forgets his party an' that he ain't on the ballot in North Car'lina. Man name Breckinridge run. Few folks recalls him.

Before the war, some folk say we gonna leave the Union if Lincoln get elected. They concern 'bout what gonna happen in that November election.

Us colored caught up in this mess. Some reads the paper when we gets a'hold of it, but most come to us in drips an' drabs. Overhearin' white folk talk an' listenin' to each other gossipin'. Plenty of it.

There be the Whigs, which go by another name. Hmm…. Can't recall. Them Democrats breaks in two—Northern an' Southern. We all for Breckinridge—that I know. He a Southerner. Everybody gabbin' 'bout the election an' what a cold fall we havin'.

Some say that Mister Lincoln gonna take down the South. Some even say that he gonna outlaw slavery. An' 'course, that what he done. An' there them colored that wus against Lincoln. Even now.

These times nowadays be so hard that some black folk think it all go back to Mister Lincoln—it all his fault. They thinkin' they be better off if he ain't never been elected. *[Some scratchiness is heard on the tape, but no words appear to be lost.]*

Not me. Not then, not never. No. I thinks a lot 'bout slavery, 'bout growin' up, bein' a child then. These times plenty difficult, but them times wus worse. An' I lives through two big wars an' some smaller ones. But the Great War don't compare to the War Between the States. Don't compare 'cause the nation split in two lak a oak by lightenin'. Which I once see'd on the Smith place. Big bolt sever a chestnut tree. Then it catched on fire an' burned lak Sherman hisself come marchin' through.

Well, this wus all happenin' as my story unfold. There lots of nervous folks, black an' white. There a mess of political parties, an' lots of war talk. Also, yo' gotta remember when a slave run, everybody git nervous. An' Run'way Johnny—takin' off when he do—stir folk up when they stirred up enough. One man run, they think their Negroes all gonna go rise up an' run.

I go back now to that Thursday, when I supposed to meets the Hurt. The day begin, an' I still has no plan. Don't even knows exactly what time the A. P. Hurt due. I axe around, but all I hears is "mid-day." Sometime boats early, sometime late.

I do my mornin' chores—lak usual. Patsy say I gotta to do some washin', scour some pots, then check back with her later. All the while I'm a'plottin' hows I gonna gits myself down to the Cape Fear River dock. Mind yo', I wus thinkin' up some lie, but not quite sure what it might be, or who to axe for help.

So I comin' up the path back from the wash line, an' I stumble into the very person I needs to meet—Mammy Rae—saunterin' in her big-bone way down when I comin' up. I know she suspect what I might be up to, an' she catch my eye. Then wink.

"Good mornin', Mammy," I say, an' I stops.

"Mornin' yo'self, Sarah Louise," Mammy Rae say. We both standin' there. An' there be a pause. "I be goin' back down to the dye shack," Mammy say, an' she put down the basket she carryin'. Seem to be out'ta breath. "I gonna needs some help today. Check with Patsy. If she ain't in the kitchen, she there soon. Missus want them fabrics done for the seamstress."

"Mammy," I say. An' what come out surprise me. "Why yo' turn yo'self in last week 'bout that run'way? What yo' do that for? Ain't no one gonna believe yo'."

Mammy Rae wipe her brow, though it cool outside. "Gal," she say. "Lots yo' don't know. Yo' still a child."

We standin' there, sun out, but still cold in the mornin' with winter comin' on. I ain't mad at Mammy, an' she seem ol', sweatin', tired out. An' then I thinkin' this conversation beside the point. Don't even knows why I brings it up. I look down at the dirt path.

Then Mammy Rae take my arm an' say, "Yo' at the age for trouble, gal. Need to take care. Us colored here, we all be watchin' over yo. But we can't do but so much. Yo' take care now. Don't do nothin' stupid. An' she let go of my arm an' gives me another wink. "Check with Aunt Patsy about yo' chores. Tell her I needs yo'."

I nods. That's all. Mammy picks up her basket, an' off she go down the path. I make my way to the big house, gonna axe Aunt Patsy, an' puts my hand in my apron pocket to feel the two halfs of David letter, all folded up—my good luck charm.

Well, everyone young once. Yo' thinks Mammy sideway warnin' gonna stop me? Make me think twice 'bout lying again, lightin' out? No, no, an' double no! I don't think 'bout it no longer than it take for me to say "Yankee Doodle Dandy." No stoppin' a gal that think she in love.

My head wus swimmin' with ideas. I seein' Mammy Rae just when I need her, that be a sign. So I begins to hatch out a plan. Mammy Rae a ways up the dirt path, so I runs up to tells her. When I does, she ain't too happy none 'bout what I say, but she agree.

"Lawdy, Lawd, have mercy," she shakin' her head. Then she tell me I gonna do what I want even without her, so she might as well help.

So I goes back to the big house, quick, to finds Patsy. She talkin' to someone, an' tell me to finish hangin' out the wash line an' puts the big pots away. After that, I can go down to help Mammy Rae at the dye shack. She gonna see me later.

Ma outside, not near Patsy, but around the back. So I have to calls to her before she go down the back veranda stairs. "What yo' wants, gal?" Don'ts yo' has enough to keeps yo' busy?" Aunt Patsy give yo' chores? Ma gots her feet spread, arms crossed.

"I ain't feelin' so good, Ma. Come to tells yo'. Come at me all a'sudden. I'm gonna finish up my mornin' chores; then I goin' to Mammy Rae that need me at the dye shack. But I ain't feelin' well. I might just has to lie down. Don't knows if I make it through." I holds my belly an' makes a face.

"Gal trouble?" Ma axe.

"Don't know, Ma. Just hurtin'." I grips the skirt' gathers round my middle an' makes another face.

"Well, I supposin' I can tell Patsy yo' ain't well." She look at me, only half convinced. "Yo' wanna go ahead home, lie down now? An' I cans check on yo' at dinner. Yo' milk this mornin'? Tote all that kindlin' yet? How about the line, yo' finish that?"

"Yas, ma'am. I done them things. Patsy tell me to put the big pots away, which I gonna do now. But Ma, I gonna go down to Mammy Rae an' rest there. I just seen her an' she got a potion for some healin' tea. I could rest there an' have some company. That way if I feelin' better, I can help her too."

Ma shake her head *no* but say, "Yo' do as yo' lak, Sarah Louise. Yo' do as yo' lak. Always do." She glide down the big house veranda stairs.

I should'a felt good 'bout how smooth it all go, but I didn't. I stands there in the mid- mornin', chill finally gone, an' I feelin' rather low. Lyin' again, I tells myself. An' remember the words of Mister Crow: *bad gal, bad gal.* "No good can come from deceit," I say out loud—it somethin' the preacher tell us.

I put them pots away—take me but a few minutes—then begin my walk to Mammy Rae, an' I be thinkin' that nothin' is gonna keep me from seein' David—even if I has to do wrong—which I wus clearly doin'.

It lak I got me two souls—one that wanna do the right thing an' knowed better, an' the other drive me to mischief an' ain't no good. But the bad *feel* good, so I does it anyway.

It were a quiet fall day. Some Negro men folk be gatherin' fodder in the low land. Summer corn all harvested an' shucked, but there still be some dry stalks with half ears. Women an' gals this time of year ain't workin' as hard after harvest as before. Some already thinkin' 'bout Christmas time, Marster an' Missus Christmas ball be comin' up. Always plenty to do, but it slow toward winter, an' that one reason I figure I can be sick.

After a few minutes, I on the lower path toward the dye shack, all alone. Blue sky, warm sun. I forgets all 'bout Ma. Forgets 'bout chores. Even Run'way Johnny fadin'. Even Mar, Kate I forgets 'bout—everythin' fall away. Somethin' powerful pullin' at me.

David. I thinks 'bout how he look at me with those strange green eyes, his smile almost sly—lak he know some secret 'bout me, but weren't never gonna tell. An' when he talk, his words come out slow, thoughtful, fine, as if he prepared them all in advance. Make me wanna keep listenin' to his every word. I walk, an' there a lightness make me feel floaty. Maybe I gits it from Ma. Maybe I gonna be a graceful woman lak Ma when I full growed.

Well, I gots to walk by the li'l garden that way below the summer kitchen, so I bends down to pluck up some Hogweed an' stuff it quick in my mouth. It be so sour that I knows I gonna look pretty sick now. An' I slows my pace to show I havin' a difficult time.

An' sure enough, I see Marse George by the stable mountin' block, 'bout to ride Slim, his new roan gelding that weren't but 'bout five year ol'.

"Mornin', Sarah Louise," he call when he see me walkin'.

"Mornin'," I calls back, tryin' not to be too gay.

But Marse George don't notice nothin' suspicious. He look all dashin' an' full of pep. Ready for adventure.

I thinks for a moment that Marse George be about the same age as David. An' I imagine that it be David mountin' Slim instead of Marse George. I squint to blur my vision an' think: *What if Marse George an' all the white folk wus slaves an' us colored folk wus all marsters?*

I can see David in them clean, starch britches, with brass buttons shinin' on his tailcoat. See Ma orderin' around Missus. She say, "Yas, ma'am" to Ma, head bowed in respect. I thinks Pa would lock up Mister Hardin, catchin' him in a lie or some misdeed. Then, Pa would be generous an' let him go. An' I could be free, an' marry David…. Mister… didn't even remember his Christian name… so I pulls out my love note to looks it up. Augustus. A good name. Then, Mister David Stephens Augustus could come courtin' me proper. I be a lady.

By now, I be on a small knoll that raise me up so I could see the big house, sittin' in its shallow valley. Look lak a picture painted. Could use some fresh paint, I thinks, but still look mighty grand, with the big back veranda, an' tall windows open for some fresh mornin' air, white curtains blowin', wavin' to me, not a care in the world.

Mammy Rae be standin' over the iron dye pot when I arrives. She, lak Ma, shakin' her head. She look hot an' tired, though it still cool an' still mornin'.

"Yo come to make trouble, gal, yo' sure do." An' she don't look up. Just stir.

"I ain't gonna get caught, Mammy," I say right off. "An' if I don't sees David now…well…I won't sees him again for a long time, maybe never. It just a small fib I gonna tell—so small. I knows it don't look good. But yo' understand, Mammy. I knows yo' do. Weren't yo' in love once? Didn't yo' has a beau?"

Mammy just say, "Yo' ain't to do no dilly-dallyin', Miss Sarah Louise, Miss Mind-of-her-Own, Miss Gal-in-Love." She stop stirrin' long enough to looks at me.

"Only gone a short time, promise." I grabs Mammy arm, soaked with sweat, steamin' lak she in the pot, not just standin' by it.

"I gots yo' a clean dress. Be hangin' in the shed. Yo' watch the pot for me, Sarah Louise, an' I be back in no time." She slip me a apron from the peg, help tie it in the back, an' hand me the turnin' spoon. I feels her special touch settle me right down. A gift, she sure did have.

But just as soon as Mammy help me slip on my apron an' leave for the shed, I feels good, somethin' swoop down—some blackness.

Yas. As soon as Mammy Rae gone, who be payin' a visit to Miss Sarah Louise Smith? Yo' guess it. Ol' Mister Crow—debil, he is, he takin' this opportunity to swoop down on me again.

"Caw, caw, caw," he cry. But this time I ain't scared, so I says to him, "Mister Crow, I ain't bad, an' nobody nor nothin' gonna talk me out of this here errand I 'bout to do. Not yo', Mammy Rae, no one!" I starts stirrin' quick, excitement, anger, fear right beside me, helpin' stir up the pot.

"Sad gal, sad gal," Mister Crow say; he perched on the shelf ledge. "Sad gal, sad gal."

"Them all the words yo' knows? I ain't bad, an' I ain't sad! Now flies away ol' crow before I makes yo' sad an' sorry for ever comin' my way. Shoo, shoo." I takes the huge, wet wooden dye spoon an' holds it up, cuts the air with it lak a sword. Again an' again. "Shoo, shoo!" An' he flies away, leavin' me feelin' pretty bold an' satisfied.

Mammy Rae come back, but I decides not to tell her nothin'. Don't needs her mistakin' ol' Mister Crow as a sign of ill omen. She gots a nice gingham dress folded over her arm. Clean an' pressed.

"Puts this on, gal," she say, takin' the dye spoon from me an' helpin' me out of the apron an' my dress. The gingham one must be owned by Miss Mary, I thinks, but don't wants to axe. It fit good an' sure make me feel fine.

"I knows when the Hurt come in," Mammy say. "Hears about it from folk at the big house." She tie me together with a big bow over my waist, hangin' down the back. The dress weren' too fancy, but it starched an' clean. Red gingham look pretty an' fresh. She give me a small white bonnet to puts over my head. "If yo' gets stopped," she tell me, "yo' just say yo' pickin' up some piece goods for Missus. Off the boat. Yo' gets that? Piece goods."

I nods, an' go to leave, but Mammy catches me up one mo' time. "Hurt comin'," they think, at half past noon. Yo' see that David boy for a few minute only. Yo' don't do no foolishness, bring any attention yo'self. An' carry this—"

She hand me a basket with a white sack cloth over it. Inside there be couple of yards of linen, folded. An' beneath that, there is two cooked yams an' couple of dry biscuits. Mammy look at me an' nod. "Yo' be careful. Yo' ain't gots no idea what yo' doin'. Don't knows why I helps yo'. No I don't."

It be a hour walk down to the wharf if I takes the shortcut, which I plans to do. There a narrow dirt path that I catch just south of whar' I be. I ain't expectin' no trouble. Paterollers not out middle of day, just at night. Most folks that sees each other knows to minds their owns business.

I lookin' fine when I sets off. Perky an' feelin' lak I owns the world. Guess I too young an' stupid to knows better.

It be a trip worth tellin' about. Yas, but I be tired out with all this talkin'. An' my bones ache again. Lawd. We gonna need to stop here for this day. It be the last day of August—ain't that right? Gots the doc comin' out this way—checkin' on folks. House call around the neighborhood—he comin' to me too. *[There is a break in the interview, silence, and then some garbled voices are heard along with some other noise before the tape is shut off.]*

September 1, 1937

Yo' be early today. Just as well. I be ready for yo'. Thinkin' last night 'bout this tale of mine. How much to say. How I gettin' caught up in it. September already. Time movin' too fast—that haven't changed. Fast back then, fast now.

Yesterday, I left off as I were 'bout to meet David. An' I mention them ol' timey paterollers be out catchin' up Negroes. Not so much daytime, an' that be when I be going. They ride at night. A sorry bunch. Whippin', stealin'. If a slave get caught without a pass—yo' knows 'bout them passes? If a slave ain't got one, it ain't good. No. But they be easy to fake if yo' can read an' write an' can gets a'hold of clean paper.

I tell yo' 'bout them another time. This here trip I make be in the day. I ain't worried about them. An' I wus just plannin' to be away for such a short time.

So offs I goes in my gingham dress. An' I gets there with no problem along the way. Didn't see no one. It be lak God hisself had planned it. I arrive, an' that ol' Hurt pull in a minute or two later. When I see'd it from the woods, I start runnin', but then I catched myself, thinkin' back to what Mammy Rae say 'bout not drawin' attention. So I smooth myself over an' try to blend into the crowd.

Mess of folk. Every which way. Black an' white. I stands back by the tree that we et at before. Everybody movin', scurryin' around lak ants—white ones an' black ones. I remembers standin' there—changin' my focus, makin' the whole scene blurry—that way, I feel removed, don't appear nervous. I be lookin' for David, but I don't see'd him anywhar'. Then tap, tap, tap! I startle an' turn around.

It be David! An' he give me such a look that it make me blush. He take my elbow, gentle an' say we better sits down.

"I so glad yo' here, Sarah Louise. So glad! Did yo' gits my note? I weren't sure 'bout sendin' it, weren't sure whose hand it might fall into…"

"I gits it. Have it right here." An' I pulls out the two halfs of the folded letter, an' I begins to open them on my lap.

I look at David with the sorry thing spread out on my lap, an' he smile. Then I smile, an' we suddenly laughin' lak we has some long-held secret an' we just gittin' around to share it.

"I don't know why I sent it, Miss Sarah Louise, but I mighty glad I did." David say, an' he take my hand. "I knows this sound real forward, but I can't helps myself." An' he lookin' at me. An' we settin' there, moonin'. Lookin' into each other eyes lak sweethearts. Yo' can reads a person soul.

"Yo' don't has to save that silly, ripped-up note," David say. "There'll be mo'—I writes to yo' again, Sarah Louise. Better notes than this here one. I promise." Someone yell in the distance. Some ugly, angry shout. I look up. Remind me that I ain't supposed to be out. A sign.

"I gotta go," I say. An' the spell between us broken. David gots work to be done, an' I gots to get home quick.

"Yo' comin' back?" I axe as we gettin' up. Me smoothin' my fresh gingham dress, David still lookin' at me.

"Yo' so pretty," he say an' squeeze my hand. "I'll write. The Hurt be back soon—about three week, one last time. Should be Thursday, three week, that in November. Cans yo' remember that, gal? Can yo's gits away?"

"I be here. I good with dates. Half past noon. I be here."

David squeeze my hand again. He brush his face up to mine, an' Lawd, he kiss me on the cheek. One small dab.

I don't recall what all we says after that kiss. Happen so fast, it 'bout burn my cheek. It be a dream—an' I 'bout to lose myself in it. Dream so real when yo' dreamin' it, but when it gone, yo' can't quite trust it happen.

Then, I'm on the path home. Happy. I rememberin' that ol' Mister Crow an' thinkin' I ain't the sad gal Mister Crow predict. He get that wrong. I skippin'. Singin'. Hummin' some li'l tune. That be a fine day. An' I thinkin' I escape my fate.

Which I done. When I gits home, no one miss me. I come to Mammy Rae dye shack, an' there she be, stirrin' the pot lak I never left. She smile at me, an' I knows everythin' all right.

"Yo' meet yo' beau?" She axe, an' barely look up.

"I meet him, Mammy." An' all I can do is grin. "Yo' wants this dress back? I keeps it nice an' clean."

Mammy dry her big hands on her apron, reach behind her, untie it, an' take her dirty apron off. Put it on the bench an' help me out of my dress. I puts on my ol' one, an' off I goes to my cabin. I knows it way past dinner time, but not yet time for any supper preparations. But I needs to pick up an' make my presence known. I has to remember not to let any skip into my walk. I sick with gal trouble. I tries to makes myself look ill an' downcast.

It late afternoon. Ma still not at the cabin. No one there. I just stop an' rest on the stoop, on the large stone in front.

Well, that be a day. I ready to stop now at this happy part. Before any trouble start, which it always do. Trouble never far behind.

Turn off that machine. I needs to collect myself. *[Ms. Augustus stops speaking, and the tape is clicked off, then on again. It is obviously the same day but difficult to know just how much later.]*

…Stiflin' hot. Hmm… Good about this here break. *[Some crackling sounds are heard, and someone is speaking. Then the tape is turned off and then clicked back on.]*

Well, I left off at the front door of my cabin, whar I settin', recollectin' my li'l scene with David. I pattin' myself on the back, thinkin' I outwit everybody—Ma, Marster, the whole lot. Mammy Rae, she even come behind me with support. I knows she gonna helps me the next time too. We in this together. Even ol' Mister Crow don't bother me now.

Then, I sees Kate walkin' up the path toward the cabin. She swishin' her skirt an' singin' a tune when she spy me on the stone.

"Hears yo' ain't feelin' well, Sarah Louise." An' she give me that twinkle in her eye. Hears yo' gots the female ailment. That true?" Kate smile.

"That true, all right," I reply, gittin' up, but I now grinnin' too. Can't help myself. Can't lie that easy to Kate.

"So yo' go an' meets that beau, Sarah Louise? Yo' sneak away somehow. I just knows it." Kate look at me—she know that I know that she know.

"Right…" she say, an' we begin down the path toward the well. We be needin' some water for supper before too long. I grabs a big ol' tin bucket settin' by the side of the cabin.

"Kate," I say. "I meets him. I slips away with Mammy Rae help. She gits me a gingham dress, all starched an' fits real good. Don't knows how she do it, but she do."

I lightly smackin' the bucket against my side as I walk. Late afternoon chill in the air. Folks be comin' our way soon.

"Gonna tells me? Yo' in love? Yo' gettin' married. Yo' too youn'! What happen'? Yo' tells me!" An' Kate nudge my arm.

"There ain't nothin' to tells. Mammy Rae help me get away—she the only one that know—an' yo. I meets David down at the dock. Gits there right on time. I lookin' for him, an' he sneak up behinds me—surprise me, just lak that." I gets behind Kate, an' tap her shoulder.

"Anyone sees? Yo' two just meets, an' ain't he got no one lookin' out for what he doin'? Boss man? He just goin' 'bout his own business? What 'bout his masser? Whar' he at? What he say?"

We at the deep well by the cabins. It a stone well, the kinds yo' don't sees no mo'. An' there be a crank, with rope gits pulled up with a handle an' hook. I hooks on my tin bucket an' cranks down the handle—way down it have to go. Kate settin' on the stone well wall.

"He don't has a masser," I says. "He a free colored man from New York an' Baltimore. Work as a stevedore on the rivers, an' he even been across the ocean. Been all around the world, Kate."

"How ol' he be?"

"I thinks he 'bout twenty." The bucket up now, ready to be unhooked. I bends toward the well. "Kate, yo' gonna helps me or not?"

Kate bend over an' help hold the weight while I unhooks the bucket. It splashes an' we lose some—always happen, gits some, lose some.

This whole conversation takin' just a few minutes. Then we back on the path.

"No masser? How he be free? He fair?"

"A li'l darker than high yella', an' he gots him green eyes, Kate. He yo' age, but he know a whole lot 'bout the world. An' this war comin'. Lincoln gonna gets hisself elected, an' the South gonna pull away."

"That just talk." Kate take the bucket from my hand, carry it for awhile.

"Talk is how things happen. Folks gotta talk."

At the cabin, Ma be outside, pullin' clean, dry clothes off the bushes behind the cabin. Hannah be with her, settin' on the stone stoop, gabbin' baby-talk to her pins. When we come, she quiet down. Ma look at us. Kate go to the side, put down the bucket. I look at Ma, but I ain't ready to speak to her 'bout David. She think I still a child—too young for such things.

"Awfully quiet, yo' two," Ma say. It dark earlier, an' 'cause the time of year, we don't has lot of evenin' chores. Ma axe me to go to the creek. Kate suppose to fold laundry.

"We gots a bucket of drinkin' water already, Ma." An' I point to it beside the cabin.

"I gots eyes, child," she say. "Go gets some creek water. Well fixin' to go dry again. "

So I picks up another bucket an' sets off to the creek. I still has the two pieces of David letter in my pocket, an' I touch them, just to be sure.

On the way down, the hoot owl hootin' his question. An' I say aloud, "David, that who!" Maybe Ma be right, I just a child.

I fills my bucket up, kneelin' on the river grass, mostly turn brown. It damp an' soggy. I still wet from the first bucket. I guessin' that why Ma send me.

So when the bucket filled, I stand up an' goes off back home, with this bucket sloppin' against me too in the chill air'. I feels awake, real awake—senses tuned, alert. The light almost gone now, but a searchin' wind come up sudden, shakin' the brittle leaves. Can't see nothin', but I know the path so good, I can follow it blind.

Yo' can guess what happen now—who I sees along that path. Them faceless angels—they dancin' in front of me. In them white dresses an' in the darkenin' sky, they be makin' their own light. Ain't moonlight exactly. The light come from within them. The angels is lit up inside, as they be doin' some strange dance.

"War," one of them say. But she sing it lak a song.

"All around the world," another say. An' *war* sound lak *world*.

"I can't hears yo'" I call out to them. I put my bucket down. "I can't hears yo' real good."

There lot of motion swirlin' with them. Maybe there four of them, an' they movin' slow, floatin', dancin' in a circle, almost lak they feet lifted up from the ground. An' they wearin' white gauze gowns, dresses flowin'.

I see'd them, clear. Sure of that. For two minute, maybe less. I standin' there, bucket beside me on the path. Them angels has a gentle feelin', even when they whisperin' 'bout war. I ain't afeared. No. Not lak with Mister Crow. Fact is, them angels bring a calmness. Hard to explain. It sort of lak summer. Stillness on a summer night. Yas, that mo' what it lak—suddenly, it high summer.

"Say what yo' tell me before," I call to them. "I ain't heared yo' real good." Don't know why I so bold, but I is. Guess I see'd them angels ain't be comin' for no evil purpose.

"World in a whirl," one of them say. Then, "War, war, war," another one sing out. "All around the world."

I lookin' at the angels, straight at them—an' then as swift as they come, they sort of get soft an' disappear, fade—gettin' fainter an' fainter, till their own lights inside gits so dim that they completely gone. Then the chill come back, an' the wind pick up. An' I all alone again.

Now I don't knows why, but when I picks up my bucket, the water feel lighter, though the pail still filled. An' as I heads for home, I feel lighter, even gay. I thinkin' that Lincoln gonna gets hisself elected, an' David right—there gonna be war. But instead of frettin', I be feelin' good. Fact is, I be happy, lak everythin' in this crazy world *just is*, whether I likes it or not. So I better accepts it, I tells myself. I remembers back to the cart when we comin' home from the hangin'. I hears the mournful sound of the wheels turnin', an' thinks back to how one of them wheels always out of true, but that cart still movin' forward.

An' when I thinks about it, I can sees that this a moment when things start turnin' for me—lak them cart wheels. Nothin' completely right, but I be movin' forward. Growin' up. So much sufferin' come from not acceptin' things.

I thinkin' 'bout this, ponderin', as I makes my way home, bucket bumpin' against my right leg, splashin', as I ploddin' up the path, till the whole skirt of my dress wet. But I don't mind; I feels protected an' wide open, lak I can takes on anythin'.

Home, it be a different story. Ma angry 'bout somethin'—she an' Mar snippin' at each other heels lak barkin' dogs. Mar axe Kate if she agree with her, an' Kate say she do. So it two against Ma when I arrives.

Mar must'ta come home when I out at the creek. An' I look at her an' sees her dress torn by the hem. Claim she catch it in the door at the big house. But it too dirty for that.

"I knows whar' yo' been." Ma have her big, broad back towards us gals as she tend the fireplace.

"I ain't been nowhar', Ma. I swear. I git ripped in the door jam. Miss Ida tell yo' that." She almost yellin' now, standin' near Ma by the fire.

"Yo gits some pone off the table now. It hot. Yo' do whats yo' told."

"Yo' can't just believe me, Ma. Yo' can't. Lak it against yo' religion. No one but Kate believe me. She know I tell the truth. Yo' believes what I say, Sarah Louise?"

An' she turn to me. I left the bucket outside for later. An' I pulls up a chair close to fire, 'cause I damp an' cold. Gets myself settled.

"Don't know what gonna on," I say. "What happen, Mar? How yo' dress get tore?"

"That what I tryin' to explain. But I needs some understandin', sympathy, not this here…what I gits. I feels bad 'bout this dress, an' Ma actin' lak I done tore it on purpose, out of spite, an' now I lyin' to cover up the truth." Ma with her back toward us, blowin' into the fire to spark it up before she lay on new wood an' put in the closed pot.

"It 'bout ready now. Whar' that pot?"

Mar has the cast-iron dish with some kind of ham hock in it. She hand it to Ma, who reach behind her—not lookin'—an' snatch it.

Outside there a half-cellar whar' we store meat an' root crops. Ma get up to go fetch somethin' from there herself—onion, I thinkin'. When she out'ta the cabin, I axe Mar what happen.

"Yo' don't wants to knows, Sarah Louise. Yo' just tell Ma that yo' believes me."

Hannah by the fire, still caught up with her dolls. She got a whole plantation full of them that she fetch out'ta the clothes basket. Some with painted faces, an' some plain.

She talkin' to herself, hummin' a li'l tune.

So when Ma go out, Mar an' Kate sneaks over to whar' I set. We makes a plan to talk later when Ma go to bed. I see that Mar gots lot she want to say. An' quick, she take a folded piece of newspaper out'ta her apron pocket, shake it, an' nod her head an' stick it back real quick into her apron. "Later," she whisper.

Ma back inside now. She gots a peeled onion with her. She chop it up quick an' drop it into the pot. When she lift the lid, the ham smell real good. She stir once, an' close it up. My stomach growl. I real hungry. *[Some throat clearing is heard.]*

Now, it must'ta be late October, almost November then—hog-killin' time—Most years we kill the hogs around Christmas, but some years, cold early, we don't wait that long. Sometime we trade out, an' get meat early from other farms. So I don't remember that year real good.

I ain't talks before about hows we kills our hogs. Thank the Lawd that be men folks work. But when killin' time come, I sometime watch them. So I pick up some.

Guess I needin' a break. Throat gittin' sore. Next time I gonna tells yo' 'bout hog killin' an' the newspaper Kate hand me—what we learned that night after Ma git to sleep.

September 2, 1937

I back. Drinkin' a cup of this black coffee my neighbor give me. Wants some? *[The interviewers says, "No." The tape is clicked off, then on, and the interview continues.]*

The men slaves kills the hogs we keeps. Every year there be shoats fattened up for slaughter, an' long ago, I hear they would catch up wild boars. They good meat 'cause they gets plenty to et, roamin' the forests an' woodlands around these parts. But they dangerous.

Now in late October, or November, even December, if it a warm year—soon as it get cold enough, they start the hog slaughter. They big, these hogs. To kill them, yo' gotta stick them so they bleeds an' yo' can catch up the blood. We always used the shed far behind the upper pasture. If you kill them too close to the pen, them other pigs smell death an' panic.

But the day before they do this, they dig a pit, an' they has a big vat inside it. The vat made from wood planks an' some iron in the bottom, sunk into the earth, filled with hot water—fire lit underneath, so the killed hog gits puts in, scalded. Then when it scalded good, there be a platform for the hog to be put on, an' slaves use iron scrapers to take off the hair an' bristles.

After that, the hog be hung on a pole, high up, an' a gambrel stick put through the hamstrings. It viscera get slopped out with a dull knife, put into a bucket, rendered the next day. While the carcass still steamin', the body cavity git washed real good. An' the animal be left lak this overnight to cool down in the air. Small intestines from one or two hogs—an' the large intestines—wus all saved. Some smaller casings used for raw-meat sausage. Large ones for liver an' blood sausage. Stomachs for headcheese or scrapple. Organs wus turned inside out, put on a board, scraped, cleaned, then put into salt-water. We keep the pig feet too—take a cleaver to the hooves. Make soup.

But time I gits back to my story. We ain't butcherin' no hog today. [*There is a pause in the tape, but Ms. Augustus quickly resumes.*]

That night late, the night Mar show me the newspaper, after Ma go to sleep—an' she always sleep real sound, nothin' trouble her— Hannah sleep sound too. Mar, Kate, and me, we lifts our heads from the sacks an' nods to meets outside.

It cold out, so we gits down to business. Mar pull out her newspaper, an' we struggle to reads it by moonlight.

"How yo' come by this, gal?" Kate want to know. Me too. "An' that a lie yo' done told Ma? I knows it is."

"I see James Henry, that whar' I be. Ya'll knows that. An' ya'll knows I can't tells Ma. Mar sound irritated. Lak we rubbin' her face in somethin'.

"Whar' yo' go?" Whar' yo' meets him? I wanna know. Now, this here the very same day that I lit out to see David, then lie about it. So I ain't gonna act lak I better than her. No, I has my own worries.

"We meet at the fence down yonder. At the lower field. I catched the dress across that wire fence. It snag me, an' I fall in the dirt. But we gots a plan now. That what I wants to tell."

She unfold a sheet of newspaper an' smooth it against a side of the cabin, pick it up, move it around, lookin' for moonlight enough to make out what it say—'cause the type be awful tiny. But finally, we able to reads it. Two short pieces 'bout "disunion"—on the same page. Talk of *ardent believers in the South who would joyfully hail the day of separation, though it were black with impending disaster.*

The words wus boastful—white folk words. No colored gonna talk lak that. I has to axe Mar what "ardent" mean. An' I ain't rememberin' it all. But yo' gets the idea. It all 'bout how the South gonna pull away from the Union.

"Who give yo' this here, Mar?" Kate have the paper in her hand, tryin' to read mo', shiftin' around for better light as the cloud cover come on.

"Quiet! Can' yo' sees I tryin' to read?" I standin' over Kate, but I snatch the paper an' walks a ways a bit. I reads somethin' 'bout North Car'lina not wantin' to leave the Union—but it might if it have to.

"Sarah Louise. Kate." Mar come an' snatch the paper. I tryin' to tells ya'll somethin' important. A secret." We look up at Mar. "Yo' has to promise me that yo' ain't never gonna tells," she say.

"Tell it quick—cold out here." A shiver run up my back.

"Gives me yo' hands. Puts them right here. An' we puts out hands together. "Yo' swears on yo' lives an' on the lives of Ma, Pa, an' Hannah that yo' ain't gonna never tells?"

I sees it ain't no use arguin' 'bout how we swears or who we swears on. It late an' cold, an' I gots my own problems. Kate must'ta be thinkin' the same things. She nod. I nod. We both say we swear.

"Well, James Henry an' me, we got us a plan." Mar look at us real good. "Can't say a word, neither of yo'. Yo' has to swear."

"We hears yo'. We swears. Ain't gonna say nothin'," Kate say, an' I nods.

"After the election, an' Lincoln git in—which I knows he will—James Henry an' me, we gonna run away." She say this in one breath—lak she done run up from the lower pasture this minute.

"Whar' yo' gits this paper?" I axe.

"Did yo' hears me, Sarah Louise? I sayin' James Henry an' me gonna elope an' runs away?"

"I hears yo'! I hears yo'!" I say.

"When yo' gonna run?" Kate axe.

"She ain't never gonna do it," I say.

"Ya'll don't believes me, do yo'?" Mar gots her hands on her hips. She take a step back. Her whisper be a shoutin' whisper—coarse, angry.

"Shhh! Yo' wants to wake up the world, Mar? That satisfy yo'?" I axe.

Mar turn on me. "Well, I happens to knows what yo' be doin', yo' li'l ol' self, Sarah Louise. I do. An' yo' ain't got no right to…."

"What I be doin'? What yo' hear?" I up in Mar face now.

"Look, yo' two," Kate chime in. "This ain't no time to fight. Sisters gotta stick together."

She right, a'course. Kate be sensible for a change. We needs to stick together. We is family, an' there ain't much use fightin'.

"Tells me what yo' knows," I say. But I tone down now.

"Sarah Louise, word gits out that yo' ain't sick today. No. Yo' lit out with Mammy Rae help. Lit out to see yo' beau. So yo' ain't gots no right to tell me 'bout mine." Mar git this satisfied expression on her dark face. An' she nod her head a couple times to make her point, an' that no one now can say nothin' against it.

"How yo' knows this? Who tell yo' this? Kate, yo' know too?" But our voices gettin' raised now. We ain't so much whisperin'. We all look at each other an' naturally quiet down.

"First I hear 'bout it is now." Kate look at me lak it time for me to come clean—have this whole thing verified. Kate usually the sassy, troublesome one. Now she be actin' mo' growed up, lak she the adult with two unruly children to tend.

"We has to swears to stick together," I say. Mar an' Kate nod an' agree. I lowers my voice. "I done as Mar say. I lit out to the river an' meets my beau. Mammy Rae, she help. But I be back on time—weren't missed. How's yo' hears, Mar?"

I seen yo' on the path. I seen yo' in a red gingham dress, all ironed an' smart. An' yo' walkin' on the river path lak yo' own the world. I puts it together. Ma say yo' sick with gal problems. But it ain't yo' time of month. No one tell me nothin', an' I ain't say nothin' to nobody 'bout what I seen." *[Some throat clearing is heard; then there's a long pause.]*

We stands there for a long time in the cold. Seem lak James Henry is the one got a'hold of that torn-out newspaper, but he can't read none. So Mar do, an' then together, they come up with a plan to run, elope when Lincoln become president, an' North Car'lina pull away from the Union. That way, in all the mess an' confusion, it would take mo' time for anyone to know they was missin'. An' even if they do, most folks gonna has enough to do, lookin' out for theirselfs. Just lak the angels predicts, I thinkin'. But I ain't tellin' no one about no angels. I keeps that to myself.

Kate an' I listen. It were a silly plan Mar an' James Henry hatch up. They fools to think it. But we alls wus young, all too stupid to knows better. So when we hears the plan, it make sense to us. We so full of ourselfs that the plan sound good. Oh Lawd, when I thinks about it now.

We all decides that night that I gonna belong with David—whenever he comin' back—an' Mar gonna go with James Henry. An' they gonna run when the time come. Soon as war break out.

"What 'bout me?" Kate axe. "Yo' an' Mar gots yo'selfs beaus. What 'bout me?" Kate stand there lookin' pitiful.

But no one answer her. We ain't got no beau for her.

Then a wind pick up, an' it die right down in a swirl of fallen leaves that reminds me of my angels. Seem lak a lot time passin' quick. *[There is a pause in the tape. Then Ms. Augustus's voice is heard.]*

Thinks that enough for the day. Rest awhile. All right with yo'? *[The interviewer agrees to end for the day, and the machine is turned off.]*

September 3, 1937

Oh…. We on? *[Some clicking is heard. The interviewer confirms that the tape is on.]*

Well, I just gonna finish that night, what happen next. Us gals out by the side of the cabin for a hour. We done make plans that Mar gonna elope, head up north with James Henry McNeil, an' I gonna gets with David—though how an' whar' exactly, I ain't sure. Only thing I sure of is I goin' that Thursday to meet David when the Hurt suppose to be at the dock.

So Mar gots a beau, an' I gots beau. An' Kate be upset that she ain't. She the sister in the middle—stack up between me an' Mar, an' now she stuck in the middle of our arrangements. She feelin' low, 'cause she older than me. But the Lawd work in His own way. He gots His own plan.

Next day, we set about our chores. It were a regular weekday, an' rainy. Cold. Gettin' real cold. We been havin' frost a couple time before that night, an' it become the time of year whar' we wakin' up, an' it still dark out.

Now, I shoulds tell yo' 'bout the corn. It all harvested by end of October. But there always some stalks left standin' in the field. Slaves go out an' finds them stunty ears. Usually, the corn whats left stay dry enough to keep through most of winter, till it git too rainy—an' the damp rot it. But there a dish we makes from the rotten ones too.

Sometime we soak them ears, boil them up, or we put them in the ashes to cook. Or we shuck them an' makes the flour that we ground by hand, makes meal, what we use for mush, bread, an' pone.

So early mornin', Ma axe us to go finds them in the field an' gather what we can before chores. She wakes us up early, so we still in the moonlight before dawn.

It dark an' cold. We grabs all the layers we can, an' we complainin' to Ma how it too early—but mostly we like this work. It give us time to gab with each other. So we go off, even with our complainin'.

Ma up early first. She the one to tend the fire from the night before. It don't never last. Ma would bank it, so the embers stir easy, an' then she'd poke it till it flare up an' catch. I watched as she looked out the door to see if there enough moon for us to go out this mornin'. There wus. She gently shake us awake but let Hannah sleep. So we real quiet, gettin' up in the chill. Shiverin' a bit—as the cabin begin to git warm from the fire.

The mornin' moon wus almost full. Ma make sure we have shawls, then she shoo us out'ta the shack. The night shadows wus castin' on the path whar' we walks. So quiet out there. Too late for bugs to be makin' their racket. But there a owl hootin' in the distance. We ain't talkin' yet, too sleepy. Mar, Kate, me walkin' the path, an' the dirt squeakin' beneath our feet.

When we at the middle field, whar' the last corn be, the stalks brittle—sharp, could cut—an' sound lak dried ol' paper when we fold back the husk to get at the ear. We gather them up in our skirts, each gal with 'bout a half dozen. Not much left, an' they hard to find. A few is the real puny, dry ones, but Ma plan on grindin' these.

We work with a small huskin' hook. Knows 'bout them? Ever harvest corn? *[The interviewer says "no."]*

Well, I tells yo' 'bout it. It be a metal band that yo' keeps in yo' hand lak this. [*Ms. Augustus must have done some physical demonstration because the interviewer says, "Ah, yes."*]

The band small an' sharp. There were a leather strap to fasten, keep it in place. Sometime we use just a peg—sharp on one side, an' yo' slice the ear. Then twists it lak this to breaks off the ear. [*There is probably another small demonstration.*]

If yo' hasn't never done corn harvest, I should tells yo' 'bout it. Hows we work in the field at harvest time. But I be short here—this ain't part of my story, just what I live through.

We has two field planted with corn. Each field come to harvest a li'l different time because it growed different, an' we plant it over weeks. That way we ain't got too much to harvest at once.

So when we come to get it, we walkin' sometime with the mule cart goin' slow out in front. Them corn ears need to be left to dry on the stalk for long as possible, but before they gits damage by rain. They has sturdier corn these days, but back then, the ears wus real particular 'bout the weather. We pull all the full ears, but leaves them few puny ones or thems that ain't quite ready. We gits 'bout two cart-load a day. An' we leaves the stalks for shuckin'—which happen later. We gots corn cribs to store the corn ear. Wooden board slats with open air so the corn ear don't rot. We shuck some for meal, which go to the mill, an' some we leaves for later—cookin' an' what not.

So much hard work we done by hand on the farm. An' it all done by slaves. [*Ms. Augustus sighs, then continues.*]

When the weather good, corn harvest be a fine day, exceptin' when yo' hand get hurt from the strap cuttin' yo'. Some white folk has a special glove, but we colored just use the strap. Sometime the peg hurt mo' than the hook. It smaller, an' the strap that hold it cut mo'.

Well, that day, it weren't till we ploddin' back home, ears held in our apron skirts, that we awake enough to talk. Before, we wus just workin'. Early mornin' silence sort of holy, an' it feel lak a sin to talk. Only sound be the dry stalks rattlin' as we walk through the rows, then the sound of us cuttin' ears. An' the hoot owl every once in a while.

Then, I remembers, I just starts singin'. Come natural. We sing in meetin's an' in the field. So I takes up this one, near 'bout dawn. [*Ms. Augustus's voice is thin and high, but there is a sweetness in it as well.*]

Oh, do Lawd, do Lawd, Lawd, 'member me,
Do Lawd, oh do Lawd, do 'member me,
Hallelujah!
Do Lawd, do Lawd, do 'member me,
Oh do Lawd, oh Lawd, Lawd, 'member me.
When I in trouble,
Down on my knees,
When I in trouble,
Lawd, 'member me,
I gonna take a li'l journey,
So Lawd, 'member me.

Then, Mar an' Kate joins in. This a song we sing in church mostly. But that mornin', we walk back an' sing together on the road. At the edge of the field, we stop.

"When yo' sees James Henry again?" Kate axe.

"Don't know. We ain't made plans. Guess before too long." Mar turn to me. "When yo' sees yo' beau?"

"I set to sees him when the Hurt come in next."

"How yo' gonna gets away this time?" Kate axe.

"Can't think that far."

We gots the corn ears folded up in our skirts an' aprons. Still icy out, too chill to stand around for long. Then Mar chime in.

"We gots to stick together, right? No matter what. We needs to keep our family business to ourselfs. Too much talkin' around this place, an' it gonna brings us down. If not today, then tomorrow." Mar lookin' from me to Kate an' back.

It brightenin' up—sky turnin' red as she speak. Mornin' light hittin' our faces. I can sees them now lak I still in the field, an' it a new day—that day in late October, 1860. This burn into my mind. If Mar an' Kate still alive, I knows they remember it too.

Then Kate say, "I agrees. We can't trust no one."

"What 'bout Ma or Pa?" I axe.

"No one, not Ma, Pa, or even Hannah—she too li'l," Mar say.

"But what 'bout Mammy Rae? She know most it already.

"How much she know, Sarah Louise? What she know? She don't know nothin' 'bout James Henry an' me? Mar be shiftin' around, nervous. It full light now.

"Ain't sure, Mar, but she know 'bout me an' David. She gots some conjure, so I can't say what she know. What she finds out."

"What we gonna do? Sun comin' up. Ma expectin' us," Mar nudgin' me with her shoulder. "I gittin' hungry!"

"Let's swear a oath," I say.

"Oath?" Mar axe.

Then Kate take charge. "Yeah. Oath. Of allegiance." An' we turn to her. Each sister know that this gonna bind us. "Repeats after me," Kate begin. "We Smith sisters do solemnly swear…on…"

"What should we swear on?" Mar chime in.

"We swears on the holy Bible, lak they do in courts," I say.

"That ain't good enough," Kate say. "How about this? We Smith sisters do solemnly swears on the holy Bible, on the lives of their Ma, Pa, an' baby sister Hannah…"

"An' on our own lifes… Pa too." Mar add. "An' we needs to puts our hands together."

"I gots it now," Kate say.

"Puts yo' hands out," I tells them. "In the middle here." So we shifts our corn an' each sticks out a hand so that one is on top of another.

"Repeats after me," Kate begin again. "We Smith sisters do solemnly swears…"

An' as she make our oath, we repeat each phrase: "We Smith sisters do solemnly swears…on the holy Bible, on the lifes of our Ma, Pa, an' baby sister Hannah… an' on our own lifes…that from this day forward… to eternity… we Smith sisters will abide by our own secrets…to keeps them secret…till death do them part. Amen."

Then we takes our hands away.

"Sounds mo' lak we gettin' married," Mar say.

But we done it. We all takes the oath. An' then we walkin' home again, the new sun cast a thin line of shadows across the dirt path, an' there be some loud cawin'. I knows what that is. Crows. An' that ain't no coincidence. I thinkin' that this be a bad omen. Mister Crow showin' off his handiwork. I look up, an' the sky be black with them.

I don't say nothin'. No point. Mar' an' Kate think they just birds travelin' south for winter. Don't expect they believes me anyway if I begin talkin' 'bout the debil being some big crow. So I alone with these thoughts, an' ol' Mister Crow showin' off 'cause he got some special purpose in mind. *[Ms. Augustus lets out a long sigh, then continues.]*

When we gets home, Ma already wonderin' whar' we been so long, but she don't scold 'cause there work needs doin'. We sits down in the cabin an' et some breakfast quick—just mush an' left over bread from the big kitchen. It taste good. Ma a good cook—she can take any ol' scrap an' make it fine. I see Kate gobblin' up her mush an' bread lak she starvin'. She a gal who hate to do without.

Don't remember much mo' that day. Guess it go lak most do. That time a'year, the weather unpredictable an' chores slack off—at least for the gals. Hogs is mainly men folk work.

Well, them angels an' Mister Crow must has other folks to see, 'cause they leaves me alone for awhile. But all the time I thinkin' 'bout how I gonna gets away on that Thursday to see David. Can't tells folks I sick with women ailment again—that excuse used up. An' I thinkin' 'bout my sisters an' our oath.

What I recalls most about the end of that October, early November, is the rain. It rain hard. Most of the harvest in—the corn—so we all grateful about that. But the banks of the creek overflow an' take some bottom land whar' we has the county fair one year. Marster in charge of it one time, before the war, but I can't remember what year. He appointed the… chief… marshal—or whatever they calls it. Chief Marshal of the agricultural fair. It a important job. Marster a man everyone trust. When he wus chief, I just a gal, an' we never go to the fair, just heared 'bout it.

But I be movin' back an' forth. Gots too much to tells. *[Ms. Augustus sighs again and then is quiet for a few moments. The interviewer asks if she would like to break for the day, and Ms. Augustus says "yes." The tape is clicked off.]*

September 6, 1937

It been so hot. Hows yo' stay cool? I stays here by the door that catch a li'l breeze come this way. *[The interviewer explains that she has a small electric fan, and she offers to get one for Ms. Augustus. Ms. Augustus refuses because she says that they make people sick and that they are unnatural. Then Ms. Augustus says that she is ready to begin.]*

Back before the war, we sometime have to fan the white folk. Especially if they sick. One of the house gals would takes a large lady fan an' sweep it for hours so that the patient don't git too hot. Fever in the summer wus dangerous.

But whar I pick up now, it late fall, almost winter time. We has the agricultural fair in November, after the election for president. Lincoln git elected. But it just don't change nothin' lak we thought it would. So Mar and Henry James decide to wait. There ain't no commotion for thems to make their run. Everythin' die down lak a calm before the storm.

Let me go back to Friday, when we last talk. I tellin' yo' the oath, the pact we make—Kate, Mar, an' me. Then time go by, an' we close up to that Thursday whens I suppose to go to see David at the Hurt.

That week wus rain. Bad rain, cold rain bringin' in winter. Hard to imagine in this heat. Here we are settin' with the widows open, the room lak a oven that stay lit a hundred year. Hard to think about the cold.

Chil'ren nowadays spoiled. They got indoor heat, light, plumbin'— everythin'. Most got coats before Depression. Some I know done has sold them off or couldn't replace them when they gets worn an' tattered. Just saw a li'l gal the other day, she barefoot, makin' her way across Raleigh. Baby in her arms. She a baby herself, but she already gots herself a baby. I invite her in for some water. She so tired out an' worn, couldn't let her just pass. I axe her how come she ain't got not shoes, an' she tell me she sold them last week so she could gets somethin' to et. The father, he left her to find work—she don't knows whar' he go. She all alone. Family in South Car'lina. No kin here. Husband come up to works tobacca, but there ain't no work, so he left. It a mess now, I tells yo'. Don't knows no one ain't sufferin'. *[There is a brief pause in the tape.]*

Now…I decides not to tell Mammy Rae 'bout this next meetin' with David. Plan is I gonna tries to run to him somehow on my own. But it so rainy an' cold all that time. An' a darkness come over the place—everythin' git drab an' gray, lak ol' wool. I has lot'a trouble concoctin' a plan, but I come up with one at last. I wus a crafty gal back then, an' I caught up in the workin' of my heart. I makes my plan, but all the time I thinkin' I gonna keep it secret—even from Mar an' Kate. Even with the oath. No need to trouble them till I needs to.

It November now, an' at the Smith place, we be preparing for Missus Christmas ball. They has fabric for new dresses—Mammy Rae dye some, an' some they sends for from far away. They kill another two hogs that month. So while it pourin' rain, most of us gals inside helpin' at the shacks or in the big house—sewin', takin' stock, cleanin'.

All this goin' on that first full week in November. White folk 'bout to vote—goin' for Breck'ridge. There mo' political parties than I can recalls. Democrats, Whigs, Republicans. An' them parties, they be separate for North an' South. Us slaves, we knows what we hears an' what we can reads in the newspaper scraps we gets a'hold of.

I fifteen still. Ain't turn sixteen till that April, at the start of war. I still learnin' my sewin'—which I weren't never no good at. Still can't sew good, though I trained an' knows how. But I learn some fancy stitch—an' that I do real good. They would tell me, "Sarah Louise, draws me some flowers with them fancy embroidery threads." An' I could do it. I would sees them flowers in my mind—an' I draws out a pattern.

So all this rainy, cold week I embroider green ivy vines around the collar of Miss Ida dress, settin' by the window near the kitchen alcove on a ol' wood chair. An' stitchin'. Fire goin'—Missus keep the fire goin' all day long. Most of the house slaves wus workin' inside. The summer kitchen all but closed up. We got some laundry lines strung up inside too. Mar pull sheets in, an' I takes time out from stitchin' to iron. 'Course Kate there. She learnin' to cook good.

Aunt Patsy be there, an' some other gals I ain't remember now. But… there be one gal who name Baretta. She always wear a bonnet. She from a family… can't recalls which. Baretta thin lak a stick. She older than me, but not by much. Her folk live in them cabins across the small field, off a ways. Funny hows I can't remember. We only got 'bout twenty slaves, but I can't remember them all. They just now lak some characters in a movin' picture show. *[There is a long pause. Then, Sarah Louise lets out a long sigh and resumes.]*

Well, one day—a few days before I suppose to meets with David—we all goin' 'bout our chores—ordinary day—an' a carriage come up. Afternoon. The rain beatin' this earth lak Jesus hisself take issue with the way the world goin'. God take a bucket an' scoop up the rivers an' dump them back down. So it strange to see travelers in this bad weather. They ridin' in a fancy black carriage, an' the driver, he just 'bout froze—soaked to his bones. First, they comes up to the front to unloads the white folks; then they sends the driver around the back.

Everybody up all at once. Aunt Patsy leave her cookin' pots at the back door, an' there be a young slave we ain't never see'd before. We invites him in, but he worried 'bout his two geldings shiverin' outside. Aunt Patsy call for Tibs, the stable hand. Her voice strong an' carry through the poundin' rain.

Tibs come from the carriage barn enough to sees. He run to grabs the reins an' trots them horses, already unhitched, to the barn. He carry a flat plank over his head to protect hisself from the downpour, an' he sloshin' through the mud with them horses to the barn.

"We take care of yo'," Aunt Patsy say. An' she pull him by the sleeve into the kitchen. He drippin' an' shiverin'.

"I'll gits some hot tea," someone say. "An' some dry clothin'." None of us gals wus workin'. We too excited by the visitors.

Before yo' knows it, the stranger out of his pants, jacket, an' he standin' there in some rough sack short-pant an' hemp shirt—an' he have a knit item in his hand that he stuff into his pant pocket. He have smart eyes, an' he be a handsome young man, standin' there. Not fancy but clean. He cuppin' his tea an' go to sit on the bench by the kitchen fire. Silent a bit before his tongue git loosed. Aunt Patsy must'ta put a dram in that tea.

"We come a ways. From Virg'nia. Weather bad, an' we couldn't takes the main road, so we takes a narrow, high one. It turn an' turn. Then it gets low an' flooded, so Mister Hunter have us cut across a field. We gets lost. Somehow end up here."

The stranger say his name is Marcus, an' he from a large plantation up Virg'nia. They on they way to Charleston, South Car'lina. He say his marster is a political man, an' he have important business. He gonna be down there for the national election—might even stay a while.

By this time, Marcus etin' bread an' sweet taters. An' Miss 'Lizabeth already done told us: "Get a meal ready; we have company stayin' the night."

There be the one gentleman, lak Marcus say, an' another, younger man that he ain't mention by name—the older man son, we think—almost grown. Marcus, he turn out to be a interestin' fellow that got a lot to tell.

We all move pretty quick, 'course, when Miss Ida say we havin' company. We has goods stored, but I knows Marster wants some fancy stuff to treat his guests right. That man, his name wus Mister Hunter, an', lak Marcus say, he some important man in the state of Virg'nia. He go by initials, lak Marster—J.B. Hmm… don't remember them. But everyone could tells by the fancy carriage that he rich an' important.

Marcus done drinks an' ets his fill, an' Kate comin' an' goin' all the whiles I takes up my stitchin' again, till Aunt Patsy, who in charge, say, "Sarah Louise, gal, ain't yo' gots no sense? Gets up an' fetch some bed linen an' yo' makes yo'self useful. Stitchin' done later, gal. Yo' oughts to know better!" An' she sweep by me an' give me a li'l shove off the chair.

So, I do as Aunt Patsy say. Puts down my stitchin', smooth out my apron an' dress, an' goes into the hallway past the parlor. It just afternoon, but candles an' the big fireplace all lit. Blazin'. Shadows everywhar' lak it dead'a night. Dreary is what I call it. But I rushes around, an' meets up with Baretta. She gots some blankets an' is makin' up the guest room up near the attic stair.

"Yo' hears what they all talkin' 'bout?" Baretta move close an' whisper. She smell bad, lak something dead.

"I ain't heared nothin'," I say. But I turns away from Baretta.

"Ain't Mister Hunter driver say nothin' 'bout war?" An' Baretta move in close again.

"Gal," I say. "What smell so bad on yo'? Sort'a lak a drown rat."

Baretta say she don't smell nothin'. Must be me. But I tells her, "It sure ain't me! No ma'am. If I be smellin' this bad, Ma ain't let me inside the cabin. No, she ain't."

But Baretta back away. So I switch the subject. "Tells me about the war," I say.

"Nothin'. No war, no nothin'," she say an' return to her makin' up the bed. A candle on the nightstand beside her. I picks it up. Keeps my distance from ol' smelly Baretta. No, I thinkin', she gots a problem.

"Yo' needs me to make up the cot?" I axe. There a small cot we use, can puts in this room. It store in the attic.

"Yo' never mind. I do it by myself." I see Baretta cryin'. Big ol' tears comin' down. But she quiet, not make a peep.

"I didn't means nothin' by it, Baretta," I says. An' smell or no smell, I goes to her. She backin' up though till she up in a corner. I touches her shoulder, but that smell be powerful bad.

"Yo' can tells me, gal. Really."

"I bleedin'…" she say an' sink down to the wood floor. She still cry, but she ain't make no sound. Just shakin' her head back an' forth.

"Yo' monthly, Baretta. That what this about?" *[There is a pause, and the tape is clicked off and on a few times. Some indistinct sounds are heard, and then Ms. Augustus continues.]*

Yo' probably thinkin' it peculiar for me mention women problems. But this my point: it ain't only slavery makin' this gal suffer—though that sure is part. Big part. But she kept down by her people too. They don't know no better. She ignorant. Her people ignorant. This only the second time she get her monthly, but she ain't got nobody to show her what to do. She ain't got no rags, an' ain't got no sense neither.

I tries to help. Baretta come from bad stock. Her kin, what she have, live in some shacks off the dirt road. They field hands, her folk is. None them read nor write, an' they marry each other—brother an' sister, uncle an' niece. This Baretta gal—an' I hates to says this about my own—she trash. Her people just hands, an' no one know why Baretta get picked to work in the house. It above her station.

But here we is, fixing up the room together, fixin' up, so I says to her she need to get some rags. Don't her folks has none? She say she don't know an' can't talks to no one. She has her ol' undergarments been wearin' all week. She stuff ol' newspaper from the big house in them, but they is soggy, stained through. After we makes up the bed an' gets the cot down, makes up that too, we goes to Aunt Patsy. She know what to do. An' make a long story short, Aunt Patsy take care of Baretta problem. I whisper to Aunt Patsy, an' she find plenty of clean rags. She also give Baretta some slippery elm for the pain. An' she show her what to do next month. When Aunt Patsy finish with Baretta, she turn to me an' make a face lak she ain't sure what the world coming to.

After awhile, we gets the company settled—an' there mo' to do, with clothin', supper, an' tending to them, but Marcus all the time stay in the kitchen. When things calm down for us that workin', I sees him still by the kitchen fireplace, just lookin' out, lak he rememberin' somethin'. Everyone else gabbin' about all the commotion them new folks makes. Marcus though, he take out that knit item—it wet, but he don't seem to care. He put it on his head. It a knit cap, lak none I see'd before. Black with green an' red stripes along it, made from embroidery threads, an' fit sort'a tight.

When Marcus take it out of his pocket, he kiss it, before placin' it on his head. Then he say, "I gonna pray."

That just stop the gabbin' cold. We all turns to him, an' he nod, get down on his knees, facin' the alcove an' he bend his head down—head an' arms—an' he recite some mumbo jumbo ain't nobody understand. So we lookin' at each other—still ain't no one talkin'. Almost seem rude to axe questions or be talkin' when this here Negro with his cap on his nappy head be prayin'. We just lookin' around lak we ain't believin' what we seein'.

Then he stand up as if nothin' happen, an' he turn to Aunt Patsy an' say somethin' in some foreign tongue, lak, "Abso.. absoo, what not." An' he bow, take off his knit cap, an' sip his tea.

Aunt Patsy be the first to speak. "Marcus, what the debil, yo' doin', boy?" An' she only wait a moment before he answer.

"I a Muslim, Aunt Patsy." He know her name by now. "It the one true religion, an' it pass to me from my grandpap, who I live with when I a young child, before I get sold."

Baretta, ignorant, still standin' there, shakin' her head. She make tisking noises lak she is 'bout to lower herself to some ol' fool.

"Muslin ain't no religion. It the cloth yo' wearin'. It what yo' shirt made from," she say. "Even I knows that!"

Marcus don't answer right away. He bow his head to her. Say his mumbo jumbo again. We all quiet. Aunt Patsy by the pot, stinky Baretta with her arms crossed, me an' others lookin' on.

Then Marcus speak slowly. "My grandpap come from Africa, Fula from Futa Jallon. He a man of learnin', who be stolen from his tribe, an' sold to whites. He cross the Atlantic lak yo' kin folk—slave ship. He a young man. Sold again, an' he end up in Maryland. That happen many, many year ago." Marcus look at us. Turn from one to the other, startin' with Baretta. "He learn us about Mohammad, an' he ain't never become no white man Christian. He Muslim. He pass down what he know to my pappy an' me. Pappy dead. I the only man-child from his line, an' it my duty to pass down Allah law to my children when the time come." Marcus real solemn. Yo' can see he be different than thems that usually come our way.

"Yo' marster know about this here religion?" Aunt Patsy begin. "He let yo' go on with' it? I ain't never heared 'bout no Muslim."

The back door open, a cold wet wind follow. Tibs come in, all wet, for it still pourin' outside.

"Ain't never seen it rain so," Tibs say. He about twenty, but real slim an' puny. He a strange fella. Mo' to say 'bout him later. How he take up with Sammy. Try to run away. Git sold.

"It have to quit soon. Lawd ain't gonna drown us again." Sofia say. "No, He ain't." She a middle-age gal, usually work in the field.

"Just maybe He will. For all our sins," say Marcus. His knit cap gone off his head.

"What sins yo' talkin' about?" Tibs axe. "I only gots me one sin…" Tibs look around at all us gals. "Well, better not say!" An' he laugh. He nod his head toward Marcus. "We gots ourself some righteous company!"

"Now I ain't talkin' about *our* sins," Marcus say. "I talkin' about white sin."

"Yo' hush yo' mouth now, boy!" Aunt Patsy stop stirrin' the pot, turn to him. "I ain't allow yo' come in here bad mouth our white folk. We has a good marster."

"I ain't bad mouth *yo'* white folks—just white folks general. There gonna be war, an' my master think he gonna be president of this new south. That why we be travelin' to Charleston. He gots this war business to tend to. Yo' ain't got no idea what goin' on." Marcus turn to us, get quiet for a moment. Then he continue. "None of yo' does." Now it seem Marcus the one above, lookin' down.

"I knows 'bout a war comin'," I say. "We ain't all ignorant as yo' thinks."

Aunt Patsy at her pot, holdin' her wood spoon, still ain't stirrin'. "It just all talk. Things heat up, an' they dies back down—I seen it before, an' it happenin' again now. Ain't nothin' ever gonna change."

"Whar' I comes from, war ain't just talk. So I tells y'all. Warns y'all—Allah gonna take his revenge against them that enslave us."

We all in some huddle. Moths to a flame, whisperin'—drawn together. We ain't never heared no one lak Marcus before—gabbin' 'bout the war. Out in the open. It scary, but give us courage. *[There is a long pause in the tape. Then some clicks are heard, and Ms. Augustus clears her throat.]*

That about it for today. I done, done. Talk too long. Needs me a break. It past dinner time. *[There are some scraping sounds heard—perhaps the chairs scraping against the wood floor. Then Ms. Augustus's voice is heard.]* We picks up tomorrow. *[Some indistinct sounds are heard, and the tape is clicked off.]*

September 7, 1937

Well, it Friday. I glad it here! I gonna picks up right whar' I leaves off. We was in the kitchen with that Marcus fella, an' he tell us 'bout the war comin'.

But he also tell us 'bout he bein' Muslim. Since that time, there be other Muslims I come to know. From New York. But Marcus sure surprise me. Now I weren't no fool lak Baretta, thinkin' he gab 'bout no homespun shirt! An' it almost lak he try to convert us. But I is a Christian believer. Then an' now. Ain't never changin'. But I respects what folks believes. We got a right to decides for ourselfs.

When Marcus tell us about his grandpap in Africa, that Fula people he from, he kind'a remind me of Uncle Cicero, who wus descended from a prince. In the kitchen that day, I wus thinkin' how there be a whole lots I don't knows. Abouts whar' I from. What my people lak—don't means Ma an' Pa. I means back through generations. Africa.

I don't cares much these days. Just want to gets by. I ol', gots trouble enough. But when I a gal in slavery time, I wants to knows everythin'. I full of myself, thinkin' the world spin around me.

The folks that come—Mister Hunter an' his son, they only stay with us one night. It still rainin' the next mornin', but they say they gots to leaves on urgent business. So Marcus leave too. He sleep that night in the horse barn close to the big house. He sleep near them geldings he so prize.

Before he go, he tell us that South Car'lina gonna disunion. Other states gonna follow too—the ones far down south. Miss'ippi, Louis'ana, Georgia. North Car'lina, he ain't so sure. But South Car'lina all charged up, an' his Mister Hunter part of some delegation, an' he been down Charleston a few months earlier in the spring. Right now wus almost 'bout the time Mr. Lincoln get elected.

I ain't clear on the politics. Weren't clear then, 'cause it kept from us, an' I don't even thinks our own white folks knowed. But people wus gettin' all riled up—dogs before a hunt. Lak they get in a pack, barkin'—not thinkin' 'bout what happen, but wantin' somethin' to happen 'cause they all worked up. Men mostly. Women folks, seem to me, they just goin' along.

Bad. The whole mood then wus bad. Turn the house inside out. I tells yo' whats I means later. Beginnin' of the end is what it were. For Negroes an' whites. Different but the same. *[Ms. Augustus lets out a big sigh and then resumes.]*

It rain an' rain all night, hard, an' it occur to me that even if it stop the next day, I ain't never gonna get to David. I had a plan to get away, but I now realize that even if the rain stop, there ain't no way I could walk them flooded roads with all that red clay mud. Though Marcus probably get by on the main road if he good enough driver to reach it.

On Wednesday mornin', I awakes with another plan. I thinkin' there ain't no time to waste with the Hurt comin' in on Thursday, the next day. It a long shot, but the plan sort'a make sense. I gonna write me a note an' gives it to Marcus. He gonna gets it to David somehow. Marcus a good man. He pray an' seem trustworthy. He be tellin' us how Mr. Hunter gonna has one mo' delay, that they gots to stop by the dock tomorrow. An' there be Negroes there Marcus can just pass a note to.

So that mornin', real early, before anyone awake, I finds me a candle, a scrap of paper, an' a ol' stub pencil I keeps hidden near the wall. Miss 'Lizabeth give to me when I li'l an' we play. It be pared down to a small nub, but it still write.

The rain wus just a light drizzle, an' I goes to the privy, whar' I can be alone. I shiverin' in a flour sack blanket, but I sits there an' writes out my letter to David, pourin' out what buried so deep in my heart.

I writes that he must somehow gets back in touch with me. An' that he right 'bout the war comin'. I even tells him my sister Mar gonna elope.

I writes this last part thinkin' that if Mar do it, maybe I put a bug in his ear that it somethin' we could do. I usin' my best flowery words. I ain't has much chance to writes, so the punctuation give me trouble. This bein' my very first love note an' all, it take me a long time to write. But when I finished, I feel proud of the effort.

That mornin' right after sun up, I lookin' to check if the carriage still there—it is. When everyone get up, we has ourself a slow mornin' 'cause of the rain. But I soon make up some excuse why I needs to go to the big house. But before I gets there, I finds Marcus near the horse barn, in the breezeway. It early, an' he alone.

I thankin' the Lawd an' sweet Jesus both, 'cause once again, I carryin' out my plan. The angels with me, clearin' the way.

We by the pantry—the breezeway by the pantry—an' Marcus shinin' his boots. So he bendin' down.

"Marcus," I say.

An' he rise, "Yas, Miss Sarah Louise," he say. An' we stand there while the rain begin to come down heavy again.

"I knows yo' leavin' today, goin' south. I knows yo' passin' the dock at the Cape Fear—I wants yo' to takes this letter for me—gives it to a Negro that work there. Tell him to pass it along to David Augustus—everyone know him—he a free black man that come through today on the Hurt steamship, an' I wants him to have this note." It all come gushin' out. Then I takes a breath. I gots my note folded real small, an' it look neat. I hands it to him

"I can't take this," Marcus look at me, still one boot untied.

"Ain't yo' gonna pass the river dock?"

"We gonna pass it, all right. But Mister Hunter say we ain't has time to stop." Mister Hunter, he has important business. There a war comin', gal. Everythin's gonna change." His mouth still open lak he gots mo' to say.

"Yo' takes my note. This here to my beau. He expectin' me to come today—me, myself. An' I trustin' yo' with my…"

"Look here, gal. Don't tax me with yo' troubles. 'Cause that exactly what yo' doin'." Marcus look away toward the road, lak he seein' somethin' through the heavy rains. Then he snatch the note from my hand. "Yo' a pretty gal, so why yo' gonna make me do this foolishness? An' I ain't promisin' this'll get whar' it need to go. What this fella name again? What he go by?"

"David. David Augustus. He a free man from up north, work at the docks an' his boat, The Hurt, come in around half-past noon. He fair skinned an' got green…"

"I ain't gonna see him, so I don't tell me what he look like. I run this errand at my own peril. An' I only doin' it if Marster stop at the dock. So what yo' full name?

"Sarah Louise Smith," I tells him, but all sudden I feels my heart flutterin' as he look at me. He lookin' an' then break out in a wide smile, lak I done tell a joke.

"What yo' laugh at?" I axe.

"Yo'," he say. "Yo'." Marcus get a strange look in his eyes. An' I look back. Somethin' powerful 'bout him. Somethin' different.

Then he shake his head, bow to me, bend to finish up his bootlace—an' he gone. Didn't even say goodbye. He walk back inside the horse barn. I standin' there. The rain get light, almost stop.

But that bow, that strange li'l bow—mockin'. I thinkin' it must be part of his religious duty, so he donc it. But he done it playful. Odd. An' that the last I ever see'd or heared from Marcus.

Later, in the afternoon, before dark, the rain stop an' the evenin' sun come out, right before it set, turnin' the sky orange. Way we all actin', might well has been rainin' for forty days an' nights. We all forgets just how bright the sun can be. It change things. The whole plantation spring to life. Still muddy, cold, an' wet, but that sunshine spread it wings lak a promise.

But that promise, it ain't get fulfilled. No, it don't. This wus the beginnin' of all the bad what happen. After the carriage leave an' the rain stop, at sun down, Marster call some of us Negroes out—not all—just the house servants. He calls us to the veranda near the rear of the big house. When this kind'a thing happen, it usually ain't good news. An' it weren't this time neither.

Missus wus there too. The sun near settin', a bright orange globe hangin' in the deep blue sky, castin' its last glow.

"There work to be done, so I'll keep you here just a moment," say Marster. He got on his dark navy-blue great coat. His hands behind his back. Missus stand by his side, not movin', no expression on her face. She in a gray wool dress, her shawl pull tight. "As many of you are aware, we just had a visit from our Virginia neighbors, who are travelin' a long ways to Charleston." He pause.

There 'bout seven, eight of us standin' there in the cold. No wind blowin', with that big ol' settin' sun in the sky, waitin' on Marster words before it free enough to set. Aunt Patsy there 'course. Mar an' Kate.

"Missus an' I," Marster begin again. "We've decided that it would be best to cancel the Christmas ball this year. There are to be no more preparations—no more dress making, no more planning for this event. All work for the Christmas ball is to cease—as of now. I hope that I make myself clear. I don't want no gossip neither. Nothing concerns you except what I tell you." Marster stern, lak we slaves done cancel his fancy party an' now he upset. He pause again, lookin' around for us to make objections we ain't entitled to.

"And your own celebration this year, your Christmas…—whatever ya'll call it, that is cancelled too. Ya'll can have a small religious gathering, but nothing else. No party, no frolicking, no gathering other than for the express purpose of prayer." Missus drop her eyes. But not Marster. No, he in command of all he see.

"Make certain everyone receives this message. That's all. You're dismissed." Marster look over the small crowd of us. Turn his back, an' he an' Missus go inside.

No one say much at first. When Marster an' Missus go, there some mumblin'. Mostly surprise. An' disappointment.

"Less work for me," Aunt Patsy say, but anyone can see she angry at the whole business. She still have work to do in the big house, so she go there. Mar, Kate, an' me, we takes off for home. It dark outside now. That sun dip down an' finish off the day.

I gonna skip around now. Lak I say, all that rainy weather stop that afternoon, an' we now we gettin' clear, sunshiny days. Cold an' dry. All up through Christmas, which come real somber this year. There be the usual distribution of shoes an' clothes, an' we does get some time off. But it all somber. Days short, an' snow come late, but it come bad that year.

We has two things that happen. One 'bout Mar an' how she gets married without elopin', an' the war. War, war, an' mo' war. An' David—how he vanish in thin air.

It happen plain with Mar. Us slaves, we usually has us a Christmas dance, with fiddle playin' an' good food, around the time the white folks has their ball. But this year, we has nothin' but a camp meetin'.

Take place in the horse barn. At evenin'. We builds us a big bonfire outside the paddocks an' leave both big doors open. Folks fills the barn with plenty of clean straw, an' we lets the horses out to pasture.

Lak I told yo', Christmas ball cancelled. We all thinkin' it gonna be a big splendid affair, but Marster cancel it after Mr. Hunter come. He ain't never tell us why, but everyone get wind of what happenin' in the country. Even us slaves. Even them lowly ones, lak Baretta, that ain't got enough sense to keeps herself clean.

What I means to say—well, I'll just say it. South Car'lina gonna quit the Union. Maybe before Christmas. Maybe after. But times is tense. We all feel it. An' we readin' from newspapers, listenin' to gossip.

There a tightness everywhar' around. Marster an' Missus is watchin' us, watchin' the land as if some stranger gonna snatch it from them. No frivolity now. Everyone just be goin' through the motions of livin'. Sun stay shinin', but the spirit gone dark.

Then trouble. We gonna has us a service for Christmas, lak Marster say we can. An' Henry come. He always invited when he around. He the fiddler player. Best in the county, best in a few counties. I already tell yo' 'bout Henry—how Marster hire him out sometimes for weddin's, balls. Usually at Christmas time, Henry gone. He get so many calls, he never around this time of year. But he here for this Christmas, 1860. Not enough white folk celebratin', I guess.

Henry—as I say—he play real good, it hard to describe. It lak Heaven burstin' down into the world to give us joy. So even though we has this here impendin' doom, we all lookin' forward to Henry playin' at our meetin'. No one say he can't.

Now we always had us a good Christmas party—an' most year it wus fine with Marster. He like us to cut loose. If we has us a good harvest an' been workin' hard, Marster let us has us some fun. Not all masters allowed their Negroes to celebrate. Some be thinkin' we gonna rise up. Fact is, some do. There a story that very year about a John Brown—a white man—an' he got to killing people up in Virg'nia not long before. We all heared about it. He a crazy man, an' he storm the federal arsenal up that way. He thinkin' he gonna get some slaves to rise up too. He sure stir things up. Folks got killed—even a free colored man, I heared. But Brown get hisself caught, an' next thing, get hanged.

Yo' hears 'bout our arsenal—Fayett'ville? It wus taken by Confed'rates at the start of the war. I tell yo' 'bout that later.

It didn't take much to get white men talkin' 'bout their slaves. An' there be free colored in Fayett'ville too—white folk thinks they gonna take the Union side an' rise up—if it come to war. They ain't got no masters, but they ain't really free neither. An' some wus plenty discontent. It that feelin' white folk afeared that gonna sweep across the land.

What I say here is that everyone wus scared. Marster take precautions lak everyone else. No Christmas celebrations for white nor black. The world seem lak it holdin' its breath, stop turnin'. An' there weren't a soul that didn't feels it. *[There is a long sigh and a pause. The tape continues to run though.]*

This our last Christmas as slaves. There be other Christmases during the war, but this were the last one before the change.

Not all slaves come to this Christmas service. Most do, not all. We wus in the horse barn, lak I say. An' we has our meetin' on a Saturday night. It weren't Christmas, but close. We wanted folks to come from neighbor farms, plantations. That way it feel mo' lak the celebration we ain't supposed to have. They'd gets passes an' come out to pray, an' we'd have us a sense that it be Christmas.

The paterollers wus out, 'course. It bein' Saturday night, especially this year—not just on our plantation, but all over Fayett'ville, Cumberland County. White folk nervous. Everyone alert for anything out of the ordinary, might be trouble. An' what they on alert for, they sure gonna finds.

Some slaves that come wus from Harris McNeil farm. Mar beau come. An' the trouble start after he arrive. When the paterollers come drunk an' finds our meetin' in progress, hear our ring-shout.

Mar with James Henry, they standin' on the side. Big blaze goin' outside the barn. We start with a camp meetin', which begin with prayer but just turn a li'l loud. An' that what attract them no-good paterollers. Drunk white paterollers, they probably in Hell right now.

This ring-shout somethin' we do to get the spirit. I seen plenty white folks do it after slavery times. Baptists mostly. We pray an' call out. There some dancin' in a circle, but it religious, an' without fiddlin'. Usually. We just has Uncle…Uncle…. Well, I can't recalls his name. He our preacher, a ol' man from another plantation. Come only a few times.

Well, he do the shout first an' we join him, holler back. It go… I gonna sing what I recalls. [*Some shuffling noises are heard, and Ms. Augustus clears her throat before her high, thin voice comes through.*]

By myself, by myself, by myself, by myself…

I singin' both parts—if we wus doin' the shout, preacher say it first, congregation follow. Has to imagine…

> *Yo' know I've got to run. Yo' got to run.*
> *I got to run. Yo' got to run.*
> *By myself,*
> *By myself.*
> *I got a letter,*
> *I got a letter.*
> *Ol' brownskin. I'll tell yo' what she say,*
> *Tell yo' what she say:*
> *Leavin' tomorrow, tell yo' goodbye,*
> *Leavin' tomorrow, tell yo' goodbye.*
> *Oh my Lawdy, oh my Lawdy,*
> *Oh my Lawdy, oh my Lawdy,*
> *Well, well, well.*
> *Well, well, well.*
> *I got a rock.*
> *Yo' got a rock.*
> *Rock is death,*
> *Rock is death.*
> *Oh my Lawdy, oh my Lawdy,*
> *Oh my Lawdy, oh my Lawdy.*
> *Run here Jeremiah,*
> *Run here Jeremiah.*
> *I must go. On my way, on my way,*
> *On my way, on my way…*

It call "Run, Ol' Jeremiah." An' it that singin' that git us in trouble with them drunk paterollers.

Marster, as I say, give us his permission for a service. So we has it. We goin' back an' forth, lak…. [*Ms. Augustus repeats some of the song she just sang.*]

Run here, Jeremiah. An' we call back louder:
Run here, Jeremiah! So on.

Meanwhile, we in a circle around the preacher. Henry, the fiddler, off to the side, ain't playin' nothin'—but pretty soon, he pick it up, an' he playin' along with this here shout. Most time we just sing out, but with Henry here, an' this bein' Christmas, it natural he join in. We wus in a circle this night, but sometime we do ring-shout in a line. We shufflin' our feet an' gettin' the rhythm. The spirit. Jesus wakin' us all up inside.

I can't do it for yo' now. Yo' needs mo' folks—can't do it alone. An' my bones ache, knees bad. No, that beyond me now.

Sometime we lift our arms. Move them around, lak this. [*In all probability, Ms. Augustus is demonstrating the movement she describes.*] I knows we must'ta look crazy. Crazy folks, out of control, when the paterollers show up. Two of them, workin' together.

We has, lak I tells yo', James Henry here—an' he wus without a pass. An' two other slave fellas from some nearby farm. Baretta kin. They wus liquor up already—even though this be a religious service.

Now, them paterollers ain't never a good lot. An' these here wus particular bad ones. They liquor up too. An' has them a foul smell. Bad as Baretta wus that time.

Our barn lit up by the fire outside, so they can see us off from the distance. Through the piney wood. We has us our ring-shout—James standin' next to Mar. Remember that 'cause Mar grab James Henry when the fat pateroller strike him. They both carry whips, long horse whips, what they call buggy whips.

We singin' when they comes in, chargin' on horses, galloping through the open the barn doors, whoopin' an' hollerin'. "We catch yo' Niggas red-handed," one yell. We hear yo' from the wood, shoutin' yo' conjure Voodoo."

They ride around us in a circle, lak herdin' cattle. Then one take out a rifle an' aim it at the crowd of us. We huddle together.

"Which ones yo' Niggas ain't from here?" The older one yell.

Quiet all around. No one answer.

"Which ones yo' ain't from around here? Ain't belongs to J. B.?" Older man aim his rifle at each us, even at ol' Henry standin' with his fiddle. "Yo' Niggas up to no good. I know yo' ain't no black cows here to shit up the cow barn . Yo' can talk. So talk!" That the way they go 'bout, swearin' an' talkin' foul. Even as we do our prayer meetin'.

"Shoot one, Jeb. Shoot one in the foot an' see what happen. All these Niggas the same. They debil worship. They fixin' to rise up. They all the same."

"Which one yo' Niggas ain't happy? I gonna gets yo' to dance. Which one of yo' is a lazy, discontented Niggas is up to no good?" older white man say.

They move toward us an' seem to picks out James Henry, though James don't do nothin' to provoke them. He got strong eyes, an' he must'ta been glarin' at these men. An' he holdin' hands with Mar.

"That yo' cow, Nigga?" The white man say to James Henry. "The cow yo' gonna milk?" He laugh. "I tell yo', she ain't no milk cow. She dark meat for white men. She don't belong to yo'. She belong to a white man. Yo' just a bull Nigga, an' I tellin' yo' to let her go" He look down at Henry James an' Mar clasped hands. "Hears me, Nigga?"

It mo' than poor James Henry can takes.

Now it cold in that barn. With the doors flung open, an' no one stokin' the fire. I be thinkin' how cold it wus an' how I should be shiverin', but I ain't. No one shiverin'. Don't know if the heat come from fear or anger. We all riled up. If that white man ain't have himself a rifle, I thinks we would of charged up against him. It become the insurrection them paterollers wus here to prevent. It weren't before, but now we wus all burnin' with hate.

Next thing, James Henry let go Mar hand. He step forward—out of the crowd.

"That right, Nigga. Come here!" The older man with the rifle slam the butt against James Henry head. "Yo' is a stupid fool of a young bull Nigga. Ain't worth the grits it take to keep yo' alive." Ol' man laugh an' rear up his horse, so we move back.

Not Mar, though. She move forward to catch James as he fall. She kneel down beside him, his head in her lap. She don't look up them white men, only lookin' at James Henry. He out. Ain't movin'. But yo' can tell it ain't serious, though there blood whar' the rifle hit. He moan, lak he ready to come around. But Mar sooth him; it better for everyone that he stay out.

The one with the rifle, he next aim his gun through the barn doors an' fire. "Yo' don't tells no one about this. We knows yo' Niggas up to no good. Incitin' the debil with yo' mumbo jumbo." He pause, an' the only sound were the cracklin' of the bonfire dyin' right outside the open doors.

"Some of yo' ain't belongs here, ain't gots no passes neither. Do yo'? Breakin' the law. Next time yo' won't get off so easy."

They wearin' wide brim hats, so I can't sees who they be—most folks—white or Negro—I would recognize. Not them. Thinks they might be part of the McLean clan, but this be far for them to travel.

But before I can catch their faces, the one without the rifle, he walk his horse up to Mar, almost on top—horse doin' a high side step to avoid steppin' on her an James Henry. Horse have mo' sense than the rider do.

"I comin' back to snatch this ripe one—she askin', no she beggin' for a man," he say. "Ain't yo', honey?" He look down at Mar, then around at us. I try but can't make out his face under that big hat, even as he lift his head, lak he surveyin' property he just bought. Ma in the crowd, but Pa ain't come this night. Aunt Patsy there, an' she hold Ma arm. Holdin' onto her lak Ma 'bout to jump off the Clarendon Bridge. "I'll be back, Niggas. Yo' ain't goin' nowhar' now, an' yo' ain't goin' nowhar' never. Yo' just born to pick cotton—an' breed. Right gal?" He look at Mar again. "Sure lood good for that."

The other one make a whoopin' noise—they both spur their horses, an' off they go at a gallop out the barn.

Ring-shout over. Christmas service over. Cold air keep rushin' in through them wide open doors, an' now we feel the chill. Soon, James Henry moan again an' seem to come to. Our attention go to him. No one sayin' nothin'. No, we just tendin' to James. *[There is a brief pause.]*

I gonna take me a break. *[The tape is abruptly turned off. When it is turned on, Ms. Augustus resumes, and it seems that just a few moments have gone by.]*

It become a dangerous world out there. After this night, Mar an' James Henry Harris decides to get theirselfs married whar' they are. They been thinkin' they elope an' run off to the north. But after this here incident, they decides to gets married right away. We thinkin' James Harris, he gonna recover an' do just fine. An' his body do recover. But he become a angry man—always be hatchin' plans. Mar tell us them. All we knows is that the future be leanin' on us heavy.

Poor James, he weren't fit for this world. Didn't see nothin' comin'. Guess yo' never do. [*A rather long pause follows; then Ms. Augustus begins again.*]

The wedding take place on our plantation. James Henry an' Mar, they gets their permissions, an' the followin' week they already married. Quick, it seem, as God in His heaven say, "Let there be light," weddin' gonna happen. Some provisions suppose to be meant for the white folk Christmas ball gets put to use.

So it be New Year time. About to turn 1861. They marry New Year Eve. It ain't on that Saturday, happen another day. Can't remembers well, 'cause I ain't attend that weddin'. I take up with the croup. Maybe it be the chill from the open barn doors Christmas service. Maybe it punishment that come so I ain't able to attend. But my own sister weddin', an' I miss it.

Mar wus a beautiful bride. She come in with Mammy Rae to the cabin, whar' I wus fevered on my pallet. People comin' an' goin' with all them preparations. What I remembers is Mar wearin' Missus graduation dress. It white an' long an' flowing, an' has lots of lace trimmin'—down the sleeve, around the high neck collar—all white. Mar happy, an' she look lak one of my angels—floatin' above the ground—when she walk across the yard.

Ain't got a lot to tells 'bout that weddin'. It pass in a haze; I so sick. Mar come in glowin', an' I lifts my head. Mammy Rae tell her not to come close, but I want her to. Never see'd her lookin' so beautiful as she do on that day.

There plenty of good food. Some Harris slaves come, an' James Henry marster show his face. Pa come. An' he come to see me too. He open the door an' axe in his gentle voice, "How my gal is? My Sarah Louise?" He give me a hug, even though I so sick.

They has the ceremony an' broom jump on the front veranda, then move to the horse barn. With fresh hay spread out. No one say nothin' 'bout what happen the week before, an' far I know, Marster never heared nothin' 'bout the trouble that night. James Henry have hisself a bad headache, but it clear up before too long. At the weddin', his cut almost healed over—yo' couldn't scarcely see it. But his hurt wus still there. *[Ms. Augustus lets out a long sigh and then resumes.]*

I recalls that Aunt Patsy bring me ham an' fixin's, but I couldn't ets none. She put the plate down top of a low wood stool, milkin' stool, whar's I could smells it—hopin' that would whet my appetite. It pipin' hot, an' look good, but I too sick.

At one point Hannah come in an' sit beside me—though she shouldn't. She just a li'l gal, an' I axe her if Ma know she come.

"I slip away, Sarah," she say an' take my hand, kiss me on the forehead, lak she growed up an' in charge. Then she squeeze my hand, an' off she go. That all I 'members. Sweet Hannah. She a baby then, but she come to good in the world.

I runnin' a fever all that night. Mammy Rae an' Aunt Nancy brings me herbs an' foul tastin' potions. An' I dream of the faceless angels—they on a cliff at the Cape Fear, by a ferry at Carver Falls. I been there once, but it come back in the fever dream. Them angels wus dancin' in their circle, but the circle kept movin' like a spiral, an' the angels movin' slowly toward the edge of the cliff. I tries to warn them, but I ain't got no voice. I keeps on tryin'—callin' out with all my might, an' I gittin' panicky, 'cause they close to the edge, an' I wants to prevent them from fallin'. Then, all a'sudden, I part of their circle—dancin' with them, lak I one of them. An' the dance get faster an' faster—an' as I swirlin' around in a frenzy, my features becomin' a blur till I lose my face too. Now, I ain't got no eyes to see the cliff edge, an' I ain't got no mouth to scream. An' just as I realize I can't save the angels an' I can't even saves myself—we lost forever—the angels silently let go of my hand, an' I dance over the edge, an' as I fallin' toward the water, I wakes up.

It dark out when I shoot up on my pallet—sittin' right up now. Alone in the dark cabin, moonlight comin' through the window. I sweatin' somethin' fierce, but then I realizin' that my fever break. Later that night, when everyone come back, I already feelin' better. *[There is a rather long pause in the tape. Ms. Augustus clears her throat, then resumes.]*

After a few days I out of bed. Croup gone. Mar stay in the small tool shed by the barn. Folks clear it out for her an' James Henry, who build hisself a fireplace out'ta stone that work at the back. An' folks gives them some rough furniture so they could stay with each other for a couple days. Then she move back in with us. Mar married an' officially a growed woman, but she still live with us mostly. James Henry try to come every Saturday night, an' they stay in the tool shed. Ain't never seen Mar mo' happy than she be then.

I gonna stop. I talkin' about Mar all mornin', an' I tired out. Tired an' gonna nap. Lie down in this heat an' takes me a good nap. We gets together tomorrow, same time. But I finished now. *[The tape is immediately turned off.]*

September 8, 1937

I has nightmares all last night. I dreamed that same dream I telled yo' about yesterday. About them faceless angels an' how I join them in their circle dance an' falls off the Carver Falls cliff. Except this time, I dream that I found my voice, an' instead of joinin' the angels, they stop an' listen to me sing. An' when they stops, David is among them. He wearin' a white angel robe, an' he has his face. When I singin' an' sees him, I overcome—screams his name. He turn to me—still young an' handsome—an' he say, "What took yo' so long, Sarah Louise?" Before I answer, I pop awake.

This my dream, but I can't make no sense of it. It wake me, an' I sweatin'—though ain't got no fever—an' I ain't been back to sleep since. Must'ta wake me around four in the mornin'.

I do believes them angels is with me today. They knows how to speak with dead folks, an' they tellin' me somethin'. Sure as I be here today, I knows they still with me. Thought they might have give up, but I guess they hasn't. *[There is a brief pause. Some clicking is heard. Then Ms. Augustus resumes.]*

My dates ain't right, but I gonna tries my best to remember. About Mar—how she married James Henry, how they live the married life in the tool shed on Saturday nights an' Sunday mornin'. With passes to let James come. Mar stay with us rest of the time. That the way it were. Mar get to have herself a baby—but that sad…. *[There is a brief pause.]*

Things happenin' fast. South Car'lina—done leave the Union right before Christmas. When that Mister Hunter an' Marcus come, South Car'lina wus already gone. After Mar get married, other states follow—lak the string of my angels off the cliff. They dance theirselfs off the edge. There be Miss'ippi, Florida, Al'bama… whole string of slave states. Tense times. Soon, no slaves gittin' Saturday passes, so that be the end of Pa visits, an' James Henry visits too.

Lincoln git elected—I tells yo' that? Gets hisself elected president in Washington, though he ain't even on the ballot here. Don't knows no Southern state that has him. He a northern man from out west whar' there ain't no slaves. But he elected an' take his office that spring. Breckinridge wus elected president here. But far as I know, he ain't never serve.

An' all this time, I be thinkin' of David. I still don't know if my note ever get to him. I wus hopin' that Marcus, with his knit cap an' Muslim religion, might make good. It weren't no promise he make, but it clear he gonna do his best. With all his prayin' an' how he got the one true religion an' all—well, I thinks somehow that note must'ta got into David hand.

But the weeks an' months go by, an' I don't hears nothin' from David. Still, my heart is hopeful, an' I be thinkin' some good gonna happen soon. Every time a wagon or a carriage pass along the road, I be thinkin' I gonna gets a message, another love note. It wus almost spring. A season done roll by, an' I ain't heared nothin'.

Then the weather turn bad again. A late season snow an' a deep freeze. Everybody seem to go on with their chores, but we all drug down by the cold, dank weather an' talk of war. It dismal, short days, an' everyone trudge on. We doin' what we can, stay warm. Baretta family, they all come down with the same sickness I gets. Exceptin' they ain't so lucky. A boy child in that family die.

Before the war, when a white person die, the colored wus sent walkin' if we in a town home, or ridin' from farm to farm, if we out in the country—tellin' other white folk that a person die. We carry a book an' pieces of black crepe in a bag, an' when we go to a house, somebody white have to sign the book, make a cross by their name, write a note, an' takes a piece of crepe to keeps. They pins it on theirselfs to show they in mournin'.

An' when rich white folk get buried, family borrow or rent theirselfs a hearse an' black horses to pull it with—for the procession to the graveyard. Black folks wus mostly the ones what got the body prepare for burial—washin' the dead, shroudin' the body—or dependin' on the family, sometimes white folks want to do this work theirselfs.

Someone else die too, I rememberin'—other than that baby from Baretta family. There at least two deaths among the colored. We lay them to rest in the slave cemetery. Don't think anyone could find it these days. The crosses wus rough wood, an' they ain't last all this time. It a pity not to remember the dead. All of them gone, an' no one to keep the memory.

I thinkin' 'bout my grandma. Never yet tells yo' 'bout her. Ain't sure whar' she buried. She a McDonald, an' she go by Sarah—like me. She have fifteen children in her time, but not all live. That the way it were. A woman would birth her children every two years—comin' regular. But so many die before they turn a year or two ol'.

I don't recalls my grandma too good. Ma say that she work as a wet nurse—'cause she gots so many children her own. That way she stay full of milk. She live till after the war. But then she catched pneumonia an' die. Waitin' for a train to Fayett'ville. She move to Raleigh, lak me, then goin' back home, she get ill, never recover. I guessin' she must'ta been over a hundred year ol'. She wus owned by a family further south, out Elizabethtown way, but that all I knowed. My family weren't in touch with her.

My granddaddy, he be a Fuller. Owned by a lawyer in Fayett'ville. Don't knows much about him neither, only that everyone say he wus a very good man. Also, he live south too, near my grandma place, but closer to the coast. I only see granddaddy one time when he passin' through. I so li'l that I don't remember him. He wus spoke 'bout by Ma, 'cause he Ma father. Wish I'd knowed him. [*Ms. Augustus lets out a long, deep sigh and pauses. She then resumes. The tape continues to run.*]

Don't know whar' they all buried neither—nor no one in my family. We spread out an' die in different places. Ma, Pa, Mar, Hannah, Kate. Sometime I think we stars in heaven—all shinin'. Bodies in the ground, spirits up high. Wood crosses gone, an' the worms done et the body in the fields. [*Ms. Augustus lets out another long sigh. This time the tape is turned off, but when it is turned on, it is clear that the same day's interview continues.*]

Winter linger on. But I still don't hears from David. Lak I say before. Then it just about spring—that time year, maybe February, March. Past

February, I thinkin'. I sad, real sad this time. Sad as Mister Crow predict. I sure is a sad gal. He right about that.

Fact is, I gets myself a case of the hypos. I be draggin' around—doin' chores, but my heart ain't fully present.

One day in particular—I recall it good. We havin' spring weather, warm spell. Don't know if it March now or still February—weren't April. Know that. Well, I on the path from the big house whar' I workin'—must be dinner time, an' I be returnin' to work. I wus out fetchin' somethin'.

Kate wus there—on the path. Then, Mar appears. Lak we plan on meetin' up. Mar gots her a load of washin'. Kate—don't know what bring her. It a sunny, warm day. Sheet of blue sky, ain't a cloud in sight. We standin' together at the fork in the path—yo' coulds either go back to the big house, whar' I goin', or yo' could go on to Mammy Rae, whar' the path fork off again. Yo' could follow the creek to the Cape Fear River or go on up to the main road. But we together, an' stops by that first fork.

"Remember when we swears that day?" Mar axe. She wearin' a cornflower blue dress that match the sky.

"Sure," Kate say.

I standin' with my hang-dog look, ain't contribute to the conversation. Ain't in the mood.

"I a married woman now," Mar say, lak someone done axe her.

I ain't say nothin', but I thinkin' how it agree with her. Then I think about David—just for a moment, an' I feels my tears well up.

"Tells me about bein' married," Kate say, an' Mar get this faraway look in her eye. She put down her load, rest it on a big stone that mark the fork.

"Don't knows what I can say, really I don't." Mar still lookin' at the sky lak there be a small bright speck up so high up she have to strain to sees it.

"Well, say somethin'!" I chime in. "Yo' standin' there lak yo' dumb struck."

"I ain't dumb struck—just can't find the right words, Sarah Louise. An' what yo' so angry 'bout? What yo' problem anyway? Least I ain't goin' around lak some big mopey-dopey." Mar look me up an' down. A challenge.

"What yo' call me?" I axe.

"A big mopey-dopey. That just how yo' actin'." Mar get her attitude up. Seen it before. She get it when she think she right, an' no one can tell her no different.

"Least I ain't goin' around lak my head way up in the clouds…an' with a war comin'. Yo' walkin' around hummin', singin'. Lak the debil hisself put a spell on yo'. Bet yo' carryin' his child." I raisin' my voice. Gots my hands on my hips, ready to fight. But I ain't got no idea whar' this hate comin' from. Seem to spark up all at once.

"Yo' just sad 'cause yo' ain't heared from yo' sweetheart. Yo' upset, an' yo' puttin' it on me! I ain't to blame, Sarah Louise."

When Mar say this, I stop. She be right, a'course. An' in one breath I go from mad to sad. Tears now streamin' down my face, an' I start ballin', coverin' my face with my hands, slumpin' to the ground.

Kate bend to comfort me, but I shrug her away. "Don't needs nothin' from yo'," I tell her.

Mar join Kate, so we all down there on the ground together. I keep shruggin' them off, but Kate an' Mar stroke me—my back, my face, an' soon enough I gives in. They huggin' me, an' now I huggin' them.

"We Smith sisters do solemnly swears…on the holy Bible, on the lives of their Ma, Pa, and baby sister Hannah…an' on their own lifes… that from this day forward…to eternity…these Smith sisters will abide by their own secrets…to keeps them secret…till death do them part." Mar say the whole pledge.

"Amen," Kate say.

"Amen," I say. But rather than us gettin' cheered up an' return to happier times, now it seem that the sadness in the world catchin' up to us instead. We all weepin' now, squattin' there in the dirt, huddlin' in our li'l group, crying our eyes out on such a beautiful day.

Mar stop her sobbin' long enough to say she ain't really married. It be slave vows—an' they don't mean nothin'. She can't see her husband 'cause ain't no slave can gets a pass to travel. I say that sure better than what I gots—less than nothin', in my case.

"Hasn't yo' heared from David since yo' sends him that letter?" Mar want to know.

"Hurt been back here two time at least," Kate say. "I knowed it has—come up from Wilmington."

"Probably that ol' hocus-pocus Marcus never deliver the letter yo' writes. "He no good. I coulds tell." Mar add.

"Why didn't David write me even if he never git my letter?" I axe. By this time we composed a bit, stand up, brushin' off our skirts, dryin' our eyes.

"It hard times. Gonna get harder," Mar turn to me. She take my hand, an' I takes Kate hand. We in a circle. I looks at them an' sees somethin' strong in both Kate an' Mar eyes—we all bound together an' strong.

"Amen," I say.

"Amen," Kate repeat. An' Mar do too.

We hug goodbye, say we see each other later—go our separate ways. *[Ms. Augustus announces that she is through for the day; she is exhausted. She lets out one of her long, deep sighs and then says rather sharply, "Turn that off." Clicks are heard, and the tape machine is off.]*

September 9, 1937

It weren't a long day yesterday. I know. But it tire me out an' give me mo' bad dreams. I wus up at three an' been up since.

In this dream, there ain't no angels. It begin with the war—an' it 'bout to end. The white folks—even them that died in the war—is comin' home to the Smith Plantation. Marster, Marse George, neighbor folk, they all walkin', marchin' up the road to the big house. Me, Ma, Kate, Mar, an' li'l Hannah start runnin' to meet them. But as they gets closer, we see that they all colored. They turn into black folk. We hang back to watch.

An' when they pass through the front gate—we has this a white picket fence—they all collapse, pile up on top of each other, a big stack An' as they fall on the pile, they die. They die as black men.

It all so real that when the dream wake me, I sweatin'. So I sits up in bed, an' then gots to get up 'cause my legs cramp up. Yo' knows how stiff my knees get, so I stumblin' around in the darkness. I gets myself a glass of water, an' I go to sits here on the front porch, whar' I sittin' now. When it light out, I make me some coffee an' breakfast, but I really just waitin' for yo'. *[There are some shuffling sounds, then crackling sounds, but the tape continues.]*

I ready to begins. I ready to talks 'bout the war.

First off, I wants to say that the war didn't have no clear beginnin' an' no clear end—especially the slavery part. No clear end to that. Colored an' white…well, still ain't the same. Ain't equal. Lincoln done outlaw slavery, but that ain't change the way folks act.

Now I weren't gonna say this—but slavery done go underground. An' we all half colored, if yo' axe me. Ain't many Negro today that don't has his momma or gran'momma taken by a white man.

Some folk say we much worse off now. Others say we ain't. Some say the whole world in depression. White an' colored—we all worse off. Maybe it bein' poor that keep folk in bondage—an' this be a money war.

One ol' man, I know, he part Indian, Cherokee—now he in a bad way too. He wus a slave before the war, live in Chatham County, to the west an' south of here. His great gran'ma wus a full blood Cherokee, but he end up a field slave. Don't know the family name, whar' in Chatham he from—south of Pittsboro, wanna say. Now yo' should talk with him. He tell yo' that he so poor he can't feed hisself but once a day, if he lucky—he on the street beggin' most of the time, can't work none. Got the rheumatism bad, an' there ain't no work anyhow. Nobody got no money to give him. So he go hungry. But he swear up an' down that he a free man.

He tell a story how he learn he free. He a boy—out at a farm postal drop whar' the stage deliver—an' his white folk, his marster, wus with him that day. They go to pick up the mail, the newspaper, an' his marster unfold it an' read the news.

"Boy," he say. "Yo' free. I don't owns yo' no mo'. Don't owns yo' or yo' ma or any yo' poor Niggas." Then the marster throw down the newspaper an' walk away, leave him by a tall longleaf pine near the delivery stop. The boy, he sit down an' lean against the thick trunk of that tree, an' he sit there hour or so—no one around, no one bother him—then, he pick hisself up an' walk home to his ma. It happen in the middle of a afternoon. One afternoon, just lak that.

Eventually, his family leave. Not right way. They ain't got no place to go, but they just strike out, on foot—no wagon, buggy, no mule. Don't have no kin folk to go to, but they leaves.

When this here ol' gentleman tell me his story, tears come to his eyes. Growed man 'bout to weep when he say he rather starve to death than be a slave—even if he did have enough food to et back then. No matter. His white folk ain't no good. They whip their colored, mistreat them, an' keeps them in chains when they act up. They even had a jail on the plantation whar' he were. They beat them if they don't works hard. [*A brief pause is heard, then a sound like a chair scraping against the wood floor. Ms. Augustus quickly resumes.*]

I tell yo' another time about this overseer business. We got a couple at the Smith farm. One ain't so bad, but the other wus. One make a show of his whip, but don't hardly use it. The other…well, I be tellin' that story before too long.

I heared many tales 'bout overseers. They sometime low-life white men, come from bad families, or they just scrapin' by. Some black, picked because they mean-spirited. Whites picked because they lowdown, with no education, no property. Sometime the colored given extra privileges to whup the field hands, keep them in line. [*Another long sigh is heard. Then Ms. Augustus begins again.*]

Now… it be… sometime early spring. War comin'. My angels knowed it—remember how they swirl around, tellin' me about the war?

David—never heared from him that spring. Weren't till beginnin' summer that I gets his news. Spring, we go gets to plantin'. Corn go in. Beans. Cotton. Tobacca. The weather get warm in fits. Then rainy, so we good with the crops.

Marse George—he the one talk most 'bout North Car'lina an' disunion. He at his age, must'ta been seventeen, full of hisself. He want to prove he a man. Somethin' wrong with boys that age.

I spend most time in the kitchen, learnin' hows to cook good, an' learnin' my fancy stitch work—I has such a steady hand an' a fine eye for that.

Kate in the kitchen, workin' with me. Mostly she bakin'—breads, pies. But Mar, she work as a housemaid. Git to hear mo' than us do.

One evenin' that spring, we off early. Finish chores—must be first week in April. That what I thinkin', but I coulds be wrong. It before the war, right before. An' it before my sixteenth birthday.

After we leaves the big house, an' after we home with Ma, an' when we cleanin' up, us gals gabbin'. Ma an' Hannah—that just be ol' enough to be talkin' up a storm—she lak a parrot, repeatin' back anythin' yo' say. Lak this machine.

Ma send us to gather washin' hung over bushes, near the path. We has a line now, but it so full that Ma put some washin' out over them nearby bushes—that way they dry. The sun, I knows, goin' down. Small chill in the air. Mostly we gabbin' 'bout nothin'—Aunt Patsy dress get stained with a pot of blueberry jam that broke fallin' from a shelf, an' she can't get the stain out. The hall clock ain't keeping good time lak it used to, an' it drivin' them that needs it crazy. Kate, who still ain't got no beau, get herself all caught up gossipin' about Marse George. There rumors that he keen on this gal that live near Raleigh. Pretty with blonde ring curls, an' come from a important family, lawyers. On occasion, them folk come down, talk politics.

"Marse George," Mar begin. "He ain't really got no time for ladies. All he talk 'bout is war. He, Marster an' Missus arguin' today."

"What he say?" My mind turnin' to thoughts of David an' how he gonna be situated if war come here.

"Marse George say he ain't afraid of no infernal Yankee cowards, that he plan on fightin' for the South, for the new Confederacy with Jeff Davis." Mar shake out our ol' ragged winter quilt. "Help me fold this," she say.

So I takes one end, an' we make neat work of the foldin'. Puttin' it away till next year. This one be a woolen blanket. Too scratchy, except when it real cold.

"What Marster or Missus say?" Kate axe.

"Missus always tellin' Marse George to watch his language—there ladies present. Marster say there ain't gonna be no war, so he better get his mind on his own business. Marster want Marse George to go off to school lak Marse Harry is—to Chapel Hill, become a lawyer."

We has a big basket with us. It made years ago by my gran'ma Sarah. Before I born, before any us born. It made from reeds, an' it real light. It woven an' got two handles. We loadin' it up, havin' this war talk—lak nothin' ever gonna change. Laundry, slavery, nothin'.

"They say anythin' else?" I wanna know.

"Yup." Mar go on. "Marster don't want no war. Neither do Marse Harry. Marster remind Marse George that Harry go to last spring commencement up in Chapel Hill, an' President Buchanan wus there. He speakin' an' tellin' folks how he want peace. Marster say he too ol' for any war. He say South Car'lina wrong—other states too. He say North Car'lina ain't no sheep, ain't gotta follow the rest to slaughter. He say they all hot-headed. Especially the youn' men, lak yo'—an' he turn to Marse George, raisin' his voice up. Then he drop his silver on his half-eaten plate so it make the sound of a bell. Then, he push his chair out an' get up from the table.

"Miss Ellen an' Miss Ida upset, real upset. Others lower thems heads, say nothin'. Quiet. An' mo' quiet. Whole two minutes must'ta go by—Marster in the hallway, rummagin' for somethin'. Missus hear him an' she done call him back. Say that it ain't good manners to just to pick up an' leave before a meal done, an' she ain't gonna have none of it at her table."

"Marster come back?" I axe.

"Yas, he do. He come back, an' sit right down, lak Missus tell him. But Marse George, he get the last word in. He say that there gonna be war whether Marster lak it or not. An' he goin'. He gonna defend his home an' the way of life he come to love. Ain't no man gonna stop him. He look right at Marster an' say, 'I follow God's will.'

"Then he look around, an' he axe Missus if he could be excused, don't wait for no answer, but he leave. Throw his napkin on his chair, tossin' it down lak a enemy flag, an' he done finish with it."

"Wish I could'a been there!" Kate say. She enjoyin' this. We both stoppin' our foldin'— we done. It dark out by now.

"Whar' wus yo', Mar? Whar' wus yo' in this mess?" I axe.

"I standin' off to the side, whar' I usually serve. By the great sideboard, the butler door. Don't think no one see'd me at first. When Marse George leave, then they do. Missus, she look lak she 'bout to cry, say that I needs to return to the kitchen, an' she ring her bell when she want me. They wusn't through with their meal, Missus say, an' they don't need nothin' cleared yet."

As Mar talkin', I just standin' there, half listenin', half daydreamin' 'bout my David. Rememberin' his bright green eyes. They the color of afternoon grass, shiny an' calm before the sun go down…

"Let's go home," I say. Then add, "I thinks Marse George right."

Mar just shakin' her head, grab the basket handles on one end. "I think so too," Kate say. She grab the other end. I carry the folded blanket. An' off we sets out for home. *[There is a long, scratchy pause on the tape, and then Ms. Augustus resumes.]*

That wus the first we heared serious talk 'bout war. An' the next week it start. North Car'lina still part of the Union—stayed in till after Fort Sumter battle. We the last state to withdraw. Don't know exactly when our white folks knowed all that wus goin' on. But they wusn't good 'bout keepin' secrets—though they try.

Hard times come. Here wus spring, an' most years, we happy—colored an' white—that winter finally over, an' what illness come, usually gone. This year the weather wus especially favorable for crops. But white folk real nervous. There ain't been no colored passes for a long while. Mar ain't see James Henry, an' Pa ain't comin' his Saturdays.

The day we gets the news, it be a terrible blow. Nobody know what to think. No. Nobody do. Everybody that gots any sense is scared. Others, they fools.

Mar say she overhear snatches, other colored do too. Reports that Lincoln done send out troops against South Car'lina. An' Jeff Davis say the Union troops attackin' can only mean the North want war.

Fort Sumter get surrendered to the Confed'rate States. But before it do, Lincoln tell North Car'lina to send their troops—'cause we close to South Car'lina—an' we suppose to fortify the Union. President Lincoln tell us this.

But instead of us goin', we join the other side. This the moment we leaves the Union. That how it happen.

Lots of talk 'bout stayin' with the North, but there no way North Car'lina gonna fight against its sister. Ain't gonna do it. Can't fight against them Southern states. An' we have us slavery, so the only thing left is to declare ourself for the Confederacy, an' take up arms.

This happen in April an' May of 1861. It a perplexin' time. By end of May, North Car'lina officially out. But the fightin' start before—April, but North Car'lina, it don't leave the Union till May. That what I recall.

A mess of stuff must'ta been happenin'. But I tells yo' only what I knows. Can't gives yo' no history lesson; I be a ol' woman. But when war declared, I remembers the day. An' when North Car'lina pull from the Union, I remembers that day too. Seem lak the world done turn upside down.

We gits two calls to war—the first wus Sumter. News spread we wus at war, but folks ain't yet sure what that mean.

Seem lak for some folk the war begin in earnest when North Car'lina leave the Union—that day…now, I remember it good. Can tells yo' 'bout it an' what the colored folks thinkin'. It a mess.

It Monday, I remember, 'cause it washin' day for Missus, an' it always start early. Mar an' some other gal—not Baretta, I'd recall if it were her. Poor Baretta.

Mar come outside in the mornin' chill with the laundry bins—they straw too, woven tight, different from our baskets. We wearin' shawls, rough woven shawls that we drape over our heads. The bed linens, table cloths, all pile in one bin. Mar put the bins on the back veranda for us others to take to Mammy Rae. We sometime do our washin' there, especially if the weather bad. We gots big iron pot we hang—separate from the dye pot. Mammy Rae always get start early on wash days, so by sun-up she has her a steamin' hot iron kettle of water. It were a rainy day. Drizzle mostly. All gloomy, the kind whar' the sun never shine all day. The sky hangin' low with cloud cover, an' heavy lak wet wool.

As I says, them days I just walkin' around sad. Still nothin' makin' me feel good. It just past my birthday. I turn sixteen. Imagine that. Sixteen. So young but I feels lak a woman, with powerful emotion that stir up easy. I wus real skinny back then, but I has me a good figure. I uset'ta wear my long hair in braids, then twisted up lak a halo around my head. Didn't half know how pretty I wus. Guess us young gals ain't gots lots of notice, less spoiled. Though some of them white youn' ladies, they spoiled enough for everyone. Not the Smith gals. Missus not in favor that.

I workin' outside in the dye shack again. Mammy Rae, she somewhar'. I dumpin' the first load into the big iron kettle pot, take out the long paddle to stir when I hears a whistle. It sharp an' sound a few times.

There a ruckus, sound of voices. Also the dogs barkin'. I wanna go, see what the commotion 'bout, but I just put the linen in to boil, an' the low clouds turn to drizzle that now be turnin' to light rain. I goes to the edge of the dye shack, listen, an' only heared mumble. "Tarnation," I says aloud. Then I thinkin' I ain't never use that word before. "Tarnation." It just come into my head.

Kate show up next. An' she carryin' a pretty parasol. A real parasol. She scurrying toward me, holdin' her skirt up out of the puddles she walkin' through.

"War," Kate say. "We done join the Confederacy—we done join the rebels. I come to tell yo'." Kate under the shelter now, in the dye shack. She shake out the parasol—this the first time I ever see'd her with one—but she shake it lak she done it a million times.

"How yo' hear? I'm still holdin' my big paddle, so I gives the pot a quick stir.

"Two men show up on horseback. They say the news come through on the telegraph, an' they tellin' all the folks around." Kate out of breath.

Now with these two gallopin' right to the big house, there ain't no way the house slaves couldn't knows. So Marster, inside in his study, when he get the word, figure that he need to spread it. The men, they stay for only a few minutes; then they off to the Ellicott Plantation." I turn to Kate, who look scared.

"I don't knows what to say," I tells her. "I knowed it gonna happen. I knowed it…"

"The men say that we at war now. Real war. We done join up. Then I heared guns goin' off, but Aunt Nancy later say it just folks celebratin' up the hill. Sound lak firecrackers on the Fourth of July. Folks excited, takin' up arms, an' they shootin'."

"What's gonna happen? Anyone say? What Marster sayin'?"

"He say that we darkies need to go 'bout our business. He don't want no worry from us. He got hisself in the parlor right now—with the doors shut tight. Missus upset, she in her room. The young misses chatterin' in the parlor. They suppose to stay together, that what Missus say before she go up."

"Missus tell yo' to come here—how'd yo' gits this parasol?"

"It by the back veranda, an' I snatch it. Gotta get back, Sarah Louise. Gotta go. Yo' keep on with the dyin'. Don't think much mo' gonna happen today. Not lak the war be right here in Fayett'ville. Ain't at the farm." An' Kate pick up the pretty parasol that got some pink lace ruffle to the edge, an' off she run into the rain that comin' down again. Liftin' her skirt lak a lady as she go.

I still by myself, at the wash pot, stirrin'. Which be fine, really. Stirrin' suit me. I could hears the rain beatin' against the shack roof. All them other voices die off. Dogs ain't barkin'. Only the sound of that rain. I thinks it right for the mood. An omen for what gonna come.

At some point, two young Negra gals come that mornin' with another bin to dye. Them two li'l gals, must be eight, nine. They giggly, don't understands whar' day this be. They might'ta been twins, though probably weren't. Don't recalls the names neither. They both soaked, but ain't got a care in the world. Drop the bin by me, then scurry off, lak I weren't even there. I just invisible.

Don't remembers much mo'. Funny how yo' gits a picture but don't recall the frame. *[There is a long pause and a sadness is almost discernable. Nothing is heard for a rather long moment, and then the scratchy tape is clicked off and on again.]*

I gonna end the day. Right here. I been talkin' a long time, an' I feels tired. Yo' turns this off now. That all I has. *[There is the sound of a chair scraping against a wooden floor. Ms. Augustus clears her throat, and the tape machine is turned off.]*

September 10, 1937

Glad it Friday. Last weekday. I ain't gonna see yo' tomorrow. Fact is, havin' a neighbor stop. Miss Nellie Mae. She down the street. We goin' to the open market together. Lookin' forward.

Well, yo' ought'ta be happy, 'cause I in a better mood today. I sleep real good. No bad dreams. I feels rested.

Thinkin' to all I leave out yesterday—my birthday, the takin' of the arsenal in Fayett'ville. Don't know how I leaves out that.

So I guess I gonna starts in about the arsenal. Yo' might be better off consultin' a history book for that. Somebody done wrote it down, be my guess.

We uset'ta to have us a federal arsenal. It be a large property, an' I only been there once, that first year of the war, after it taken by our Fayett'ville men that come marchin' up the Hill.

Miss Ida, she watch it happen. I tell yo' what I knows. When it occur, I ain't yet ever seen the place. Seen it later. It be one evenin' Miss Ida, she come to slave quarters an' tell us her story.

Now yo' know that them white chil'ren sometime come to get home-cooked food at slave quarters. They calls it "Auntie food," an' though we ain't got much, we always share.

Mostly, the white chil'ren loves the pone, baked fresh. An' they come when they gets a hankerin' for it. We et pretty easy, not lak the white folks, with the fancy tableware an' cloth. So Marster, Missus children come to relax some. Say our food always taste better. Ain't so sure, but it were a treat for them.

That April—after Sumter, before we leaves the Union in May—that the time I tellin' 'bout. Miss Ida come for a bite after her supper. We about to et—has us ham hocks an' chittlin's, pone—she welcome to. She join us on the stoop.

She a youn' gal, older than me…don't remember exactly what her age. She sittin' on the stoop in a indigo cotton dress, skirt full, with a apron tied around her waist in a big bow. A full apron, 'cause I remember wonderin' how she keep it so clean. Maybe it new, put on after her own supper—'cause she et already, an' she ain't the most lady-like of the gals.

"What you staring at, Sarah Louise?" she axe, noticin'. An' I blurt out 'bout how clean she is—ain't carin' if I rude or not. Ma, she ain't around for some reason. Miss Ida just settin' with her plate on her lap. I there with Kate, Mar, Hannah. In fact, Hannah be so close to Miss Ida, she foolin' with the spring curls in her strawberry hair.

"I starin' at how fresh an' clean yo' apron is," I say. Ain't no reason to lie. Miss Ida ain't gonna take no offense.

"Well, it just get put on by Baretta. I made a mess of my other one," Miss Ida say. Then, "Oh! Oh! Oh!" an' Miss Ida start to squirm, dancin' around, though her fanny still setting. "I gotta tell you. I come down to tell ya'll…and I almost forget." Miss Ida take a big ol' bite of corn pone, stuffin' half a piece in her mouth all at once. Crumbs fall over her.

"Look lak yo' 'bout to dirty this one too." I say.

Miss Ida laugh so hard she spit out some of the pone she try to swallow. It blow so far, it almost go down the path.

Hannah be the next to start laughin'. Then Mar, Kate—we all join in. Corn pone be flyin' everywhar'.

"Let me tell ya'll!" Miss Ida put her hand up, cover her mouth. "This is serious business!" But we still all laughin'. "Shh! Shh!" Ida say.

"What Missus gonna say when she see yo'?" Kate can't get herself quiet.

"Shh! Shush!" Miss Ida try again. An' this time we hushin' up lak she want. "I go to Miss Wharton today in town. For my piano lesson." Ida look around at us. She serious now.

Hannah pullin' at Miss Ida curls. She one li'l annoyin' gal. Ida shake her head an' go on to tell us 'bout how all the men folks assembled below Hay Street an' they marched up to the arsenal.

"Marster there, Miss Ida? How 'bout Marse George, Norman, Harry?" I axe. Marse Harry home from school 'cause all the problems we havin'.

"Yes, they were all there. But I didn't see them. They come separate. Momma took me by carriage. I was safe where I took my lesson. In town. But I did see some..."

"What yo' see?" Mar axe.

"Not only what I saw but also what I heard..." Miss Ida continue.

"Well, tell us!" We all move closer in to Miss Ida, who put her plate down on the floor, inside the cabin door.

"Well, at first it seem like a parade. But it weren't. Our men folk were there to fight the Union."

"What the Union doin' there?" Mar axe.

"They were the federal troops run by old Mister Bradford—he's a drunk. That's what Pa says—and he and his men are part of the government. Federals. Our men were there to take the arsenal for the South. Claim it for the Confederacy. I saw them marching—with my own eyes. Some of our fellas were in fancy dress uniforms, with black feathers in their caps. Others didn't have no uniforms. Dressed regular. Over a hundred men. Took the arsenal and run up our flag on the pole. North Carolina. Momma an' Pa say this is the first step."

"First step of what?" Mar interrupt.

"War, silly. War!" Miss Ida say, an' she shakin' her head to get li'l Hannah off her again.

"What this war about, Miss Ida?" Mar cuttin' in. She sound upset.

"You, silly. This war is all about you!" Ida lookin' angry at all us gals. "It's about you!" she say once mo'.

"Miss Ida, we knows..." Mar begin. Then she stop. All quiet. The sky gittin' dark, but it a bright, clear night. Evenin' comin'. We all stay quiet for another moment. This a line we all knows not to cross.

Mar begin again, but she say this low, in a whisper. "We knows 'bout the North. Ain't no fools."

Miss Ida lookin' down. "We shouldn't talk, Mary. I already said too much." There another moment, an' I thinkin' Miss Ida 'bout to excuse herself.

Then Hannah pipe up, tuggin' at Miss Ida dress sleeve. "Tell us again 'bout the men, how they look, whar' they march from." Hannah snugglin' against Miss Ida, who still got herself ham left on her plate, which now notice and pick up off the cabin floor.

"Some of them were in uniform, like I said. They looked grand. Our women folk have been working to change them out from their parade dress. But a few of the older gentlemen, like Mister Paul, the banker downtown, he was too portly and was struggling up Hay Street in his Sunday clothes and dress boots." Miss Ida take a big bite of ham an' lick her fingers. "It was a hot day, and he wearin' his winter overcoat." She look at us for effect, smile, an' continue. "Some of the other men, the young ones, were in uniform and awfully good looking." Ida raise her eyebrows at us. She tilt her head off to the side. "They were very gay in plumed hats, carrying big bayonets."
"Tell us mo'!" Hannah cry out. She nudgin' up to Miss Ida, tuggin' her apron. "Did we has us a war? Who won? Was there guns gittin' shot off? Blood over all them fancy uniforms? Who die?"

"No one died, Hannah!" Miss Ida say. Then she pause long enough to finish off her ham. But Hannah full of herself, won't quit.

"Somebody must'ta get shot, Miss Ida? Tell me who?"

"Shh!" Miss Ida say. "Hannah, you sure is one gabbing child! Shh!" But then she motion us to gets closer. She put her plate down on the ground by the stoop. "I ain't supposed to say nothing. But you colored are going to hear this anyway.

"One reason we took the arsenal is that white folk say the Negroes are going to rise up, and we all have to be prepared." Miss Ida stop. "Not that anyone is really scared. And it's nothing bad against y'all, but we got to be ready to fight."

Even Hannah git quiet. She sure ain't understandin' much, but she get the general idea.

"Some white folks are counting on you Negroes to stick by us," Miss Ida say. "Because them Northerners are some mean folk. You don't know that now, but you will. You don't want no Northerners down here...." Miss Ida stop. She ain't quite sure what she sayin'.

"Ya'll know Momma and Pa going to have some big old fit if they catch me talking to you like this." She don't raise her eyes none now. She lookin' inside the cabin at a wide plank floorboard come loose.

"We ain't gonna say nothin'. Ain't gonna tells no one nothin'," Mar say." "Yo' know that." We all nod. *[There is a brief pause. Then Ms. Augustus lets out a sigh.]*

Soon, Miss Ida get herself up an' go home. But before she go, she take out two glass marbles that she been carryin' in her petticoat pocket, an' she leave them with Hannah. She say they is toy cannonballs, an' they signify that the South gonna win the war an' that Hannah an' all us Negroes gonna be safe. She put them in Hannah hand whar' we coulds all see them—then she close Hannah li'l fist, put her own li'l hands up around Hannah fist, give a squeeze. Then she off—say her goodbye, go skippin' up the path.

We must'ta been a gabbin' at the stoop a long time. When Miss Ida go, we lookin' around for Ma. It completely dark out, but it a clear night with a big ol' full moon.

Later, we find out that Ma gone to a meetin' at the barn that evenin'. That why she away so long. They has themselfs a secret meetin' 'cause they hears about the arsenal an' what happen that day. News travel fast.

All the slaves at our place be thinkin' about war. There a buzz. Some say white folk take the arsenal to control their colored better. Some say they want those weapons just in case.

But right now, Marster ain't threatenin' no one; no one threatenin' him. Nothin' changin' at the Smith Place, an' it better, we decides, to just go 'bout our chores.

Miss Ida is the only one that tell us what she hear. Next time she come, she tell us about Marse George—who we ain't seein' as often as before. He got what they calls the "war fever"—it come lak a sickness an' carry him off. *[There is another brief pause during which a few seconds of silence pass before Ms. Augustus resumes.]*

The next day, it Tuesday. An' Baretta an' me has to work together 'cause Missus say she want the summer kitchen open. We havin' a spell of warm, lovely weather. I tell Missus, "Yas, ma'am," an' off I go, passin'

Miss Ida in her fresh apron, comin' in from the veranda. She nod an' give a li'l grin.

Baretta, already inside the kitchen. She hummin' some spiritual an' swipin' a rag over a window sill.

"Yo' hears 'bout the war yesterday," she axe me, not lookin' up, but she keep wipin' the same clean sill with her dirty rag.

Now I just pass Miss Ida, an' I promise her last night that I won't be talkin' nothin' about no war. So I says, "What war, Baretta? Ain't no war!" 'Cause, in fact, there ain't. I'm at the next window, an' it stuck. I begin tuggin'. "Help me," I say.

Baretta put down her rag, an' join me. "Yo' gotta knows something," she say.

We alone, workin' at the window by the big stove. It stuck shut, an' we has to yank hard.

"Yo' mean yesterday? The arsenal?" I axe, an' bump the heel of my right hand against the bottom, whar' it seem caught. "Push," I say.

"I is pushin'!" Baretta yell back. The window creak. Almost come loose. "Yas," she say. "The arsenal."

"That weren't no real war," I tell her, an' give a big shove. The window pop open. It the kind that move up an' down.

"Sarah Louise, I ain't no fool. I heared 'bout the war. Pa tell us that he see'd them soldiers come up the Haymont Hill to take the arsenal—we won it. There a battle, with guns go off…" She take a step back, nice breeze come through the window now.

"Yo' believes what yo' want. But that weren't no real war."

"How yo' knows that? People say they see'd the North Car'lina flag go up, an' the war done won. We gonna get extra rations…" Baretta puts her hand on her hip, an' go "Humph.…" She look her usual mess, though she don't smell too bad today.

I wants to tell her 'bout what Miss Ida say, but I knows I can't.

"Baretta, yo' a gal that is always gonna learns the hard way. Same for all yo' folks. What happen yesterday, it weren't no war. Weren't even the first battle."

Baretta open her mouth lak she plan on catchin' house flies. She just stand there.

With the window open, I take a cloth an' wipe the sill. Then I take up the broom by the doorway, start my sweeping, then say, "Baretta, get the pan. It behind the stove." [*Ms. Augustus makes a "ahem" noise, not really a word or a sigh, then continues.*]

That be how I come to know everybody already heared 'bout the arsenal. Not even one day, an' even Baretta know. An' folks all got somethin' to say. Uncle Cicero, Aunt Nancy son—I mention him before—he all growed up, an' lak his Pa, he take to trainin' mules an' breakin' horses.

They call him Swell. Don't knows if that his given name, but that what he go by. An' after his Pa die, Swell take up with Sammy. That right—li'l Sammy, that work as a stable boy. When it plantin' season, though, he in the field. Probably gets to know Swell down in the barns. These two spends what free time they has in each other company. Now I thinkin' Swell has hisself a banjo, homemade out'ta a can, an' maybe he learns Sammy to play.

Swell, he become pretty uppity after the arsenal got took. Least at camp meetin's when he be with his own. Say that slaves gonna has to rise up, take their own freedom if the north ain't strong enough. If there be war, he say, he gonna join the other side—the north—fight for what he know is right. Swell say that slavery lak a big ol' alligator lurkin' beneath the surface—no one can sees it, but it there—in the dark water, always hungry, gonna bite.

There some that with him, some against him, an' some afraid to say.

Baretta think we already have ourselfs a war, done fight it, an' won.

But it wus hard to know what to think. It all confused. Life movin' fast. Swell, he full of swagger. An' li'l Sammy, he full'a hate. A mean dog nobody trust.

White folk, all this time, they mostly think the South gonna triumph, but Marster don't wants to fight. Don't believe in it.

No tellin' what wus gonna happen. Should'a been clear, but it weren't. [*There is a very brief pause in the tape; then Ms. Augustus resumes.*]

The arsenal fight give white folk courage. North Car'lina flag flyin' high on Haymont Hill get most folks thinkin' the South can win the war.

Then come the battle in South Car'lina. Fort Sumter. Lincoln wus made president, an' as I say, he send troops down, an' when they lose, he order North Car'lina to send men. But Governor Ellis won't do it. Before long, we has ourself a war.

Now, I has a birthday in April. Some slaves don't knows when they born, but we keeps our dates in the Bible. All the family but Pa knowed how to read an' write. We mark births, marriages. I born April 22, 1845. Ninety-two now, ninety-three if I make spring next year.

Slaves on the Smith place didn't has no real birthday celebration. We do small things—make dolls for the gals when they young. Other toys. Ma, Mar, or Kate would take over chores when it my birthday. I do the same for them. In camp meetings, we get praised.

But that year they forgets. All day I thinkin' they gonna surprise me. Give me somethin' special. Then come dinner. Nothin'. Supper. Nothin'. An' I think I too big a gal to care 'bout my birthday now. But finally, right before I goes to sleep that night, I bursts out, "Ma, ain't it my birthday today—yo' forgits?"

She by the fire. I in my sack, alone. Others tryin' to gets to sleep.

"Oh, my Lawd!" Ma say, an' she whip around. Her face lit up—shadows playin' on her face. "What day is this? April what? Oh, my Lawd, it the twenty-second April. Gal, oh gal. Yo' is right. What kind of ma yo' has?" Ma come over, kneel by me, give me a hug. Wrap her strong arms around me.

"This gonna has to be yo' present this year, Sarah Louise," Ma say. "Till I thinks of somethin' better. Yo' sixteen year ol', an' yo' own Ma forgit yo' birthday. What this world comin' to?"

Before I knows it, Mar, Kate, an' Hannah gits up an' they be huggin' me too. I weren't too sad no mo', an' didn't mind their forgittin'. Really, I didn't mind.

But the world wus changin'. That we knowed. We a close family, an' we already breakin' apart—spinnin' out of control. I changin' an' spinnin' too—sixteen, a growed woman, I thinkin'. Birthdays wus for small gals, I tell myself.

One day after my birthday, maybe it be May by now—Ma an' me out walkin' the path to the big house. We totin' water together—not much, we has our big tin buckets, walkin' in step. Ma glidin'; I tryin' to match her smooth way.

"Yo' mo' lak me every day, Sarah Louise. Yo' sure is." Ma say.

"What yo' mean? I axe, 'cause this surprise me.

"All I say to yo', child, is yo' frisky an' smart. Good lookin' too. Pretty. Now yo' ain't alone; yo' sisters has these qualities, but yo', well…yo'…." Ma smile at me, an' her face light up lak a bright star.

"But Ma…" I begin to say. She turn away, an' I see she still smilin', though she be shakin' her head.

"Yo' almost growed up. But yo' ain't gonna has it easy. Yo' too much lak me. Gonna get there, but I afeared yo' gonna suffer along the way."

When we at the big house—I realize that we ain't barely spilled no water. An' somehow we been walkin' in step the whole way. *[Ms. Augustus clears her voice, then continues.]*

I gonna takes me a break. For the weekend. It Friday, an' I tired. *[Ms. Augustus clears her voice again, then resumes.]*

Monday, I gonna start the war. *[There are some muffled voices, and the tape is shut off.]*

September 13, 1937

I glad yo' here. Both Saturday an' Sunday at church, I rememberin' the war. Them five years pass slow when we livin' them—a lifetime—but now it seem lak scenery on a fast-movin' train. Mountains, pine barrens, barns in the distance. Rivers, fields, an' all the blood an' scorched land, broken men, hunger.

But I gonna slow it down. We at the church yesterday mornin'. There wus a warm rain outside, preacher tellin' us some verse from Matthew 13, how the sower went forth to sow, an' how some seed fall on rock an' some fall on good soil. We mostly ol' folk there. Done sowed whatever seed we has. Memories is mostly what we has left.

I walk home after church. The air, mistin', rain stopped. I gonna tell my story before it lost. *[There is a pause, and the tape machine is clicked off and on again. Then Ms. Augustus speaks.]*

The first big battle we fights—I means that North Car'lina send her troops to—is Big Bethel. Two regiments up Virg'nia, while folks here thinkin' that they can sign up for half the year, an' the war gonna be over. Six months seem 'bout right to have themselfs a war.

Beginnin' May, it getting' warm. By now, everybody know North Car'lina goin' with the Confederates, so talk 'bout sidin' with the Union die down. Even Marster hisself think about fightin'.

Yo' remember me talkin' about Cicero son Swell? He a man what can reads an' writes good. An' Sammy. I got a story 'bout him. But first I tells yo' 'bout the start of the war.

At the beginnin', the housemaids an' cooks wus called to action. We all preparin' to do mo' cannin' this year, an' Marster buyin' mo' goods than usual. Misses have a fit about prices goin' up. We gonna gets new paper money, we heared. Confederate money. But by the end, that new money, Jeff Davis dollars they call them, weren't worth the paper they printed on.

One afternoon, women from the McNeil farm come by to sew, an' I overheared Missus say that the price of flour 'bout double in one month.

But there be two incidents I recall good. One happen when Marster rings his iron bell outside the summer kitchen to gather us up an' tell us 'bout the war, how it gonna be, sacrifices an' privation. Then there wus that time when a few of us gals be sent into the attic to finds ol' clothes, drapery, and such to get sewn up into blankets, coats, bandages for soldiers.

He ring the iron bell one mornin' early. Must'ta been May, right when we go to war. Happen few days after the men come by an' Mar find me at the dye shack with her parasol.

It sun-up, an' he call us to the veranda before it get too warm or we gets too busy.

He an' Missus there, but the chil'ren ain't. Also, one ol' hound dog that Marster love so much he allowed inside the house. Only one. Now he stand by Marster side an' be waggin' his big tail.

"You colored. You colored going to hear your fill about what is going on in our part of the world. You going to hear—that is, if you listen," Marster say.

The hot sun comin' risin', take the early chill out'ta the air. An' yo' could tells it gonna be a hot day.

"Ya'll come closer," Marster say, an' he take a step forward. But he motion to Missus that she stay back an' keep the dog back too.

A few shuffle forward to do what he order. I standin' off to the side, by the edge. We all hushed, 'cause we got our opinions already—so we just gonna be weighin' them against what we hear.

"Most of what happens doesn't concern ya'll. You'll have lots of work to do. No shortage of work. There are going to be new restrictions too. Some Niggas still will get their passes, like they're accustomed to—but they will be in strict control. At this place and at other places. You'll expect that now." Marster look around at 'bout twelve of us. We listenin', waitin' to hear something we ain't heared before.

"But Missus and I will make certain that ya'll be safe. Masters from all these parts will be protecting you from those who started this war. Protects you with our very own lives." Marster has a big boomin' voice, an' he near to shoutin' now. Can't tell if he angry or just firm.

"I want ya'll to know, to hear it from me—that we here in North Carolina, your home, are at war." Marster pause, glance at folks. Nobody say nothin', 'course. An' none of us move.

"Probably there will be rumors to this effect—that we're at war. So you need to know it's true: North Carolina has officially joined the Confederacy and the other Southern states to oppose—to stand up against—President Lincoln's act of aggression against our neighbor state of South Carolina. I say it again—we are at war!" Marster definitely shout now, but then he lower his voice an' go on.

"Your labor and your loyalty will continue to be required. Some of you will be asked to do chores that you haven't done before. You will do these without complaint." He stop for a moment to emphasize his point.

"Missus here will be directly involved in seeing that the household service is completed to her satisfaction. We have our young men—*our very own young men*—that will be putting their lifes on the line for us all—including you colored. And no foolishness will be tolerated."

At this moment, Missus step forward an' tap Marster on the shoulder. Marster nod to her that he 'bout to give her time if she just wait. She take a small step back.

"I don't expect any questions. I do expect absolute obedience. I've put up with colored nonsense before, but not now. We are at war, and foolishness could endanger the lives of others. Your disobedience could be fatal." Marster pause for us to gets the full effect of his words.

"Take this as fair warning. We give you darkies your very lives, and you owe us everything." He wait another moment for his message to sink in. Which it do an' don't. Then he nod to Missus, she come forward again, an' Marster takes his step back.

"I have here a list of how you women, the gals, will be reassigned. So when I call your name, you stay here so I can give you new orders. Marster will dismiss you boys to do your usual work." She nod to Marster, who now come forward to stand by Missus.

"You boys knows what you need to do, so I will simply tell you again that your work will be watched carefully. We're going to have a new overseer here. He is a colored man and will be joining you soon." Marster stop. He pausin' an' peerin' over us from the veranda. This new part 'bout the overseer, that get us. Come as a surprise. Nobody heared nothin' 'bout that. Not a murmur.

"Dismissed," he shout. "Now you men, you darkies, get back to work!" Marster clap his hands three times in a row. Never done that before—clap his hands together. It sure peculiar. The men folk go, but they movin' mighty slow. Some be thinkin' that this be a white man war. But really they mo' concerned 'bout who this new overseer gonna be. We ain't never had a new man brought in lak this. Marster must'ta purchased him, or maybe—we thinkin'—he paid. Some men folk seem mo' concerned 'bout him than the war.

The gals stay behind, an' Missus give assignments—some new, some ain't. I gets taken from the housework an' gets sent up to the attic, to sort ol' materials for sewin'.

Kate, she get puts with me an' Baretta too. There plenty of cooks. Mar still has her ol' chores, 'cause we havin' women comin' all the time. To sew mostly. They sittin' in the parlor or out the front veranda. Makin' uniforms, quilt blankets, knittin' socks, gloves, covers for canteens. All sewin' together. Miss 'Lizabeth, Miss Ida, Miss Mary, an' Miss Ellen too. Some neighbor gals goes to relatives, but they be mostly at home all through the war. Miss Ellen, she git engaged at some point, but her beau get killed. Must'ta been in '63.

Up in the attic—that first week, Baretta, Kate, and me, we sortin' through trunks. Some stuff must'ta been there from before the Revolution.

We finds these ol' worn dresses. An' Baretta, so silly, she take it upon herself to tries one on. Some ol' ball gown, out'ta fashion. It bright red shiny fabric, with lace around the neck, an' long, lacy sleeves. She even find a hat to match.

"Help me get out'ta this raggedy smock," Baretta say to Kate an' me. Baretta pullin' off her gray sack dress. So we helps her out'ta her dirty apron—she never wus quite clean, an' she still smell a li'l. It be all her people; they just ain't right, an' everybody know it.

But when Baretta get her fancy dress ball gown on—well, she turn into another gal entirely. We amazed.

"How I look, ya'll?" Baretta can't see her own self. Ain't no mirror there. So she take on struttin' between the trunks an' dusty furniture. She prancin' with her shoulders movin' to an' fro—lak she the finest lady.

Baretta stop, rummage through one trunk, find a couple mo' fancy dresses, throw them to us. "Yo' get dressed too. Or yo' be late for the ball!"

So Kate an' me pick up some elegant ol' dresses, an' we pulls them on. Don't needs much encouragement. Before yo' knows it, we all dressed lak ladies that livin' a hundred year ago. In our finery.

Kate tryin' to speak lak a lady—she talkin' of her "splendid time" with her "beau who named Beauregard." We laugh at that.

We be havin' such a good time that we got to remember to keep our voices down. Don't wants to get ourself caught. It were a fun time, except at the end.

Kate take off her gown an' hold it up close to her face—the bright blue one with the fancy stitch work.

"We ain't never gonna be fine ladies," Kate say. An' she sit down on the dirty floor by the front window. Dust go floatin' all by her pretty face.

"We can pretend, Kate. We can have us this same fun some time again." Baretta say. I just keeps quiet beside her.

"That ain't the point, Baretta. I don't wants to just pretend." Kate 'bout to cry now. Her voice start to waver.

"Maybe this war gonna change things, Kate. Maybe we all gonna be free one day," I say.

Both gals look at me.

"I don't know," I say. An' we fall quiet again.

Soon, we puttin' the ball gowns back in the trunk, an' we searchin' for mo' suitable items. We finds ourselfs a ol' wool blanket that the moths done got to—still some good to it though. An' Baretta find a big bolt of undyed linen buried beneath some dusty hats. I take their feathers from them, 'cause Missus say they needs them too. Ain't nobody gonna wear them outdated hats anymo'.

Only sound now are the floorboards creakin' an' some muffled voices from below. We puttin' the goods together in a big pile, an' then Aunt Nancy peek through the attic.

"Missus wanna see what yo' finds," she say. "Load up them goods an' come on down." It only her head peep through the open hatch. But then she swing it full open an' leave it that way as she go down the rickety stair to the kitchen hall.

When we down, Aunt Nancy say we to gets clean up an' have us some dinner on the back porch. She take these here to Missus. *[There is a brief pause. Ms. Augustus clears her throat and continues.]*

So the war begin. We has the battle at Bethel. A few of our boys come home after that victory, an' we has ourself a parade downtown, many thinkin' the war over.

After each battle, there folks be thinkin' the South won. Everybody ready to celebrate. Some boys comes home after six month—the period of their enlistment. Early on, none of them die. White folk talkin' about God bein' on their side an' how this war lak the Revolution them grandpappies fights in.

I tell yo' next 'bout David…how I finds somethin' out that gives me great hope. It happen in June, the weather hot, an' Missus axe me an' a few others—can't remember who—to go on a wagon ride.

We has ourselfs a different driver that day. I think he belong to Baretta family. Her older brother Tom—he a good driver.

We supposed to brings them goods that the ladies sewed to the Cape Fear dock. To ship it all out. Flour an' supplies too. Missus ain't goin' herself, so want me along to hand off the letter she attach. She know I read, an' she afeared the dock workers ain't gonna be able to. So I in charge of the letter. The goods is all goin' to Virg'nia. But they divided into different regiments. I put in charge of dividin' the parcels, accordin' to the regiments. There three or four us on this trip. But I wus the only gal. The others there wus men to do the haulin'.

When we gets to the dock, it buzzin' with activity. There be a ship in, an' I wus hopin' that David might be there. But I knowed that ship ain't the Hurt, so I try not to get too excited. It be the Dawson, an' I ain't sure whar' it from.

Tom an' me gots to finds the regiment clerks an' sort out the goods right. There be food stuffs to consider an' piece goods.

After a while, Tom told to wait outside the dock house—maybe he suppose'ta be gettin' his receipts. I told to wait in the wagon, while the fellas do their work.

But as I waitin', I spies the willow oak—that very same willow oak David an' me sit by. An' now it beckonin'. So 'course I climbs out'ta the wagon. I knows I shouldn't, but there ain't nobody to stop me.

It a sunny, warm June day, early afternoon. An' the oak has bright green new leaves that shimmer in the sun an' light breeze. The tree invite me over, glorious as it wus, with wide reachin' branches, lovely leaves, and knotty roots stickin' out of the dirt lak the knuckle bones of a giant.

The dock wus so busy; nobody take no notice of a young colored gal.

When I reach the tree, I walk around it, thinkin' of David, the starched gingham dress I wear that day, his love note…. Then, I take a notion to rub my hand against the thick bark by the back of the tree. It real rough, an' there, in a certain place, I notice, whar' there initials an' hearts carved all along the side. So I trace my hand in all them initials that cut deep, but I can't read, an'…goin' along the bark, I discovers, among the initials, some writing. A message. A message for me.

Me—Sarah Louise Smith. Sure as I know my name, I certain the message is for me. Yas. There carved into that tree—a message. I thinkin' that my angels must'ta brung me here to read this.

SL I LOVE YOU WAIT D

The world start spinnin' around when I reads this. I by myself, an' I slide down along the tree until I sittin' there. The June sun filtering through the leaves. Sixteen year ol' an' in love. "David," I say aloud. I feel my heart beatin', an' I feel suddenly that I on top of the world. There ain't nothin' I can't do.

Front of me is the hub-bub of this li'l port. The Dawson docked. Men, colored an' white, small as Hannah pin dolls workin'—dust stirred up as they movin', swarmin', a blur. But I feelin' absolutely alone for a moment. I just with myself. Feelin' as strong an' sturdy as the tree I up against.

Then David is there. Not really him, but his presence. I still don't knows if he receive my love letter that I send with Marcus so long ago. Don't knows when he carve this message, ain't no date on it. But he surely carve it, so deep an' clear, knowin' that my journey gonna take me to it.

So this is how we finds each other again. How we communicatin'. Ain't sure he get my message, but I sure gets his.

I stand up to go; the clear blue sky is so high, an' there ain't a cloud can reach it. Before I leave, I turns first an' I kiss that tree. An' that huge sad weight I carryin' for so long—just lift.

Right then an' there I swears to myself that I gonna live for my freedom. Don't know why I gets this idea. But I know that someday I gonna finds David. Somehow, we gonna be free together, an' so I know this for certain because it now carved into me lak the words carved into that tree. [*Ms. Augustus stops abruptly. All that can be heard is the sound of the scratchy tape as it winds. Then Ms. Augustus resumes, picking up right where she left off.*]

Baretta brother Tom find me as I be walkin' back toward him. He axe whar' I been. Say he worried, lookin' all over for me, think maybe somebody grab me. Say he checked the wagon half dozen time, an' I nowhar'. Then he say that by accident, he peer up the embankment, an' he see me walkin' back from this big ol' tree.

"What the heck yo' doin' here?" he want to know. "Yo' has women problems?

I looks up to answer, but nothin' come out my mouth. I only smile.

"What goin' on with yo', gal?" he shakin' his head, lookin' at me lak I something different on earth.

We go over to the dock whar' we finish our work, most goods unloaded. Two white men give me separate receipts to take to Missus. Goods an' supplies all set to get whar' they need to go. It be a hour ride back. Clippity clop we go. [*The tape machine is quickly turned off.*]

September 14, 1937

Hate this. Rain hard. Bones ache. An' the week just gettin' started. Take my pill earlier, so I be all right soon. If rain git real bad, we moves inside. Yo' chilly? I got a throw. *[The tape machine is turned off and then on a couple of times. Ms. Augustus resumes.]*

Our life then—it wus a whirlwind, catchin' us all up, Negroes an' white. An' nothin' we could do were gonna stop it.

Swell, like I say, he wus the first to run. A hothead. He thinkin' he be real smart, an' do all he thinkin' out loud. That wus what git him in trouble.

Marster at home. Ain't gone off to fight yet. Yeah, he against the war, but he go fight all the same. Missus, she wus goin' half crazy—she wanted the war but weren't so sure she want to lose her boys. Marse George, he just crazy for war, all for fightin'. Yo' could pack him up an' ship him overseas, an' he'd be ready to fight whatever war yo' put him to. An' Marse Norman, he wus for the war too. Only Marse Harry, he weren't so sure.

Then Marster find out Marse Harry 'bout to quit school up in Chapel Hill. Yo' knows they close that school durin' the war. We wus out on the veranda, me an' others—maybe Kate—an' through the wide open window I hears them discussin' what Marse Harry gonna do. He speakin' to his Pa an' say he gonna quit school. At first, Marster proud, thinkin' he have such a brave son, willin' to die for the cause.

"But that just it," I hear Marse Harry say. "I ain't gonna quit to join the troops. I quittin' to go teach school out west."

I got a small rug in my hand, 'bout to go tie me up a line to beat it. But I stop—we all stop to listen. The white gauze curtain be blowin' gentle, an' we all be findin' stuff to do near that window.

Then boom! Somethin' slam down. Maybe a book. Don't know who done the slammin'.

"What I'm saying, Pa…" Marse Harry voice so loud, it almost quiverin'… "is that I'm not quitting school to soldier. I got a friend, Thomas Phillips—you remember me talking about him—he and his kin are Quakers. They're all living out in Caldwell County. They need school masters there. Especially now, with the war. And this teaching post Phillips got lined up is going to exempt me from serving. That's the point. Tom and I are going to wait out the war and meanwhile do some good where it counts."

"The heck you are!" Marster voice carry. Another slam. "And don't walk away when I'm talking to you, young man!" Silence for a minute.

"Pa, the truth is, I'm against the war—on principle. I hate those Yankees; we all do, but I got to follow my heart. I'm against war—period. This war, all wars." Marse Harry calmin' down. "So I hope you understand, Pa. And you'll give me your blessing. I've already talked to Ma. She understands."

"It isn't Ma who needs to understand, son. It's you. You must realize that your people need you. Duty is calling. It's time to answer. Be a man." Marster ain't yellin' now. But his voice angry, low, full of hurt. "You have to see reason, son. Duty, honor first. I can't give you my blessing. Not to a man who won't serve his country when it needs him. You think about that."

That the end of what we hear. The curtain still blowin', an' we all gets on with our li'l chores. Later we finds out that Marse Harry quit school in Chapel Hill—an' he depart Fayett'ville for Caldwell County. But he didn't get away from the war. He end up conscripted a year or two later. After the war, he marry an' become a Quaker. Live out west part of the state. Can't remember if he have four or five chil'ren. Think his wife might'ta die of the flu. But Marster never forgive Marse Harry.

Come into late May when Swell finally run away. He some hothead, an' no surprise he the one that take it upon hisself to up an' leave. An' he try to takes someone with him, but that don't work out—an' yo' knows who I mean.

When I arrives home after that day—that crazy day I gets David message, well, I comes home ready for anythin'. Ma notice somethin' new in me right away. Same with Mar an' Kate. Even Hannah see I different.

Weather wus hot that time of year. Crops planted same as they wus before the war. Thought they wus goin' to plant mo', but ain't enough field hands. Some Negroes take up with their white masters for the war. Not at our place, but there be a shortage of hands if we need to hire.

White women folk gatherin' on the front veranda mo' than they uset'ta—sewin' for soldiers. Our young misses join in too—Miss Elizabeth, Miss Ellen, Miss Ida, Miss Mary. Others come too. At one point, Missus write off to Raleigh, an' join some Soldier Aid Association or Society.

Then, we gets clean materials sent down from Raleigh by stage. I remember big parcels tied up in plain brown paper an' how the stage driver hate to bring them, 'cause they so big an' cumbersome.

Then the youn' boys started takin' off—all fired up with soldierin'. 'Course they ain't got no notion of war. Their heads in the clouds. Some take their slaves along, as I say, but none of our does that. I hears that some Ellicott fellas do.

An' we gots ourselfs a new overseer. Marster say that he ain't tolerate no foolishness. He find this man, a free Negro, an' pay him wages to keep us workin'. Marster set him up in a cabin down a ways from the summer kitchen. It weren't nothin' but a ol' storage shed we use for household items. No windows, an' it sort of creaky. But Marster has it clean up good.

Uset'ta be that we rotate field men—ain't had no real overseer. So it a peculiar situation that Marster gonna pay good money out for the job.

His name wus Marvin. Some call him Mister M. An' he brought from Bladen County, south of Cumberland. They's a li'l backwards there. It in the country, rural, an' the largest town 'round them parts is Elizabeth.

Marvin a big man—dark-skinned, an' I remember hows he would sweat. Even if there be a evenin' breeze or it be a cool time a year. No matter. Mister M. would be in such a sweat that he work with his shirt off. Bare to the waist. He got big muscles an' them snake marks on his back. Same as Johnny.

Once when I goin' past Mister M.—he have his back by me, an' he gittin' water from the pump—I go by an' it seem to be that his snakes are letters. Words.

I can't helps myself, so I stops to read them. They spell out something. Marvin sense I behind him, an' he flip around with the meanest look in his eyes I ever see'd on man or beast.

"What yo' starin' at?" Mister M. snarl.

"I just lookin' at yo' back, Mister M. Them scars somethin' awful."

"They's what give me spirit, gal," he say. "Make me powerful. Drive me to drive yo'." Mister M. look me up an' down, then right in the eyes. Pierce me lak arrows.

I just nods an' move away, tryin' hard not to run—which I feels lak doin', but somehows knows that I better not. Never got to know what them letters say.

Marvin—he drive the field hands hard. No matter what our folks do, ain't good enough for Mister M. He has hisself a wagon, an' he ride it whar' they workin'. He stand up half naked, an' he crack a long bull whip.

"Yo' lazy, good-for-nothin' Niggas, ain't worth the food yo' white folks give to sustain yo' unworthy selfs." That the sort of thing he tell the field hands.

I see'd him out there. Mo' than once. Marvin, dark, sweaty, with his whip—crackin' it in the air. An' I seen him use it.

I passin' by the field, one whar' we gots corn planted. Hands out weedin' that day. Hot afternoon. Sun beatin' down, air thick so that it waver when yo' looks across the field. I be carryin' water. Never works the fields myself—none my folks do. We all trained for the house.

This day—think it still June—Mister M., he off his wagon, shoutin' at some gal. Wanna say it Sally, but that don't make sense. She gotta be Baretta people.

Well, he got this gal pinned to the ground, an' he shakin' her. Ain't usin' his whip. Just shakin' the life out'ta her. She a small thing, an' she shakin' lak a rag doll. Marvin, he rip her shift. She must'ta passed out, 'cause she gone limp. He have her down on the ground.

Folks around stop their work. But ain't nobody come to rescue this gal. Everyone scared, including' me—froze up, watchin' Marvin.

When he see us, he lift his head an' yell for us to go back to work. "Ain't no concern ya'll!" He look lak he the debil possessed, an' he 'bout to drag her off.

Swell, he at the end of the field, last row, almost at the lower pasture. Don't know how he see'd this, but he do—an' he come runnin' over, stompin' through the new corn. He hoppin' the rows, almost flyin'.

When he git to Marvin, who still on top of this gal, Swell 'bout to pull the gal out from under him, but Marvin—in one swift motion, almost lak he see'd Swell comin'—he swing around, an' he strike him full in the face. Smack in the jaw, an' I sees Swell knock backward from the blow. But he don't fall. He just steppin' back, in some crazy dance as he recover his balance.

Then the men is on top each other. Same moment, two womens git the gal, an' I there be too, with some water. I dabbin' her face. We pull her ripped dress to cover her. No, it weren't Sally. It a younger gal.

The men folks rush over, try to pull Mister M. an' Swell apart. But they strong men, an' they stick lak magnets.

We off to the side, revivin' the gal. She come to.

Two men finally hold Marvin an' Swell apart. They ragin' bulls, but it hot out, an' even they is tired. When Marvin return to his wagon, Swell stand there. Mister M. callin' back that he gonna get Swell horse whupped, an' Swell ain't never gonna walk again when Marster get through.

Swell shout out that everybody see'd what happen. Mister Marvin hisself hired to protect Marster property, an' look what he done—'bout to rape what he suppose' to protect. Swell say Marster gonna hear the truth.

A few minute pass when two hands come an' take Swell away across the field. Swell go with them, but before he leave, he shout out that God an' everybody here be his witness.

"Anyone got somethin' to say, better say it now." Mister M. yell out. Stand up tall on the wagon.

Then he continue, "If I hears one mo' thing about today, I gonna git all yo' hides whipped. 'Cause what I sees is a slave revolt. An' that a dangerous thing."

Marvin look at the gals. "That go for yo' too, especially yo'. An' he wink.

Then he make a big show of dustin' off his pants. He pick up the water bucket that almost empty in the wagon. Instead of raisin' the dipper, he lift the whole bucket, take a drink, an' splash what water left over hisself. Empty the bucket.

"It gonna be one sorry mess of Niggas when I git through," he say. "Ya'll gits back to work now! I has enough to worry 'bout without yo' sorry Niggas makin' mo' trouble."

Few minutes go by, an' Swell still in his rage. He a bull that don't want no pen. Wanna charge. He on the edge of the field whar the hands left him. An' he bend to do some weedin' right there. But his mind won't let him. He has to stomp off. I wus with my water bucket, almost empty, near by. So I follows him. Walk first, then has to lope to catch up.

When Marvin see us go, he shout, "Whar' yo' goin', Niggas?" He been sittin' back down on the buck board, but he raise hisself up his full height.

Swell keep walkin', an' so does I—hurryin' to keep up, till Marvin give up an' sit down.

So Swell an' me, we followin' the edge of the field. Hot sun beatin' down, bugs bitin', mosquitoes, field flies, as we makin' our way to the dirt path whar' we can cross. There a few folks around, not many. In the summer garden, some gals bent over with them big-brimmed straw hat they uset'ta wears.

And at the path, right as we about to go, Swell gently take my arm an' stop me. He look down right at me. He pantin' still, tore up an' sweaty. Me, I in a plain sack cloth dress with my half apron on.

"Gal, I gonna tells yo' somethin'."

I look at him. Swell ain't much of a talker. I just stands there.

"I gonna tells yo' 'cause yo' seen what done happen. An' yo' with me now. Ain't nobody else." Swell face drippin'.

"What yo' knows 'bout freedom?" He axe. "Yo' knows what it is?"

"Ain't ignorant," I says.

"When the time come, I wants yo' to tell my ma, Aunt Nancy, that I gonna be fine. That I comin' back to get her. She ain't to worry." I puts down my empty bucket.

"Whar' yo' goin'?" I axe. But I alreadys knows.

Swell bends down to me. "Tell Sammy I be back for him too. He ain't gonna understand—too young. He gonna miss me, but he can stays with my ma till I comes back. Got that?"

I repeats what he say, an' Swell seem satisfied.

"I goin' to Fort Monroe, up Virg'nia. Gonna fight for them Yankees. Tibs should do the same, maybe take Sammy up. Or maybe Sammy just wait for me. Swell speakin' slow—we face to face.

"Yo' ain't a child no mo', an' I trustin' yo' with my life. I might be crazy. Probably is."

"I gonna be free too, Swell," I say. The words just fall out'ta my mouth. Swell stare at me.

"I suppose we both crazy then." An' he smile. Real big.

"Yo' can trust me, Swell," I say. "I ain't gonna tell Marster or Missus— they ain't gonna know nothin' by me."

Swell take my hand in his, an' press it tight. He give me that wide smile again. "Gal," he say. "It take a long time to git whar' I need to go, but I gonna get there. An' sure enough I'll sees yo' again."

But that be it. The last time I sees Swell. Never made good his promise, never came back. But that be all right. I knowed he done meant what he say. [*Ms. Augustus takes a deep sigh, pauses for a few moments, then resumes.*]

'Course this incident has powerful ripples, but them ripples settle out before too long—lak castin' a stone into deep water—stone sink, an' sooner or later, them ripples disappear till all yo' see is calm.

Marster hire a slave catcher to brings Swell home. He post a notice in the Fayett'ville paper, with Swell name an' a description of the way he look. Man done track Swell to Virg'nia line, then he lose him. Rumors travel around that Swell must'ta made it to Fort Monroe, joined the Northern Army. No one knowed nothin' for sure, but Uncle Cicero would'a been proud of Swell for tryin'.

Next thing happen is Sammy try to run away too. He full of raw emotion, another hot-head. It be me that tell him 'bout Swell an' how Swell say he should stay put till Swell hisself come for him. I do lak Swell axe me to, but Sammy ain't a boy that thinkin' with a cool head. So he run, but he didn't make it no further than the Ellicott place. He leave in the dead of night—but some paterollers finds him right away. He come home beat up. Eye swollen, an' he got whip lashes all up an' down his li'l back. His clothes all tore up, an' he look pitiful. But that ain't break his spirit. No. Nothin' do that till Sammy get sold. Along with Tibs. They both gets sold to no good speculators—white men that gots nothin' better to do than to trade in human lifes.

Never knowed what happen to Tibs or Sammy. Sofia—she a mess. Don't knows if I tell yo' that Tibs is sweetheart to Sofia what work in the field. Somewhar' along in all this, they take up together. When they sells Tibs, Sofia one sad, sad gal.

So there don't be no fuss, Marster take them away early one Saturday mornin' before sun-up. By time we wakes, they gone. We gits to gossip, fret, but that ain't do no good. They ain't comin' home. Marster don't wants any troublesome Negroes with a war goin' on. An' he decide to join up hisself right after this happen. He too ol', but believe it be his duty to serve, an' he want things smooth while he gone. Missus an' Mister Marvin be left in charge to run things day to day.

Folks real upset about li'l Sammy an' Tibs. These—an' that Sandy gal, gone before my time—the only colored Marster see'd fit to sell. It a sad day when we finds out. Somebody say they put Sammy in chains—li'l Sammy. Whar' they gots chains to fit him?

I gonna takes me a short break. Not ready to finish up. Just a break. *[The tape machine is immediately snapped off. Ms. Augustus resumes after her break.]*

But all that wus at the beginnin' of the war. We colored all upsets 'bout Sammy, Tibs, Swell. An' Mister Marvin. Then Marster gone. Need to tell yo' 'bout that. Nobody know what gonna happen. Some hears 'bout them Yankees, how they lawless. An' I keep thinkin' 'bout David, how I miss him, that I be waitin' for him, some word.

We ain't gettin' much news. Some get a'hold of scraps of newspaper, but them stories don't make sense. Reports of battles in places we don't know. Some colored thinkin' that we gonna be shifted further South— them notions goin' around—some thinkin' we gonna get sold off, others thinkin' we gonna gets our freedom. A mess of ideas. There be mo' than one Negro thinkin' it be the end of the world. A field hand at the Smith place, he be prayin' in the field instead of choppin' weeds. Mister M. get wind of that, an' he done whip that man till he bleed.

But there so much hard work to be done that we has to settle down. The work keep us goin'. Can't be worryin' all the time. Everyone have to pull together. Work hard. Live day to day.

At first, white folks wus full of hope. Confederate soldiers winnin' battles, an' the women busy at home sewin' uniforms, piecin' blankets, makin' caps, knittin'. Spirits wus high, an' nobody guessed that the war wus gonna last.

There be privations. White folk couldn't get no coffee. Use chicory an' corn meal. Come out mo' lak stew. Even okra seed. That sure a strange tastin' brew! Suga' get low. Use cane molasses. Flour scarce. Aunt Patsy, she havin' to change all her recipes.

Marster join the second North Car'lina regiment. He kept sayin' he too ol', an' we thinkin' he gonna stay an' be part of the Home Guard, but he join up. Other men, landowners join too. Folks doin' what they gotta do.

An' now by the middle of that first year, all the boys gone. Marse George—no surprise, get hisself killed. It a woeful sad day for Missus when they brings him home. An' he wus lucky; not all the dead got return. But Marse George wus killed close by, so he get to come home. Marse George—pains me even now to thinks of him. He nice an' gentle when he a small boy. But he turn out to have hisself a mean streak. Never knowed what happen to make him such, but he be a disappointment to Marster an' Missus.

Marse Harry, Marse Norman—they all goes. Marse Harry, he take up with them Quakers, west part of the state. Take that teachin' post after all. Marse Norman fight in the mountains.

So the big house seem empty. Everyone whats left wus goin' about their chores, workin' harder with less. Fields to tend—the crops wus good that first year. An' I done told yo' 'bout them sewin' bees. Sewin' an' quiltin' out on the front porch. Women supportin' them needy soldiers.

An' things changed—for the worse. Soon it all be drudgery. Even them high spirits come down pretty quick. Didn't take much—a battle lost, a neighbor boy wounded or killed. Drudgery wear folks out, lak we travelin' some dirt road an' them wagon wheel ruts be cut too deep.

In slave quarters, things gittin' real dull. Mister Marvin take up with the liquor. Mornin', noon, night, Mister M. drunk. Sometime he so liquored up, he fall asleep in the wagon mid-day. It be right with the fielders.

An' there be them Negroes we heared 'bout that livin' in them rough camps to serve their masters. It discouragin' when they get killed. Some colored up an' leave, especially if they close to the line. But come to find that they be diggin' trenches an' doin' the same mess they do in slavery, just now for the Northern side.

Some blacks fightin' for the Confederacy. Arm against the Yankees. Colored ain't suppose to carry no rifle even for them Yanks. But they do. By the end of the war there be whole Confederate regiment an' Union one.

Some men desert. Them that can't soldier no mo', take off somewhar'. Home Guard pick them up, or sometimes they come home an' then go back. Or never return. We has ourselfs a deserter come to Smith Plantation that very first year. He from Georgia, an' he tryin to travel through Car'lina to his home. Come walkin' all the way from Virg'nia. Bedraggled an' weren't right in his head. *[There is a pause and a long sigh. Then, Ms. Augustus resumes.]*

I tired out, gonna takes a break. Evenin', tonight, I plan on thinkin' back. It some tangled chain, this story. Gonna wiggle out the knots. *[Ms. Augustus laughs, and the tape machine is promptly snapped off.]*

September 15, 1937

Gotta tells yo'. *[Some scuffling and scraping sounds, probably of chairs being adjusted, are heard.]* After yo' leaves, I don't has no visitors yesterday. By myself. It start to rain. Yo' know how my bones aches, an' them pills give to me by the doc don't help too much.

I creakin' around. Got enough for supper, I thinks, so I be all right. Haves myself a can of beans an' some salt crackers that comes in a box. Halfs broke, but I don' care.

I et my meal on the front porch whar' we sittin'. Not at the table inside. Too gloomy. It rainin' all day up through evenin', but it weren't fallin' hard, just a patter, an' the air good to breathe. Sometime can't get the right air when it close. So I sittin' here thinkin'— memories floatin' back—yo' heared of them fishes that find their way up from the ocean? What they called? Smelt? They swim their way up creek. That be my memories. A blur of li'l fishes, bits of color, an' I can't catch them or grab hold.

I recalls mo' today than I dids yesterday. I tell yo' that. An' I has me another one of them dreams. Tie into what Mammy Rae say at the end of the that first war summer. I wants to tell yo' that, only I gonna tells yo' this here dream first. Won't make no sense if I don't.

Strange thing is that this dream don't keep me up all night lak them others. It were a bad dream, terrible—yet somehow I falls back asleep, real sound till this mornin' when I wakes, the sun done already rise, so I get a late start.

Told yo' 'bout Pa an' his stories before the war. When he come on them Saturday night passes an' us gals gather around him to hear. How he tell us 'bout the debil shoes from the smithy. And how hangin' the horseshoe, ends up, outside the door, keep him far away.

Well, it be the debil from Pa stories in my dream. That an' what Mammy Rae tell me. All mixed with conjure. Aunt Patsy daughter, Sally, she in this dream too. Hadn't thought much about her, but there she were.

Well, I back on the Smith Plantation, a young gal—before the war, it must be. I goin' to my cabin from the big house. An ordinary day, but as I walkin', I notice it look lak rain 'bout to pour itself out from the heavens. *Big storm coming*, I thinks. So right quick I starts to run.

In the dream, it mo' gloomy than it were yesterday. Maybe that what trigger this dream.

So, I runnin' home to my cabin. In the dream, it about to pour, an' just as I runnin', not paying attention whar' I goes, I bumps full into Sally, walkin' the other way. She completely drenched, lak a well bucket been turned over her, though whar' we standin', it ain't rainin'. She wus just strollin' along, soakin' wet, not even mindin' it much. But I wus in such a hurry to gits home before the storm catch me that I smacks right into her, knocks us both down. Boom! An' there we be, sittin' in the dirt.

Sally turn to me. "It pourin' debils an' dogs, Sarah Louise," is what she say, an' she say it real calm. An' she don't seem angry at me for knockin' her off her feet.

"Debils an' dogs?" I say, tryin' to grasp her meanin'.

Then she say, "Don't take that path, Sarah Louise. Stay put." Sally calm an' sort'a detached, lak she sleep walkin'.

We sittin' in the dirt lak two dumb chicks. "Sally," I say, "We gots to gets ourselfs up." I nudge her.

But Sally don't say nothin'—she still in that other world—but she grab hold'a my arm, lak she gonna help me stand, or maybe she grab onto me for her own support. But she don't rise. "Ouch," I say, 'cause it hurt.

"Don't take that path, Sarah Louise!" she repeat again, this time real stern, lak she is gettin' angry. An' when she look at me, she lookin' past me.

"Why?" I axe. "Why can'ts I go home?" I now thinkin' Sally look lak a haint.

"Can't go home, Sarah Louise, 'cause this here is traveling rain," she say. "An' yo' don't wanna it ever to catch yo'. If it do—these debils an' dogs gonna change yo'—an' yo' ain't never gonna be the same.

"Travelin' rain need to stay behind yo'," Sally say, an' she now sure look possessed. "See what happenin' to me." We standin' on the dirt path. An' time is standin' still. Except that dark cloud seem to be movin' closer an' closer.

"Sally," I say. "We gotta go, gal. Can't be here with that storm comin'."

Sally still holdin' my arm real tight—never let it go. So I think she'll just come with me, 'cause she sort'a attached. I try to move, but Sally yank me back. Then, Sally turn sheet white. Lose her color; she bleached out. An' when I look at her, I notice how her clothes has all dried up. Her soaked clothes, hair, drippin' face—all dry up, lak she been in sunshine the whole afternoon.

Then I notice that she wearin' the same gingham dress I wear when I goes to meet David that second time. Miss 'Lizabeth dress it were, an' Sally, now she almost look lak Miss 'Lizabeth, 'bout as white an' fair complected.

An' I knows now that I be seein' a ghost.

"But I gots to git home," is what I yell in my dream. "The sky got its mouth wide open, an' it about to swallow us up!" An' as I say these words, the black sky take on a shape an' become a monster. Sure enough, we in its mouth.

"Yo' ain't never goin' home, Mrs. Augustus," Sally say in a deep, unnatural voice. "Travelin' rain gonna gets yo' if yo' do."

"Sally, yo' is the debil," I call out.

But she don't say nothin'; she just grippin' my arm, squeezin' so tight it stop the blood.

"Sally, let go! Yo' hurtin' me bad!" I screamin' 'cause my arm in such pain.

Then I thinkin', *Why she call me Mrs. Augustus*—that my married name. An' I ain't married yet when this dream take place.

I about to faint dead away when the first big drops fall. They ice cold, an' they wakes me up. I sit up here in bed, still dark out. But then lay my head down, an' off I falls back asleep so sound that I sleeps till late.

Weren't till coffee an' my toast this mornin' that my dream come back.

Now, I thinkin' that the debil ain't through with me yet. Look at my arm—it bruised. [*Before the tape machine is turned off, there is much clicking, and there are some very muffled, indistinct voices that can be heard. Then Ms. Augustus seems to begin mid-sentence.*]

…by the late summer crops need to be harvest, same as the year before. Some of Baretta people get sent to Raleigh to help the war effort, so we end up short-handed. Everybody get to work in the field. Even the young misses. But mostly they just tend to the summer garden.

Mammy Rae, she still at her dye-pot most days. Lots of cloth gettin' dyed gray. 'Course I wus sent there to helps her. So before I tell yo' about the harvest that year, I gonna tells what happen at the dye pot. How it connect to my dream.

Kate say she give up on boys—but I tell yo' 'bout her young man. Go by the name of Dirty Bones. That right. Dirty Bones, which ain't such a nice name for a beau. An' Kate, she want a beau that handsome with a nice name. She want romance in her life—not no Dirty Bones. So I tells yo' 'bout that next.

Now Missus that first year, she always in a fret. Take to yellin' at us. When she ain't sewin', she walkin' around, givin' orders. One time she catched Mister Marvin sleepin' in his wagon, an' she give him a rakin' down on the spot. Front of the fielders. Ain't help Mister Marvin none. No one wanna pay attention to him before, an' now they barely listenin'.

Anyways, I be by the dye-pot with Mammy Rae when she axe me 'bout David. It late summer, hot as a witch fire.

"What yo' gonna do 'bout him?" Mammy wanna know. She stirrin' the pot—me, I sittin' on the bench inside the lean-to, catchin' what small breeze come by.

"I gotta wait. That what I do. I wait. Yo' knows this message he carve out for me, so I waits. Can't do nothin' else." I swingin' my legs, but my feets don't touch the ground on this here high bench. No dirt stirred up. Only that soft breeze.

Mammy has herself a rhythm to her stirrin'. She got both hands on the big ladle she use.

"Yo' young," Mammy Rae say. "Yo' sure has time to wait. Ain't no reason to gives up yo' hope, child." Mammy start hummin' *Swing Low, Sweet Chariot*. She got a nice, full-body voice, real soothin', lak touchin' velvet. [*Ms. Augustus, in her high, wavering voice, begins to sing, interrupting herself with the story.*]

> *Swing low, sweet chariot,*
> *Comin' for to carry me home…*

Swing low, sweet chariot,
Comin' for to carry me home…

"But yo' ain't never goin' home," Mammy say.
"But I am home," I say. My cabin right down that dirt trail."

I looked over Jordan, an' what did I see?
Comin' for to carry me home…
A band of angels comin' after me,
Coming for to carry me home.

"I talkin' 'bout yo' angels, Sarah Louise," Mammy say. An' she stop her stirrin' for a moment. "Yo' band of angels is gonna carry yo', but yo' ain't never gonna go home."

"I don't understand," I say. But I rise up from the bench an' stand beside her.

"Yo' wait for David. It the right thing to do. Yo' gonna live a long time, longer than any us, Sarah Louise." Mammy stop for a minute, catch her breath. Her words hang in the air. Seem to me she talkin' riddles.

"An' yo' gonna travel through some dark, stormy weather, an' there ain't nothin' I can do 'bout it, ain't nothin' anyone can do. The angels gonna carry yo', but not to home the way yo' might think."

Mammy turn around, leaves her ladle in the pot, an' give me a hug. She gots tears in her eyes as she press her big warm body against me, an' I smells her salty herbs an' fragrant, spicy skin. There ain't been no one since lak Mammy Rae.

Mammy begin to stroke me lak I a li'l kitten again. She ain't never got no chil'ren of her own, but she sure know how to make a chil' feel fine. She don't last long though—no. I ain't tell yo' this earlier. She gone soon after this talk we has. Lawd call her back. Wish there a Mammy Rae around today. Yas. We needs mo' Mammy Raes in the world. *[Ms. Augustus sighs, and then she continues after a short pause. The tape sounds very scratchy, but just continues to record.]*

Now, 'bout Kate an' Dirty Bones. It happen that first war summer after Mammy gone an' before the Missus take me away.

[Ms. Augustus laughs a little. She clears her throat and then resumes.] I tell yo' 'bout how I leaves. But first, I starts with Kate.

Yo' recalls how Mar married to James Henry, owned by the McNeils that lives close by. War start an' they don'ts get to see each other real often for awhile—can't travel without no pass. But after our white men leave to fights the war, mo' colored starts gettin' around. First, white folks think colored gonna rise up, an' they clamp down—no passes. Then it fall back to the way it wus, get pretty lax. Especially here when Marster go. An' folks too busy with the war. Less paterollers. Everyone caught up an' makin' do on the home front. Ain't enough white men go around. Field hands needed mo' than ever. No one want to punish the colored much.

It wus that summer Kate has herself a idea. She thinks that she need a beau, an' she axe James Henry if he got hisself a young friend she coulds meets. We still ain't allowed no dances. But we sure is havin' some lively camp meetin's.

Well, James Henry, he nice to Mar, nice to all folk. He just a shy, humble ol' boy. Everyone like James.

One day, James Henry an' Kate gets to talkin'. An' Kate complainin' that she ain't never had no beau. She be too plain. So James, he tell Kate that no, she real pretty, an' he know just the man for her.

James tell Kate that this boy, a manservant, ain't no fielder, an' he good-lookin' besides. Just her type. Only he a bit older than her, maybe twenty-five. Ain't never married or nothin', just God-fearin', quiet sort, respectful, with good manners. He so good, in fact, he attend to Mister Harris McNeil hisself. But Mister Harris gone, an' this here man, he become a driver, an' he drive this way often. Just this very same week, he come with Mrs. McNeil 'cause she a regular in the ladies sewin' circle what meet at the Smith place.

Now, Kate, Mar, an' me, we settin' outside the tool shed that become their cabin. Must'ta been Saturday night, late. Mar an' James Henry settin' on the stone stoop. Kate dress up with a clean shift so as to makes herself suitable for courtin', though she ain't exactly courtin' yet. She settin' on a stump of a cut down pine. I perched on half-broke child chair that I found an' brung with me.

"How tall is this fella?" Kate wanna know.

"He tall an' slim. But he strong too," James Henry say, Mar settin' now on his lap.

"Yo' ain't tell me his name," Kate say. "What his name? Has I seen him before?" Kate lean forward lak a horse ready to leaves the gate.

"Yo' probably seen him, Kate. But lak I say, he uset'ta be with Mister McNeil, an' he ain't been allowed to much dances."

"His name, James Henry! Yo' gonna tell me, or I has to begs yo' for it?" What he called? Do he know about me? Did yo' tells him anythin'?" Kate talkin' before she thinkin', which she often do.

"Well, I gonna tell yo, Kate. But it only the name he called, ain't his real name." James take a breath, then he just say it. "He go by Dirty Bones."

Kate drop her mouth lak all a'sudden she hungry for flies.

"I ain't goin' with no man name Dirty Bones!" Kate say, an' she raise herself up. "What the matter with him? Don't he wash hisself?"

"His real name—is Abraham Walker. Dirty Bones what people calls him. Don't mean nothin'. Just a nickname. "Ain't yo' got one, Kate? What yo' go by?"

"Why they calls him that? Kate got her face screwed up lak she just et some of Aunt Patsy horehound stew. She up an' prancin' 'bout.

"Don't gets yo'self all in a mess! He gits this name when he a boy an' uset'ta play by the shoat pen. His ma say he dirty in his bones. Don't mean nothin'. She make the name up. It stick."

"Well, I gotta thinks about it. Growed man allow hisself to go by a name lak that ain't got no self-respect." Kate come this conclusion, feel pretty much satisfied. She go, "Humph!" An' she set herself down again.

An' that be it for awhile. Next day, James leave, an' there no mo' talk of Dirty Bones or beaus for Kate. But a'course, she get to eat her words. Yas, she do. *[There is a pause, and the tape keeps playing. Then, Ms. Augustus says that she is at a good stopping place and done for the day.]*

September 16, 1937

No mo' dreams last night. I happy 'bout that. I gonna tells yo' now how I leaves the plantation. Remember how Sally come to me in the dream as a debil haint, tellin' me I ain't gonna go home? Never finds me a way home? An' that what Mammy Rae tell me too, in real life?

Well, Mammy Rae die soon after that conversation. Breathin' one day, dead the next. Maybe it weren't the next day exactly, but I never see'd her alive again.

Mammy Rae… what can I say? I hope that generations gonna hear 'bout her 'cause the good Lawd ain't makin' folks lak that no mo'. He give Mammy a heart full of love, then He give her conjure power. Her big ol' self, with her big bosom, always at her dye pot lak she could change the colors in the world.

Somebody find her when she don't show up for her chores. She live alone, an' someone go to her cabin to check if she have herself a problem. Mammy always on time, could sets yo' clock by her—if yo' had one.

Might'ta been Sally who done finds her. Mammy passed out—dead on her cot. Calm as anythin'. When Sally finds her, she think Mammy just sleepin' sound. But she gently shake an' know right away Mammy dead. Go in her sleep. Nobody know how ol' she is. There weren't no family Bible with her dates.

Folks say death just another stage of life. Movin' through to the other side. Jesus come down from His heaven an' give us His hand to lift us up to the final restin' place. Sweet Jesus be with us for that last journey home.

Can't thinks of her none without gittin' teary. [*Ms. Augustus lets out a deep sigh before continuing.*]

I knows yo' thinkin' this happen a long time ago, how can a skinny, dry-up ol' woman find the tears to cry. After all I been through. An' if I has any left, why waste them on those that passed so long ago?

An' who gonna mourn for me? I so close now that if I had me a stepstool, I could climb up to Heaven myself.

I tell yo' what I thinks. Life ain't no long flat road. It mo' lak the night sky with stars, an' we all shinin' an' connected. Most don't see how, but Mammy Rae did. She a seer—conjure up the universe—till she see how we all connected.

I wanna stop. [*The tape machine is abruptly clicked off and then on again a few times before Ms. Augustus continues.*]

When Mammy Rae die, we has us a funeral. Nice. A camp meetin' service, then another service graveside. I wus pretty broke up. It wus a hot day in late August.

No white mens at the funeral, a'course. We bury her in the li'l slave cemetery whar' Uncle Cicero rest. They sleepin' side by side—neighbors. It were a big coffin, an' somebody painted the outside red—in honor of all the color Mammy Rae brung to people lives with her dye pot. Ain't never seen a red coffin before or since.

Each of us that loved her carried a flower to her grave, an' after the prayer an' Bible verse get read, we step forward to give a testimonial. I had a white gardenia, picked because it the color of undyed cloth—I wanted somethin' natural. An' there ain't nothin' sweeter smellin' than a gardenia.

But soon enough we had to go back to work, so it wus "ashes to ashes, dust to dust" an' somebody lay in the first shovelful of dirt. That first thump always hit hard. We each take our turn, then sing. *[Ms. Augustus pauses for a moment, seems to catch her breath in preparation of the song that follows. Again, Ms. Augustus's voice is high, wavering, but very clear.]*

> *Hark from the tomb, a doleful sound,*
> *My ears hear a tender cry—*
> *A livin' woman done comin' through the ground*
> *Whar' we may all shortly lie.*
> *Here is the clay, may be yo' bed,*
> *In spite of all yo' toil,*
> *Let all the wise bow down a reverent head*
> *Must lie as low as ours…*

Wish I could remember the whole song. It bring me back. *[There is a brief pause before Ms. Augustus continues.]*

After Mammy Rae die, I couldn't et no food for awhile. Belly always hurt too much. Folks today, with all our medicine, forgets that when the body ain't well, we need to look to the heart. When I comin' up, folks understood that. Didn't need all these pills what docs give now.

It be just a few weeks later that Missus get a notion that she an' all the young misses should go to Virg'nia to stay with kin. Summer 'bout gone, an' they gonna wait until most of the crops get harvested, then go before the weather turn cold.

Marster wus expected home any day to take care of things. He comin' on leave. So it wus all suppose to work out. Meanwhiles, Missus busy gettin' herself ready. Trunks down from the attic—they needs to be cleaned, fresh'ed up. Some harnesses need repair. Carriage too.

But September come, an' Marster still don't arrive. Missus find me out by Mammy dye pot. I be helpin' Aunt Patsy who took charge in Mammy place.

"Sarah Louise, I want a word," she say.

I dry my hands on my stained apron an' go to her. She alone, standin' in the heat an' sunshine. She have her hair all neat up, no bonnet though.

"I ain't so presentable, ma'am," I say.

"That's all right." When I by her, she nod at me an' begin to walk the path toward the big house. So I follow, walkin' a li'l behind.

"Now, you know that we plan to leave soon for Virginny."

"Yas, Missus, I sure knowed."

"Well, I want you to come with us. So do all the young misses. We took a vote this morning, and of all the Nigga gals here that could attend to them, they want you." We near the summer kitchen, an' I cans smells fresh bread. All my goin' without eatin' suddenly catchin' up with me.

"I heared you're still mourning for our Mammy Rae. You aren't eating or taking care of yourself. That right, Sarah Louise?" Missus axe.

"Ma'am, I done lost my appetite when she die. But that bread sure smell good."

"I'll call a servant to get you some—right after we finish. That sound fine? Time to stop this foolishness." Missus look at me, an' I nod my head. I ready to agree to anythin', that bread smell so good.

"So that's how it is. You will be coming along. You're certainly old enough to leave your ma. Why, you must be sixteen years by now—that right? Almost a woman. Look at you!" Missus stand back lak there a crowd waitin' to come an' admire me.

"Ma'am," I say. "I ain't never been nowhar' before. What Ma gonna say?"

"You never mind. I tell her myself." She walk behind an' call out to the kitchen. Sally there, an' she come wipin' her hands on her apron. Missus tell Sally to git me some of that fresh bread, other victuals too. Sally look up to see me an' Missus, curtsey, an' go to the kitchen to do what she told.

"Sally will bring you something, and when you're done, I want you to go back an' help Aunt Patsy finish with that dye lot. No dilly-dallying. You eat first. Then get yourself moving right along."

"Thank you. Yas ma'am," I say, doin' my own curtsey. But as Missus leave, I axe, "Excuse me, ma'am, when we gonna leaves?"

"Just pack up your things tonight and be ready. We leave when I say so. I'll have someone get you when I'm ready. One of the servants. That's it, Sarah Louise." Missus voice firm. "Ah, here Sally comes now." Missus give me a small smile, lak she got a twitch in her mouth—she ain't got the same generous spirit her gals has.

Sally bring me a plate with some ham an' fresh bread. Taste awful good. Sally leave me on the stoop without axin' anythin' 'cause she gots somethin' on the stove that need tendin'.

By the time I go returns to Aunt Patsy at the dye pot, she already knowed I wus goin'.

I didn't has much to pack, just a few things, an' I puts them in a ol' straw basket with a lid an' a oak branch handle. Ma help fancy it up by weavin' in some rags. By time she done, that basket look real pretty.

Just three of us go to Virg'nia—Aunt Nancy, to help with the cookin'; Tom, Baretta brother, who ain't as bad as some of Baretta kin, to drive an' do repairs if we need them, an' me. I goin' as a lady maid.

Ma cry when I tellin' her I 'bout to leaves. She call me her "baby gal," say she sure gonna miss me. Hug me tight, an' spend almost a whole week tellin' me all the things I needs to beware of…what not to do, what to do, how to watch out for bad menfolk—that her biggest concern. An' she wus right 'bout that. *[Ms. Augustus abruptly stops speaking. The scratchy tape is heard and there is silence. Then, Ms. Augustus begins speaking again, just as abruptly.]*

It wus the last of September when I get word we be leavin' next morning. Still no Marster. 'Course, Mar an' Kate wus there when I leaves.

The carriage were repainted a glossy black, an' two gelded horses wus harnessed up, stampin' in place, ready to go. Tom load the baggage—take a while an' there plenty of goods piled on top whar' the carriage got some rails to strap to. There a back place that hold luggage too. Tom use our hemp rope—the rope we make right there. An' he gots plenty to tie down.

Others come too—most the plantation, exceptin' them in the fields. Oh, an' li'l Hannah, she take herself a big runnin' leap right into my arms when I on the carriage steps, goin' in.

It wus very early, barely sun-up. Ol' man rooster still crowin'. The air damp an' chill, almost cold. We wus all gathered by the big house, an' everyone wus wavin' to us after we gets ourself settled in the carriage—yas, I wus in the carriage with the white folks. An' as we pulled away, I could hear them callin' out their "good-byes."

Turn the thing off. Needs a quick break. Take some water. Throat dry. [*Before the interviewer can answer, the tape machine is shut off. There are a few more clicks, along with some dead scratchy tape, and then Ms. Augustus resumes, seemingly refreshed.*]

We on the Raleigh Road north at first. Then we take another road to the east. Never been so far from home before, an' I ain't recognizin' anything. We on the road two hours, an' I feels homesick already. The trees wus lookin' different, an' the earth wus mo' red clay the farther north we gits. The carriage ride ain't smooth, so we jostled half to death. I remembers Miss Ida curls—bouncing up an' down as we move.

It a long day. We stops to feeds an' water the horses. We also has us some food we et by the roadside, a creek whar' we water. We make good time, but the trip take almost three whole days.

By that first night we wus north of Smithfield, a long ways, an' we be stayin' at a distant relative home just south of Wilson, I recalls. It a big white house, but us slaves didn't go in it. We has our supper in the back yard, by the piazza, what they call it. The slaves there wus sort'a uppity, an' I was real homesick, thinkin' of Ma, Kate, Mar, Hannah, an' all that's left behind.

An' by the next evenin', we already in Virginny. It wus a long day in the carriage, but we made it past the line. I never been no place lak this.

The land rollin' on an' on. We stay at a farm outside a small town. It just a farm; Missus got no kin there. But she knowed the family.

Next evenin'—after another day of drivin' an' bumpin'—we got whar' we wus goin'. We wus somewhar' south of Norfolk, Virginny. That what I remember they say. Back Bay Plantation—they call it. The place got a big house, red brick an' stately. Not lak the white wood houses yo' see in North Car'lina. The main road to the big house wus gravel, not dirt, an' the whole place look elegant. So pretty an' fine that nobody never think a war wus goin' on.

The land wus green, an' the soil look rich an' dark. There must'ta been a hundred slaves livin' there in quarters, half mile down from the big house, whar' a river run by.

But I stayed with the white folk in the big house, on a cot set up in a hallway. It connect the regular kitchen with the rest of the house. Then there a outside covered walkway they calls "the dog-trot," 'cause they had plenty of dogs, all kinds, an' they always trottin' between the house kitchen an' the summer kitchen, lookin' for scraps—which they sometimes gets.

It a different life there, with its own set rhythms. I mostly learns how to helps our young misses get dressed, fix their hair, tend to them in any way they wants. I weren't allowed to mix with the rest of the slaves. I just suppose to mind the Missus an' stay around the big house.

I could tell I weren't in North Car'lina. Here they has all kinds of slaves—an' each one gots a real particular service he give. Back home, we got our regular chores, but we always doin' other stuff to make ourselfs useful. Here, a slave do one thing mainly. So if yo' ain't called or needed, yo' has plenty of time to be shiftin' 'bout. An' that the way it was.

I gonna skip around to the part I remember good. That be when a deserter from the Union come by for sanctuary. We had one at the Smith place, but he just a boy goin' home 'cause he young an' miss his folks. It wus around November that year. Maybe end of October.

They opens up a hospital nearby—it a makeshift place to serve the Confederate boys wounded in battle. I thinks they has one or two Bull Runs, an' another in Balls Bluff. I don't has a map of them parts, an' truth is, I ain't good at maps. Yo' can comes behinds me an' check them history books what were written down by them generals. They gives the place names an' dates—I ain't seen many of them. *[Ms. Augustus clears her throat, and there is a long pause, but the tape machine is not turned off. Ms. Augustus resumes where she left off.]*

Ain't never read no history. Of this war, nor no other. Ain't interested. It be white folks history that they tell—ain't colored. It go from battle to battle—them that won, numbers of men what die or gets theirself wounded. History be better if it wus told by common folks, black or white. Them that live it.

Yo' puttin' my story on this machine. Maybe folk one day gonna listen. Hear what I say.

Next birthday I turns ninety-three. Day I turn a hundred, I gonna be a century. Yo' come back then; I gonna still be around. Tell yo' mo'. If I remember. *[There is a short pause, and Ms. Augustus continues.]*

Well, that winter, early, must'ta been December by then—yas—when that wounded soldier, a blue-coat, come wanderin' down the drive. Some of us see him, an' hell break loose. Ain't no men at the place, an' the Missus that in charge—name McKethan—she get her huntin' rifle an' meet him on the front porch. Some slaves be watchin' from the side whar' they gots a large brick shed an' walkway.

Missus got her rifle cocked an' shouldered, an' the door wus closed behind her. She ain't sayin' nothin', an' we all be still as painted flowers on a wall. But when this Yankee come up close, we can see that he all bedraggled, wounded, draggin' his left leg behind him lak it ain't quite attach. He gots some white rag tie to his rifle. The bayonet wus gone, so it wus just the rifle. He got a Yankee cap on, but his uniform be ripped all through the hurt leg an' some by the sleeve.

"I come to surrender," he try to shout, though his sorrowful voice ain't none too strong. "Peace!" he say, as he come up the gravel drive, limpin', draggin' his left leg an' usin' his left hand to pull it along.

When he get closer, Missus put down her rifle. His face just filthy an' distorted, wracked with pain—a sight. He make it up to the front step an' collapse. He done carry hisself much as he could, an' he ain't got no strength left.

Missus won't go down to him. She call for a manservant from her household to go. He come an' prod the Yankee with a broom. The slave wus dressed in his fancy waist coat an' he don't wanna bend down, so he just poke him with the broom handle.

The soldier moan, so we knows he still alive. I gets a pretty fair look at him later. Two colored men come with a ol' barn door they use as a stretcher, an' they carry the Yankee around the house to the dog trot, which wus covered. They puts him there. The weather that day wus pretty warm, so they leaves him there till they can move him to the hospital set up near by.

I never speaks to this man, but them that do, tell me his story. He a young man, but he look scary, lak he right from battle, an' I ain't never see'd no one wounded, all tore up. He a Fed'ral soldier but wus raised in South Car'lina, near Charleston. He join up with the Union 'cause his family live in Pennsylvania. But he have a uncle in the South, an' after the South win Balls Bluff, he desert. He wus already wounded, but when the Confed'rate troops saw him, they shot. Left him for dead.

His commandin' officer wus Colonel Stone. An' he make the regiment charge across some river—an' they all gets shot an' wounded up the bank. The Confed'rate troops ain't showin' no mercy, an' they stabbing Yankees with them bayonets, killin' them. Many injured an' left to drown, theys bodies floatin' down river.

This man, name wus Smith. Ain't no relation. He has his whole left leg almost shot off. Blood everywhar'. When one of them McKethan slaves open up the ripped pant of his uniform, they finds a bloody mess. It a wonder he alive.

By afternoon, this Smith soldier get taken by some stretcher-bearers to the hospital close by. He look dead by then. Ain't even conscious. Eyes shut. Never finds out what happen to him.

Soon after this incident, we leaves to finish out winter in Fayett'ville. But we comin' back, Missus promise, next year, after spring planting. Mrs. McKethan take up helpin' at the hospital after this soldier get brung to it. Find she needed. An' our Missus decide she gonna help out next year. Gonna nurse the sick an' wounded. too. *[There is a short scratchy sound, then a long pause. Ms. Augustus seems to pick up in mid-sentence.]*

…Takes me a good break. Turn this thing off. *[The machine is quickly snapped off.]*

September 17, 1937

Friday, an' I ain't gonna make it a long day. I gotta go to the market this afternoon. An' this dry, cool weather gots me up an' movin'.

Now… it be near the end of that first year. Southerners still thinkin' they gonna win. On the way back, we take the same route, stoppin' at the same farmhouse, then at the other big house near Wilson. The same tiring three long days. The only eventful thing happen wus we meets Rebel cavalry. Don't knows what they doin' or recollect whar' we meets them, but they surely look lak lawless heathens on horseback. Drunk, dangerous men let loose on the world.

It wus on our second day. Ways to go yet. The road wus nearly empty, a few carriages, carts comin' through. We wus jostlin' through potholes wore by rain an' years of heavy travel. At some point, we needs to stop, water our horses an' us takes a break. An' there other needs to takes care of. We all lookin' forward to seein' kin, see what changes time done wrought at home.

The road come close to a river, an' Missus announce this a good place. Ain't sure if it a creek or a river; it wide but ain't deep. The bank kind of steep, so Tom unhitch the carriage, take the horses down to drink while we get out, stretch. Miss Ellen an' Miss Ida take themselfs off to some bushes. We got some food an' start snackin'. Missus look around for herself for a private place, not the bushes, but in the woods nearby.

Tom be the first to spy them. He call out, "I see soldiers! Soldiers comin'!"

When the Missus hear that, she order us inside the carriage, though it still weren't harness yet, an' Tom wus quick comin up the bank leadin' the horses with both hands.

I ain't exactly sure why Missus want us back inside. If there danger, we couldn't go nowhar'. But we all scurry. My heart a'pumpin' so loud I could hear it.

The youn' misses crowd in, gigglin' out'ta nerves—all sittin' close. Miss Ellen say that she should stands outside with her Momma, 'cause she the oldest. Miss Ida upset 'cause her new-sewn dress got catched up on a hawthorn bush an' ripped. She show me her skirt, near the back hem, an' I tell it but a small tear, nothin' we can't fix.

By the time we all settled, Tom begin to harness up the horses. Just Missus an' Tom outside. We can hear the cavalry comin' an' men callin' in the distance.

"Can't you move any faster, boy?" Missus axe.

"I movin' 'bout as fast as these ponies let me, ma'am," Tom reply. But Aunt Nancy an' I look at each other. We know that Tom be workin' slow, thinkin' he a man, ain't gonna be scared off by no soldier, think he can handle whatever comin' up.

An' sure enough, when the cavalry arrive, Tom still dawdlin'. Missus stand up in front of the carriage when the first soldier come 'cross the river, gallopin' up. The rest on the other bank, an' they ain't in any regular formation—not what we can see. They seem to be lollygaggin', jokin' on the other side. Some let their horses drink.

"Ma'am," the officer say. "I Colonel McSomething or Other, and we are the something cavalry of the Confederate States of America." He tip his cap. Ain't quite a salute. "Please state your name, where you are from, where you going, and your purpose."

"Sir," Missus begin. "My name is Henrietta Smith, and these are my daughters and my property. We are going home to Fayetteville, to our farm. We come from Virginia, where we were staying with kin on Back Bay Plantation, south of Norfolk. We all full-blooded patriots of the Confederacy." Missus next give him a official lookin' salute from beneath her bonnet, lak she a soldier herself.

Now this all takin' a few moments. Tom finish his harnessin', but he just standin' there lak he ready for action, soon as he called. Though this ain't the Fed'rals, he waitin' for a opportunity to prove hisself.

This officer standin' close by, but his men on the other side be noisy an' disruptive. An' then, as I lookin' at them, I see that they all drunk an' sort of disorderly. Some can hardly stay mounted. Others leanin' over the pummel, half asleep. I seen one fella reach for a flask, take a sip, an' pass it along to another.

"Do you have any papers, ma'am?" Mister Officer axe.

"Papers! What papers would you expect a lady to have?" Missus put out by the question, an' now she sizin' up the whole lot of them. She seein' what we seein' from the carriage.

Missus turn to Tom. "Are you finished with those harnesses, boy? Get on the bench and drive. We are leaving for home. We going back to the civilized world!"

"Ma'am, I need to check that carriage for contraband before you pull out," Officer say. "Contraband," he say again an' nods lak he official.

"Sir," Missus say. "You'll do no such thing. Your men are intoxicated. Drunk, drunk on duty. Anyone can see that, and I'll not have a single one of them—you included—check either my carriage or my property. If you make a move forward to molest us in any way, I'll report you!" Missus stop, give a sharp look around, lak she too good for the likes of them; then she get into the carriage.

By this time, Tom done finish his harnessin', an' he up on the driver bench. "Giddy-up," he say, an' off we goes down the road. As I look behind—an' we all see this—the officer standin' sternly, while his men be laughin'. One man actually slip off his horse, he be laughin' so hard. Then in the distance, we hears the officer shoot off his pistol in the air, tryin' to git his dignity back. But it ain't no use. It clear that Missus win her first battle of the war. *[There is a brief pause, and Ms. Augustus resumes.]*

When we finally arrives home, folks wus very happy to see us. Hannah growed so big, I barely knowed her. She speakin' clear now, an' she got a lot to say. Ma keep lookin' at me though, axin' how I been keepin', what I up to. If there be anythin' I needs to tells her.

Then there Kate, she lookin' lak the cat done swallow the canary bird—tell yo' mo' 'bout her later. Bet yo' can guess.

An' Mar, I quick finds out, is expectin' a baby in the spring. She still slender, so yo' couldn't half tell.

We has us a wet winter, which is good for the plantin'. We gonna plant extra sorghum this year. An' Missus say we gonna sow the seeds closer together. Harder to weed but get mo' yield. She say they do this up Virg'nia.

So this year we put in a whole field of close planted sorghum. Before the war, we never growed half as much. Now we already low on sugar, so the sorghum juice be good for molasses. When we harvest it, we has to strip, cut, head, an' load the stalks—difficult work. Then we grinds it real good, an' we has ourself a make-shift grinder an' a mule to turn. Then we boil the juice down in pots we keep near the field. The only good part is the eatin' we do afterward. We bakes us some sweet molasses bread an' make molasses taffy for the chil'ren. We et the sticky sweets, an' we has ourselfs a time then.

It wus good to be home. Though, truth be told, the place look a li'l weary, rundown than I remembers when I left. House need paintin', a front stair begin to split. Fences need tendin' to.

An' 'course, I thinkin' back to what Mammy say before she pass, that I ain't never comin' home. She usually a seer, but this time, I thinkin' she wrong.

But I gettin' ahead of myself. Gonna go back to a day—soon after I gets home, maybe a week or two—Ma an' me be standin' in the cabin, preparin' supper. Kate, Mar, an' Hannah been out late to the big house. They suppose to tote some fresh water an' kindlin' back home. It pretty cold outside, so we don't expect them to dilly-dally. An' we has a good, hot fire in the cabin. They knows they gonna get warm when they gits here.

Ma quiet, then she axe me if I needs to tell her somethin', 'cause if I do, I better hurry up an' get it off my chest.

"I fine, Ma. What yo' worried for? I be all right. Yo' knows that." I pourin' some corn meal batter into a pot, gonna have ourself some gruel—hot with butter an' smoked ham. We also got ourselfs some winter greens in a stew pot an' mush cookin' in the fireplace pot between the ashes. Ma been grindin' dry corn with a oak mortar an' pestle that Pa done carved for her. She ain't got no ready flour.

Ma puts down her tool an' come on over. I stirrin' the pot with the first batch of corn mush. Gotta keep stirrin' to keep it smooth. She give me a hug, an' she tell me that she just waitin' for a moment we alone, 'cause she gots to talk to me.

"I needs to know the truth, Sarah Louise. I sees yo' a big, fine gal, an' I needs to know." Ma got her serious face on.

"Ma, yo' gots to talk mo' plain," I say. "I don't knows what yo' mean."

"I meanin' this!" Ma reply, an' she fish somethin' out of her apron pocket. It a piece of paper, folded real small an' tight, an' I knows right away what it is, who it from.

"Ma," I say, "Let me explain."

"First, gal, yo' needs to read the thing; then yo' can explain. I gonna be waitin'." Ma done finish with her hug, an' now she seem cross. Ma hand me the note. "I'll take the spoon, Sarah Louise." Ma begin to stir now, but I feel her eyes on me good.

Carefully, I unfold the letter, an' yup, sure as yo' sittin' here, it another of David letters. Somehow it find his way to me, an' he expressin' his love.

I still has this letter—somewhar'. I searchin' for it this mornin' an' must'ta tore the house up. But I couldn't finds it. I got it somewhar', just can't lay my hands on it. I hopin' to read it to yo' when I finds it, 'cause it be a fine letter. I gonna has to tells yo' the best I can, 'cause I remember it good.

> *My Dear Miss Sarah Louise,*
>
> *Forgive me again for trying to write to you like this. I put this here letter in the hands of a woman who works in the kitchen at your plantation. She say you are gone to Virginia for a spell. I am at your place now as I write this quickly, because I must return to Wilmington before I am missed.*
>
> *I can't explain how I have come, but I want to profess to you again my love, tell you my news, and when you can expect to hears from me next. So I'll be brief, though my love for you is anything but.*
>
> *I am going to join a group of free colored soldiers—a regiment up North that is soon forming. Our goal is freedom and equality for our race. That means you and all your loved ones. The Confederacy will fall, and if I live to see it, I will come for you. We will marry and live in freedom with our children, in a future home I will build with my very own hands. My family has land in Maryland and in New York, and they have already promised some to us.*
>
> *So, Mrs. Augustus—for that's who you've been in my heart from the day we first kissed underneath that big oak tree—I close this letter with all my love, and I trust that you, my sweetheart, will wait for me.*
>
> *Sincerely in the Lord, Ever More,*
>
> *Your husband-to-be, Mister David Stephens Augustus*

Well, after I finish readin' this note, I look up, an' there's Ma lak she a kettle about to boil over. She got the pot off the fire an' stopped her stirrin'. She standin' there, starin' at me. Her arms is crossed, an' she tappin' her right foot lak she keepin' time to some distant drum.

"So, yo' near to be married—just 'bout—just 'bout, from what I readin'! An' course, yo' Ma, she the last one to knows."

"I wus gonna tell yo', Ma. It all happen so quick. Then, the last time I go to look for David, I couldn't finds him. So there be there nothin' to tell…"

"Glad yo' think this nothin', gal! Wonder what other li'l ol' nothin's yo' ain't tellin'! Yo' been with this no-good, Northern trash that call hisself a man?"

By this time, by this part, the whole family—exceptin' Pa, 'course—must'ta be home an' listenin' outside. Ma yellin' so that they prob'ly don't wanna come in. Rather stay outside.

Ma don't care; she too caught up. But then she say, "Whatever yo' tell me, yo' can tell the rest of yo' family—if they listenin', Sarah Louise. Everyone here know somethin' 'bout what goin' on—everyone but yo' very own ma." She raise her voice so that thems outside can hears. "Why should yo' ma know anythin'? She just the person that give yo' life."

"Ma, it ain't lak that," I begins. But Ma, she on a roll, an' there ain't nothin' gonna stop her.

"Before yo' leaves with Missus up Virginny, I knows somethin' up by the way yo' actin'. Carryin' on lak yo' a growed-up gal. An' to thinks it goin' on right before my very own eyes. Yo' ought'ta be ashamed of yo'self. Yo' better get down on yo' hands an' knees an' axe the good Lawd for forgiveness—'cause that certainly what yo' gonna need!"

"Ma," I say. "I'm sorry! But I ain't done nothin'." I wishin' Mar an' Kate would come in.

"Yo' better be sorry," Ma continue. "Yo' better be sorry 'cause yo' ain't marryin' no Northern black man I ain't never even laid eyes on. An' yo' think Marster, Missus, gonna say: *Oh, Sarah Louise, sure yo' cans marry yo' free black beau from New York, Maryland, or whar'ever he from. No problem, we just let yo' run off.*

"Ma," I say. "Yo' through? Yo' finish yellin' yet? Yo' wanna hears what I gots to say? Or yo' just wanna keeps on goin'?

"No, I ain't through. Yo' axin' me, an' I tellin' yo'—I ain't through! 'Cause when this note come to me, I tryin' to speak with yo' sisters, but they ain't tellin' me nothin'!" She raise her voice again. "They don't knows nothin', an' they ain't sayin' nothin'. Never seen such nothin' all the way around!" Ma let out a big breath, an' she take to pace back an' forth the way Marster sometime do. Her arms fold across her chest lak she a general takin' down her army.

"Ma," I say, "I can explain. I can. Yo'd lak David…"

"Sarah Louise, I gonna axe yo' to tells me the truth—I ain't axin' for no lies. I gots plenty of them already. The only thing I gets is from Aunt Patsy, an' she tell me that Mammy Rae—God rest her soul—she the one to axe. She know. But she dead! It hurt me to thinks how yo' own ma know nothin', an' Mammy Rae, that ain't even kin, she knowed what wus goin' on."

Ma look around the empty cabin. "An' now, whar' yo' sisters at? They gonna gives me trouble too." Ma sit down, hold her head in her hands, an' rub her temples.

"Ma, I hears yo' out. Yo' ready now for me to explain, or do yo' just wanna go on yellin'?" Then I lower my voice; I ain't so angry, just wanna say my piece.

"Suppose I say enough for now, so go ahead!" Ma quiet; the storm die down.

"Ma," I say. An' I take the greens out the fireplace, place them on the stone floor right by the fire. I go over an' sit by Ma. "I sorry," I say. An' I rub her back. She turn to me an' we hug. I sorry that Ma gots to learns 'bout David this way. But I pretty happy 'bout that love letter, which I keeps in my hand, folded again, an' puts in my dress pocket.

I tells Ma the whole truth—at least, most of it. Soon, Mar, Kate, an' Hannah come in, bringin' the cold air with them. They gots two big buckets of fresh water an' loads of kindlin' they get by the horse barn. A oak tree come down a month ago, an' there slow-burnin' wood that come from it. They bring some of that too.

We all sits down to supper by the fireplace. Li'l Hannah an' me sit on the floor, while Ma, Kate, an' Mar huddle around on the three only chairs we got.

The fight is over—an' they all glad to hear that Ma know most everythin', no big secret left. Durin' supper, we continue the talk. It take all night to settle down. Main thing is I has to convince Ma that David intentions is good. That we kiss, nothin' else. So Ma know I ain't a gal with loose morals, that I ain't gonna bring shame on myself an' the family. We go on—stayin' up later than usual. But by the end of the conversation, Ma all right with what happen, an' she say she gonna talk with Pa 'cause he ain't knowed nothin' 'bout any letters—she didn't wants to upsets him before knowin' the whole truth—from me. But Pa ain't no fool; he know somethin' up.

An' Ma ain't convinced 'bout this marryin'. Me an' David. Say it ain't gonna happen. David a young boy, thinkin' he can change the world. But the world don't change that easy. Ma say that the South likely gonna win the war, an' colored folks gonna go on lak they always do. *[Ms. Augustus pauses, sighs, and the machine is clicked off.]*

September 20, 1937

That on? Good. I picks up whar' I leaves off Friday. First, I gots to tells yo' that I search for David letter, but I can't finds it anywhar'. I rip out the lining of my trunk, but it ain't there. About drive me crazy. Looks inside the seam an' under my mattress—but it ain't there neither. It gotta show up, but it gonna to take me to my grave worryin' 'bout it, so I gonna has to lets it go for now. *[Some scraping sounds are heard, but the tape machine is left on.]*

It prob'ly 1862, whar's I leaves off. We home from Virginny that fall, 1861, an' it turn the next year. Missus uset'ta say "Vir-ginny." Lak it some person name. Virginia split in two. Lak the state.

We spends our Christmas home. No celebration. Nothin' but news of war. It a cold winter, but it quick.

No word from David. I carry his love note with me day an' night. Ma get right with the situation, an' she tell Pa, but we all be movin' on. Plenty else to do an' worry 'bout.

Kate take up with Dirty Bones, only she won't call him that. No. She call him Bram, short for Abraham. Another nick-name, an' it sort of stick. He come by nearly every day, 'cause he be the coach driver of the women an' young misses do the stitchin'. We has ourselfs a government contract for makin' uniforms, an' pieces come already cut to the plantation, but they needs to be sewed together. I do some stitchin' too sometime. Ain't so good at a straight sew.

When Bram arrive, he unharness the horse—a chestnut mare go by the name of Maggie—an' he visit Kate in the big house kitchen. That whar' they do their courtin'. Now, Bram ain't a handsome man, no. He got these buck teeth stick out when he smile, which he do a lot. He very sweet an' bashful. Smart too, though he can't read or write. An' if he laugh real hard 'cause Kate cuttin' up, he turn away lak he embarrassed to be havin' a good time. He ain't slender, but he stocky, strong, an' mo' serious than Kate, who always like to tease. But mostly they get along.

I thinks I told yo' that Mar get herself in the family way. She tall an' slim, so early on, it don't show. She get this glow, so it just look lak married life agree with her. Then, she fill out, least in the belly, an' she give birth before I leaves again for Back Bay.

Midway through, Mar seem lak she growin' a small watermelon inside. She take to wearin' loose-fittin' smocks with big ol' aprons tied up high beneath her bosom. She begin to waddle when she walk, has trouble with her chores. By then, she sure showin' good, an' Missus, the young misses, Ma, Pa—everyone knowed.

Don't wanna say much about this 'cause it sad. It a difficult thing for a gal to carry a baby for term, especially if it don't come right in the end. Not all babies get born—or live. Not all mothers neither.

Right here it wus a cold spell—thinks it middle of March, real changeable weather—when Mar has her baby in the privy. She think she havin' stomach pain, an' she go out to privy in the dead of night, alone. Next thing we hear is Mar stumblin' in, moanin' in pain, an' she callin' us, weepin' somethin' pitiful. She got a still-born infant daughter swaddled in her bloody nightgown. She wearin' her underclothes, barely make it through the cabin door.

Everyone wus fast asleep. When I hears her—I the first to rise—I off my pallet quick, an' there is Mar with her baby, lak I say, in the dark cabin. Mar sit down, almost collapse on a chair, baby swaddled on her lap. Bloody. Then Ma rise, Kate. Hannah sleep right through it.

The baby gal wus tiny but perfect. Her eyes wus closed. She copper-colored as Cape Fear. She born in the cowl. But Mar take it off by time we see the baby. Ma start up the fire to warm Mar, an' we has some candles. I drags my pallet close to the fire, an' get Mar to lie on it. She still bloody an' clingin' onto her baby gal.

We gather around her, an' Mar get into my sack, shiverin'. She show us her li'l girl. Blood all over Mar. Kate fetch some clean clothes, an' Ma take the baby, puts it in a basket an' return to Mar. We slip her out'ta her dirty clothes, get her into fresh ones—and get her some rags. Ma know what to do. She seen birth from when she a gal an' her ma wus a midwife. We heat some water, help Ma clean her up. We cover the baby gal, an' the next day burn all the bloody clothes outside.

Nothin' to say, really. Babies die all the time. This one die before it ever has a chance. Mar name it Wednesday, 'cause it wus born on that day, an' Mar say she always wanna remember an' say a extra prayer every Wednesday. This name help her remember. An' sure as I sittin' here, she pray for her Wednesday every week for the rest of her life.

There wus only a small ceremony. A handful of us family by the grave. Missus don't come—'cause she think it bad luck. Especially in war-time. Baby that born with a cowl bring sorrow. Especially if it die. *[There is a short pause in the tape. Then Ms. Augustus continues.]*

Mar got real sick with bleedin' after the baby come. She very weak. Aunt Patsy come take care of her. Give her herbs to stop the bleedin'— chokeberry an' sumac. Mar take it a few time a day for a week. Missus almost call Doc McNair, but Mar get well, so ain't no need. Aunt Nancy, she come too. Even Baretta come out of respect for Mar—they work together. Sally come. Others too.

The tiny coffin buried with Uncle Cicero down past the lower pasture. It were a gray day, cold, wind blowin'. We put Wednesday into ground, bury her in the basket closed up over with a cane lid. *[Ms. Augustus falls silent for a short time, then speaks.]*

This here part of her prayer. *{Ms. Augustus clears her throat and continues.]*

Lawd, yo' behind all creation,
before all creation,
yo' next to it, above it, an' within all creation.
Let the dead be blessed, Jesus, amen.

[There is another brief moment of silence.] Should be Wednesday today, but it ain't. It Monday. *[Another very brief silence follows. Then, Ms. Augustus resumes.]*

By spring—late spring 1862, May—after plantin' done, we take off for Virg'nia again. Same place, an' same people travelin'—me, Tom, Aunt Nancy, the Missus, an' all the young misses.

Mar recover. She a strong gal with strong faith. But she never get with child again. Somethin' gone wrong with this first one, an' it ain't never been right for poor Mar since.

So it be May 1862. Middle war. There wus some battles close to home. Not in Fayett'ville, lak when Sherman come later, but on the coast an' in the mountains west. It all hushed-up, but we knows there wus fightin'. Sometime the servants from the big house filch a newspaper. Think Baretta a culprit once—an' once Bram come to the house with a sorry li'l ripped-out article he got from somewhar'. Neither of them could read, so they pass what they has to the colored that can. Bram hand over what he got to Kate. Also, we listenin' close to the white folks, though they careful not to say much.

There be some fightin' on the Neuse River, near Goldsboro. Seem lak this be a sign that the end of the world be near. Certain colored believe this. White folk too. Some talk that way to scare people—thems that ignorant, especially. Believes the war gonna bring in the Second Comin', an' God be punishin' us for our sins.

Most slaves couldn't read, couldn't even write their own names. Many folks get religion. Look to the Bible, Old, New Testament. Gonna be the end, brought on by the wrath of God. Every notion pass around. Some colored thinkin' they gonna be set free, or thinkin' they gonna gets sacrificed—a Voodoo, conjure thing—even burned alive—I heared that—or sent down South.

Then, May, spring, 1862, Missus say we goin' to Virginny, return to Back Bay. Must'ta been the middle of June, 1862, by the time we actually leaves. Marster, he finally home from his service—around Christmas, before the year turn over. With Mar baby an' stuff goin' on, I almost forgot to tells yo'. Marster come home. But he doin' poorly. Never the same man. Ain't wounded—in his body, at least. An' Missus always say, "Thank God for that." But he seem despairin', take to bein' alone, an' he got a small painful catch to the way he walk. He take over runnin' the plantation again, an' he join the Home Guard, whar' he stay for the rest of the war.

At first, Marster fuss 'bout us travelin' north to Virg'nia at such a time. They's fightin' a big campaign, he keep sayin'. Ain't safe. But Missus tell him that we ain't aimin' to *go into the war*. Don't he know his geography? We only goin' south an' east of whar' the fightin' wus. So Marster give in—he done fight his battles.

So Marster only insist we wait a bit, which we do. Missus, meanwhile, she insist that the war comin' south eventually, so we might as well get to it. An' she tell Marster that she plannin' to do some good—hospital work, takin' care of our wounded soldiers.

We leaves early in the mornin'. Pretty day, plenty sunshine. This time we haves lots of boxes to be loaded—supplies, 'cause of Missus arrangement to works in the hospital. It take a long time gettin' the trunks an' boxes packed. Marster there, tryin' to give orders. But it really Missus that give them now. Marster take charge of the field hands, an' there no mo' Mister Marvin. He git his sorry self fired. When Marster come home, he hear 'bout Mister Marvin whippin', drinkin', sleepin' in his cart. Story go that Marster find him with a half-drunk corn liquor bottle in his wagon, sleepin' so hard, he snorin' up a song. Fielders uset'ta call it "Marvin Song." That bottle wus his only friend. He a hard, brutal man.

Folks say that Mr. Marvin come up from the deep south—that he a man with Indian blood too. An' when Marster fire him—he do it one mornin' right then an' there—in front of the fielders. Marster say that Swell escapin' be his fault. An' Marster blame him for harvest bein' so bad, though I don't remember it bein' so.

One of Baretta clan, Marster put him in charge of the field cart. But Marster watch over him close. Marster would hobble out to the field most days. Had to put a colored in charge 'cause there be a shortage of good white men. Only the rounders wus left.

This fella, this one from Baretta family, he a drunk too, but he knowed enough not to gets hisself caught. The family wus a sneaky bunch. Sometime they stealin' chickens, even hogs, an' cookin' them at night. But they never gets themselfs caught. This fella, can't remembers his name—but at least he ain't a mean drunk, just sort of ignorant lak all Baretta people.

Before we left that day in June, I recalls overhearin' Marster tellin' Missus how she shouldn't go north again, 'cause it too dangerous.

Marster an' Missus by the back veranda, an' I comin' from the dye shed to picks up some materials Missus want. When I hears them talkin', I stops.

"Just wish you'd think about it again, Henrietta," Marster say. He standin' real close to Missus, has her elbow in his hand.

"I have thought about it. A million times over. Sister says the fighting isn't close. You know I'd never take risks, J. B., not with the girls. We'll be safe, I promise you."

"You can't make that promise," Marster insist. But there ain't no liveliness in his voice. "You're all I have."

"Dear"—or some such she call him—"please remember that we were there last year. We were safe then, and Margaret says that it's fine safe. Our boys need us. Especially in the hospitals…"

"McClellan is having his campaign, and, I say that it isn't safe," Marster explain. "And don't tell me that our boys need you. Plenty of Virginia ladies are available to nurse."

"I am doing it for *our* boys, J. B., the ones we have and want home safely. What if everyone thought like…"

But then come Aunt Nancy, sayin' that Baretta done burn the tablecloth she iron. Nancy tol' that gal before, but she don't listen….

Missus leave Marster in the room alone. An' that the end. It be next week that we leave.

The day begin early. Sun just come up, an' the whole mornin' sparklin' lak it scrubbed clean. Birds chirpin', the big ol' magnolia tree has its shiny saucer flowers open an' smellin' sweet. Nature don't care if Mar baby is still-born or if boys is dyin' in some battlefield.

I come out from the path, near the summer garden, I takin' it all in, movin' slow. I see Marster an' Missus sayin' good-bye, the young misses fixin' themselves an' makin' sure their boxes get loaded.

I ain't in the mood to go this year. No. I rather stay with Mar, Ma, Kate, Hannah. I knows the journey gonna be long, an' there ain't no excitement in the adventure. Ain't even gone yet, an' already I homesick. That what I thinking as I approach the wagon. An' just as I thinkin' this, I hear a sound in the distance. It Mister Crow with his caw, caw, caw—cawin' loud an' shrill.

I look, see one li'l ol' bird up so high, it seem lak a speck in the blue sky. Ain't that bird callin'. Then a big dark shadow swoop. An' I hear the word, "Mad."

I be whippin' my head around, see if anybody notice this here crow or hear what he just say. But I ain't quite with the others yet. I on the path whar' it turn the corner to the big house; the stage wagon wus in the front, up by the stairs. All a'sudden, I feel lak I'm standin' outside myself. I ain't inhabitin' my body.

Just then I hear: "Sarah Louise, we wus lookin' for yo'." It be Ma that walk over to me an' break my mood.

"Yo' hear that, Ma?" I axe. "Yo' see that ol' Mister Crow? Hear what he say, Ma, did yo'?" Ma shake her head, tug me by my puff sleeve, try to wakes me up.

"Yo' better puts yo' head on right, gal." Ma be take me by the arm, walk me over to the carriage. "Everyone waitin' for yo', gal."

"She here now," Ma say.

"Sarah Louise, where have you been?" Missus turn an' pat the seat across from her, near Miss Ida. Young misses, everyone waitin' for me. "In here, Sarah Louise, before I lose my patience."

Ma turn me around by my shoulder an' give me a hug.

"Baby gal, I wants yo' behaves yo'self. Keep yo' head. There a war goin' on, an' rough men be afoot. Yo' hears what I sayin'?" Ma pull me away, give me a shake, then another hug, that feel powerful an' soothin' as any that Mammy Rae give.

"Ma," I say. An' big, fat tears start wellin' in my eyes.

"We gonna miss yo', Sarah Louise," say Kate an' Mar. They come up, an' they huggin' me too. Hannah sittin' on a tree stump by the edge of the dirt path I come from, pickin' some dandelions from a clump. She won't look at me.

I step up into the carriage. Tom fold the steps up. The carriage shake a bit as Tom move to the driver seat. Then I hears his "giddy-up," an' we off. [*Ms. Augustus pauses. Nothing is heard, except the old tape creaking and scratching. Ms. Augustus then continues.*]

Think I done for day. I picks up tomorrow with Mister Crow, what he say to me, an' what it come to mean. When we begins our journey that day—we didn't knows it at the time—but we movin' straight into war—just lak Missus say we wusn't but Marster say we wus. [*There are some scratchy sounds, and the machine is clicked off.*]

September 21, 1937

I tells yo' the truth. I thinkin' yesterday that I gonna brings myself bad luck. Mister Crow know that I talkin' about him, an' I afeared I conjure him up. Sometime it happen. So I wus reluctant to talk yesterday. But here I is this mornin'—after a good night sleep. No bad dreams. Wakes up to this fine, cool mornin', feelin' rested an' ready to go. [*There are some shifting noises and the sounds of chairs scrapings as Ms. Augustus pauses for a moment, then continues.*]

Now this first day of the second trip to Back Bay—wus pretty somber. We rollin' on that bumpy road, squeeze pretty close inside the carriage. A beautiful, clear day that turn hot. Ladies wearin' too much clothin'. It the fashion back then, an' that day did start out cool. Bodices, back then, they has to be laced as tight as yo' could pulls them. Barely catch yo' breath. So we wus rollin' along lak this, maybe a hour, when a wheel break. Crack on that bumpy road, an' we all hears it.

We just north of Fayett'ville. Tom, the only fella we got to fix it. The gals inside wus throwed all over to one side—colored on top of the young missus, an' Missus, she slide over first, an' land herself on the bottom of the heap.

"Whoa, whoa," Tom call out. He off the driver bench, try to calm the horses, an' quick is helpin' us all out. Door barely would open, but he get us out. When the horses still seem upset, Tom unharness them, stake them to a nearby pine.

The road wus empty. Nobody around. No house, no people. Just a large, open cotton field, a stand of pines across the road, an' a smaller cane field on the other side.

"Tom, you know how to fix this wheel?" Missus axe, when we out an' lookin' at the broken carriage, off balance, leanin'.

"We hit a big rock, Missus. A bolder exposed in a rut." No way to avoid it. It just be there. The horses ain't seen it. We lucky they ain't lame." Tom kneelin' down, surveyin' the wheel, which look pretty bad to me. One of the spokes is cracked, an' outer wheel rim is split.

"Can you fix it, Tom? That's what I'm asking." Missus stand there, waitin' on Tom, who still lookin' at the wheel an' shakin' his head.

"I thinks I can fix it so that maybe it last for a while, ma'am. But I gonna needs to repack the bundles to free up some hemp rope. It strong. I thinks I can wet it so it binds the rim. But we gots to replace both the rim and a few spokes before too long. Maybe when we gets to Wilson. They has a wood shop an' a smithy there. But, yas, ma'am. Thinks I cans handle this one." Tom noddin' his head lak he a man that can takes care of any problem.

"How long you think it will take?" Missus wanna knows.

"About two hours, at most. That ought'ta do it. Wet rope need to dry when I gits the rim bound up." Tom standin' up, his cap off as he talkin'. We all watchin' by the dirt road—if yo' can call it that: two gullies an' a ridge of dry up dirt an' grass.

Not much shade, an' Missus an' them young misses gettin' overheated. So we told to fan them. Back them times, ladies carry fancy imported fans made from whale bone an' silk. They open an' closes. So, Missus sit by the road, near some bushes by the pine stand, an' all the youn' misses sit around too. Aunt Nancy an' me each takes a fan an' commence to fannin' them.

Missus say somethin' 'bout how black skin made to take the heat. That we done born for it. That what the climate back in Africa is—swelterin' heat. So we wus made for this work. We listen, don't say nothin', just keep fannin', but we hot too.

Aunt Nancy, she sweatin' somethin' fierce. An' Miss Ida, she start complainin' 'bout how the fan ain't helpin' much, an' can't Aunt Nancy fan any faster?

Now, war or no war. This road deserted. We don't sees no one the whole time Tom fixin' the wheel. Tom, he drenched in sweat too. If he work at home, in the field, he take his shirt off. But here, ain't right to be half naked in front of ladies, so he keep it on. After 'bout half hour, Tom so wet, his shirt stickin' to him, an' it seem lak he take a dip in the Cape Fear.

An' just before Tom finish, that when it happen—Aunt Nancy give a swoon, an' there she go—down onto the soft pine straw in the stand. She give out a li'l sigh, a moan lak she wanna say somethin' but ain't sure what—then she fall slow in a gentle swirlin' motion—swoon. Strangest faint I ever see'd. Look lak God hand smooth her way down she land so soft.

Tom didn't see it. He wus loadin' up the carriage again, tyin' up boxes, except this time he don't has as much rope. Missus get up, but not the young misses. They just sit up. I stop my fannin' an' lift Aunt Nancy head. It real hot. Missus standin' there.

"Aunt Nancy," she call. "You wake up! Can you hear me?" Missus hot an' she say she ain't got the patience right now for no Negro shenanigans.

I take off my half-apron an' sit down to wipe Aunt Nancy brow. Her head is in my lap, an' she moanin', lak she tryin' to say somethin'.

"Loosen her dress some," I say. An' Missus come forward, take Aunt Nancy arms an' pull her up so I can get to the back whar' the buttons is.

"Aunt Nancy," I say. "We gonna give yo' some breathin' room."

"I be all right," Aunt Nancy whisper. "Just need a minute."

I be tryin' to unfasten the dress, an' a few buttons pop. I gather them, then go back to moppin' Aunt Nancy brow. She now sittin' up, an' she lean against me. The young misses seem unconcern. I guess they thinkin' Aunt Nancy just fine. They annoyed, thinkin' there gonna be a delay.

Tom come back to us an' say that he ready, the carriage ready. But then he see Aunt Nancy an' hear what happen, so he say he gonna carry her back into the coach, which he sort'ta do, one arm draped over his shoulder, an' he walkin' her back to the carriage, supportin' her weight.

Somehow we all manage to gits backs in. Aunt Nancy rousin', comin' mo' awake with a li'l water we give her. An' I leaves her dress undone 'cause she a big woman, an' that tight dress ain't help her none. Must'ta been over a hundred in the sun.

We all pile inside an' get ourselfs goin'. It still mornin', but we already tired out. Tom has us loaded so that the broke right wheel ain't got much weight on it. He bind it with the hemp rope, which he thin out by unwindin' the strands. He do a good job, an' we movin' again, though slow as any Sunday. An' yo' could hear the creakin' of the hemp rope as it stretch an' feel the thumpin' whar' the wheel wus bound. For a moment I begin thinkin' back to that day we watch the hangin' on Ramsey Street, an' how the cart wheel were so untrue. Thump, thump, thump.

So it take all day, but we gets to the Wilson place. The missus there, she be, I thinkin', some distant relation.

By time we arrive, the sun 'bout down. Missus an' other folk come out an' make a fuss about whar' we been —she wus expectin' us early for supper, an' we late. So on an' so forth. But she happy to see Missus an' the young misses is arrived safe.

Tom get to unload again, exceptin' now he gits help. His rope hold on the wheel, an' they has a small blacksmithy shop on the plantation. They take off the wheel an' fit in a new spoke. Then they clamps a new oak rim all around. I watch a smithy do this one time in a Fayett'ville shop on Hay Street.

Neither me or Aunt Nancy allowed in the big house. First, Aunt Nancy wus put in the summer kitchen, which were a big buildin', very big. But she ain't stay there but a couple of hours. It so hot in there with them bakin' bread, an' the oven heatin' an' all. So she get a cot in the yard. Aunt Nancy, she revive good, an' they's got a seamstress that fix the buttons on her dress.

We only stay overnight—an' we off the next day. Repairs made, we et a nice late supper an' has eggs an' biscuits in the mornin'. A treat. Everyone spirits revive.

Some of the goods, we leaves there—an' all the soldier uniforms that the ladies stitch down in Fayett'ville. They wus to be sent to Raleigh, I thinks, but I don'ts remember why we leave them all in Wilson. Maybe a stage come through.

Anyway, it soon be another steamin' day, just lak the one come before it. Sun boilin' hot by midmornin' an' stay that way to sundown.

By nightfall, we arrive at that same Virginny farm we stay at the last year. Seem they take in travelers. We beds down for the night in the barn. It cool for a summer night, an' we leaves the barn doors wide open, 'cause it had been closed up an' smell of manure. Not many slaves on this farm. Think there be three, one family, kept together.

We wakes up to corn mush fried in butter on a griddle. They has sorghum syrup what gets poured on top. It real good. We et our breakfast, say our goodbyes, an' soon we goes off again into another hot day. We begins on a long gravel driveway, turns on to a dirt, rutted ol' road, but at some point, it join again to the big road, made of hard-pack dirt, wide an' smooth.

We wus travelin' toward the war. This day, the road weren't deserted, an' we seen soldiers—especially when we cross over the North Landin' River. This wus all south of Norfolk—that the big city an' the Peninsula whar' all the fightin' be. General McClellan—he wus the Union man in charge. I knowed this 'cause David, after the war, had a saddle named for him.

We see'd soldiers, in gray, a couple dozen regiments maybe, marchin' north. An' when we gets across the river, we see lots an' lots of soldiers—whole regiments. Bedraggled—some of them. There be a stench 'bout. The battlefield wus miles off, but yo' could smell the fightin' on them. Blood, gunpowder, sweat, dirt, an' stinkin' flesh.

Missus, she has Tom stop the carriage, an' she speak to some officer. All them soldiers nearby, they takes their caps off to us. Their sweaty hair all matted.

Then we movin' again, gettin' closer. When we finally arrives at Back Bay, it ain't quite sundown yet. That last day seem to go by pretty fast. Things at Back Bay wus all a'buzzin'. Plenty of change from the year before. We come down that long drive, crunchin' the pea gravel, an' all the white folks come greet us—the young misses, Missus.

Me an' Tom an' Aunt Nancy wus hungry. We got us salt pork an' buttermilk biscuits. Uhmm, I remember how they good! Makes them with bacon fat.

That night—lak the year before—I sleepin' on a cot in the hallway. An' the house slaves they got wus happy to see us. Ain't so quick to put on airs. The war been ragin', they tells us. An' after every big battle, the Confed'rates brings wounded to lay there on the lawn till transfer to the hospital. That the hospital whar' the Missus gonna work. Me too. I gonna tells yo' 'bout that. What happen. How I does the nursin' with Doc Goldstein—an' what happen there. [*There is a brief sigh and a pause.*] First, I gonna tells yo' 'bout Tom.

Tom found hisself a gal here, an' they in love. Met last year, though I never knowed it till now. Her name Stella. She dark-skin an' work mostly in the summer garden. What she do other times, I don't knows. It about a acre or two, an' they grows squash, tomatoes, an' they has fruit trees all different kinds. They even has orange trees—in a makeshift green house. Other trees too, plum, apple, cherry. Slaves git whipped if they get caught stealin' fruit. Which they do. Stella bein' the main culprit I hears, though, far as I knows, she never git caught.

This here is a prize garden, so it be a privilege that Stella get to work there. Tom has his duties in the livery—that what he done last year. Groom them horses. They got big mighty work horses, Belgiums, with great big hooves, not lak the kinds we has in Fayett'ville. An' they has ponies an' regular horses—all sorts of fine animals. The stable made of stone an' brick, with lots of stalls, an' a ridin' ring inside. Must be three dozen horses they got stabled inside there.

The livery wus down a long path that go by the summer garden—that be how these two hook up. Yo' got to walk right by the garden to get to the stable.

What I hears—'cause there be lots of gossip here—is that Stella father be the marster of the house hisself. She dark complected, but she favored the marster, who work part time as a Presbyterian minister. That kind of thing seem common with them that preach. Don't know why. But it happen in Fayett'ville, Virginny, all over. *[Ms. Augustus sighs, hesitates, and then resumes.]*

But something bad wus 'bout happen on this trip. Lak Mister Crow say. He always right. I gonna tells yo'. But not yet. Ain't time. *[Ms. Augustus stops. She takes a breath, and there is a rather long silence before she begins.]*

Gonna tells yo' about how I gives a few of the Negro slaves here a education. Some of the housemaids. Gals. How I learns them to read an' write. I step outside the law, but them gals begs me. So I does it. An' I proud for what I done, an' later when I tells Ma, she proud too. *[There is another considerable pause, though the tape keeps running.]*

Whar' wus I? Gettin' jumbled. Wanna tells yo' 'bout Tom an' his new love, Stella. But I thinks I tell yo' next 'bout the great Atlantic Ocean. *[The tape machine is shut off and then clicked back on.]*

Now Back Bay Plantation be near Norfolk, an' that located by the ocean. Atlantic Ocean that I heared 'bout but ain't never see'd. They calls this whole area we in "The Peninsula." This whar' big battles wus fought in '62.

That Union general, the one with the saddle, he has his big campaign when we there that year. I knowed it recorded in history books, so yo' can check what I says. But I pretty sure I right.

This one day I wanna tell yo' 'bout, must'ta been in September. We take a trip from the Plantation 'cause Mrs. Smith say we all ready for a li'l break. A "outing," she call it.

First, we suppose to go to the docks near Virg'nia Beach. North of there, whar' they has deep water for the big ships that dock. Supplies be comin' there, an' Missus say we need to pick goods up.

We go by carriage, a big one, so there Negro gals lak myself, riding on the back bench outside, an' white folk ridin' inside. It were a long drive to get there, but we could see the beach before we even on the docks—which wus big an' very busy. White sand an' that big green-blue ocean.

This wus suppose to be a outin' for *our* young misses—docks, beach, somethin' they ain't never seen before, an' somethin' to gets their minds off the war. But by time we set off to go, all the gals from both plantations wanna come. Can't blame them. I goin' along to attend to our misses, an' there be two housemaids from Back Bay. Other gals wanna go when they finds out we visitin' the beach, but there ain't room for everyone. We have a full carriage, an' we gots to leave room on top for the supplies we pickin' up.

The carriage wus painted bright green, an' it wus big an' comfortable. The dock pick-up don't take long. Two men in uniform come toward us, an' the Negroes unload. There a small wagon there that pick up the packages, an' before yo' knows it, we leave the dock an' arrives at the white sand beach. I must'ta napped for some of it.

The beach—Sandbridge, it called—wus a long strip. An' as we gets off the carriage, a soft gusty wind greet us an' snatch up a couple of bonnets off the young ladies' heads. Them young gals is gigglin' right away, an' run to catch them up, tie them back in place. I remember that it be just us—our party—on that wide ribbon of sand, stretchin' far as the eye can see.

Nothin' as grand as that ocean. I stand there—ships out in the distance, an' the white sand beach beneath my boots lak fine sugar. There be shells too, pieces mostly, an' one of the young misses—a child around six year ol'—she take off her high-top shoes an' start runnin' an' twirlin' 'bout. Her name wus Sarah Louise too—lak me. Accordin' to Ma, I wus named after my great aunt. But she wus named after the white gal that owned her. Ain't sure what the relation wus for this young gal, but we end up with the same name.

Anyways, this is li'l Sarah Louise—when they call her, I be turnin' my head too—she take off her shoes an' go runnin' down the strand lak some wild, untame creature. She fly lak her powerful soul released. Her ma, the Missus, be shoutin' for her to come back. One of housemaids, a young Negra gal, take off down the beach, chasin' her.

The roar of the ocean wus callin' out to me. It in the air, carried by sea, wind, an' in them high white fluffy clouds. Waves seem to lift as they come to shore, crests with white rims, then they lower, sometimes crash down, claw themselves into the sand, an' pull back again.

An' there I be, watchin' this here li'l barefoot white gal, Sarah Louise, runnin' barefoot. Natural an' in the moment. Then I sees myself as her, runnin' up a ribbon of sand—travelin' that coast to somewhar' else. *[Ms. Augustus's voice here is high and strained. She takes a deep breath, and hesitates a moment before resuming.]*

As I stand there, I think maybe after the war, David an' me gonna visit here, returns to this same beautiful beach. We gonna be free. An' I gonna take off my shoes, feel the hot sugary sand between my toes. Even run an' twirl around lak this li'l Sarah Louise.

An' when David see me barefoot, he sure gonna axe, "Ain't yo' got no sense, gal?" But I gonna see he smilin'.

"No," I'll say. "I married yo', didn't I?" An' I gonna laughs an' takes off across the sand. David, he gonna takes off his boots an' follow me.

Turn this off, why don't yo'. *[The tape is snapped off. When Ms. Augustus resumes, it is the next day.]*

September 22, 1937

What yo' say 'bout this rain? Come pourin' down before dawn. Get me up early. My neighbor Mr. Plotkin—just move in—he say the rain gonna be here few days. See if he right. He from Russia. An' whar' he from, folks predict the weather by listenin' to birds.

Don't know 'bout that. But I pretty sure this cold rain gonna bring the fall. Cold rain bring cold weather'. Ain't look forward to winter this year. Hard time now, gonna git harder when folks needs to keep warm. *[There is some scratchiness in the tape and just a slight pause.]*

Whar' wus I? *[Some background noise is heard.]* No, don't turn it off. We just gettin' started.

Last night, after yo' leaves, I sittin' here, an' I thinkin' again how it don't make sense Missus take us north at such a dangerous time. Marster right.

We headed into war, not out'ta it. Men folk should be sendin' the women folk the other way. Make no sense. Marster so protective with his gals—the young misses an' Missus. But there we be.

Back Bay—it ain't nowhar' on the map. People always talkin' 'bout Norfolk. But Back Bay Plantation weren't a city or a town. Probably gone by now.

It must'ta been June—whar' I leaves off yesterday. Sometime in June, toward the middle. Spring plantin' in the ground, an' corn, sorghum comin' up good. There a lot of rain that spring. Almost too much.

Well, them slaves at Back Bay, lak I be tellin' yo', they be gossipin' an' gabbin'. Men folk, talkin' big 'bout how some of them gonna join the Union Army, gets theirselfs to Fort Monroe when the Yankees come to give them arms—which they wus expectin' to happen soon.

Fort Monroe be whar' Swell run off to. It located close by, an' slaves from all over take to runnin' to there. We hears that the Union soldiers wus acceptin' run'way Negroes. Men, women, an' chil'ren. Call them contraband—that something between slaves an' free.

A few men already lit out from Back Bay—that what get the gossip goin', boastin' 'bout who leave an' who leave next.

One fella, one of the slaves at Back Bay, a young blacksmith name Jukes. That what they calls him. About sixteen year ol', an' he be a smart boy, could do sums in his head. Add, subtract any numbers—without paper an' pen.

But Jukes ain't got no common sense. Good brain, but he never take the time to think anythin' out. He all action. Maybe that why he do sums so fast—didn't have no patience.

I only seen him a few times. He'd be workin' an' singin'. Had a good, strong voice, an' strong build. Dark skin an' handsome.

Story go that Jukes be one of them that take it in his head to run off to Fort Monroe. Exceptin' he leave so quick that he never bother with no directions. Ain't got the sense to axe which way. Just lit off.

So Jukes be thinkin' he travelin' north an' west, but he really travelin' south an' west. End up in the Great Dismal Swamp an' starve hisself to skin an' bones. Then the fool, he axe directions. Gets hisself caught up by some Rebel soldiers that cart him home in chains. Meanwhile, white folk in Back Bay publish a notice, offer a reward. Then Jukes arrive home, behind the stage that bring the mail. They has him walkin' in chains, hitched by a rope to the coach. He look ragged an' scared.

Everybody feel bad for Jukes 'cause he such a young man full of promise. He come home beaten, but that ain't nothin' to what happen next.

Now yo'd think that bein' in the middle of a war, white folks would has enough on their minds not to bother none with a fool Negro boy lak Jukes that ain't got hisself no sense. But no, they gonna make a example out'ta him. Tensions be so strong that folks think it a fine time to learn all colored a lesson so that nobody ever wanna run again.

Them white folks wus real scared—scared as much as Jukes wus when they brings him home. Only Jukes ain't got much to lose. White folks fear they lose they whole way of life.

We so close to the Union line, it don't take much to run. Everyone jittery. Armies here fightin' right next door. Men wus dying, an' when slaves lift their head, they always lookin' toward the sound of guns.

So Jukes, he come back hands chained, feet hobbled, trailing on a rope lak some stubborn mule behind the mail stage. He chained all up, an' he got on this big spiked collar. Iron an' heavy.

Yas, he a run'way an' gonna gits hisself freedom if he could. But he didn't know which way to run. Young. Ain't a bad fella. An' he now tells his white folk that he wus 'bout to return home on his own accord. That what he say. That he realize his mistake in runnin'. An' he wus sorry, weren't never gonna run again. That what he be sayin', anyways.

No one believe him. Maybe he weren't tellin' the truth. Maybe he see what in the wind. Scared.

He want leniency, but his white folks say he don't deserve none.

Instead he git whupped. His skinny, ratty, half-starved self. It wus pitiful. An' it seem to make the world seem harsher than it were.

We all called—no, *ordered*—out to watch. It wus the afternoon before dinner, just past noon, hottest part of day. It were the Missus at Back Bay that ordered us out there. She want Jukes gits his whippin' in public. I didn't wanna go. Maybe no one did. Ain't no joy in seein' a boy suffer.

When I see my Missus, I axe her plain if I gots to watch the whuppin'. She say, why yas, yo' better go. Everyone required.

Even my Missus—she watchin' off in the distance 'cause I see'd her—everyone look ashamed at what they doin'. Missus too. But nobody say nothin' to stop it. [*Ms. Augustus stops, and the tape is stopped and started again a couple of times before she begins again.*]

I seen hogs behave better toward their own than us. We all sinners. [*There's a rather long pause, and then Ms. Augustus continues.*]

So, Jukes gits hisself whipped bloody that day. Boy that can't find the right direction to run. Only hope that when he travel to Heaven he gonna get some direction. An' find his salvation for all he suffer on this earth.

This the first time I ever see'd someone git whupped. Run'way Johnny, he show me his scars along his back, them purple snakes. But them wus scars. I ain't seen wounds cut fresh. [*Ms. Augustus lets out a long, deep sigh, and she pauses.*]

I tell yo' mo' 'bout Jukes whuppin'. By sun up, folks already talkin' 'bout it. We has to do our chores, so we all scurryin' around. An' all the while Jukes chained in plain view to the large chestnut tree that by the front drive, right at the fork, whar' the pea gravel road splits to the big house an' off to the stable. He sittin' down, lookin' pitiful. Though Jukes ain't got no ma or pa, he gots his uncles an' aunties that love him the same. Night before, they sneaks him some food—nothin' much, biscuits an' water. He slunk down from bein' almost a man to a li'l bony, half-naked child.

At one point, I pluck up my courage—just after breakfast—'cause I see folk hands him nourishment—so I gives him a piece of cheese from the summer kitchen. He never look at me. I tell him, "Jukes, I knows. An' I sorry for yo'.

Jukes don't say nothin'. Don't look up. Just extend his bony arm out an' take the cheese.

"I is Sarah Louise Smith, an' I here with my Missus, her gals, an' couple other slaves from North Car'lina, Smith Plantation. Yo' know we here?"

"Don't knows nothin'," is what he say. Don't even look up. His face starin' into the crook of his other arm.

"I sorry for yo' pain…"

"Ain't nothin' for yo' be sorry 'bout. Yo' ain't do nothin'," Juke say in a muffled voice. Then he toss his head in a small nod, signal I need to go.

An' that it. I see'd how ashamed he be. I leave. Got to help Miss Ellen. She suppose to wear her new dress today. It come from material she send for last week, right here at Back Bay. With the war goin' on an' supplies short, she didn't know when it get shipped or if it gonna arrive safe. So she thrilled. I see the fabric. It a nice shade of blue, with li'l yeller dots woven in. Swiss dot they call it.

By mid-mornin' we all knows that before we has our dinner, we gonna have to gather by the deep well. By the chestnut tree that ol' as time. It mark the path whar' the stage coach road come by.

It wus still June. Warm day. Everythin' around full of glory—leaves, flowers, an' there be Jukes   so skinny yo' could see his ribs through his worn sack cloth shirt. The overseer, a ol' white man, with white hair but a stocky build, he unleash Jukes from the tree, an' he push Jukes toward the crowd that there. Jukes have his wrists bound behind him, an' the overseer give Jukes a small kick, just enough to makes him stumble, then fall.

"What you see here is degradation. Sin and degradation. This is what happens to them that don't follow God's will. Gather around, everyone! Come here, closer!" The overseer lift Juke arms lak he want him to praise the Lawd.

Some folks make a shufflin' with their feets, but no one move closer.

"That's right! You folks got to see good because what I'm going to do is for the good of everyone." The overseer take up a long cowhide that stuck in the crotch of a nearby tree. Jukes on his knees, hands tied behind. Overseer, he move back, look out across his audience; he on stage, 'bout to perform.

"I want two darkies to come forward. Two strong darkies to help me now. Show this coward that the Confederacy knows how to deal with those that run." He offer a wide grin.

No one come forward, an' no one say a word. All hushed. I standin' by the young misses, 'cause I been with them most the mornin'. We preparin' supplies for the hospital, whar' we goin' later that week.

Then the overseer crack his whip an' tell Jukes to rise, pick hisself up from the ground. Juke be kneeling there, his face cover in dust. Shirt filthy.

The overseer pick two field hands to hold him up. Say if they don't, they gonna git some of this too. He crack his whip again couple times. The sound as sharp, loud as rifle shot.

"Untie this boy's hands," overseer say. Then he tell the two field hands take off his shirt. Tell them to rip it, which they do.

"Jukes," overseer say. "I want you to strip down naked, boy. Naked as the day you were born."

"There women folk here…" Jukes begin to say. He cut off 'cause the whip strike him across his shoulder. He cower lak a pup, the fielders support his arms as Juke raise his untied hands over his face.

"You do what I say. These women and gals have seen men before. Ain't nothing new. If the ladies wish to look away, they can please themselves."

The white folks—young misses—they escorted into the house. Somehow I left there. Not axed to accompany them inside. The missus of the house, at Back Bay plantation, she the only white lady left.

Jukes is turn away from the crowd, an' he remove his pants, which wus dark stained in the crotch. The overseer then make the field hands take Jukes to the chestnut tree. He standin' so his naked back wus toward us. An' I see that he sweatin', an' his skin gleamin' in the hot sun. Then, the field hands instructed to tie Jukes to the chestnut tree, which they do an step aside.

"Who among you darkies can count?" overseer axe. "I need someone to do my counting."

Now I can counts good, but I ain't steppin' forward. An' I thinkin' there plenty that can count that won't come forward. I can't tells if the ignorant overseer can't count hisself, or he just want someone to do his work.

Finally, a ol' gentleman that look lak he ol' enough to seen the Revolution step out'ta the shadow of the large tool shed nearby.

"I can count," he say simply. "I can count this man way to salvation." I heared the words clear.

"Uncle," say the overseer, "I want you to count these stripes and shout out each one loud enough so the devil can hear you."

The ol' man wus crook-backed an' walk with a cane. His skin wus ebony. Darkest man I ever see'd. Look lak he a original from the bottom land of Africa. Yet had a way 'bout him. Dignified.

A woman near me say, "That Uncle Shofer. He gonna sooth Jukes just by bein' with him. A blessin' Uncle Shofer here." A few Negroes nod.

So it begin. Overseer take the whip an' lash poor Jukes. Uncle Shafer begin his count. "One!" he call out.

"Louder, Uncle," Overseer demand.

"Two!" Uncle Shafer raise his quiverin', ol' man voice up a notch.

When the stripe make contact with Juke back, I feel it. I think we all did—an' that the point. We watch Juke try to be a man, take his lashin' without a peep. But soon he utter some low moans, an' his body shake shake an' shake.

I feels each stripe go through me, the sting, sharp as a sewin' needle, an' there be lines of blood across Juke back an' shoulders.

The sound of the cowhide cut the air lak rifle fire—each stripe snap an' echo in the hot noon air. Other than that crackin', there be silence, exceptin' for Juke low moans what he couldn't help. It sticky an' hot that day— overseer hisself sweatin', right through his jacket, till he take it off.

We standin' there a long time. When I first come, I real hungry, but now my hunger gone.

Uncle Shafer face be lak a slab of stone. He just do his count, loud an' clear. An' there be Juke, all bloody, tied to the chestnut. [*Ms. Augustus pauses, clears her throat, and continues.*]

Overseer, he do his job thorough—forty lashes, then he stop. No mo', no less. Juke back a horrible mess.

We all numb—an' Jukes hisself—half dead. There be blood everywhar'—runnin' down his legs, puddlin' in the dirt an' in sparse grass by his bare feet. He barely conscious, slumped over, knees give out. The only thing keepin' him up is his tied hands. Look lak Christ hisself after the Roman soldiers done nail him to the cross. [*Ms. Augustus's voice is very high here, and she sounds very upset. She pauses for a moment, then resumes.*]

Needs me a break. Look at that bright sun shinin' out there. An' here I is, talkin' 'bout this terrible thing.

I wouldn't hurt a mangy ol' dog come up here beggin'—a stray. No. I'd find him a crust to eat an' water to drink. *[There is a long pause, and the machine is clicked off and on a few times. Some muddled voices are heard. When Ms. Augustus continues, it is clearly the later that same day.]*

At the Smith place, life weren't never so brutal. Now I thinks maybe we wus the exception.

Yo' a woman. Look to be chaste. An' yo' knows to stay clear of men that ain't up to no good. Ain't honorable. But slave gals at the mercy. A woman owned. Ain't no such thing as honor.

Jukes survive. But when the overseer done an' cut the rope from Jukes wrist, Jukes fall down lak he dead, a sad heap of flesh an' bones.

Some folks—them that knowed Jukes good—rush in. They carry him, bloody an' groanin', back to a cabin. I knowed it must'ta take months for cuts lak them to scab. An' that night Jukes come down with a high fever. Aunt Nancy called to help. Which she do. After that, I lost track.

Two days later, we wus ready to leave for our nursing duties. This trip gonna be me, the Missus, an' Miss Jo Ann—the eldest daughter at Back Bay. She weren't but twenty year ol' then, a pretty gal, school teacher before the war. We has lots of supplies to carry, an' there ain't much room. Missus—my Missus, who in charge—thinkin' we need to check out the situation, before we bring the young misses or Aunt Nancy along.

Missus say it gonna be hard, sad, dirty work, an' the young misses ain't up to them livin' conditions.

But Missus—she plenty stout an' ain't exactly the sensitive type. She take charge. Put together five big trunk of fresh washed linens an' ol', clean bed sheets for bandages. Put in some corn liquor too. An' second-hand clothes that wus worn, but still good. A collection. Plus, there be new uniforms—not the ones we sew in North Car'lina—them already sent to Raleigh. These others made local, ain't as good.

McClellan wus the general from the North, an' the battles we goin' near is part of what they call the Peninsula Campaign. The other general, Lee, he the Confederate one, an' take the lead. This wus the last part in the Seven Day Battles that go from the end of June to early July—right before Independence Day.

The hospital wus south of the real fightin'. Wounded soldiers wus sent back this way. There be a road an' a rail. Boats that come through inland rivers, creeks—all branches of the James, but most of them what wus wounded come by wagon road. We gets some men that be almost dead an' there weren't no hope, an' some that only injured.

It take us all day to get to this hospital. We supposed to stay there for two week at a time—live there, then return to Back Bay for mo' supplies. Maybe even lets the young misses come.

The hospital ain't a regular hospital—it a ol' brick church set up as one. Presbyterian—go by the name of Benns Church. Real grand—got a balcony, an' the whole place, up to the roof, brick. They sets up quarters for the white folks in the manse. Slaves stay in the carriage house, which were the stable in back. They ain't got no horses or livestock in there, just some pallets on the floor. Fresh hay an' pallets.

The church proper, it set up with cots, muslin stretch' over a wood frame with a joint that bend so it can fold up. The countryside around Benns wus beautiful—wide stretches of rollin' hills, green, lush, an' split rail fences. James River ain't too far to the north us. Look around, an' yo' couldn't tell there wus war close by—or anywhar'. But when them soldiers show up, they brung the war with them. Over the hillsides, they trash the green fields as they come. Inside the church, all them soldiers stink.

This the place whar' Mister Crow get his say. The debil live in places of death an' sickness. He love war an' soldiers.

Yo' axe me the other day to define history—an' I still ain't got no answer. I just a ol' Negro woman that come up when history bein' made.

I can tells yo' how legs an' arms git sawed. How soldiers die with their eyes wide open an' have nothin' to say. What happens when brutal men think they the ones in charge. [*Ms. Augustus's voice trails off, and she stops speaking for a few moments. Then, when she resumes, her voice no longer sounds sad but rather resolute.*]

Turn it off. This Wednesday. I be expectin' yo' back on Friday, not before. [*The tape machine is promptly clicked off.*]

September 24, 1937

Chill in the air feel good today, lak fall. Rain gone, air real fresh. This the way I lak it. Bones don't ache so. *[The machine is snapped off and on a few times.]*

Yesterday, I doin' laundry, straightenin' up, thinkin' 'bout my story, an' I hangin' out a bed sheet on the line. Early mornin', an' I alone in the back yard, with song birds chatterin'. Then I hears a lone crow. Ordinary crow, I think. Not my Mister Crow.

Clouds movin' across the sky. When I wus a gal, I thought them movin' clouds wus the earth movin'. Thought I could feel the planet shift.

I hang one sheet on the line, my pale blue one, an' I had to go in the house an' cry. Just thinkin' back. An' how nothin' in this world ever perfect. *[Ms. Augustus's voice is high, almost as if she is about to sing. Then, she stops speaking for a moment, clears her throat, and continues.]*

It wus summer 1862. An' lak I say on Wednesday, we nursin' some at the makeshift church hospital. The weather wus hot an' stifflin, an' we got real sick men—them with arms or legs blown half way off an' need to be sawed. Jesus done save them, but he ain't save their every part.

We charged with nursin' the ailing soldiers that come in. When we first gets there, just a few mens in our care. After the first big battle, they starts pourin' in. Camp packed with all sorts of wounded. I just a slave gal, but I soon charged with helpin' the doc—they so short-handed.

Some men that straggle into camp ain't even wounded—they tired mostly or gots the dysentery, an' they sets up field tents nearby. Some could be getting' back to fightin', but they linger. So pretty, peaceful by the church. Beautiful, not lak Fayett'ville, with its sand an' piney woods.

There a wide stretch of rollin' meadow whar' the soldier tents is—so different from them battle scenes. Nothin' burned or ravaged here. *[There is a lot of scratchiness on the tape here, and some words seem to be lost. When Ms. Augustus continues, she is mid-sentence.]*

…come on two stage coaches we hire at the rail station. Left Back Bay by coach, then travel by rail, then coach again.

The coaches let us off in front of the church so the mens can unload supplies. There a doc, Doctor Goldstein, come to greet us. He a young, new doc, Jewish, I hears later, he come from Germany. First I thinkin' he a ol' man, but whens I gets myself a good look, I see how young he is. He has wild dark hair but kind eyes. It wus only his long beard that make him appear older. He wear a leather butcher apron when he work, an' it wus covered in dry blood.

When he first come out to greet us, he wipe his hand on a cloth stuck in a pocket in his bloody apron, an' he extend it to us. He even put his hand out to me. But Missus stop him, an' we never shake. Which wus all right.

That first day wus overcast outside, air heavy, threatenin'. Men come to tote our bags—mine get carry over to the manse stable. Missus an' Miss Jo Ann, has their things brung to the manse. It must'ta been late afternoon, 'cause we has time to et an' do only a bit of work that first day.

We tired an' hungry from the long trip. They has makeshift tables set out on the property, away from the church. When I first walk by, the door wide open, an' I hear groans of misery an' sorrow issuing from within.

I hesitate at the open door, down the many brick steps that lead up. Doc Goldstein see me. "You ought to wash up and get some food before you start in," he say, an' give me one of his kind smiles. He come to be known for them. They nothin' I ever see'd before or since.

"Ain't so hungry," I say, an' cast my eyes down quick, 'cause there somethin' very personal 'bout the way Doc look at a person, an' Negroes wus taught not to look white folks in the eyes.

"You'll get accustomed to the smell," Doc say. "There is a large table and some hot food by the holly tree. Have a bite; then come see me. I'll put you to work." Doc still smilin', still lookin' at me.

"Whar' yo' be at?" I axe.

"Inside. You'll find me. What's your name?"

"Sarah Louise," I say. "I belong to the Smiths. Missus is the lady directin' them men there." An' I point.

Doc nod. Then he go walk up the brick church stair an' disappear into the dark.

I see the whar' the food is. There be covered dishes on a plain board table. Missus show up, an' so do Miss Jo Ann.

"Are you washed up?" Missus say to me.

"No, ma'am. Whar'?"

Missus point off, an' I see that we near a creek bank. Miss Jo Ann must'ta just come from there, she wipin' her hands on a clean flour towel. She pass it over to me.

"Go ahead," she nod. "Keep it." An' I take the towel, go off to the creek to wash.

The bank is steep for such a small creek, so I take my care steppin' down. The water ain't like the creeks in Fayett'ville, sluggish, brackish an' all. This one is clear an' fast movin'. I see li'l minnows dashin' 'bout. Holdin' onto a small saplin', I lean down, dip in one hand, switch, dip in the other. I dry my hands, an' come back to the table, whar' white folks is settin' down to et.

Missus turn to me. "I fixed you a plate, Sarah Louise. You go off and find yourself a spot." She hand me a small plate piled high with biscuits, cured ham, an' watermelon slices.

I weren't hungry before, but with this plate in my hand, I starvin'. My belly rumble. "Thank yo' kindly, ma'am," I say.

"Don't dilly-dally, Sarah Louise. Just eat your food and get to work. Lots to do."

"Yas, ma'am," I say again, thinkin' I should mention that Doc Goldstein tol' me to report to him after.

I finds me a green spot beneath a maple, an' I sits down on a big root near the trunk. I alone, birds chirpin' without a care in world, before I hear a voice, which I quick recognize.

It David voice. Here I be settin' on this root, ready to et, an' David find me. Come to remind me that we has our first meetin' on tree roots by the Cape Fear.

I begins to et, but I barely taste my food, thinkin' 'bout David an' the slop I offer him that first day.

"I still coming for you, Sarah Louise," the voice say.

"I hope yo' is!" I say aloud. But as I look up, instead of David soft, lovin' face, I finds Missus—hands planted on her hips, frown on her face, standin' lak she already had enough of my foolishness.

"Sarah Louise, I hope I'm not disturbing you! Who are you talking to? Miss Jo Ann and I are already inside working. You finish up and come on in that church. Doc been asking about you, think you good for something. I'm not convinced."

"Yas, ma'am. I comin'!" I stand up, stuffin' the rest of the food in my mouth. It sure is good. I gives my empty plate to the mess cook—they has a mess soldier in charge an' a colored fella washin' up. The mess tent wus by the side of the church whar' the creek bend. Makeshift kitchen there too.

When I walkin' up the stairs, I almost bump right into Doc Goldstein, that' be walkin' down. He stop, reverse, an' we walkin' up together.

"You ever change bandages, seen any wounds—I mean profound, deep wounds? You aren't afraid of blood, are you? Faint-hearted?"

"Not much for faintin'," I say. "An' I never change no bandage. But I ain't afraid to learn."

"Good," he say, an' we enter the church.

Nothin' prepare me for what I sees. First off, there shadowy light cast by two large stain glass windows. They plain but cast deep blue light. I can't see good till my eyes adjust. Then I see them dull gray flannel shapes—rows of them. Cots with men, blankets, an' a disarray to the whole affair. Comin' into focus slow, my eyes pick up the details. Men are shapes sittin' up. Some shapes become boots, others piles of uniforms, rucksacks, all piled underneath an' beside the cots.

An' the smell. Bad. Only a few bottom windows wus open, so it stiflin' inside. I smelled blood lak from hog butcherin'. But this smell wus much worse. When the viscera come out, it send up a peculiar odor, one that hang in the air. That what happen in the hospital. Smell lak the inside of a huge dead hog.

"You doing all right, young lady?" Doc Goldstein axe. I'd pulled up my apron to cover my nose an' mouth'.

"Sir, yo' speakin' to me?"

"I've forgotten your name." Doc motion his head for me to come outside with him. My eyes wus gettin' adjusted.

"More wounded men are coming today. You can see how overcrowded we are," Doc Goldstein begin. "So I need every hand. Truth is, I was told that Mrs. Smith was bringing additional young ladies to nurse. Told she had three daughters. We're short-handed."

"Ain't never been called a lady," I says, droppin' my apron from my mouth so as I cans speak clear, though the smell still linger.

"Tell me your name again," Doc say. "Promise I won't forget this time." An' Doc Goldstein give me his smile.

I look at him then—a good look. An' I see a youn' man, maybe thirty. The beard made me think he older at first. An' I notice that he talk strange, sure ain't from around here. Ain't a Yankee nor Rebel.

"Sarah Louise," I say. "An' if yo' gots work for me, I do it. I ain't scared."

He motion again for me to come inside. This time my eyes adjust mo' quick, an' I ready. Ain't such a shock.

We only has a li'l while before evenin' come. Doc tell me to go around to all the men, see that them that need water gits a drink. I gots a full bucket an' a tin to dip. When I runs out, I told to go fill up at the creek.

If I finds anyone dead, I suppose not to say nothin', just note whar' he lay an' git the doc. He need to make the pronouncement. There another man to fill out papers an' send word to the soldier next'a kin.

That night I beds down in the brick stable by the wall inside a wood stall. Half the buildin' arranged with them, other part empty, whar' there be a rough table set up, a dining room for when it rain.

Each stall wus lak a room with a hay pallet—straw stuffed inside a sack. But it wus new straw an' clean. Just a few colored here. Men an' women. There be a stable boy, Jeb, an' the mess cook assistant, go by "Cookey." Two stable hands wus there, twins that look exactly alike. They go by "twins"—an' nobody bother to tell them apart. They somber Negroes who work together to diggraves.

There three stalls for horses an' a open cart kept to the side near the table. Twins use it to take the bodies. In the heat, they gets them in the ground quick. Holes most time dug a day ahead.

When we arrive that first afternoon—Missus, Miss Jo Ann, me—there 'bout thirty wounded men inside the church, an' two empty surgery tents set up outside. *[There is a brief pause, and Ms. Augustus resumes.]*

I gonna gets the tea. Hot. Take a break. Want some? I gets it. I takes my medicinal tea; yo' wants the black?

Stretch… wait a minute. Turn that off. *[Some scratching noise is heard, and the tape machine is clicked off and on again. Ms. Augustus resumes.]*

Well, the next day… we wakes up fine, but two men die durin' the night, so we has us a burial before noon. We collects their papers, letters, an' one of them have a photograph he die with in his hands. Some die that way. There a clerk to fill out death papers, an' a couple men on horseback come to pick them up, file them, an' notify kin.

One of the dead men wus a officer, an' I be the one that tend him. He a older man with gray hair an' a beard. He gots all his limbs, but he wounded in his chest, an' Doc told me he ain't got a chance. But we suppose to pretend there always hope. Doc say everyone need hope. The officer axe me for water that evenin'; by mornin' when I check on him, he gone.

Sad thing to die without kin present. Sometime a soldier mutter a woman name to me. He have his eyes closed, got the fever. An' I ain't got the heart to tells him I ain't his ma, sweetheart, sister. So I just say, "I here for yo'. Yo' all right." Once, a soldier axe me to recite a prayer I knowed, so I did. Ain't much to do when the end so near. *[There is an audible sigh, followed by a rather long moment of silence. Ms. Augustus then resumes.]*

The thing 'bout the burial is Doc Goldstein. He ain't a Christian; he a Jew, so he don't know what to do or say at a Christian funeral.

We standin' around at the north end, by the church cemetery, to bury the men. Group of us. One man there, a commander. We got maybe three, four ol' torn hymnals at the service—left behind in the church. Missus has one, but don't knowed who got the others.

Black folk that attend this, they standin' at the rear, while the few white folks gather up front. They maybe eight, ten us folks, includin' Missus an' Miss Jo Ann.

Doc Goldstein say he know a Hebrew prayer, an' since there only be one all-knowin' God that understand all languages, he gonna recite it.

We all nod, except I noticin' Missus—who be wearin' her light green fancy brocade dress. She look around lak she want someone to say something mo' fittin', mo' Christian. When nobody do, she step forward to say a few words 'bout honor an' the Southern cause. She then sing a verse out'ta the hymnal. Others that knowed it, join. Then, she step back so that the twins can lower the bodies. *[Ms. Augustus clears her throat and speaks.]*

Ashes to ashes, dust to dust. *[There are some long pauses, some shuffling, and the machine is clicked off.]*

September 27, 1937

I knows I axe for the weekend, an' yo' give it to me. But I havin' a rash of nightmares again. *[Ms. Augustus sighs but quickly continues.]*

I leaves off at the burial, an' that wus end of June still or beginnin' July. That night, the rain start—slow with a warm drizzle, but soon big drops fallin' hard—it become that heavy, wet, slanted rain, a storm. Tents collapse. It pour down lak them travelin' rains I tells yo' 'bout. A few white soldiers has to bunk with us colored in the stable.

Nobody like that. The soldiers take up our dinin' table—which wus a big barn door set on saw horses—an' they use that lak a wall to keep separate from us. For almost two days it rain hard. Then it stop, sudden. Sun come out second day afternoon. Table back, an' them white men gone.

When the rain clear, we all see that the camp look a wreck—muddy tents mashed into the ground, tree limbs everywhar', with big branches down, an' the land turn to muck. Everyone get busy cleanin'. I walk over to the hospital to check on the men—hadn't been there in a day. I take my water bucket, but ain't find no one dead. A miracle.

Later that same day, afternoon—before we can gets the camp cleaned up—a new mess of wounded soldiers come in—thick as the rain—streamin' into camp. They come on foot, horseback, an' wagon. I just leave the hospital. Walkin' down them church steps, the afternoon so clear, the way it get after a rain, all the humid air gone, an' I stop in my tracks 'cause I high up enough to see them over the rise, dottin' the hillside, bedraggled, small as ants at first, but gettin' bigger, swarmin' over the hillside into camp. I scurry to find Doc, who washin' hisself in the rear of the church. Gots his bloody apron off, an' Cookey wus there, pourin' hot water over his hands.

"Soldiers over the rise yonder," I say. "Lots."

Doc don't even look up. "I've known since yesterday afternoon that they were on their way, Sarah."

"Yo' want me do somethin'? Go fill the bucket?"

"Don't see why not." Doc look up, his face wet, an' he smile.

By the time I finish with my bucket trip down the bank, gettin' two buckets, 'cause I gonna needs them, must'ta been a hundred new wounded in camp, an' everythin' still in disarray. Blood lak I never see'd. Ain't room enough in the church. An' the grounds swarms with men. The ones that ain't badly wounded help us set up tents, an' the lawn out front look mo' lak a battlefield than church yard. We still cleanin' an' fixin' our soggy tents. Some we has to hang on lines to dry out. Branches, leaves, mud everywhar'. Most of the soldiers tents they brung with them wus wet an' dirty too, but none wus soaked bad as ours.

Men keep stragglin' into camp, arrivin' alone or in groups—two, three, even as much as ten. With horses, wagons, or on foot. An' they muddy from the rain.

We ain't much mo' than a dozen that run the hospital—black an' white. So we spread thin to tend them. Doc Goldstein direct the healthy soldiers to town or to private homes nearby. Thems that ain't bad injured sent off too—in the same wagons they come in on—to places south.

It take hours for all the last of them soldiers to arrive. Missus, she good, a real nurse, order the wounded onto the empty cots we has. When we runs out, she have men put on blankets an' tarps on the church floor. The pews wus long time gone. Anywhar' there space, we now has wounded soldiers. Before yo' walk in, yo' could smell the blood, hear the moanin', the cryin' out.

Miss Jo Ann, she get a pile of ol' cloth we keep in the supply house, an' she get busy bindin' up the worst wounds. Doc tell me to keep goin' around with the water. So many thirsty, moanin' men, blood-soaked an' filthy. I skittin' from one to the other. Some has holes from Minie ball blasts through their chests, stomachs.

Miss Jo Ann an' now the twins take to bandagin'. We all be doin' what we can. Tying up head wounds, splintin' broken limbs with any piece of wood we got handy. Two men nurses—don't know whar' they comes from—arrives in a hospital cart to carry off some soldiers to town. An' there is them that needs amputations—arms, feet, legs. An' them that is dyin' already.

I wus at one soldier cot, readin' him a letter from his sweetheart, when Doc Goldstein find me. "I need help," he say an' take the letter, fold it, place it by the soldier side. "She'll be back, Johnny," Doc tell him.

The boy we go to, ain't even has his face hair to shave, 'bout sixteen he look, layin' on a cot, in the high part of the church yard, near the cemetery. A youn' Missus from a neighbor place that come to help, beside him, with writin' paper an' ink, writin' down his letter home. She has a li'l canvas seat that she use, an' she movin' from one soldier to the next, writin' down their letters home. Doc nod at her, an' she excuse herself, tell the soldier she return soon.

The twins also carry the stretcher. Doc want them to tote this youn' boy carefully down the stairs to the outside tents, freshly staked, whar' the surgery be done. Doc nod at me, an' I follows them out.

I still gots one of my water buckets that I brings with me from the church.

"Sarah Louise, set that bucket down and get me my tools in that case—by that wagon." Doc point.

"I comin', yas, Sir," I say, an' puts the bucket down, which Cookey find quick an' carry off. I walk over an' finds the wooden case, packed with instruments I see'd before. There a few dry tents up now, I notice, as I walk back to Doc an' the boy.

Inside the tent, Doc Goldstein take his case from me an' hand me a bottle with a cork an' a thin rag. The boy is groanin' an' has his eyes shut tight. He don't seem to be strugglin' much, but in a lot of pain.

"Sarah, I want you to put the rag over this soldier's mouth, hold it firm, and drip a few drops of the medicine from the bottle until I tell you *enough*. Then I want you to come around this side and assist me. I may need to take this leg off, right above the knee." Doc take his hand an' draw a line across the boy knee. Doc jacket off, I notice, an' he got his sleeves rolled up, apron on.

"I ain't never…" I begins.

"That's all right. Just do as I say." Doc turn to the boy, tell him to relax, go to sleep, Doc Goldstein in charge, everythin' gonna be fine.

Doc nod to me, an' I take the rag an' cover the boy mouth. Doc nod again, an' I drip the medicine. It stink so bad I can't smell the blood no mo'. A few drops, an' Doc nods, so I stop.

"This will help you rest, son. Go to sleep." The boy fight me the smallest bit. But he weak as a kitten.

Ain't take long. The boy out. Few breaths an' he open, then quickly shut his eyes. Doc take his scissor an' cut his pant leg off to the waist. I see what he want me to do. So I step to the side, pull off the pant leg.

Doc right away clean the leg. I see it has a open gash—muscle, no skin. Lots of dirt, an' yo' could see bone. Meanwhile, Doc don't say nothin'. He look at it an' reach to his open wood case I put on a small nearby table. There wus a saw, other tools—knives, other sharp instruments, a drill.

Doc tell me to take out the scalpel knife an' pour some bucket water over it, which I do. He take it from me an' dry it with a clean linen he got. He got a clean linen to dry them with. Then he turn to the boy, take his pinky finger, an' simply put it into the worst part of the wound, the part blown open. He dig in with his other fingers, most of his hand, an' touch the bone.

"I've got to feel the damage, Sarah Louise. Got to see if that Minie ball is intact or if it's exploded into fragments." Doc looks up to the left, the corner of the canvas tent. He be seein' with his fingers.

"Needs to come off," he say.

I stand by the youn' boy side. My mouth open wide enough to catch a sparrow.

"This will take ten minutes, Sarah Louise, and you'll assist me. If you do a good job, I'll keep you on. We gots lots of boys. Give me that sponge."

Doc Goldstein take his scalpel, make his cut through what left of the muscle, the tight part, 'cause some wus blowed away. He cut deep. It turn my stomach, an' I could feels my biscuit risin'.

"Close your eyes for a minute if you want," Doc say. "Just a minute though. Because I'm going to need you again soon. First time always seems hard."

But it strange, 'cause I don't close my eyes. I takes a deep breath, an' feels this powerful sense of doin' good.

Next thing, I watchin' Doc take his bone saw out the case. He don't axe for bucket water; he sawin' through the bone. The sound somethin' terrible—an' flecks of bone, muscle, flesh fly off. But Doc don't care. He file up the stump bone to make it smooth. If he leave it ragged, pieces would poke. He leave a flap of skin to stitch up over the stump. He have some special silk thread for stitchin'. Doc make a hole for drainage, an' he bind the stump up with isinglass plaster that has in a jar.

The boy still out. Ain't wake till later, after the twins carry him by stretcher to the hospital proper—whar' now, thankfully, there be a empty cot for this boy. When he come to, he in pain bad. An' thirsty. When I ain't needed to help Doc with surgery, I still goin' around with my water bucket. This soldier live; some ain't so lucky.

On the surgery table, men become flesh an' bone, what we all is. But when I gives them water an' talk to them, it clear to me that they be somebody brother, father, son.

Leg amputation take about ten, fifteen minute. That it. Arms go faster. Man get delivered to camp with all his body limbs, but by the time he leave, he might be missin' one.

That first boy done fine. An' we do another, also good. We do a bunch this first round, after this battle. Ain't even sure which battle it were. Or how many exactly we do.

Later that week, I recalls another boy, a li'l older an' blond—he come in almost dead, an' he pass on the table. I about to administer my chloroform, an' I see his eyes open, plead with me to wait, which I do. Then he smile at me as if he wanna say somethin'. He try to lift his hand, but he close his eyes, shudder once, an' die.

Now Doc only has to look at me, nod. I puts down my cloth, go outside to call the stretcher bearers—or the twins or if there nobody else around.

Curl an' Sampson—two Negroes from a nearby Virginny plantation— come, lift this blonde boy on a board, an' take him straight away to the makeshift graveyard by the church cemetery. No time for much preparation. There too many dead for the twins to dig separate holes. They has to bury them together in a single big grave. No service neither, but a few of us come to say a prayer.

Arms an' legs get piled up outside the tent—tossed to the side. We cover them, out'ta respect. At night they get burned outside of camp. Way off, near them woods to the north. Most time the wind carry the smell away, but sometime, it shift, an' the whole camp smell of roasted flesh. Stench make yo' gag. It get into yo' stomach lak yo' swallowed it. *[There is a scraping sound. Ms. Augustus says that she needs a break and tells the interviewer to turn the tape machine off. When Ms. Augustus resumes, it is later that same day.]*

So much sufferin'. A young boy look up, give yo' a helpless smile, mutter somethin' 'bout his sweetheart or ma. Then yo' overhear two soldiers talkin' 'bout a skirmish in the field that day. Maybe yo' be helpin' a boy lift his head to swallow a sip. Maybe he dead the next time yo' see him. Enough blood spill in that war to fill the big ocean. *[Ms. Augustus sighs, and there is a short silence before she begins again.]*

That week—I wanna say—we amputate fifty limbs. Six or seven men die while Doc cuttin' them. Must be that we has at least a hundred men at camp. Maybe mo'.

There be work without end. Lots of sick, injured men, cryin' out, even screamin' in delirium, high fever. We 'bout out of supplies, though there be folks around that come to help, bring what they can.

Missus exhausted. Same for Miss Jo Ann. We lookin' forward to goin' to Back Bay, whar' we ain't touched by this misery.

But then it happen—the second week, right before we suppose to leave. [*There is a short pause; then Ms. Augustus resumes.*]

The soldiers call Doc "Sawbones." A nickname. It common at the time 'cause the way they amputate with the saw. So by the end that first week, Doc Goldstein answer to "Sawbones" or just plain "Bones." Me, I calls him "Doc"—always. Missus call him "Doctor Goldstein" as do Miss Jo Ann. But the men love nicknames. An' I be workin' with them gets the name "Gal."

Ain't so bad, I think. Could be "Nigga," what most Negro gals called, 'cause no one bother to learn names. Some call the men "Jimbo." Older women gets called "Auntie," out'ta respect. But us youn' gals called "Nigga." We all the same. But 'cause I come with the water, help Doc, an' has the reputation of bein' such good help, I gits called "Gal." I even reads and writes for the men. Doc even teach me to how to sew up a stump flap—which I do for him when he called away.

The men mostly all right. Thems that is wounded. The mens that isn't, sometimes they full of spite an' meanness.

Now, we suppose' to stay only two weeks. Battles movin' south. So this wus just before we plan on leavin' for Back Bay. We gots a mess of Confed'rate Calvary soldiers, an' their horses, which we mainly keeps out to pasture. We still got lots of oats, enough to spare for them horses.

It start with one man that grab me when I in the stable fetchin' oats. We alone, an' it mid-day.

"Hey, yo'," a soldier call out. He gatherin' up things in a rucksack. Squattin', an' he rise. "Hey, yo', '*Gal*,'" he say with a snigger an' come toward me. He alone, an' quick, he shove me up against the stable wall. My oat bag ain't fill yet, but I drop it to push him away. I ain't got enough strength, an' he start puttin' his hands all over me. He smell bad, an' I strugglin'. In a few seconds, though, one of twins comes in whistlin', an' the man back up, kick my oat bag that on the ground, take up his own rucksack, an' walk out. I tidy my dress up, an' the twin don't even knowed what go on. I gather the oats I come for, an' leave.

Now, there always soldiers around the stable. Another time, mornin', I walkin' from the stable to the creek to get me my bucket of water for the men. Make my rounds. A soldier must'ta follow me, 'cause he come up sudden, grab me by the wrist, swing me toward him. "Whar' yo' off to? Got yo'self a pass, Nigga?" Again, I pull away, an' this man let me go too. But he bruise my wrist, he grab me so hard. "Next time…" he call after me, but I be runnin'."

Most days I be the one to feed the pastured horses. I always did lak horses, an' I wus good with them. Also, the pasture wus away from the wounded soldiers, all that blood an' sickness.

One afternoon, Doc tell me I can goes, take a break. So I finish up a few chores an' gets the oats. When I walkin' up, the horses alert to me right away. I always shake the feed bag, so they be trottin' over, ears pricked up, real pretty, exceptin' when the crowd up. They puts them flat an' nip an' buck at each other. Gotta keeps yo' distance 'cause they sometime kick. So I spreads out most of the oats on the grass, an' backs up. I leaves some in the bottom of the bag for the lame horse that never get any. She a mare named Lulu. Buckskin with a white patch on her rump.

I walkin' with the bag to whar' the creek run—before the bend. There a deep thicket off to one side whar' soldiers drink whiskey, an' the pasture go all the way down, almost to the creek. It lak a li'l pocket whar' the fence is, an' some green grass left to nibble. It be near a bend in the creek, a elbow, an' nobody go there.

At first, I walk slow toward Lulu. Just so she see me. When she do, she lift her head—she got a blaze down her front—an' I show her the bag. Lulu shake her head, neigh, an' she hobble along, followin' me, hangin' a few steps behind, lak she always do.

"Lu," I sing out. "Lulu." But I don't dare shake the bag, lest all the others come at a gallop. I only hold it up every few seconds so she see'd it an' follow. Folks say she got the thrush bad an' ought'ta be put down, but I think it only in one hoof, an' already it dryin' out since she been restin'.

We at the bend, an' I stop so Lulu can come over. I encourage Lulu to eat out the bag, 'cause she a sweet gal. When she eat, I stroke her.

Then—all a sudden—come a hand across my mouth. An' I ain't on my feet no longer. Someone got me over his shoulder. The feedbag drop from my hand, an' Lulu oats spill to the ground.

"Let go!" I scream. A cold damp rag come over my mouth, an' I recognize the chloroform smell.

"Nigga gal, yo' so good to help us white men," I hear. "Even if yo' ain't no doc."

Some chuckle. "Yo' ain't gonna *saw* nothin' here, Nigga. We the ones that gonna do the sawin'. Back an' forth till yo' sawed in half."

I can't speak, can't see good. Only catch glimpses of Lulu with her head bowed, gobblin' up spilt oats.

An' I see them soldier legs. Lak they detached from their bodies, walkin'.

"We got her, Henry."

"We got ourself our Nigga sawbones gal."

"Only she ain't gonna do no sawin' this time."

"She kill that Ambrose boy from Kinston, what got hisself shot in the knee."

"He dead an' buried. I hope he up in Heaven, lookin' down, smilin' at what he gonna see."

"Ambrose—he wus a good ol' boy."

Now, I drugged, but I ain't asleep. Just in a stupor, bewitched. Afternoon turn to evenin', almost twilight. An' that confuse me even mo'. I force myself to open my eyes, but I can't see nothin'. Only shapes, shadows. I wus by that north creek bend, on the ground, lookin' up at faces, white faces I couldn't make out. Sound as if they gurglin' lak the creek. I see some of their mouths open but can't hear no words.

Then I thinkin' my back is hurt. They must'ta tossed me against a branch, 'cause I feels somethin' sharp. Then I wakes for a moment, in hot pain, an' I sees what they gonna do.

I struggles. They must be five of them. Maybe mo'. Can't tell. I try to crawl, but they got my arms an' legs pinned.

My fingers be diggin' into the earth, tryin' to steady myself. But it real slippery, an' no matter how hards I try, I can't do it. My back wus hurt bad, the ground all muddy, an' my dress wus wet an' ripped.

One man turn me over, start snatchin' at me. It dark out now. I hear the creek rush loud, unnatural, lak it in my ear.

Then I sinkin' into the soft earth. Not against the branches, I on a river of soft, spongy earth bein' carry off somewhar'. I floatin' down some current, dreamin' I on the operatin' table, an' Doc 'bout to do surgery, while he got me floatin' on some board in the middle of a stream.

I think I must be dyin'—this floatin' be the Lawd hands carryin' me so smooth to Heaven. I feel hands lift me. For a moment, I thinkin' I already dead, an' some beasts of the forest is pickin' my bones for what meat there might be left.

When the pickin' stop, I on a hard surface, lak a flat boat, the raft ferry they has on the Cape Fear, an' someone takin' me across. But I scared. I wanna paddle off somewhar', flip myself over, use my arms to paddle the raft away. But I can't. I lak a June bug can't right itself.

Only thing I feel is the stabbin' pain. A blunt stabbin' deep inside. It come at me with such force, I sure my insides is bleedin', my life blood flowin' out.

Then a stench—corn whiskey an' manure mixed up—an' some man scratchy whiskers rubbin' my face raw, back an' forth, lak I a piece of lumber bein' sanded to nothin'. [*A scraping sound is heard, but the tape continues to run.*]

Stop for a moment. [*Ms. Augustus clears her throat, sighs, and resumes.*]

Ain't sure what happen next. I has a memory of Mammy Rae at the dye shack. But the memory drift into a dream: Doc doin' his surgery on me, an' I half asleep, listenin' to him. Doc is hummin' a hymn, sawin' off all my limbs, an' filing smooth the stumps—lak they horse hoofs—an' as he hummin', another man say, "No need to dress her up for no party now. She ain't never gonna dance again."

In the dream, I wanna open my eyes—bad. I strugglin', but they glued or stitched shut. So I tries to talk—but my mouth be shut tight too. I tries to scream, but can't do that neither. I just the trunk of a body, helpless.

Now come silence—a welcome guest. An' I be give up my struggle. No use. I gives up. No talk now 'bout no party nor dancin'. I drift to a place whar' I be safe. In my mind, I mean.

The ground whar' I lays is damp, spongy, except for that branch, every once in awhile stab me in the back when I tries to roll. I in a stupor. Sort of wakes up every so often, then drift back to sleep.

Night pass, 'cause I remember sun-up. At some point before dawn, I hears a hoot owl. An' he the one that wake me with his "Who, who, who"—a question I needs to answer.

So I does. I open my eyes, surprised that they ain't glued nor stitched shut no mo'. Then I try my mouth, "It me, Sarah Louise," I say.

I comes to, on that bank, that muddy, damp bank, while the moon still out, an' night shadows just leavin'.

I sits up. Painful. My back near broke in two. I hears the creek babblin'. Ain't sure whar' I is, so I sits up, try to look around. Trees comin' into focus. "Who, who, who," I hears again through the forest.

"It me, Sarah Louise Smith, an' I still alive on Earth," I say.

These words help me, an' I think 'bout gittin' up. I must be by the pasture, the creek bend.

I try to stand but can't quite get my legs under me. They almost wooden. My knees ache. I notice dark dried blood on my thighs. Black in that early light. Blood mix with creek mud.

I ain't dressed proper, so I grab my muslin shift that cast nearby. It ripped an' dirty. I try to put it on, but I weak as a kitten. An' in pain. I know what them soldiers done. Pieces come back to me: them sandpaper whiskers rubbin' against my face, the foul smell of stale whiskey, that stabbin' inside.

I has to lay back down, an' I peerin' at the last bit of moon through the branches, thinkin' that Doc an' Missus must be wonderin' 'bout me. They all probably risin' to breakfast. Maybe they even miss me last night.

Them soldiers must be awake too, laughin' by the mornin' campfire, 'bout the good ol' time they has with that Nigga gal, the one so happy to help Doc saw off soldier legs. Bet she ain't so happy now. Or maybe they ain't talkin'—ashamed of theirselfs, thinkin' 'bout a wife or sweetheart back home.

By sun-up, I muster the strength to pull my legs under me, get up. Make sure my shift is on—though it be ripped an' dirty—an' slowly go down to the creek, whar' I splash water on me to wash the mud, an' I pull twigs from my hair.

Then I ready to set out. Slow. Reckon it must be a quarter mile back to the church. I feel numb, ain't thinkin' right. An' I so sore as I tries to walk, feels mo' lak a dead woman risin' from the grave.

I can't finds my boots, so I walk barefoot, an' the whole bottom half of my skirt be draggin'.

When I come upon the green pasture, it glistenin' with dew, an' I wus surprise to see it so unchanged. There a few horses yonder, heads down grazin', an' a mockin' bird callin' as it wing across the pale sky.

But I don't go through the pasture. It too open. Instead, I cut through the small forest stand by the creek bend. I stumblin' around till the forest come to a clearin', another pasture, or maybe a hayfield. The grass is taller there an' wet, but I decides to make my way through it. I ain't familiar with whar' I is exactly. Ain't been here before, though I knows the general direction to camp.

I stop every few minutes to think, get my bearin's, catch my breath. I in a daze. Can't tell if it be the chloroform that ain't yet completely worn off.

Sarah Louise Smith, I thinkin'. *Yo' all alone in this grass, an' yo' ain't never gonna be the same.* I stop for a moment; a sharp wind stir the air. *[The machine is turned off abruptly. Some clicks are heard, and Ms. Augustus begins again, without commentary.]*

I walkin' again, comin' through the field, an' now I thinkin' 'bout Run'way Johnny, how he find me that night, put his hand over my mouth. He weren't no criminal—I knew right away. I wus only wearin' a thin nightdress, but that Johnny, he knowed I just a gal. He could of done somethin', but he didn't. He a slave, but he done right when he get his chance.

Then I think to the hospital, the church ground. I wus only doin' what Doc Goldstein tell me. Helpin' thems injured soldiers. Helpin' them by bein' brave—'bout as brave as any soldier. *[Ms. Augustus sighs and resumes. The tape does not stop.]*

Sun full up now, an' the walkin' help clear my head. First, Johnny in my thoughts, next Doc. But then I thinks to Ma—how mad she'd be at me, how she blame me for what happen. Maybe she be by the bushes out behind the cabin, layin' out washin', shakin' her head. "I warned yo' 'bout them men, Sarah Louise. I told yo' to stay out'ta trouble."

An' Pa. I see him walk through the cabin door. I be a li'l gal again, an' it Saturday night. "I is home, ya'll," he say. "Yo' pappy come to hug his darlin's." His face bright as a penny, shinin' at the doorway.

I think of David, too. I see his green eyes, his slender body. Hear his voice. "Sarah Louise," he say. An' I turn to him. He standin' by me—tall an' clean an' upright.

"You ain't a Smith no mo', gal." He take my hand. "Yo' got my letter. I knows yo' did," an' he grin.

"David," I tell him. "It weren't my fault. I'm sorry."

"Yo' all right now," David say. "Yo' strong. I love you." He kiss my forehead. "Yo' Augustus now," he say an' squeeze my hand. "Don't that sound good? *Sarah Louise Augustus.* Say it for me."

"Sarah Louise Augustus," I say.

"Now sing it," David insist.

An' standin' there in that empty hayfield, stupid though it be, I begins to sing. First, I just hum, but quick it turn into a song. *[Ms. Augustus pauses and clears her throat.]* I gonna sing it now. *[Ms. Augustus begins to sing. Her tone is high and strained. But there is a sweetness, too.]*

> *Here I is on my weddin' day,*
> *Here I is on my weddin' day,*
> *Jesus, won't yo' join me an' pray,*
> *I jumpin' the broom today.*
> *Here come my groom, handsome an' clean,*
> *He polish his shoes, he come with his dream.*
> *I stay with him till Judgment Day.*

[The tape machine is abruptly turned off. When it is turned on, Ms. Augustus is speaking on the next day.]

September 29, 1937

Warm already. Sorry 'bout yesterday, but I ready today. Now. Goin' back to that day, the field. We still in the middle of the war. *[The sound of chairs scraping a wood floor is heard.]*

After I sing the weddin' song, I sit down a spell. Head clearin', but I ain't got my strength back.

It there that them angels come swirlin' around me—as I sittin' in the tall grass. They surprise me, ain't expectin' them. They startle me, so I get up, thinkin' I got to get back to the church. Then I hears them say—though not out loud—"Sarah Louise Augustus." An' I come to know that very moment that gonna be my name now. It what David wus tellin' me.

There be a circle of angels floatin' around me. The bodies feel warm. Warm me, 'cause I chill. Then one faceless angel whisper, "*Go to David, Sarah Louise Augustus.*"

An' when she say this, I knowed that I wus married now. David done take me for his bride. It only a matter of time before it official.

An' right then, I realize that I gots to run. Not to my white folks but to David.

Birds chirp—mockin' birds, sparrows, maybe even some crows. But it a beautiful mornin'. I turns myself around, an' I walkin' myself back to the forest, which I comes from. An' the angels, of course, they is all gone now.

The forest lay in shadow, an' there a thick underbrush. But there seem to be a walkin' path, so I followin' that, thinkin' 'bout my new name. Thinkin' that I needs to find David—but whar'?

Then I hear voices—they distant, but they real. Men. My heart thumpin', an' I make for cover in the foliage, under a new fallen tree— must'ta come down in the heavy rains. Still have plenty of leaves.

Soldiers is out ahead, on the path I just come from. They talkin'. Must be 'bout six or seven of them.

My heart poundin' inside my chest. I thinkin', *a run'way? Is that what yo' wants to be?*

An' sure enough, as the soldiers pass—on the way to the hayfield—I realize that they scoutin' for me, Sarah Louise Smith. But she already dead.

Maybe Doc think I got myself lost or hurt. I has a strong urge to go call to them, to go home—to the church, to Missus, to Doc, whar' it be safe. An' I hates to let Doc down when he gonna need me.

Then, just as I decide to show myself—I hear one of them call, "Over here. Come over here!" An' they move closer.

When they do this, without thinkin' I sink down. It the man voice that trigger me. A primitive force grab my spirit—his voice ring in my ears lak a repeatin' rifle.

My heart racin' now lak a colt out'ta the gate after it penned up all night. All I can thinks about is boltin'.

"Over here!" the man shout, an' I can see he got a beard an' don't has a cap on. He got a grizzly face an' long tangled hair.

I crouch down till I part of the earth. Tuck myself into the leafs an' underbrush, pray they don't spot me. Gotta be invisible, lak my angels. I thinkin', 'cause I knowed then that these be the men from last night, come back to kill me before I gets the chance to tell what they done.

Much of the mornin' go by lak this. I stays put, branches an' leaves coverin' me up. My strength ain't back lak I thought. Another group of soldiers come trompin' up an' down the forest path to the river bend, maybe lookin' to find me—or pieces of my dress, blood stains, broken branches whar' I get pushed down, boot prints whar' I violated. The forest I hidin' at ain't so far as I first thought it be. I must'ta walked in a circle. The hayfield part of the neighbor farm.

But I can't see the muddy bank whar' I gets dragged. I know the soldiers or the men must be goin' there. It have a story to tell. Lak a battlefield.

Some of the men in this next group work with Doc. I recognize them. Good men that ain't wrong me. But the terror so deep I can't come out—an' I can't think straight with my heart beatin' so loud.

Around near noon, they all gives up lookin'. But before they leaves, I hears one of them say that it the Fourth of July today. The Union day of Independence. *[There is a long silence. Ms. Augustus clears her throat and asks that the machine is turned off.]*

September 30, 1937

Almost the end of the week. Thursday already. All night I thinkin' back to that time—the Rebellion, time in the forest, whar' I leaves off my story.

I talkin' to woman next door yesterday. Name Mathews. We sit here on the porch. Warm evenin'. Nice, but right away she tell me that I be wrong to talk 'bout this. Say some stories ain't meant to be told. Say it all the past now. We Negroes got to talk 'bout what lie ahead.

Gets me thinkin'. Yo' know when I begins, I weren't never plannin' to tell yo' this. Mrs. Mathews right—some things ain't fit for talkin'.

So me an' Mrs. Mathews gab 'bout some woman kitchen garden down the street. New kind of corn seed she plant—grow tall. Good eatin' corn too. Man from my church growed it last season, an' done give me a bunch for dinner last week. I boil a couple an' has them for supper the other night. Tasty. So we has plenty to gab 'bout, Mrs. Mathews an' me. We both gonna get that seed for next year.

After she go, I gets to bed late, an' I haves me mo' nightmares. Lak I bein' warned off talkin' for today. An' beside, Mister Crow come to me again, an' that ain't a good sign.

But here yo' is. An' here I is to tells yo' mo'.

See that tree? Down the road? Not down, across, there…by the yella' house? With the fence. Yo' sees it?

That tree must be a hundred year ol'. It a maple. Solid hardwood. It strong, an' it make good wood for chairs, chests, tables, what-nots. Good burnin' wood too. Pity though, to burn it. Might even be that tiger maple inside. An' yo' never knows till yo' splits it.

Get my point? I sit here, lookin' at that ol' tree, thinkin' I just lak it. An' here I is, gettin' split open.

I gonna split myself wide open. Maybe what I got inside is lak that tiger wood. An' I ain't gonna be silent.

Mrs. Mathews, she probably watchin' us now from her window. Shakin' her head, thinkin' I should be ashamed of myself. But here I is, ain't I? *[There is a long pause; then Ms. Augustus continues.]*

It around noon, lak I say, them soldiers finally leave. When they goes, the forest silent. Pasture, hayfield—all silent. Ain't nary a bird peep nor one leaf flutter.

I lifts myself up from the forest litter. Up from the branches an' thicket that hide me. No one there; I the only person left.

So I thinkin' of that first woman. I lak Eve in the forest. Except it ain't no Eden I be *in*, but rather it be Eden I walkin' *toward*.

Problem is, I don't knows which way to go. I be thinkin' back to Jukes—walkin' the wrong direction. An' I hungry, starved really. Look a'fright. Ain't respectable. I only knows which way is camp, an' which way them soldiers come from.

Hard as it is, I walk toward the river instead. My legs ache an' I bruised real bad, but I walk to the river, thinkin' I can cleans myself up, drink if the water ain't sluggish, an' head up from there.

The river is fair wide, an' I know I gots to ford. I thinkin' the North lay upriver, an' by my reckonin' I must be closin' in on the free states if I proceed that direction. But I don't knows whar the fightin' is to stay clear of.

Well, that day, July Fourth, white folks win freedom from the British— it go by in a blur. I hungry, ain't strong, an' I don't know what I doin', whar' I off to. At some point, I do ford the river—across rocks juttin' out from the shallows near a bend. I ain't yet had nothin' to eats, so I starved an' real confused.

At the river bank—other side now—mo' grass on the bank, so I slips off my wet dress, cleans it up best I can, an' puts it on again. I walkin toward a clump of trees in the open field, an' the sun strong make me sleepy. Ain't no one around, so I lay down, sleeps awhile. By time I wakes, it a dark but moonlit night, an' I thinkin' I'd better gets myself goin' before my luck turns.

An' food—that what I thinkin' 'bout. Then ol' Mister Crow appear.

"Caw, caw, caught…" I hears.

I looks around, an' there on a barren tree branch perch Mister Crow. All them branches around has leaves. Not this one. No, it bare an' dead, stickin' out halfway up some ol' tree.

"Caw, caw, caught," he say an' flap his wings.

"I ain't caught," I say. Then realize them the first words I utter in over a day. My voice sound weak, the chirp of a fledglin'.

"Caught! Caught!" Mister Crow flap his wings again.

His words strike me as odd. Why Mister Crow take up now to warn me? Lak he tellin' me to go back to my folks—the Missus an' Doc—'cause if I don't, I gonna gets myself caught.

So what if I do, I think. I lookin' straight up through the moonlit night. "What yo' care?" I say. Mister Crow, breathe in, black feather wings shinin', a deep shadow against the sky. "I don't believes yo'," I challenge. "Yo' ain't never once on my side. Why yo' warn me now?"

It then that Mister Crow swoop down, right at my feet, an' he start peckin' the grass blades, which look as black as he do in the moonlight. He peckin' furiously…peck, peck, peck, peck.

"I ain't never gonna listen to yo' again, Mister Crow. Yo' bad, an' I ain't afeared of yo' neither!" Now I shout at him, though he still peckin' by my feet. He so close, I stomp the ground, thinkin' he get scared an' fly 'way. But he don't. So as I bend a bit to gets a better look, I sees he stop his peckin', an' he be pullin' out somethin' from the ground. I think it a worm. A long, squiggly worm that come from the bowels of this here dark earth.

Then I sees it a snake! A thin black snake. Long, very long. Ain't a worm at all. An' Mister Crow pull it out with' all his crow strength. An' it fightin' him all the way.

I steps back. Somehow Mister Crow speak. He got the snake pulled from the ground, got his beak pointed up toward the sky, an' he manage to say, "Caught… caught … caught" before he fly away, snake writhin' in his mouth as he go. [*There is a short pause before Ms. Augustus continues.*]

That the sign of the debil. Sure thing. Snake. An' Mister Crow conjure him. Let me know that he doin' the debil work.

Well, what I wants to say is that last night I sees him again. Mister Crow come for a visit. An' he say the same thing. "Caught." That part of the Voodoo. Dream whisperin', it called. That's what he done to me last night. Maybe Mister Crow ain't finished with me yet.

Fact is, I pretty sure he want me to stop talkin'. To yo'. Same as Mrs. Mathews. Different reasons, a'course. Mrs. Mathews, a neighbor; she ain't mean no harm.

In my dream, I a ol' woman, lak I is, an' I makin' coffee on a cold winter night—an' in the dream I falls asleep, an' when the coffee start brewin' I wakes up an' find all the black coffee boilin' over the stove. Then it becomes solid an' take the shape of Mister Crow. "Caught," he say. "Yo' is caught."

Now there ain't no snake in his mouth. Not this time. But he say the same thing as what he say that night by the river. An' yo' see if Mister Crow predictions come true—in what I tells an' in the dream last night.

But I tells yo', I ain't afraid. *[There is a short pause, and Ms. Augustus sighs and continues.]*

I take off walkin' through a wood on the other side of the river. Walk all night. Ain't a dense wood, an' there even a road through it. Dirt, but well-traveled. I follow along side it, hangin' back, listenin' real good. This how slaves moved when they run for freedom. In still of night, followin' roads an' stars. But I don't know much of either.

An' I ain't entirely sure I goin' north. Mostly, I hungry. Comes in waves. Right before mornin', I finds a pack house with a root cellar. Edge of a farmstead, plantation—but in the woods.

I think it dug to hide food from soldiers. It rough. Inside there a cured ham an' summer canned goods, tomato, okra. Ol' jars, dust on the lids, but I figure they still good.

So I gets my provisions—an' a clean apron hangin' on a peg—don't know why, but I take that too. An' when I out, I slip back to the woods, I say a prayer, thank the good Lawd for what He do for me, how He provide. Stealin' wrong, but this maybe be God own will. Man laws an' God laws be two different things.

I gets to the woods again, ain't yet mornin' quite—moon fadin' from the dark sky. I sits down by a big piney tree, remind me of Fayett'ville an' begins to ets what I taken. Gobblin' it up. But after a few swallows, I start to feel sick in the stomach. I stop, breathin' long, deep breaths. It what Mammy Rae taught me. Slow, deep breaths an' to look at some fixed point, don't close the eyes—make yo' swoon. So I looks down at the apron I took—it on the ground—an' notice some fancy needle work on it.

Fancy material too—silk, I think, though I ain't seen too much silk, an' the weave is coarse. Seem strange that it left whar' it wus. Embroidery on the skirt, an' it full-length, with a panel over the bosom. Ain't the kind we use at home.

So I breathe deep, lookin' down at the fancy apron, distract from my heavin', which already calmin'. I ain't bother at first to make sense of what I see, but now it look lak houses embroidered on its skirt, in many color threads. An' it sure ain't child work. It done by women that knowed how to stitch.

Soon the tightness an' sweat pass. My belly ain't yet right, but I finish what I steal. When yo' ain't et, food can make yo' sick. So I rest a bit after I finish. The food leave me with thirst, but I ain't worried 'cause I already spot a well by the farm.

Then I understand. I still lookin' at the apron when it dawn on me that it a map. A map embroidered into the garment. Ain't never seen nothin' lak it, but it a map to whar' I is. The farm an' the woods. It a map—I sure of it. An' it got two farmsteads shown in needlework. With a small road through the woods. I can't believes that I finds such a thing. A sign from my angels or from God hisself. It gonna show me whar' I need to go. The next farmstead. I sayin' prayers—thankin' God an' my angels both.

When I finally leaves, it day break. Sun-up. I in the woods, by the edge, an' I don't knows if I should try to go to the well for the water. I feelin' strong but real thirsty. It now or never.

I puts my apron down, an' lak a fox, I slink my way to the well. Still shadowy outside, ain't no one around.

The well wus a good one, with a big wood bucket to send down. The water it brung up look fine an' clear, no smell, an' it a deep well, so far down I has to turn the rope again an' again to reach the water. I drinks straight from the bucket, no dipper or cup. The day comin' on, an' it dangerous to be seen. I drink my fill, thinkin' I in the Lawd hands. He send me a map, food, an' now water to sooth my throat.

Then I in the woods again—alone by myself. *I a run'way slave*, I thinkin'. There be Run'way Johnny, Run'way Jukes, an' Run'way Sarah Louise.

I in the forest now. First mornin' light, an' the farm begin stirrin'. In the distance, a figure walk from the main house—a woman. There a horse whinnyin' in the barn, rooster already crowin'. Bird singin'. I looks up an' sees a summer Tanager, red, alone on the edge of a branch. He chirp out his song—sweet, his twill light as air.

I safe behind some scrub, way off the dirt road. I finds me a place whar' the roots of a big tree make a kind of cave, a hole in the earth. It ain't recent down, an' I afraid some animal might be livin' there, but I is so tired that I dig out' the leaves, bury myself, an' fall fast asleep.

Don't knows how long I sleeps, but it a deep sleep, an' I dream. Think sometime, most powerful dream we has is thems that come in daylight. I wus playin' hopscotch with Sally again. We on Smith Plantation, an' it early fall. I go to throw my pebble on the court, an' a big wind pick up.

"Take yo' turn," Sally tell me. "Go, Sarah Louise, go!"

But the wind swirlin', an' I think it gonna lift me up. "Yo' see that, Sally? Yo' see them angels?" I axe her. But she ain't seein' nothin'—just lak she ain't seen nothin' before. We back to bein' young gals, an' it be similar to the first I seein' my faceless angels. But these blank faces becomin' leaves. All flutterin'.

"Go, Sarah Louise." Sally give me a shove to gets my mind back on the game.

An' as she do, I fall. Lak she push me over into a cavern. Blackness, blackness. I wakes up before I hits the ground, an' it nearly night 'gain. I done sleep the whole day.

I ready to follow my map. Can't read it real good, 'cause the moon ain't out, but I gets the general idea—whar' I needs to go. There be woods an' two farmstead on either end. I at one, an' I needs to finds my way to the other.

Ain't got my bearin's yet, but there be a North Star embroider on the map. It be a sort of compass to direct me. *[There is a pause; Ms. Augustus clears her throat and continues.]*

Gonna tells yo' 'bout that, but I tired all a'sudden. Why don't we shut this machine off? Throat need tea. *[The tape machine is promptly turned off. When it is turned on again, it is later that same day.]*

Continue now. Bones achin', I tell yo', rain comin'. One heavy rain change the season.

Well, I leaves off at night. I be in the forest, an' I slink off closer to the farmhouse whar' candle light is shinin' from the window. I sneak up to read the picture an' get in my mind whar' I needs to go.

Then, before I leaves, I draw mo' water from the creaky well—still nobody hear me. Then I gets a bit of salt ham from the cellar. Wraps it in a piece of flour sack.

I slips the apron back to it hook, thinkin' it there again for a run'ways lak me.

Take me almost all night to cross that patch of woods. It a real dark an' cloudy, an' I travel by feel mo' than what I see. But I do gets to the end of the woods, an' it end at a open place by a big river. I come over a hilltop an' I see below a black river. Small house sittin' by it.

There a barn, some shacks—maybe slave quarters, I think. Ain't sure. An' I tired, so tired again. Strength ain't return yet after my ordeal.

An' I sit for a moment, against a tree, close my eyes, an' fall asleep. It still night. I lean against a tree. But the next thing I knows, I bein' shook awake by a big black man. *[The voices here are garbled, unintelligible. The machine is clicked off. When it is clicked on again, Ms. Augustus begins mid-sentence, and it is the next day.]*

October 1, 1937

…want to know whar' I from. First, I thinkin' he part of my dream, an' I sit there dumb, ain't got no answer.

"Come with me," the man say. An' he bend down to lift me up lak I a child. Hand under my forearm. He got enormous strength. An' he blue-black as stovepipe. African, I thinkin', as he pull me up.

He got a low voice, baritone. Almost lak he sing when he speak. "Gotta gets yo' out'ta here. They find yo' sure enough. Sure enough."

He lift me. I ain't resistin'.

"Gonna takes yo' to Ma Belle," he say. "She the thing."

So off we goes—the man supportin' me, almost carryin' me—down the hill to one of the shacks I spot earlier. The night air gots a nip to it. "What the date be?" I axe. "It still July?" I knows it is. But I finds myself axin' anyway.

"Yo' sure be one confused gal," the man say. "It July. Yo' gots that right. What folks call yo'?"

An' I thinkin', but then nothin' come out'ta my mouth. I knows my name, but I partly is confused an' partly wonderin' if I can trust him. So I say, "July. My name is July, lak the month."

"Ain't never heared no one name that before," the dark man say.

He go by James. Right away I see he a gentle soul, an' he take me to the shack I tell yo' 'bout—by the river. We go inside. It weren't but one room, with a slab table, an' a couple of rough chairs—two women settin' on them by the fire. Tell yo' 'bout them in a minute. The young one, heavy set, rise up to greet me.

I spends a good while with James an' his folk. They fine people, an' they be livin' on the banks of what call the James River. Start from North Car'lina an' continue through Virg'nia, the next state north.

James, he name for the river, an' he wus born on the river—call hisself a river man.

The next while go by in a blur. I ain't quite in my right mind. James has his ma an' his gal there—Ethel, that mainly take care of me. All three of them, they part of a plantation, but they work by the river. James do ferryin'. Can't recalls the family name or the name of the plantation. There be other slaves that ferry for their master, but they from a big farm wus 'bout ten mile further west.

Never learn James Ma name. We all just call her "Ma." Right down from the cabin there be a ferry that James run. It a deep, wide river here, not too fast movin', but folks cross it by flat bed. Twenty logs lashed together. James got hisself a pole, a long pole, an' there be a rope strung across it too, that he can pull on.

Ethel take good care of me. She James gal, older than he be, an' heavy-set. She very attach to James. Ethel wus married, but her husband been sold off—so now she live with James an' his ma.

That day I wus brung there, I wus near to exhaustion. I'd been walkin' the woods at night, an' I gets cold deep in my bones, take a chill. I spends the first couple of days with Ma, restin', tryin' to gets my strength back.

But the chill turn to a fever. An' I gets real bad. I wus weak when I arrives, but soon I becomes worse off, weak as a half-drown pup. Then I starts my bleedin'. Somehow I knows it ain't my monthly.

Ethel, James, Ma, an'—oh, there a shack down the field, closer in to the plantation, maybe a mile or so—with a boy child of ten, an' a ol' man—they come by some days to help with chores, brings food. They all knows I here, but that it. No one else. These folks protect me, an' I stay there three weeks, nearly a month. They all keeps me hidden.

Not many white folks come along. A few. No soldiers. Troops nearby, I hears. But the few folks that need the ferry never know I there, for I be hid inside the shack.

Folks only know me as July. I is a run'way now, so that name good as any.

But sometime they calls me Independence. I come so soon after Independence Day that they give me that name.

My time wus difficult. Lonely, uncertain. Still ain't feelin' right. Sick to my stomach an' ain't quite right in my head. Nobody bother me with questions. Just want my name. July. Independence.

I has myself a pallet by the stove. They has some fancy stove I ain't never seen before. Don't light it now 'cause it too warm. Sometime they takes me to the barn whar' they has a couple of ol' mules an' a milk cow. Storehouse there too. Weren't big. When poor whites, soldiers, or skulkers come, they hide what li'l they has there. But nobody seem to be lookin' for me. Everybody taken up with the war.

Once, I recalls Ethel git me a new dress. It blue indigo but faded, lak it been hung out in the sun. But it fine, an' I ain't never had a dress with such pretty color cloth. She get me a bonnet too, white muslin, nothin' fancy, but presentable. She a sweet, stout gal. An' I didn't yet tell yo' that she had her face burned—by the upper right cheek. A patch of angry flesh by her ear. She wear a bonnet to hide the scar. It ain't too bad, but she particular 'bout it. Nobody suppose to axe 'bout how she get burn. The bonnet she give me be same kind as her own.

About three weeks I at this place—gits my strength back—an' I remembers how we—Ethel an' me—went down to the river. We'd go at dusk. After chores when we pretty certain no one travel by.

The sun slippin' over the west—an' James tell me if I follow the river east, I ends up at the Atlantic Ocean. I that close.

But this day I recalls, it just Ethel an' me. James workin' at a evenin' chore. We be down washin' ourself in the warm river. Undress. Only got petticoats on, shifts hung on bushes. Ethel ain't got her bonnet on neither, an' I could sees her patch of rough burn skin. We wadin' barefoot in the low part of the river whar' we often comes to do the washin'. Near the ford an' the ferry raft. There wus a pebble bottom there so the water don't get muddy.

"July," she tell me. "Yo' gonna be leavin' soon. We knowed that when yo' come. But James, he worry 'bout yo'. I worry too. These parts is dangerous. An there ain't nowhar's safe to runs."

The sun gone now—sky a brilliant red, gold almost orange light hang low in the evenin' sky, linger for a time. I know that promise fair weather. I don't say nothin'. It the first that Ethel use the word "run."

We washin' ourselfs an' dunkin' in the river. Then the moon come out, half moon on the wax—shine cast all across the glimmerin' current. We quiet before Ethel say she tired out, better we should sits down awhile. If we ain't clean now, we never git clean.

So we both sits down on the grassy bank. Ma doin' the cookin', an' we ain't et supper yet. The smell waft over from the big iron pot she keep outside. We gonna haves us some fine food tonight. Mostly we et fish cooked up in a stew, an' we always has some broken up hard-tack.

Then—at that very moment—lookin' across the James an' into the moonlit sky, I decides. It come upon me. Hadn't thought much about it till Ethel bring it up. I ready to leave.

"Yo' right, Ethel. I well enough to go. Ain't good for me stay too long. Ain't safe." When I look at her, she know.

"Ain't safe nowhar'," Ethel say. "That what I tryin' to tell yo'." The warm air has a coolness to it, though it still summer.

We silent. Night quiet. Peaceful.

"I ain't never been nowhar'," Ethel say. "Don't wants to go nowhar' neither. Just gonna wait out the war right here." An' she let out a sigh. Ethel sound discouraged, an' there a catch to her voice.

"Yo' ever think 'bout freedom, Ethel?" I axe.

"Negroes always think 'bout that," she say.

Ethel nudge me with her damp body. We still in our petticoats, an' they wet.

"Bet yo' never heared this song, July. They probably ain't sing this one whar' yo' comes from." An' without me answerin' her, Ethel burst out with a song. There, sittin' on the bank with me. She gots herself a deep, strong voice that come from her stout, strong frame. *[Ms. Augustus clears her throat and begins to sing with the same high voice heard previously.]*

> *Sister Rosy, yo' get to heaven before I go,*
> *Sister, yo' look out for me, on the way—*
> *Travel on, travel on—*
> *Yo' heaven-born soldier,*
> *Travel on, travel on—*

That what she sing. Then she hum a li'l an' axe me if she right, if I ain't heared this one before.

"It new to me," I say an' wanna axe what she mean, why she sing it now. But before I can, Ethel just say, "James gonna ferry yo' across when yo' ready."

I look at her. Ethel has long hair that she put into one long braid, an' she 'bout to pin it up.

"Thinkin' to follow the river east—to the ocean," I say.

"Wouldn't do that. Go north—straight north, July. Safer. They be fightin' both ways east an' west. River be exposed, an' yo' shouldn't follow it. Yo' a pretty gal, July." Ethel look right at me. I see the burn mark etch into her cheek, an' her purple skin.

"My bleedin' stop," I say. "I only bleed a li'l them first days. It taper off."

We stand up an' begin dressin'. I help Ethel with her buttons, an' I think back to Mar, my sister. About Kate, Hannah. How I miss them. How far I come.

"Someone waitin' for yo' somewhar', July." Ethel turn to me; now her scar be covered by her bonnet—her whole face in moon shadow.

"I ain't goin' back," I say. "I got a man up north to go to."

"Yo needs to cross this river then. Yo' gonna be free before the rest of us, Independence." Ethel smile. She have a nice smile. "We all knows it. That why we gives yo' that name."

So the very next evenin', I sets off. I sick to my stomach again that mornin', an' James, he plead with me to waits. But by nightfall, I fine. There be another red sundown, an' the time seem right.

Good place to stop. Tomorrow I be movin' north, but the south gonna catch me up. It what Mister Crow predict.

Turn this off. Let's call it quits. Tomorrow market day. An' yo' gonna comes back Monday. I havin' a special church Sunday. Got chores Saturday. But Sunday gonna be my special day. Memorial for David—he die October 3. Nobody here knowed him, of course. But I tell Preacher 'bout him. Everybody got their own troubles, but Preacher promise me a prayer for the dead. [*A scraping noise is heard—probably Ms. Augustus's chair again. Then, the tape machine is snapped off. When Ms. Augustus resumes, it is Monday.]*

October 4, 1937

I light the wood stove last night. First night this year. I gots wood, but not enough. Yo' want that bark tea I makes? There a lady sell me some for a penny. She tell me it fresh, an' it is. On the stove now, hot. *[The tape machine is snapped off and on a few times, and Ms. Augustus resumes.]*

I gonna begins with the service. It nice. Our church—down the street to the left—the li'l white-washed one, is whar' we have it. Only a dozen or so is regular members, ol' folk mostly. An' the preacher, he move around, itinerant. He a young man, ain't married. Call hisself Mr. Washington Jones. Preacher Jones. Get his trainin' in Charlotte, school there. So he read an' write real good, an' he be writin' a book. Can't say why he ain't married. Always wear a blue suit to preach in, an' he has wire glasses. Book writin' strain the eyes.

Preacher, before he begin his sermon, he tell part of David story—the part I tells him. An' he end with *Amazin' Grace*. It my favorite hymn. Ain't sung till after the war— when folks free. The whole congregation there, an' they raise them voices so high, I swear they reach Heaven. *[The scratchy tape runs a few seconds. Then Ms. Augustus pauses, sighs, and continues.]*

That last night, when I leaves James place, sun go down, an' the three us walk to the bank, near the ferry.

"We gonna be thinkin' 'bout yo' an' prayin'," Ethel say an' she hug me. Ma step up an' hand me some fry fish wrap in brown paper, hard tack in a flour sack, an' water in a soldier canteen. I hug her too. She don't say much, only, "We all live under the same stars, July, an' I think they gonna shine pretty bright for yo'."

James help me onto the raft, 'bout to take me across. He load stuff on it earlier in the day so I wouldn't be see'd—sacks an a ol' wagon. He pole me across. The river low, an' when James take me, it gettin' late. But there stars out an' a clear sky.

As James an' me push off, I see Ethel an' Ma, shadowy figures on the high bank. I wearin' my indigo dress an' my white bonnet. An' I feelin' good, ain't throwed up since mornin'.

The James ain't no creek. It a wide, deep river, an' James know what he doin' when he pole. Currents make the cross waters move in different directions. Couldn't ferry without him.

When we gets to the other side, James point the way. He tell me to follow a line of stars, an' he raise his hand up to show me. "Travel at night," he warn. "Only night."

The north bank plenty steep but has rough wood steps sunk into the hillside. James help me up, an' I sure surprise when he pull out a map he draw on a scrap of paper for me. James can't read nor write, but he draw out the map fine. Tell me to put it in my bosom. If I caught, I should eat it. Be death if it found.

James see me up the top rise of the bank, squeeze my hand, tell me be safe. "God go with thee, child," he say. I hug him. Thank him for all his troubles, which was plenty. "Yo folks be in my heart," I say.

I travel—alone again, walkin' fast across the muddy fields, mostly bottomland, along the river what must flood every year—soil so rich an' black. The cane there, ain't waist high yet, an' there be dry dead stalks from last season. No buildin's, houses. Don't know whar' I is, only the map tellin' me that sooner or later I gonna come to a small town, a crossroads.

I ain't supposed to let myself be see'd. It a small place I suppose to find—should be almost deserted 'cause the war take its men. Two dirt roads gonna cross. This be a stage stop for mail, an' there be a general store run by a thief—James tell me this—uset'ta work as overseer at a big plantation to the west.

I walks all night by moonlight. I worry most 'bout snakes. But I feelin' good 'cause I know I followin' James map. When I finally come to the crossroads, I back up a ways to stop outside the town—if yo' could call it that. There a abandon stable, livery of some kind, with faded red letterin' from some bygone time. Think it a good place to stay. It off the road by a fenced pasture. Nobody near. I go in, an' it chilly an' smell. But I make myself a pallet from ol' straw an' ready a stall. I safe.

By the time I do all this, it almost sun-up. Not quite. An' I hungry, so in the first glimmer of mornin' light, I sets down an' gets out my fish an' tack. Ought'ta et it before it spoil, I think, so I decides to put the hard tack back.

I lie down when my belly full, an' tries to sleep. But as I close my eyes, I gets the sweats an' feel the fish come up. Just lak the mornin' before. I get myself to the rear door, hold on, bend over. It all come up till I has only dry heaves.

I sweatin' bad, feel weak, but I get myself into the stall. Stay there all that day. No one come by.

When night descend, I feelin' better, so I gonna travel. James tell me there a plantation with slave quarters 'bout seven mile up, an' when I take out the map, I can see the picture he draw of the huntin' dogs penned up north of the barn. He say I should go up a creek—which is the long ways around—better chance the dogs won't smell me.

So I travel… all the way till I finds myself whar I suppose to be—north of the plantation. Seem lak they seen some heavy fightin'. There a barn burned to cinders. But just lak James tell me, there be the slave quarters. Shacks really, lined up along the narrow road. When I comes upon them, already near mornin', an' James tell me to whistle an' thump the first door I come to. I gots to do it a particular way. A code. Run'ways use. I do it for yo'. [*There is a pattern of three thumps close together, a pause, three thumps, and a pause. Ms. Augustus also whistles in a thin vibrato, bird-like voice that trills quickly and stops.*]

The whistle come first an' at the end. It suppose to sound lak a bird. If nobody come, yo' do it again. But right off, the door squeak open.

Man, 'bout Pa age, stick his head out. He look me up an' down, then open wide enough to let me in. There three or four chil'ren covered in a patchwork under the one window toward the rear of the shack, on a raised pallet. They stirrin' lak a litter of pups. Ma of the house up, tendin' a pot by a small fireplace. She walk to me an' set me down on a small bench by the wall. I gonna be all right here. I weary from walkin' all night in wetness an' mud.

This stop, be the first of many I make. Don't recalls all the names, whar' exactly I stop, couldn't find these places now. But folks wus plenty nice. This family take care of me an' help me pass to the next station.

I spend all the day sleepin' while they out. When they all return at night, they brings me food—corn mush in a tin cup—an' off I go.

Over the next week, I wus still movin' north, accordin' to the map. But I wus wantin' to move east, an' the map direct me west. Folks I meets tell me the same. "Go west." Mo' than once I hear, "Head for the Ohio River. Then up to Canada."

But in my mind, I see David face. Those green eyes, his love letter that I knowed by heart: *I cannot get you out of my mind*, he write. 'Course, now I can't gets him out'ta my mind, neither. *I have no way of knowing if this here letter will reach you, but you say you can read real good, so I feel compelled to write because each word I write reminds me of you.*

Then he say—an' this his second letter: *Forgive me again for trying to write to you like this…. I want to profess to you again my love… so I'll be brief, though my love for you is anything but.* An' what stay with me most: *We will marry and live in freedom with our children, in a future home I will build with my very own hands. My family has land in Maryland and in New York, and they have already promised some to us.* An' he end with—this the part I keep repeatin' in my heart: *So, Mrs. Augustus—for that's who you've been in my heart from the day we first kissed underneath that big oak tree—I close this letter with all my love, and I trust that you, my sweetheart, will wait for me.* An' he sign it, *Your husband-to-be, Mister David Stephens Augustus.*

That what I thinkin' as I walk north. I walkin' mo' toward David than my freedom. An' that why I such a fool as to decides to travel east.

Now my travel git harder. Once I leave the route most run'ways took, there wusn't no regular stops. So I walk nights, an' days I sleep, in the woods mostly. But there be slaves throughout what helps me. I get food when they has any. Many folks take pity, hide me, protect me. They give me courage to go on.

Over the next week, I come to discover somethin'. Every mornin' no matter what I et, I sick to my stomach. I blame it on the cold fish an' soggy tack. Or once I et some spoiled horse meat that give me burnin' fever. But the truth is, ain't the food.

Yo' is a woman, yo' knows what I sayin'. After I bleed at James an' Ethel house, I thinkin' I be safe. But I ain't. I in the family way. I knowed 'bout it first in a dream—my angels come with the news. But that wus after I sees the dyin' soldier.

I wus in the middle of the Virg'nia countryside, which wus all tore up in places whar' there been battles. I see'd burned barns, houses. Deserted churches with the windows smashed. Sometimes the soldiers leave things in creeks or in the woods. I finds good boots hung up by their laces on a tree once.

One time, I wus walkin' through a gully by a long windin' creek. The gully prob'ly get filled up in spring, but in late summer, it almost dry. There be a few stars out, but it wus still pretty dark, an' as I climb down into the gully—to cross—I spots a man lyin' there. Almost stumble over him—a soldier, Confed'rate, but he ain't wearin' his uniform. It stuffed in a haversack. I knowed this, 'cause when I come on him, I think he dead—he so still, so I check his sack. That what wake him. He got a Confed'rate cap an' a jacket in there.

When he stir, it startle me. He groan an' mutter, "Who that?" Words come out slurred.

"Yo' alive?" I axe, an' I move back into a shadow.

"Water," he say. "Water."

Off I crawl with his cap to a shallow pool in the creek gully. I got the canteen James an' Ethel give me, but it clean, an' even in darkness I see this man look filthy. The creek 'bout dry, but I finds a puddle. I scoop some up in the cap.

"Ain't sure this good water," I say. Hard to see. But I has the cap full an' ready. The soldier don't open his eyes, can't lift his head, so I put my hand underneath to help. That when I feel his wound. His head been shot. My hand get sticky from the blood.

"More," he say. "More." He slurp a li'l, but he ain't got enough strength to swallow. Most of it dribble out his mouth.

"They comin' for me. Please! Please! Water!"

I give him the last drops from the cap an' put his head down gentle. I tell him I just gonna get some mo' water for him. But I really wanna clean off my hand. It feel lak a piece of the man head blown away. Can't believe he still talkin'.

I gets another cap full of water. It dank an' smell bad, but the soldier don't mind. I take his uniform jacket from the sack an' rest it behind his head so I don't has to touch him there.

"Don't leave me now," he groan, an' he try to open his eyes. But they just flutter a li'l an' close.

"I ain't leavin'," I say.

An' I give him another sip. He don't care that it got grit in it.

He make one mo' low mournful groan an' give out. I watch his body shudder an' then relax. He never knowed I wus a Negro run'way.

That day, when I sleep, I has the dream. After I leaves this dead man, I cross the creek an' push on deep into a cane thicket whar' I can't be see'd. It gettin' light out. Then I stop an' take the hard tack from my pack. Ain't much, but it somethin'. An' I feelin' sick, lak the tack might settle me.

I et it all down, every last bit I has. But less than a hour go by, an' up it comes. I sick real bad that night—sweatin' with the dry heaves again. Finally, they stop, an' I clean my mouth with canteen water.

I pull down some dead cane stalks, pile them underneath, a bed, so to keeps me off the dirt. I has to sleep with my face up, the cane so scratchy. But I thankful for it an' fall right to sleep.

In my dream that day, I be walkin' across a battlefield whar' there be bodies of the dead. Newly dead. An' the field so thick that I has to step on them to cross. The field muddy too. An' as I step on the bodies, some groan, lak my soldier. So when I hears that, I stop an' turns over the mens that groanin'. But each soldier I turn become one of my faceless angels. An' as I turn a body, it feel lak I settin' a soul free with each turn.

In the dream, all this turnin' puts me in a strange mood, an' I feel almost weightless, a angel myself. Now, I don't minds steppin' on hurt soldiers. I light, an' find myself skippin' over them, hopin' they gonna groan.

So I skippin' along, settin' souls free, when I comes upon one that cry out when I land on him. An' when I turn this one over, he shrink up, become a baby, a infant, an' she—*yas, she*—has a face. Then I hear a voice, "Pick her up, Sarah Louise. Pick her up!"

I do. An' it a perfect, swaddled infant. My breasts ache lak they full of milk.

"She yours, Sarah Louise," I hear. "Your baby."

I pop awake, sittin' up, gaspin' for air lak someone try to suffocate me. An' I knows I in a family way. [*There is a long silence, and the scratchy tapes continues for about half a minute before Ms. Augustus resumes.*]

That how Mister Crow come to be right again. Yas, I caught. Caw, caw, caw, caught. Ain't by soldiers catchin' me 'cause I a run'way. Them soldiers that hurt me, they the ones that catch me up.

By night, I gotta be walkin'. So I takes off into the woods, an' there a path I follow. I meets no one. That good, 'cause I so I numb from the news my angels brung that I ain't too careful. Just walkin'.

Close to day break, I finds a abandon cow barn. Nobody bother me, an' already I get to feelin' sick again—in the belly, heavin' with nothin' inside. An' hungry, real hungry. I finds a stall, lie down, but can't sleep.

This is whar' I break down. Summer birds chirpin'—maybe they keepin' me awake. But how coulds I blame them, singin' lak nothin' in this fine world can ever be wrong. But then I think 'bout the soldier with his shattered head.

I think again of Ma, Mar, Kate, Hannah, an' me, how we wait for Pa Saturday nights. How us gals pile into one sack, squirmin', gigglin'. How the fireplace throw out such hot heat on winter nights. How the new wash smell fresh dryin' on the bushes near our cabin.

I touch my belly—ain't no bulge yet. Then some other memories flood back. Lyin' in the stall, I feel them soldiers pinnin' me down on the muddy bank, smell the chloroform.

"Yo' just a child, an' yo' ain't up to no good," I hear Ma say. An' I put my face down into the scratchy straw an' take to sobbin'—sobbin' 'cause the child I is wus 'bout to die. Make way for the child I be carryin' inside.

"Ma," I say. "I sorry for all I done. Can yo' forgives me?" I lifts my head an' sees her clear as if she right there in front of me, hangin' washin' over the holly bushes what near the cabin at home. Her back toward me.

Without turnin' around, Ma say, "Sarah Louise, Sarah Louise, my baby gal that done left me." She a vision, an' I seein' her, but she ain't seein' me.

"I ain't left yo', Ma," I say aloud. I wanna go over, put my arms around her stout waist, feel her warmth as she hug me to her.

It look so real that I rise from the straw an' go to her, "It me, Ma. Sarah Louise. I here. I home." But as I go to put my arms to her, she vanish into air. "Ma," I yell. "Don't go! Don't leave me!"

"Ain't me the one leavin', Sarah Louise," the vision say. "It yo' that done left us. Yo' is the one struck out. Such a foolish gal. Always wus. Now, we ain't got no way to know what become of yo'."

At this point, I standin' up outside, in daylight, thinkin' Ma got the wash laid out on some nearby bushes. But it dangerous to be out lak this. I ain't in my right mind. Don't even care if I gets caught.

"That right, Mister Crow," I say. "Yo' catch me with child. Now go on an' send yo' white folks to caught me with chains."

I so full of self pity that I collapse an' just start weepin'. Cry lak I never gonna stop. Sick, alone, an' in a family way. Can't stop feelin' sorry. No. I just give in. I lak that soldier with his blown away head, gaspin' for water, dyin' in a ditch. No kin, no pity in the world for him. I think back to Doc Goldstein—it a sad world, an' no good come from livin' in it.

After a while, I stop ballin' an' drag my skinny self back whar it safe inside the barn, spend the day nappin' on an' off, gettin' ready to travel by night fall. I thin as young sapling, ain't no bulge showin' yet, so that, I think, is good.

But soon I take to worryin' what gonna happen if I finds David. How he gonna react? Does I expect him to want me now? How can he if I shows up with a child ain't his? He gonna believes it ain't my fault? I ain't to blame? An' even if he convinced, is he gonna want a tarnished gal, a run'way hunted down?

That night, I goes on, but my strength ain't there. My spirit, my will broke. Now I'm thinkin' how I even gonna finds David? Don't know whar' he is, if he alive. How I gonna knows whar' to go? I on a foolish journey 'cause I such a foolish gal. A stupid foolish gal with only myself to blame. *[Ms. Augustus lets out a deep sigh and pauses. The scratchy tape continues, and she resumes.]*

I make my way north—somehow. Still travelin' most though woods, but sometimes through fields gone to clover an' weeds. Fields that wusn't planted. Whole farms, cabins, small towns deserted.

The war terrible; chaos spread all throughout Virg'nia. Hard to describe. Can't imagine. Countryside devastated. Empty fields an' kitchen gardens. Fences down. Hen houses an' barns empty. Only ghosts. The whole country dying.

An' me—I just one sorry run'way slave gal, makin' my way through it. *[There is a brief pause in the tape.]*

Don't axe me how, but I finds my way to Baltimore. It take me a month, maybe. I lose sense of time. It wus summer still. War all around me, sounds of gunfire in the air, dead men on the fields, in the creeks an' woods. I walk through many a battle-torn place, with the spirits of the dead still lingering, unsure what to do. *[There is another brief pause, and Ms. Augustus sighs once more, then resumes.]*

I wus gonna tell yo' 'bout my miracle, how it come to pass. But I tired now, tired as the gal I wus then. End here for the day. *[There is some low, unintelligible mumbling, the sound of chairs scraping, and the machine is turned off. When Ms. Augustus begins again, it is clearly the next day.]*

October 5, 1937

How yo' lak all this rain? Mr. Jim from around the corner come by with some stove wood. He sellin' sawed up slabs to white folk, but he don't charge me nothin' for what he bring. I wanna give him somethin' for his trouble, but he won't take it. Nice an' toasty here now. I sittin' all mornin', waitin' for yo' arrive. An' here yo' is.

My ol' bones don't lak the rain. But that part of age. Doc say not much he can do. Give me pills, tell me to stay warm. Which I doin'. An' Mr. Jim brung me a penny to wear. That what they uset'ta do—wear copper or brass. The copper better, though some say the brass work too. Ma uset'ta takes the copper ladle an' rub it on her wrists—claim it help her bones. Mr. Jim, he take a awl an' make a hole, an' strung it up for me. I wearin' it now, but it ain't has enough time to work yet. Jim say it gonna take a day or so. I got yo' tea here, all ready. It on the stove top, near the kettle—there. *[A slight scraping sound is heard, then a pause, and Ms. Augustus resumes.]*

Well…I still walkin'. An' somehow I walk myself right into the great big city of Baltimore. Someone lookin' out for me. I travel by night among the slave quarters an' find my way first to Ellicott City—has the same name as the plantation—an' it a good ways from Baltimore.

I recalls comin' up on a corduroy road. Thick logs. New built for the Union Army. It were evenin' time, not quite night, an' I shouldn't been out. But I spent the day in a abandon chicken house, an' the smell got me up.

There wus Union soldiers along here, but ain't nobody takin' passes or botherin' with colored. Some Negro women wus doin' washin' in a creek beneath a bridge. Soldiers pay them ten cent a bundle. Old uniforms, bloody. Rags that can be used again. Socks. Blankets. One of the gals give me a bundle, axe if I wanna help. So I get hired.

Her name Ruth. An' after we wash a couple of bundles, she axe me if I need a place to stay, it turnin' dark an' all. I tell her, yas. Stay with her 'bout three days. Washin' an' turnin' my days around—so that I begins to sleep nights again.

Ruth has a cabin off the road, with lines strung between trees so that the wash get hung dry. Her place have a bed an' table, an' Ruth live alone. Don't remember her story, but her ma recently passed. Ruth 'bout my age.

I earn money for the first time. Ruth help me buy food, which we cook outside her place. She a quiet gal.

So lak I say, I be off after a few days. Ruth tell me the road that lead to Baltimore an' tell me that I be safe out walkin'. So many folks 'bout; no one gonna take notice. An' she give me a address of friends I suppose to locate. They gonna let me stay for a few days, she certain.

By this time, I wearin' a brown dress give to me by a Negro house slave name Bertha—Martha or Bertha. It were a white woman dress, an' she die in childbirth. Martha, Bertha, she get the dress from her white folk—brown with pale yellow stitchin' on the collar, which stand up. On the sleeves, it have flowers, delicate sewn. It real pretty, an' Martha pass it to me 'cause it too small for her. I put it away in my sack, especially when I do the washin'. But before I leaves Ruth cabin, I has it on. It good for the city. Gonna fit right in—with that an' with the lacework shawl an' bonnet I also given.

I still slim. Ain't told nobody 'bout my situation, not Ruth, not no one. An' nobody axe me whar' I come from or what I doin'. Nobody wanna know.

I finds the address Ruth give me by axin' folks. Only colored folk I dare speak to. The friends has a flat. That what they call it—room in a big brick buildin' on the outskirts of Baltimore. Flat have a stove an' some cots. Table, chairs. Family that take me in has two chil'ren—both young. Father work as a driver—don't knows mo' than that. Driver. He a driver for some white family. It a crowded, small room that ain't too clean. An' the ma, she take to yellin' at the youn'uns. So after a few days, I thank them all an' be off. Though whar', I ain't exactly sure.

Many free blacks in Baltimore. But there sure slaves there too. The streets is busy, an' I think now that tryin' to find David be lak tryin' to find a needle in a haystack.

Don't even knows if David here. Only he once live here. But that long ago. Ol' news. *[There is a short pause in the tape.]*

So, here I is—at the end of my journey, walkin' myself into the a big, big city. After I leaves Ruth friends, I decides to go to the docks, the wharf, 'cause I rememberin' that David be a stevedore before the war.

I is clean an' pert in my brown dress, bonnet, an' shawl, so I figure that no one take no notice of me. I fits right in.

Lookin' back, I think now how plain ignorant I be. Wanderin' into a city big as Baltimore, thinkin' I gonna find a black man that prob'aly ain't even there.

I finds my way again by axin'. When I there, the streets by the wharf is particular dirty, an' I has to lifts my dress hem, walkin' with care not to get soiled. It take me the whole day to walk through the city, pickin' my way, lookin' around, followin' directions.

Near dusk by the time I arrives. Big orange sun sinkin' into the ocean. Pallets an' wood boxes all stacked up on the quay. I feelin' so weary that I sits down on a crate to rest.

"Hey, yo'!" I hear.

I stand up. "Me?"

A mulatto man appear. I ain't even seen him walk up. He a older woman, rough dressed, but with manners. He tip his cap.

"I wus just sittin' here a moment. Be off soon," I say.

"No need," the man say. "I seen yo' here, an' yo' look lost. Thought I come say howdy." He sit. "Yo' mind?" He tap the spot next to him, an' I sit again.

The wood crate is big, an' so I scoot over, a li'l away. I nod, without lookin' at him. He still wearin' the cap anyway—his face in shadow.

"I Beauregard. Lightenin' Beauregard," he say, an' I feels his eyes glarin' at me. "Go by L. B."

"Nice to meet yo', Mr. Beauregard, but I soon be on my way."

"Gal lak yo' might needs some help," Mr. Lightenin' Beauregard say. "Look lak yo' expectin'. Happen all the time." He smile. I see it out the corner my eye.

I feels somethin' stir—a strange flutterin', an' I touch my belly.

"Bet yo' hungry," L. B say. "Gal in yo' condition. My wife, she always manage to cook up a good supper. An' we live close by." His eyes still on me.

I sit there, must be a full minute before I answer. "I a run'way," I say, then immediately regret it. Don't know what happen—words just slip out.

"I knowed that when I see'd yo'. Whar' yo' run from, gal? Whar' yo' from?" L. B. raise his voice. I see his head look me up an' down.

"Ain't true," I say. Now I look at him. "I just gives yo' a li'l test. See how yo' take it. I from Ellicott City, whar' I stay with Ruth, my cousin. She an' her ma, my aunt. They has a nice place by a creek there. Gotta gets back. I gonna be missed." I stands up.

"Ellicott a long ways off," L. B. say.

"I came here lookin' for a colored man, David Augustus, work as a stevedore one time."

Mr. Beauregard, he just smile—a strange, knowin' sort of grin. Then he take off his cap, scratch his head, an' I see he ol' enough to be someone gran'pap. His hair is white, lak a pear tree in bloom.

L. B. got kind eyes, but I ain't feelin' good 'bout him 'cause he seem to know too much an' make me say things I shouldn't say. An' I sure ain't ready to go on home with him. I knows that.

So I thank him an' decides to walk away—though I ain't clear what direction.

I walkin' along the wharf, mo' to look at the ocean than think 'bout David. The water calm, small peaks risin' an' fallin' lak the breath of a million kittens sleepin' right beneath the surface. Then my mind get carried to Back Bay, an' I thinkin' 'bout the day we go to the ocean an' I see'd that li'l Sarah Louise runnin' barefoot.

"Miss," I hear. "Miss, yo' forgots this," L. B. walkin' toward me, arm extended with my lace shawl in his hand. "An' I wanna give yo' this, too," he say.

I stand there in the near darkness as L. B. walk to me, give me my shawl—an' a card. A printed card. "I bet yo' can reads. Yo' just the sort," he say.

"Thank yo', Mr. L. B.," I say, takin' both items. Mr. Beauregard wink at me, then hobble away down the cobblestone street, off through a narrow alley. Hadn't noticed his limp before. *[There is a short pause in the tape. Ms. Augustus sighs and continues.]*

Why don't we take us a break? I gonna stretch my legs. Get us somethin' to drink. *[The tape machine is turned off, and when Ms. Augustus resumes, it seems to be just a little later.]*

Well, L. B.—he end up all right. Didn't know that yet. An' the card he give me read somethin' lak:

> *Dowser Extraordinaire. Master Lightening Beauregard Will Locate Water, Minerals, Buried Treasure & Persons Missing or Lost. Negroes and Slave Owners Welcome. Open Day and Night Anytime. God is on Your Side. 22 Elm Street. Reasonable Fees. No Confederate Dollars Accepted.*

I read the card. It wus ragged an' I almost tore it in half. But I read it instead, an' when I look up—Mr. L. B., nowhar' in sight. He disappear down some alley.

When I first gets to the wharf, men unloadin' a big ship at dock. Now, they all gone. Big crates settin' on the cobblestones street that wus closed off with a iron chain. No one around, the place empty. I stand by the water, put on my shawl, an' I keeps readin' the card again an' again.

At this point, I realizin' that L. B. my only choice. I ain't got no whar' else to go. I hungry an' unkempt. So I walk from the wharf to a side street an' axe directions from a woman, a middle-age Negro woman that got her door open, moppin' the hallway floor an' splashin' some dirty water out into the alley. I tell her the street address—an' she know whar' it is.

"Who yo' try to find?" she axe. An' when I tell her Lightenin' Beauregard, she know right off whar' I needs to go. "Ain't nothin' that man can't do, an' nothin' that man won't do," she say an' point me in the right direction.

I finds the place quick. Weren't no mo' than a few minute walk from this Negro gal place. It a brick row house on a narrow street. I figure the wharf nearby to the east an' south. I knock. A mulatto gal open the door. She 'bout my age, I reckon. She wear a neat brown homespun muslin dress an' a full apron.

"We expectin' yo'," she nod her head, step back so I can enter, but I stands there a minute.

"I lookin' for Mr. Beauregard," I say.

"Pa is expectin' yo'. He is home but asleep. Ma up. I get her. Come in. Don't want to stand in the street. Not around here."

So I walks in the hall, dim, but for a few stubby candles lit. It a narrow hall with wood floors, no rug, an' peelin' paper on the walls.

"Yo' wait, an' I gets Ma." The gal give me a nod, an' she off. I alone in the strange, narrow hallway.

Her ma, a ol' heavy woman, remind me of my ma. She also wear a apron, an' she dryin' her hands on it as she come. "We expectin' yo'. L. B. say yo' probably be arrivin' tonight, tomorrow mornin' at the latest." She nod too, but indicatin' she want me to follow. I do.

We end up in the back room, kitchen. It got a rough pine table an' four chair. She tell me to sets awhile. Must be tired, hungry, which I is. "When yo' baby due?" the ma axe, her back still toward me. I don't say nothin'. She axe 'gain, "The baby, when it come?"

"Ain't know nothin' 'bout no baby," I say, my voice weak.

"I got some cornmeal I fixin'. That good?" the ma axe.

"Yas, ma'am," I say. I could feel my belly growlin'. "I sure appreciate it. Seem lak I lost my way."

The young gal come in from the back yard, a alleyway really, whar' they gots a small garden. "Sit down, Ellie," the ma say. "Yo' just in time."

We et some. It good, an' I keeps it down.

What I remember next is that they puts me to bed—a big double bed, a raised pallet in a big room upstairs. Three stories to this house, an' I in the attic. The window open, but it still warm. Clean, it very clean, an' the big pallet—mattress stuffed with feathers, 'cause it soft—raised up on two boxes—wooden boxes. Maybe trunks. They gots pillows, a big soft blanket. There be curtains, an' it all be white. That what I recalls. White. Lak a big fluffy dream. Mr. Beauregard wife help me off with my dress, an' she have a night shirt ready for me. It the kind white folk wear—very white an' pretty. Then she put me to bed, an' I feels lak I put on a cloud.

"Ma'am. I never catched yo' name," I say, already feelin' drowsy.

"Ma Eve. That what everybody call me."

"Thank yo', Ma Eve," I say. "For all yo' kindness." Then the moment I puts my head on that soft pillow, I asleep.

It be nearly noon when I wakes up, groggy, lak I been drugged. An' as I gettin' up in that strange house, I notice that it very quiet, ain't a sound to be heard. Right away, I hungry again. Stomach growlin'. I touch it. Don't feel nothin'. *How'd L. B. knowed 'bout my condition?* I thinkin'. Then, I just thinkin' 'bout cornmeal an' how easy I keeps it down. That the only thing I wantin' now.

I change back into my dress. But it smell bad—hadn't realized, an' there be dried mud on the hem. Have to make do. I put it on, smooth my hair, get the bonnet layin' on a wood chair, tie that on, an' go down. Real slow on them creaky stairs.

As I go down, but it strange—I seem to be alone in the house. I steppin' down quiet, ain't wantin' to disturb no one, but then again, ain't nobody there.

That when I see him. *[There is a long pause here, and the scratchy tape is heard. Then Ms. Augustus continues in a high voice.]*

First, I don't even recognize him, an' I startle. Strange soldier settin' at the kitchen table, his head down on his folded arms, asleep—I think it be L. B. family, kin. So I tip-toe into the room. The light dim, an' I look for a candle, but don't want to disturb the man.

Then, my eyes get adjusted, an' I cross the room. "David," I whisper. "That yo'?"

The man lift his head slow, lak I rousin' him from a deep dream. Then he smile, an' I recognize those green eyes, even in the dim light.

He get up, come over to me, an' I fall into his arms. He hug me so tight, an' he kissin' my face all over. I laughin'. Joy, deep down, bustin' through. Then I'm crying. Tears come in a downpour, a terrible strong rain after draught.

"Sarah Louise, Sarah Louise, Sarah Louise," he say.

"David, David, David," I say back. An' now he start weepin'. Tears come drippin' from his eyes, but he ain't weep lak me. Just them tears flowin' slow, manly.

"Oh God!" David say. "I knew you'd come to me, and that he'd find you. I knew L. B. would come through. I just knew it, knew it." An' he start to laugh. An' I be laughin' too.

I gots so much to axe David, but for some reason, I ain't concerned. It all feel part of some dream—stumblin' on L. B., spendin' the night here in that room. Ellie, Ma Eve, corn meal I keep down, the clean, fresh bed an' night shirt. Then wakin' up alone in a dark house an' comin' down to find my David, asleep at the kitchen table.

"Can't stay but one night," David say. "I'm a soldier."

But it lak I don't hear him. Can't, won't believe him. "We all right," I say. "Ain't nobody, nothin' gonna makes us part ever again."

"Got to be quick here, Sarah Louise. But I'm not ever going to let you go." David grinnin' again an' squeeze my hand. "My Sarah Louise," he say. "My Sarah Louise. I'm going to make you my wife tonight. And not going to do it a letter either."

My jaw must'ta drop right open. An' I thinkin' that this should be the happiest moment in my life, but it ain't. I ruined.

"I gotta tell yo' somethin', David," I begin. David squeeze my hand again. He bend over the table an' kiss my cheek, look at me so close with his green eyes.

"What?" he say. Then, "Tell me later. We've been waiting for this moment our entire lives. We were born to have this night together. I loves you so." He up now. Then quick, he down on floor by whar' I sit. "I'm going to do it right. You deserve this. I'm going to ask you proper."

Time stand still. David be on one knee, kneelin' by me. I can see it as if it wus yesterday.

"Sarah Louise, you have my undying love forever and forever. I want you to be my wife. Will you, Sarah Louise, marry me?"

I look down at him, on one knee, proposin' lak a white man. An' he pull out a small box from his trouser.

"This here is for you. It once belonged to my mother, but it is yours if you say 'I do.' Open it. Before you answer, open it up."

I take the small wood box. It got a tiny hinge on it an' a rose in full blossom carved on the top. The rose painted pink, an' the box painted black. My heart heavy as I open it. Inside is a ring, a emerald ring with some filigree in gold around the stone.

"It beautiful," I say. "It the most beautiful thing I ever see'd in my life." Tears well up again an' I can't hold them back.

"I want you to be happy. I want you to say yes."

"Yas," I say.

We in each other arms again. Almost on the floor as I swoop into his powerful embrace. Then, I start sobbin'. David untie my bonnet, take it off, toss it on the table, an' he kiss my face. This time, he wild with passion—lak he preparin' to love to me right on the spot. An' it feel good, so I don't tell him. An' the whole knotted world inside me come undone. *[There is a brief pause in the tape, but then Ms. Augustus continues.]*

I gonna need to rest a minute. Get my bearin'. Need to set. *[The tape machine is clicked off. When it is turned on, it is still the same day.]*

Ain't talk 'bout this day for a long time. It all seem lak it all happen to someone else. Another gal. But it happen to me.

That Baltimore row house, we has a weddin'—yas, that night. There a preacher, an' we has it in the parlor. Official, with papers an' L. B., Ma Eve, an' Ellie as witnesses. I ain't got that paper anymo'. An' I ain't got no proof, but I tell yo' it wus a real weddin', an' there weren't no broom.

I married in a white dress. Don't even know whar' it come from, but Ma Eve get it for me. It a bit tight, but I fit myself into it. An' I still has the ring—that emerald ring David give me—but it stored in its box, with a friend daughter for safe keepin'. She in Fayett'ville. I wearin' my weddin' band; don't think it could come off. They gonna has to bury me with it.

After David propose an' we hug, I lose my nerve. Ain't has the courage to tell David I with child. An' Ma Eve, when she come in—I guess, she don't feel it her place to say—which it ain't. An' I ain't got the heart, the strength. David just glowin'. I tell yo' he a handsome, wonderful man, an' I knowed it the first time I laid eyes on him at the Cape Fear River landin', under the willow oak.

Ol' Ibo tale say that it bring good luck for gals to be under the shade of a tree. The bigger the tree, the mo' luck she get. Suppose to bring a single gal marriage, an' a married gal, chil'ren. That what Uncle Cicero say back when I a li'l child, before the mule kick him.

It all go by in a rush. David appear out'ta nowhar', an' we married that same night. They gots papers, preacher, an' even has us a cake. Ma Eve show up with a white dress, an' in that parlor I say "I do" to the love of my life.

After the weddin' ceremony, we all has somethin' to et. I keep it down. Then we has our weddin' night in the attic room. Everyone joke that we in the honeymoon suite—prepare just for us.

Done talked myself out for now. I done in. [*Ms. Augustus sighs. There is a pause and another long sigh. The tape machine is turned off.*]

October 6, 1937

Last night there were a fire down the street. House burn to ashes. You seen it? Ain't the way yo' come in. Down the other way. Commotion start after dark, maybe seven. Thank God the people didn't get burned up with it. Some say it wus white folks sets the rental house on fire for a debt ain't been paid. City fire truck show up. Whole neighborhood be watchin'. White man what own the house want the insurance money paid. These sorry times.

So I up with all the neighbors. Yo' can still smell the smoke. That burnin' gonna hang in the air for a while. People gets theirselfs work up, do terrible things. KKK. Shouldn't even talk. Bring bad luck. Ain't no crosses, thank God, when that house go. But I see'd them other times.

But I gettin' a ways from my story…. [*Ms. Augustus clears her voice, then resumes.*]

August that year. We still in '62. Lots mo' fightin' to come.

Well, it our weddin' night. We stay in that attic room—with the big, white feather bed. Come to finds out later that David expectin' me in Baltimore. The room prepared a while ago. L. B., a dowser, yo' know. An' his specialty to find folks that gone.

David has L. B. finds me. I go to L. B., thinkin' I stumblin' on him, an' I ain't gots no place to go—but that ain't the case. David ain't livin' in Baltimore lak I think. L. B. contact him through a rider—messenger boy—when he see me at the wharf. An' they related—later, I come to finds out that L. B. an' David, they be kin.

Our weddin' night—that clean white bed, an' the white curtains wus blowin' in the warm night breeze. David, he never knowed nothin' 'bout what happen to me—not that night, not then. I has my difficulties that night, but David a patient man.

When I try to fall asleep in his arms, all I see is them men an' that muddy river bank. With all my might, I try to keep that memory out'ta my head, but I can't. So I pretend, just pretend.

"Yas," I say, "Everything fine." But they wusn't. Yo' a woman, know what I mean. I ain't right, but his sake, say I is. I tryin' to make this night what he want, what I want. But I can't.

David, now, he ain't no fool. He know something wrong. But he don't know 'bout what happen or the memories I havin'. I with David, in his arms, tucked beside him on the bed, but my mind back at the creek. A slap, a shove, a hand pullin' at my hair. Legs ache, an' my back hurt, somethin' stabbin' at me.

Nobody, not Ma Eve, Ellie, L. B. tell my secret. Maybe David think I scared 'cause I still only a gal. Or maybe that I has a bad time escapin', runnin', which I do. I let him think that.

David do axe, an' I tell him 'bout what happen as I make my way north. I tells him about James an' Ethel. Other folks. But when he axe me why I run, I only say that the soldiers in camp wus plottin' against me. That I escape before they gets a chance to do something bad. I run in the nick of time.

But shame crawl all over me when I say this. Not only 'cause I lyin'. Or what wus done to me. But 'cause I ain't got the courage to speak. I thinkin' that the chloroform do something to me, make it difficult. Even the house burnin' last night bring some of it back. I didn't tell yo' that. Part the reason why I couldn't sleep. [*There is a pause. Ms. Augustus sighs and continues.*]

A white man got the palm of his hand tight against my mouth. Shuttin' it tight. Can hardly breathe. Then there be thick white clouds in front of my face—blockin' the men faces. I see shapes standin' over me, an' can feel I bein' stabbed inside. An' men is laughin'; I do hear laughin'. I try to breathe, but I can't catch my breath.

Inside, I screamin', but no sound come out. In another piece, a soldier take a long sword from a sheath, a bayonet. It shine, glisten right in front of me, an' I start to sweat, my heart poundin'. *[There is a long pause, followed by a sad-sounding sigh, different than other sighs. After another pause, Ms. Augustus resumes.]*

My weddin' night with David get filled with half dreams, nightmares. Weren't able to sleep, but sort of fadin' in an' out. I see the sword that night too. When David touch me, I layin' in the river bank slime an' the shadows be there. I struggle all that night. I haunted, but I be happy too.

David, he tell me he a military man, fight for the Union. An' I also learn that he got a brother up in Mass'chusets that wus fightin' too. I ain't never meet that brother, just heared 'bout him. He killed in South Car'lina, near the end of the war.

David brigade be buildin' a road. I figure he near the ocean 'cause he got so much experience on boats. But he ain't. He cuttin' logs for roads. An' by mornin' he need to gets back.

L. B., Ma Eve, an' Ellie occupyin' the floors below. After the weddin', they quiet, leave us be.

The hours pass. Dark, but there moonlight shinin' through the open windows, white gauze curtains swayin'. David fall asleep while I in his arms. I hear his calm, regular breathin', an' it help. Then, almost mornin', he stir a bit, then come awake—birds singin'. Still dark out, not quite dawn.

"It is the nightingale, not the lark," David say.

"What?" I axe.

"That's from Shakespeare," he say. "*Romeo and Juliet.*"

I say nothin', but it please me. We just lie there together as it turn light. That one of the best memories of my life. *[Ms. Augustus lets out a long sigh, and then there's a long pause before she continues.]*

Now, I done heared of Shakespeare, but I never read any. It ain't written regular. Once, years later, I borrow a big Shakespeare book, full of plays an' poems, but I couldn't make no sense of it, nor read any. Couple of poems, they make some sense, but that it. Ol' style, too hard. It just go to show how educated David wus. He knowed that book good enough to keep some in his head.

So we lay lak this. So nice, I ready to forgets 'bout the baby, 'bout all that I ain't ready to tell. Then come a mockin' bird harsh cry, an' David say, "I gonna go now, sweetheart." He sit up, half off the bed. "But we need us some plans." His naked back toward me, an' I run my hand over his smooth, warm skin.

"I want you to stay in Baltimore. Here. I don't want you traveling any more—isn't safe." David stand up, dress hisself. From a cloth bag he brung, he got a uniform he take out. "Lightenin' say that you can board here. Ellie knows a white woman that needs a house maid. She thinks yo'd do fine. She wants to recommend you." David turn to me. He almost dressed. His whole handsome uniform on. Hot, lazy sun filterin' now through the gauze. There street noise now—wagons on the cobblestones, horses shod feet clippin' along. Voices. Shouts. Children.

"I ain't sure I can stay here, David. These folks, nice, but they ain't kin. I a run'way. There may be people out lookin' for me. An' Ma, Pa, Kate, Mary…I miss them." Just sayin' their names make me lonesome. Tears well up; I put my head back down on the warm pillow, tryin' not to, but I weepin'.

"It'll be all right, Sarah," David say. "You're my wife now. I'll take care of you." David sit beside me. His weight pull me toward him. He stroke my head, unbury my face, takin' it between his strong hands, kissin' it all over lak it something sweet. Then, he sit back up, pull away, look straight at me. "L. B. is my great uncle," David say. "He's my father's father's brother. Ma Eve is my great aunt by marriage. They are free—my whole family is free, Sarah. And now they're your kin too." David lift my hand that got two rings on it—the emerald an' the gold band. "I wouldn't leave you with strangers."

I let the bed sheet drop, sit up, an' press myself against David, dressed in his starch uniform. He take me in his arms, an' I feel the cold brass buttons on my skin.

When David say that 'bout stayin' here with Ma Eve, I relieved at first. Mostly 'cause she know my situation. But then I be thinkin' it ain't so good after all 'cause bein' kin, she might tell David. I fall silent. There a knot in my heart, an' I can't speak.

"I've got to go, gal," David say. "Mrs. Augustus, Sarah Louise, my sweet, my fine girl. You have to promise to wait here. I'll return when I can. I'll write when I can. This way, I'll know where you'll be. You're safe here, and after the war, you're going to be free." David lift one of his boots to the chair, tightenin' his laces. Big, black, shiny boots.

"But what if people come look for me? I still a run'way. An' what I do 'bout…"

"The war is almost over, Sarah. It isn't going to last much longer, baby gal. I'm getting money for soldiering. Putting money away. And you'll be working too. That way the time pass quickly. We're going to give you a new name so that no one can find you. Fixing that now. Uncle Lightening knows his way about, how to fix such things. You're won't have to worry about anything. Trust me. I'm taking care you already."

Some dusty mornin' light settle around the room—on the bed, on the dresser that by the window. It that Baltimore summer heat come filterin' in. By mid-day, it risin' from the pavers, horse manure, stables, an' the vendors that sell fish an' chicken. When I thinks 'bout Baltimore now, what I recalls most is them summer smells.

One mo' kiss, an' David gone. Quick as he come. I lie back on the bed, tryin' to sort out what just happen. I hear house noises, muffled, from below. I can't make them out. Prob'ly Ma Eve, Ellie, L. B. havin' breakfast. Thinkin' 'bout it make me hungry, but I ain't ready to rise. So I lies down an' falls back to sleep.

Well, I must'ta sleep all the way to afternoon, late. Ellie come to check on me. "Sarah Louise, we worried 'bout yo'." Her warm hand on my shoulder, shakin' it so gentle.

"I wakin' up, now," I say, shiftin' in the bed, though I realize to pull the sheet up. But I feel drugged, heavy as a log after rain.

"Yo' ain't has to get up now," Ellie say. Her voice low, almost a whisper. I look at her face. She my age, but untouched, innocent. Her skin a nice deep coffee color.

"What time is it?" I wrap the bed sheet around me an' sits straight up. Ellie stand by me.

"It's around five, Sarah. David had to go real early, but he see us before he left. We need to talk 'bout it, but not now." An' she nod at my belly. "Ma want me to bring yo' this dress." Ellie put it on the chair by the bed.

It plain, but it look lak it gonna fit better an' be cooler than what I wearin' before.

"I'll go now. When yo' ready, get dressed an' come downstairs. Get somethin' to eat." Ellie step forward, give me a small hug lak she Mar or Kate. An' she leave quiet as she come.

I ready to rise up, so after a few minutes, I do. An' I pull on the new dress—fit good, nice an' loose—go downstair. Ma Eve there—but not Ellie or L. B. I ets some mush an' has a glass of cool milk. Ma Eve say it good for me. She fixin' stew—which be cookin' in a pot outside. Inside it too hot to cook, but there be a kitchen stove lak I ain't never see'd before.

So Ma Eve tell me the plan—what I wus to live by for the next few years. This wus gonna be my home. That attic, my room, except if we has "visitors." That what she call run'ways, deserters, abolitionists. This is a "safe house," but no one ever use it as such when I there.

Ma Eve tell me I now has a new name: Mrs. Eliza Payne—she pick it 'cause she got a paper with that name on it. "We ain't gonna call yo' nothin' else." Ma Eve say, an' I notice her strong accent. Then she add that I gots to call her "Aunt Eve" now. "An' I take that emerald ring from yo' finger, gal…. It too fancy. Yo' can wears yo' plain gold band." She tell me that she gonna stick the emerald ring safe beneath a loose floorboard behind the stove. Ain't nobody but family know it there

I look at Ma Eve. I don't wanna give her the emerald ring off my finger. I deserve it an' wants to wear it. But there be Ma Eve, lookin' at me, waitin'.

So I unscrews it from my finger, an' hands it over. She just stick it in her apron pocket an' nod.

David an' L. B. set this up. I can'ts remember all how the story go, but they has some relative in Baltimore by that name, an' she in Canada now. But they gots her papers—don't even knows what paper she talkin' 'bout. Some document I needs if someone check on me. All I remembers is from that time on my weddin' papers go with someone else, an' I never see'd them again. So Eliza I become. *[There is a short silence. Then Ms. Augustus speaks very low.]*

My name become my baby gal. Turn this thing off. [*The machine is snapped off quickly. When the tape is turned on again, it is the next day.*]

October 7, 1937

Right away, I hired out as a housemaid in Baltimore city. This part of the plan.

Now as Eliza Payne, I suppose to be L. B. niece, Ellie cousin—an' I come all the way from the west to finds proper work. I be a grievin' widow, come back to family to has my baby. Aunt Eve an' L. B. sweared to my "dead husband" that they gonna takes care of me.

White woman, Mrs. Johnson, I begins to work for, she take me in to do washin', cleanin', an' such. No cookin'. Already gots herself a cook.

An' David. I don't see him. No letters neither. Not one word. When he first come into my life, I wus a youn' gal, a slave in Fayett'ville. An' now I a married woman an' havin' someone baby.

Soon, I begins work for the Johnsons. Mrs. Johnson live there, but Mr. Johnson, he soldierin' for the Union. She gots herself one baby boy—his name…be somethin' lak Gerald. Hmmm. That don't sound right. He just a baby, an' we call him "baby." Don't even recalls his name. Wait. I think it is Gerard, Gerald, Jerome… it wuz Jerome.

She take to bed most days. She a youn' woman, but the anxious, worryin' sort. She alone—for the entire two year work there. But I never gets to know her good. She blonde, stout, an' she keep her windows drawn, even in the heat. Drapery closed. She live in a town house near Ma Eve. Close enough so that I walk there easy each mornin', early. Come home around dusk. But I ain't a slave. She pay me for my time. Union money. Fifty cent a week to start, an' half of it I gives to Ma Eve for my keep.

Well, I tell yo' now that Mrs. Johnson baby boy die. An' that when she take to her room all day. She ain't right when Jerome alive, but when he pass, she about fade away. [*There is a pause in the tape, and then some scratchy sounds are heard. There is another short break, perhaps five seconds of silence, and Ms. Augustus resumes.*]

Hate the cold. Last night, I 'bout run out'ta firewood again. Remind me of Baltimore winters. Last night, I take my cot an' I pulls it over to my stove. Stir the ashes good in the middle of the night. But I couldn't get back to sleep. I had a couple pieces of wood I stick in there, but they pine, don't last. Neighbor Mr. Charles brung them, keep me for a few days—till the weekend. Gonna come back from Hillsborough, Charles is, an' I gonna pay him for a good hardwood load.

It plenty cold in Baltimore. Them winters icy, there lots of snow. Nobody gots warm coats durin' the war. Now we gots coats, but they mostly worn-out ones. Some folks do without. But them Baltimore years I wus chilled lak I never been before or since. I think maybe the weather changin'. Gettin' warmer, or maybe it me gettin' older.

That winter, after David leave, I start to show. Weren't never fat, an' most of it out front, in the belly. But with the baby come exhaustion—tired all the time. An' I stop sleepin' good. When fall come, I all right, but it were that winter, that bone chillin' cold go right through me. An' I waitin' each day for the post, thinkin' David gonna write, but nothin' come.

About the war—some times we heared the Union wus winnin', but then it seem the Confed'racy fightin' right back. To tell the truth, I be in my own world. I got Ellie, she a real sweet gal, an' Ma Eve take care of me. L. B. come an' go. Sometime he brings men—white an' colored—to the house, but they ain't stay. Mostly, they come for meals, an' they move on quick to somewhar' else.

Ellie work at a market. She got some kin there—cousins, a uncle—that let her help out. It a rough time, an' Ellie the one that come home with food. She ain't paid cash money for her work, just food. Which wus good, 'cause food wus gettin' scarce, lak everythin' else, especially in the city.

I gonna tells yo' 'bout when Mrs. Johnson baby die. It happen after I come to work for her—three, four month or so. Four, think. Jerome take sick with the croup. It the beginnin' of winter, an' lak I say, them wus harsh times. Cold. Baby fall ill with croup in the middle of the night. I come by the next mornin', an' Mrs. Johnson in the kitchen with the baby—usually, she in bed—an' her sister with the baby. Sister from Alabama, come north. She a Collin or Collins. A Missus too. She stay just a short time, then returns south after the baby die. She older than Mrs. Johnson, with gray hair she wear pinned up in a small bonnet. All homespun, lak we has in Car'lina. She remind me of home. An' I remind her of home—which ain't good. She treat me lak Mrs. Johnson slave.

Never a please or thank yo' for nothin'. She a nervous woman too, an' I blame her for the baby death. Won't find no one else that gonna say that, but I convinced.

I get to Mrs. Johnson home in the mornin'—it right before Christmas time. Still dark out when I come in. That usual. But what ain't is Mrs. Collin there with Mrs. Johnson. Mrs. Collin holdin' the baby, pacin' the room. Baby wrapped tight in a blanket. He wailin', an' snifflin'. But can't catch his breath. There water boilin' on the stove an' the steam thick in the air. Good for the baby, help open his lungs. But he sufferin', 'cause he can't breathe.

"What wrong with baby?" I axe, takin' off my shawl, puttin' it on the hat rack at the rear hallway door. Mrs. Collin look up at me, angry, don't say nothin'.

"Up last night. Croup. Doc is coming," Mrs. Johnson say. She don't look at me neither, but I can tell she been cryin'.

"Can I helps?" I axe. "Hold the baby for a spell?" I moves near Mrs. Collins, an' she walk away.

"Eliza, I think you better take care of the house. We're just waiting for the doc." Mrs. Johnson ain't angry. She just wore out.

"Yas, ma'am," I says. "Yo' calls me if I can helps any." I nod politely an' go to the back hall alcove whar' the broom is. There a pail with some cold water in it too. I takes the broom an' go to upstairs to start my sweepin'.

I upstairs a minute when I hears the baby cry real loud. Lak it got its finger pricked. So I stops an' listen. I stands by the top of the stair, holdin' the broom. The cryin' become a wail, an' get louder. The women still downstairs in the kitchen. Their voices wus also loud. In a panic.

Then, "Oh my God," I hear. "Oh my God!" An' the baby, he begin to sound lak a cat. Ain't never heared a human sound lak that.

"Do something!" I recognize Mrs. Johnson voice. "Do something! My baby! My baby! Dear God, my baby!"

I hears Mrs. Johnson weepin'. I touch my belly. I weepin' too. Standin' there in the upper hall by the steep stair.

When the doc finally arrive, he too late. The women be in the back room, Mrs. Johnson room, so I don't know what all goes on. But Jerome gone. His wailin' stop before the doc get there.

When I come downstair, after li'l Jerome die, Mrs. Collin say. "Go on home, Eliza. You done enough." She say it lak I done kill baby Jerome.

I stands there a minute, outside the bedroom whar' they be. Mrs. Johnson wus still holdin' the dead infant in her arms. She sittin' on the bench by the closed window drape, lookin' down at the baby. She barely lift her head—ain't got the strength to look at me—she just nod. It lak she saying: *Go on home, Eliza. It gonna be all right, though we all knows it ain't. There ain't nothin' no one can do now.*

"How 'bout tomorrow, Mrs. Johnson?" I axe.

"No," she say. "You take three days off, then come back. Maybe I'll need you then." I finds my shawl off the rack—takes my leave.

I hear they has a service at the Methodist church a few streets down. The pastor, a ol' man, an' Mrs. Johnson, her sister, a few white neighbors attend.

Mrs. Johnson crushed, broken after her baby die. She wus melancholy before in that dark, lonely house. Now, she almost dead herself.

It a sorrowful time. In that *home*—if yo' can calls it that—was now just the cook an' me an' Mrs. Johnson. Mrs. Collin leave before my three days is up. Strange that she should leave with Mrs. Johnson doin' so poorly.

Mrs. Johnson—for the remainder of my time there—stay peculiar. In her room, day an' night, curtains drawn. No family, no friends. No husband. Nobody know what happen to him. I knowed he write regular for a while. Mrs. Johnson have all the letters, an' she keep them out on her desk.

I thinkin' he either a prisoner or dead in a ditch. There be dead men unaccounted for in fields, ditches, all over. At the hospital, I see'd nameless men die an' get buried in a common grave. An' later, when I return home—to Fayett'ville—goin' back durin' the war, I see'd mo' dead.

Thousands an' thousands die. Ain't never heared no official count. But I don't know one family spared. South or North. Sometime, in one family, brother be fightin' brother. Much worse than The Great War 'cause it fought on our soil. *[There is a short pause and the sound of chairs being pulled across a wood floor. Then Ms. Augustus begins.]*

But I skippin' around. I ready to tells yo' 'bout my baby, my baby gal, the one I got by them soldiers. God suppose to punish men for such terrible things. Well, maybe he do, maybe he don't. Or maybe it happen only in Heaven.

Here, we all make our way the best we can.

I be thinkin' 'bout this the other day. God plan wus for slavery when we has it. Then, when we has a law against it, His plan go another way. But I don't think so.

When I be a youn' gal, all us Negroes owned by the marsters. It be the way it were—I born into that world. Some Negroes fight against it; some accept it. But none us really understan' anything, 'cause we too busy livin'.

This the way I be thinkin': We all live with fences. Fences all around. Sometime we knock them down; sometimes others knock them. Sometime we hop the fences, but when we do, we just movin' from one pen to another—different fences, but still penned in.

Lak from the Smith place to Baltimore. I guess what I sayin' is there different ways to live, an' we all short-sighted—kick down one fence, find ourselfs held by another. An' I ain't sure whar' the blame.

As I wus growin' up, I takin' down fences. Run away—one fence. Take myself *Augustus*, a new name—another fence knock down. Marry a man I love—I hop that fence. They says I can't go home, head south in the middle of a war—but that fence I tear down too. So all my life, I surrounded by fences. Knockin' them over, but findin' them just the same. [*Ms. Augustus's voice is raised, but she does not seem upset. She lets out a long sigh, followed by a brief silence before she resumes.*]

The first winter in Baltimore wus bad. Cold. Fierce cold, an' wood hard to come by. The war makin' things difficult. Nobody gots much money. Sometimes folks travel in from the country with wagonloads cut wood, but it mostly green an' costly. L. B. got hisself a system. He an' some other men go out late at night—with a mule an' a cart. An' they stealin' wood. Sound bad, but that what folk do. It snow, an' the winds blow hard an' everythin' freeze up.

Ain't sure whar' the men do their thievin'. But it dangerous. They could gets hung. There a district by the wharf whar' they cart an' store cords on flat cars. Under tarps. They gots night watchmen, but they ain't above a bribe.

One night, I go out stealin' wood with L. B. Women ain't suppose to run errands lak this, but L. B. man sick with the flu. He recover, but this night he be sick, an' L. B. ain't got no one else to help. So I volunteers. Ma Eva—Aunt Eve—'course, won't hear of me goin', especially in my condition. Ellie think it crazy. But I convince them that the night air ain't gonna hurt me none. I ain't sleepin' well anyway, an' all I gots to do is sit on top the buckboard an' drive the cart. "I promise," I say. "Ain't gonna leaves the driver seat." So I allowed.

This night, in particular, ain't even cold. An' there weren't much moon. Ma Eva think that the full moon bring evil spirits.

L. B. ready to go around midnight. He got the mule cart hitched. It in the back alley by the kitchen. I got me extra blankets, so I prepare.

"Yo' knows how to drive," L. B. say, as I takin' the reins. He look right at me.

"I do," I say, lookin' right back, then gettin' comfortable on the rough board seat. I got a couple of wool army blankets, an' L. B. got the patchwork that he hand up. Ma Eve at the door. Ellie sound asleep.

"Yo' just stay put, gal," Ma Eve call. "Yo' drive an' stays put." She a dark shadow in the doorway. A slice of new moon barely shinin'. The air wus real still. Dead air, they calls it. "Maybe I wakes Ellie; she go instead. This just a bad idea," Ma Eve say.

"No, ma'am," I says. "No need. We been through all that. I knows how to handle the mule, an' I gonna stay right here." I pat the seat. "We pick up our load, an' we comin' right home. Gonna be fine." I lift the top blanket an' puts it over my head, keep my ears warm.

L. B., he jumps in the back. Make a clickin' sound for the mule to hear. I shake the reins. Off we go—clippity clop over the cobblestones. Some dirt roads too—bumpity, bump. Ain't but a short drive.

That trip, I can remembers it lak yesterday. The sounds, the cold, still air. Even the smell over Baltimore. A rough, burnin' wood smell that hang low, even on crisp winter nights, an' it mix with somethin' sweet. Cider, pie.

'Course, I ain't never drove a wagon. Only Marse George puny cart. An' once Uncle Cicero hitched his mule to a ol' wooden-pegged cart—I weren't but a gal, maybe eight—but he sit with me, give me the reins, We be pluckin' up stones from the lower pasture. Cicero show me how to pull back, stop, click forward. Shake them reins. Nothin' to it. So I doin' all right.

Uncle Cicero. Seem so long ago that he tellin' his Africa stories to us chil'ren. Now I expectin' my own child. "Sarah Louise," he'd say, an' shake head lak he knowed what I up to, what my life gonna be. He call me "his li'l bright angel," an' he shake his head, smile, then say, "Sarah Louise, yo' a gal that gonna go somewhar'…"

When we on the dirt road that come right off the cobblestone, L. B. whisper, "Turn right or turn left." The ride maybe twenty minute.

An' I be thinkin' back to the Ramsey Street hangin' too. Maybe 'cause them cart wheels so bad—bumpty, bump—that remind me. Nothin' in life completely right. We sufferin' even when it ain't too bad. Somethin' always be wrong, off. Bumpty bump. One wheel ain't turnin' lak the rest.

We at the depot. The wharf. There be piles of cord wood stacked under tarps. Lak L. B. predict, the night watchman sleep on the job. Ain't no one about but the sleepin' guard, an' he maybe just pretendin'. Sometimes the men slip him somethin'. I pull along the dirt road by the stacks—up to a side. L. B. order me to stop.

So I sittin' there. L. B. take his boots off. He in his stockin' feet when he run over to the edge of the wood pile, grab a few top pieces from each cord, an' run back. Dump his load quick, run back for mo'. I sittin' tight, lak I promise Ma Eve.

The mule a ol' quiet animal. He lower his head, please to be restin'. So I lookin' around. The sleepin' guard sittin' on a bench by the tarp. Young man. Negro. Still can't tell if he fakin'.

Then, I look again. Somethin' familiar. Can't quite make it out. The cart creak a bit as L. B. drop in another load. I look at the guard. He wearin' a cap almos' over his whole face, which wus in shadow.

He a big man. Wearin' country clothes. Boots. Sudden, it dawn on me. It Run'way Johnny! That who I think it be. Runaway Johnny from the Ellicott Plantation. Can't be, but I sure it is.

My heart start poundin'. About to burst from my chest. My mouth fall open, an' I can't pull my eyes away. *Maybe not*, I thinkin'. It night—I can't see good.

"Sarah… Eliza!" L. B. shake my arm. "We gotta go."

I shake the reins, make a clickin' sound. L. B. jump in the back, an' we off. L. B. ain't sayin' nothin' but "right, left, turn here," till we home. My heart still beatin' wild.

Ma Eve greet us at the kitchen door, she been waitin' up for us. Ellie still in bed, asleep. Ma Eve grab a shawl an' begin to unload. I off the buckboard an' begin to be helpin' too.

"Yo' go inside, gal," Ma, Aunt Eve say. "Yo' done enough. Yo' done good. Go inside now. Got warm bread an' stew meat for yo'." She take the wood from my arms.

L. B. ain't say nothin'. Too busy unloadin'. Good wood there—but only half a cart load. So I go through the back door into the kitchen. There a plate set, an' by the fireplace, a kettle an' a stew pot. Bread too, hot baked, an' I suddenly hungry.

My heart stop poundin' hard by then. Few minutes, Ma Eve an' L. B. join me. We all settin' there etin'. It quiet in the house. Smell warm, the fire goin'. I home an' glad for it. Nobody say nothin'. We finish up, go straight to bed.

But I can't sleep. The attic room chilled from the window. I get undressed. Got a ol' loose dress I wears to bed, an' as I changin', I catch my reflection in the dark window—the drape ain't close properly. I see my belly gettin' bigger, an' I run my hands over it—smooth an' tight. I still all thinkin' 'bout Run'way Johnny—if that wus him. I recalls the feel of his big hand across my mouth. The snakes that line his back with big welts, lak buried wire. I see him chained, roped—to the mule cart movin' along the road front of the Smith place. Me lookin' up. Him lookin' back at me, thinkin' I be the one that betray him. Them wrongs never forgotten. An' I gets a powerful, powerful feelin' that I need to tell him it wasn't me.

Let's turn this off now. Off. *[There is a scraping sound, and the tape machine is clicked off. Ms. Augustus resumes the following day.]*

October 8, 1937

Burned smell lingerin'. Carried on the wind all night. This be the last of Indian summer. Warm now, but it gonna get cold this week. Suppose to rain by Sunday. Maybe that cold wind gonna take the smell away. This time for good.

I thinkin' mo' after yo' leaves yesterday. Mo' 'bout Johnny. About the night I sees him. It come back sudden. An' I stop before I tells yo' 'bout the angels an' Mister Crow. Run'way Johnny must'ta brings them back with him, all the ways from North Car'lina.

[There are some garbled words on the tape, and the machine is clicked off and on again. Ms. Augustus continues.]

This is what I wants to say. When I in the attic, changin' my gown, thinkin' of Run'way Johnny. Window curtain ain't pull tight—an' I sees my reflection. But I also sees stars. They weren't out when L. B. an' me wus gettin' wood, but I see them now. I pulls the curtains back a bit mo'. But they ain't just stars; they be my angels flutterin' outside the window. Flutterin' points of light beyond the pane. I move close to the window, 'cause I can't tells at first if they be out or inside. Then, I turns around, check the room. I almost feels them inside, by me. But they out, beyond the window glass, in the black sky, hoverin' lak hummin' birds. I know they be tryin' to tells me somethin'. I look at them a few minutes, but I can't figure nothin' out, so finally, I shut the drapes an' get into bed.

An' that when Mister Crow come—in a dream. He come right on cue. Angels, crow. Good an' evil.

The dream go this way. Marster—ol' Marster J. B. Smith—he walkin' to the lower pasture, back in Fayett'ville, before the war. It a summer evenin' 'bout dusk. I ain't been thinkin' much about Marster or Missus lately, but when I sees Marster, he come to me real clear—lak I really seein' him, an' I ain't dreamin'. He stoppin' on that road by the mule barn. They still got the mule that kill Uncle Cicero. He inside the barn. Marster hummin' some tune, when he come upon a bird cage hangin' under the barn eaves on a butcher hook, the kind they use to hang hogs. Inside the cage is Mister Crow, an' Marster let him out.

"Fly to whar' yo' needs to," Marster say. An' there a squeak to the openin' of the rusty ol' cage door. When he hop down to gets free, Mister Crow spread his wings, ready to take flight. His wings, I tells yo', is enormous, an' my whole dream turn black an' panicky. He flap them wings, an' the sky be dark. That when I pops awake. Heart poundin'. I sits up in bed, darkness all around, lak I still in the dream. Can't tell if that darkness be the night or if I wrapped up in Mister Crow wings. I in a sweat, lak I been running fast to escape somethin'.

Nothin' happen that followin' day, except that I exhausted 'cause I didn't sleep much. And one day turn into the next an' the next. *[There is a very brief pause.]*

Winter 1863 become '64. January. Cold. I still sufferin' from northern weather. An' I still workin' for Mrs. Johnson. Nothin' change there. It dismal. Drapery stay closed; Mrs. Johnson keep on mournin' for her son. Streets empty. The city pinched. Folks feelin' lowly. War goin' on an' on. People strugglin'. An' all the time, I be growin' bigger an' bigger.

Lak I say, sometimes the war almost drop out'ta sight. Sometime, it so close that we can hear it, smell it. Day after day, life be wearisome. An' we so uset'ta this hard times that we can't remember how it be before. Cookin', washin', gettin' by. Folks needin' firewood, coal. Somethin' to keep warm with, cook by.

But nobody can be thinkin' 'bout war every minute. Got chores to do. Ol' folks die. Babies born. Horses, mules need tendin'. Chicken lay their eggs.

Maybe everythin' mo' extreme back then. War weigh heavy. Folks carry it lak a sack of stones they can't put down.

Some predict the world 'bout to end. But yo' know how that go— preachers always gonna preach.

Doom-sayers. See them out on the street corners in downtown Raleigh today. Announcin' the end is near. Usin' the Bible, sayin' it prophesize. Shoutin' at strangers passin'. Well, they had them in this war too. *[There is a long pause before Ms. Augustus continues.]*

Then the spring come on. Somethin' in the air, yo' could feel change. Folks tired, worn out, but there somethin' danglin' right beyond the weariness. Once, I hear Mrs. Johnson talkin' to a church lady drop by. She never have many guests. But this one lady—I hears the conversation they has. About slavery. About how Lincoln gonna end it. Make a law. How Lincoln wanna fight till we one country again—without slavery.

What take me by surprise is how they speakin' 'bout it, how they both seem to think this be a good idea. To end slavery. Mrs. Johnson an' this other woman say too many men die. I ain't thinkin' beforehand that Mrs. Johnson wus a abolitionist, but that get me thinkin' she wus, in her way. Too saddened in her spirit to do nothin'. But this other lady, she say that the Negroes gonna rise up, take over the plantations, get themselfs farmland, 'cause they sure knows how to work it. Negroes gonna be free, an' America gonna be one country again.

This be the first I ever hear such words from white folks. Standin' outside the parlor door, I listen. Then I heared 'bout it again through the

Baltimore newspaper. How Lincoln gonna end slavery. I think that first story appear that year. An' then it happen again. Another story. *Baltimore Sun*—L. B. gettin' some ol' newspapers.

An' I tell yo', the Negroes what could read wus starved for news. I still gots a story somewhar' clipped an' saved. Either pressed in a book or in my ol' trunk beneath my bed. I gotta remember to find it. If it ain't fall apart by now. *[There is a very brief pause in the tape before Ms. Augustus continues.]*

An' the coffins keep comin' in. To Baltimore. On trains an' by cart. I tell yo' a story 'bout a white lady I seen, pick up a coffin at the depot. About this time. Coffins would come into town in batches mostly, but sometime there be one on a train or stage. The woman wus real pretty an' young. Too young to be a soldier mother, so maybe be her husband. She dressed in black, with a black shawl, but no coat. It still cold then—think it wus late February. An' she come for the mid-day train.

The porter, he see her wait. He nod for her, seein' that she in black, mournin'. He take off his cap an' bow. When the box get unload, I see'd them from a distance. It come off the last car, an' men carry it to a open cart. The woman collapse over the box, spread her arms across it. Even distant lak I is, her cries echo through the depot. I mean she wail lak Doc Goldstein wus takin' her leg off.

The entire station stop. Everyone attention on her, lak she be wailin' the grief of the world. One gentleman near the cart, he take off his cap an' hold it by his heart. He do it, then the next fella too. Then everyone at the station, the men folk, has caps or hats held over their hearts. An' no one speak; we all takin' this moment, standin' there. Women, black an' white, lower their heads for what they see.

It close to my confinement. Early February, maybe March, by this time. The wind sharp, cuttin' the air, still carryin' winter on its back. I stood there too, big as I were, in my moment. It must'ta been five full minutes before the driver take the woman hand an' she join him on the wagon buckboard, the coffin behind. Click of the reins, off they go. Depot come back to life.

Sadden me to think it now. All them boys die. That woman. Mothers losin' sons, gals losing sweethearts, brothers. Couldn't find a family ain't lost a boy. *[There is a brief pause, and Ms. Augustus continues.]*

My confinement. Seem I past my time when it happen. White misses in Fayett'ville would have stayed home for the last month. Take to bed right before birth. Early on, it good for women to move 'bout, but later, they require to rest.

By my reckonin', I late. An' I still workin' for Mrs. Johnson—I don't give no notice because she agree that after the baby born I be allowed to bring it with me, nurse it, do my household chores—light, nothin' too heavy. I prob'ly be home at first, a couple of days. Then go back to work. She agree 'cause she ain't be wantin' to find a new gal, an' she say there ought'ta be a baby in the house. Ain't matter if it white or black. All babies God chil'ren, she say.

Near the end, I so big that I waddlin' around lak a plump duck. It hard to stand up, hard to set down. I wus huge. Can't fit in my dresses. Ellie, she a seamstress, an' she find some gowns that she alter for me. I still narrow from behind, but in front, it look lak I swallowed a whole watermelon. Most nights I wakes in a sweat. Cold outside, but the sweat be drippin' off me, an' I be wakin' to it. Pitch black, an' I be settin' up, feelin' I can't breathe. I be gaspin' for air—lak I tryin' to catch my breath after a long run.

Sometime I has nightmares—soldiers chasin' me, an' just as they 'bout to catch me up, grab a'hold of me, I wakes. This the way my confinement begin—with a real bad dream. Two months before the baby suppose to be born, the nightmare start, an' my crampin' start too. By mornin' they'd usually go away. I wouldn't have had such a hard time if them nightmares never come.

I tell Ma Eve 'bout the nightmares. Once, I even screams out. The baby would kick most when I had them dreams, Feel lak a Mexican jumpin' bean inside. Yo' put them on yo' palm, an' they'd kick up lak somethin' inside wus tryin' to get out. Baltimore chil'ren likes to play with them, race them, watch them kick an' jump. That the way the baby feel. Sometime when she kick, I put my hand over my belly, rub the spot whar' her li'l feet be, an' pray that my time go easy.

When the nightmares an' cramps come that last week, I stay inside—any day now, I be thinkin'. I ain't in bed, but I waddlin' around the house. Ma Eve, she only give me a li'l work to do—cookin', peel 'taters, sittin' on a stool, makin' bread. I stop goin' to Mrs. Johnson then, an' Ellie gets me some books to read, which I enjoy plenty. Struggle at first, I out'ta practice, I guess. But it come back quick, an' the one book I remember wus a big, thick book. Six hundred pages. Charles Dickens be the man that wrote it. Every evenin' them last weeks, I sit by the parlor fire, an' I puzzlin' the words out.

Yo' noddin' lak you reads it too. About a white boy growed up poor in London. That be in England. He poor an' mistreated, but he come into money by the end, which wus good. *Great Expectations*, it called. An' readin' it wus my way of gettin' through that time.

Sarah Louise, I remember tellin' myself, *life gonna turn out all right. That baby gonna be born, an' it gonna be a blessin'. Ain't its fault the way it begun.*

My thoughts be turnin' now, mo' an' mo' to Ma—my Ma—an' Kate, Mar, li'l Hannah. I know she must be gettin' to be a tall gal by now. She must be a sight. An' Ma, gettin' older. How I miss them. An' here I is big with child, ill-begotten.

It ain't my fault, Ma, I'd be sayin' to her. Sittin' by the fire, I'd imagine her right by me in Ma Eve house—in the parlor, kitchen, or standin' by a pot, stirrin'. First, she got her back to me, maybe hummin' to make the work go easy. Then, she turn an' see my face. When she do, she just break out her widest grin lak everythin' in the whole wide world gonna be all right. Then she look down, see that big belly of mine, an' the smile slip from her lips. She shake her head, turn her broad back to me, an' I can see her still shakin' her head, tiskin' away, lak I a small, willful child. She expect better of me. An' I be thinkin' that if I could only see her an' explain. *[Ms. Augustus lets out a big sigh, pauses, then continues.]*

Well, it be April. I so big that I cans barely get around. I has to groan each time I lifts off a chair or gets up from the bed. I lak a big box turtle get turned on its back, can't right itself. Or maybe a June bug that flip over. That the way I go through most of April, an' right through my birthday, when I turn nineteen.

I'd been mopin' around all that day an' had one of my nightmares the night before. When I tells Ma Eve an' Ellie, they say that they already plan on bakin' me a cake, with white sugar they save up. It a fine thing, with icin'.

That evenin', Ma Eve, L. B., an' me in the parlor—L. B. readin' us somethin' from the paper when Ellie walk in holdin' the cake on a silver tray. This the first real birthday cake I ever has. Ma Eve cuts a piece for me—it taste so sweet an' light. I tell them all thank yo', an' I touched. But I be rememberin' back to Kate birthday—right before I leaves—Ma has some new socks she knit, an' me an' Mar brings Kate fresh soap, a cake we mold fancy with a butter press.

I gets me some gifts too—small things, but nice. Ellie give me a new apron she sew. Somethin' I could wear fresh after the baby. Ma Eve an' L. B. give me a baby blanket sewed with yellow color thread stitched around. It beautiful, an' I couldn't axe for no better.

But all the time I thinkin' about my own ma, wonderin' if she even miss me. Don't know if she think I still alive. L. B. say he try to get word to her but that I should never write—it way too dangerous.

Later that night, the night of my birthday, I gets my first bad pains. Maybe the rich cake weren't settin' well, I be thinkin', an' I up late with a belly-ache. Ain't feelin' good at all, but I don't wanna wakes nobody, especially after they be so nice.

I plod downstair, out the kitchen door to the privy. I barely make it in. I standin' inside, in the dark, an' I clutchin' at knots in my belly. I so big an' achin'—holdin' on to the side of the privy, 'cause I almost can't stand up. Then I begin heavin' an' havin' to use the privy at the same time.

I in so much pain. Seem to be no end to it . I breathin' hard while my belly tightens. In so much pain that I weeps for myself, for my baby, an' for the whole sad world. *I ain't gonna has this baby*, I decide. I just ain't gonna do it. I too young, an' this baby ill-begotten.

"Lawd," I moan aloud, sittin' there, tryin' to stands up. "Yo' done give me this child an' yo' can take it back. I don't want it. I sick an' tired, an' I wants my own ma—not Ma Eve. I wants to go home to Fayett'ville. That all I axin' for. An' for Kate, Mar, li'l Hannah. Pa too. I knows they worry 'bout me. Lawd, yo' can makes it happen."

I try again to stand, but all I can do is rock back an' forth on the seat. Both ends of me still needin' the privy at the same time. I slidin' over an' doin' both. This a real low moment.

But after I done emptyin' myself, the pain get worse—comin' now in grippin'-tight spurts. They claw at my belly, but I has nothin' to heave an' nothin' left inside me. Only the baby an' the pains. I scared now, an' I manage—don't know how—to stands up between them pains, an' waddle back to the kitchen 'bout dawn. I sit by the stove, which needs to be stoke for breakfast, but I ain't got the strength. I cold an' shiverin'. Ellie come down first.

"What goin' on?" she axe, when she see me.

"Nothin'," I says, between groans. I still be rockin' a bit, back an' forth, back an' forth.

"Yo' havin' yo' baby," Ellie say right off. "I wakes up Ma." Ellie scurry to the bedroom.

I in steady pain now, an' my entire mood be turnin' foul. I tired an' out of patience. Feel lak I gotta go somewhar', an' quick. So I stand up an' start pacin' the floor—sort of doubled over. It still cold here. Ellie, the fool, ain't even got sense enough to light the stove. An' now gray mornin' light be seepin' through the kitchen windows. An' the floorboards look dirty, in need a good moppin'. I pace the floor, three steps one way, then three steps back. I can only look down, not up.

Ma Eve come in. She got on a clean apron, an' she tend to the stove, warmin' up the place, an' tellin' Ellie to get a mess of water from the well. She movin' so quick an' sure, I can't understand what goin' on.

L. B. come in next. "I goin' to get Granny O'Brien. She know yo' due." L. B. take me by the arm, grasp me firm, look at my downcast face. "Yo' a good gal, an' yo' gonna be fine." Then he take his hat from the wall rack an' leave.

Ma Eve got sheets on the bed in the room whar' Ellie sleep. They ol' an' threadbare, but they clean. "We be better off in here," she say. An' she take my arm too, an' steer me into the room, help me on the bed. The curtains is drawn—it dark an' the bed sheets cool as I slide into them. I gets a chill, an' then waves of pain shoot through my body, an' I starts to sweatin' somethin' fierce.

Ellie come in with a pot of boiled water, which she place on a towel on the floor. Ma Eve say somethin' lak, "She gonna go now, water must'ta broke in the night." Ellie nod lak she understand. But I don't. I be thinkin' 'bout the water Ellie just brung in. How can it get broke?

Hours an' hours go by in a blur. I in so much pain. It be lak God punishin' me for all the wrongs I ever done, an' then punish me for all the wrongs I gonna do—in the future, my whole life. I sob. An' all the time my belly gettin' tight, knottin' with them spasms. When they happen, I cry out. I didn't think I could feel worse than I did in the privy, but I do. Thought it bad then, but that weren't nothin'. *[Ms. Augustus pauses here, then continues.]*

Nobody want to talks 'bout it—what awful pain that come with chil'birth. Ain't nothin' else in this world lak it. Even Doc Goldstein told me. Say, "Sarah Louise, what you see here is awful. These men are in pain. But it isn't anything lak what their mothers went through."

At the time he say that, he speak in a whisper. I hears the words, but they travel right through me, ain't got nowhar' to land. Now them words come back to me, an' I feel them soldier pains.

Suddenly, I scream out. Ma Eve say, "She ready."

I must'ta had my eyes scrunch tight. When I open them, there a ol' woman there. One I ain't never seen before. She smile, nod her head at me.

"I want you to bend toward me. Ellie is going helps you up. When you get close to sitting, I want you to push that baby out. You hear me, gal?"

The afternoon sun now is filterin' through the drapery an' makin' dust float through the air lak li'l particles of matter, floatin' in their dreamy way.

Ellie grab me. "Push!" Ma Eve call out.

"Push!" I hear again. This time, I understand it be Granny O'Brien, the black granny that must'ta help a thousand women.

"I can't!" I yell. "It hurt!" I holdin' onto Ellie with one hand, grippin' the bed clothes with the other. Sweat pourin' off me.

"I gonna pull this gown off yo'." Ellie help Ma Eve yank off my gown, a sweat-soaked rag. I glad it off.

"I gonna push this time," I say. An' up I go. Settin' an' groanin'.

"You almost have it, gal. Push harder!" Granny say.

"I gonna rip in half," I yell.

"Push harder! It's going to be all right. You've got to push harder!" All three women now support me, doubled me over so my belly touch my chin. I naked, sweatin', tryin' to push, but nothin' happenin'. Nothin' goin' right.

"I can't! I can't! I can't!" I really tryin'. The water in the pot cold now, an' Granny take a cloth an' start washin' me off, coolin' me down.

"Ellie, get us another pot ready with that boiled water. We're going to need it soon, I hope."

The pains still comin'. But I ain't gettin' what Granny call "the urge." Exhausted, I leaned back for a time, restin'. We all takin' a break. Don't know what time it is. Don't care. The light be faded in the room now. Maybe it close to evening. L. B. should be home. "Whar' L. B.?" I axe, and must'ta pass out.

When I comes to, it dark—candles be lit on the bed table an' dresser. I can't tells if it the same day or the next.

It the pain that wake me lak a bolt of lightenin'. It has me double-over again. "Oh…" I scream out. "Oh…"

Granny, Ellie, and Ma Eve by me now. They lift me up just enough to put a clean sheet under my backside. The baby head is right against me. "I feel it!" I scream out, "It comin'!" Now I gettin' that pushin' urge. Can't stop it. "Oh!" I cry.

Somebody bring over a candle. But I can't think straight. I lak a animal.

"Push!" Granny command. An' this time, I do it. Ellie hold my elbow an' help me lean into the push.

"I see the baby's head," Ma Eve say. "It comin'! It comin'!"

"Push again, now. Now!" Granny holdin' my skin down there. With both hands, she holdin' me open.

"I gonna rip," I groan. But it don't hurt so bad no mo'.

"Hold on now, hold on!" Granny say.

"All right! All right! All right," Ma Eve voice call out. I feels a rush of somethin' warm. Blood. An' that the last thing I remembers. I pass out again. *[There is an abrupt stop in Ms. Augustus's story. Then, there is a long pause, and Ms. Augustus continues.]*

Wasn't there for the birth of my own child. Fainted dead away. Ma Eve say I bleed till I almost die. Took me two days to wake. Granny gone. Ma Eve happy to sees me when I comes to. Ellie sleep on the chaise in the parlor. I still be in her room, curtains drawn lak somebody die.

"Sarah Louise," Ellie say when she see me stir. She been settin' on a wood chair by the bed, an' she come over kneel down by me. "We're so glad yo' back. We thought…"

"Hush," Ma Eve say from the doorway, whar' she appear. "Hush. Yo' with us now." An' she come into the room, holdin' a cup, insist I drinks some tea, an' prop me up a bit, so I can stays awake.

"My baby," I say. "My baby." But Ellie cast her eyes down, an' Ma Eve just stroke my forehead, look into my eyes.

"So sorry, Sarah Louise. We done what we could."

"It wus a gal, a gal. Weren't it? Whar' is she?" But I still so tired an' sleepy, can barely keep awake. I close my eyes.

"Don't leave us, now, Sarah Louise. The Lawd want yo' to stay. Yo' got a life, an' it ain't over yet."

"Whar' my baby gone? I had a child." But my eyes stay closed, almost lak I losin' interest an' can't seem to keep awake.

"It wus a girl, a girl child, Ma whisper to me in the dark room. "Perfect formed, but stillborn. Never found its breath."

I lay in for about a week, goin' in an' out'ta sleep. An' all that time I plagued with troubled dreams 'bout the baby I lost.

They buried her in the AME church yard; plot wus free for chil'ren. But there weren't no money for a stone.

An' in one of them dreams, I'd hear the shovel what buried her. It would hit an' turn the hard dirt to loosen it, then a shovelful would lift out of the grave. I could hear the sound—hit, turn. I could smell the soil, earthy, fresh. Remind me of plantin' time in Fayett'ville. Then I'd wake for a moment, only to falls back asleep an' have the same bad dream.

"We name the child for yo'," Ellie say to me soon after I learn 'bout the baby. "We give her the name we give yo'—Eliza. Eliza Louise Payne."

Soon them April days turn warm an' sunny. My strength return. But I tell yo' for almost a full year, I gets me a stabbin' pain in my heart when folks call me Eliza. It lak the child still inside, everywhar' I go. *[There is a click, and the tape machine is stopped quickly. When it is turned on, it is another day.]*

October 11, 1937

I begin today right whar' I leaves off Friday. Lak I say, rain Sunday carry in that cold air. It sure cold. Had to keep fire lit. In the stove. Got some coal an' wood to keep me now. *[There is a brief pause, and Ms. Augustus continues.]*

All that year, I still grievin' somethin' awful for my baby gal. When yo' lose a child, it be lak a star fall out'ta the sky. A mother know how to find the hole it leave. Million stars up there, but when one star gone, a mother know whar' to look.

An' durin' this time of grief, I considerin' goin' back to Fayett'ville. Come up with a plan. Happen when I still at Mrs. Johnson house—another house empty, with no child.

When I returns to work for Mrs. Johnson, she come out'ta her own grief a bit. Once, when we cleaned the windows together in the parlor, she open the drapes. We talk a li'l, nothin' important. But soon after, she seem worse off. Maybe 'cause I return the cradle she give me before I went to confinement. She put fresh linen in it, had her driver bring it over, leave it by the kitchen hall. It wus her family cradle—wood, with fine, carved scrollwork, an' a tiny feather mattress inside. Say she ain't has no use for it, might as well be mine. It wus a gift outright, meant in kindness. But after my loss, I decides to give it back. She insist on keepin' it in the parlor, an' I think it make her sad.

The days wus gettin' warmer, an' April a pretty fair month in Baltimore. The war thin out the men—white men—but the city still hummin'. There wus even talk 'bout colored unit bein' formed, an' there wus debate 'bout it.

One evenin', walkin' home from Mrs. Johnson, I got up the courage to stop at the AME cemetery, only a few blocks out of my way. The li'l grave wus there, an' there wus a new white wood cross, with a name paint on it. Other children graves there too, most mark with white crosses, but a few wus bordered with pretty stones. So, I grab up some small stones from the dirt path near by, an' I puts them in a circle on the grave. Then, I kneel down an' whisper her name. *Eliza.* What a sound it make—all open. *Eliza Louise.*

'Course, Eliza Payne be the name Mrs. Johnson call me. But I think it the first time I say the name aloud.

Mrs. Johnson don't care nothin' 'bout the season, how the sun shine, how warm the breeze. She caught in her own woes—her baby—her husband gone. An' whatever else happen to her that I don't knows 'bout. But her house stay in darkness all that time—lak it come right out of Mister Charles Dickens, the big book I read.

I talk 'bout seein' Run'way Johnny in the winter before I gives birth. We wus gettin' the firewood the night I think I sees him. Well, I already done convince myself that the man wus Johnny an' that he still in Baltimore, an' that our paths gonna cross again. Maybe the angels give me this idea. Maybe I just has it myself.

Or maybe it be the loss of Eliza that make me so homesick, miss Ma an' kin. Maybe I thinkin' 'bout how Ma worry 'bout me, not know what happen. Ma thinkin' I surely dead or else I would'a wrote her.

Weren't my fault, I'd say to myself sometimes. I'd see Ma in my head lak she standin' there in front me, stirrin' a pot or out hangin' the washin'.

Sometime Mister Crow come to me then; he be cawin' in the background with his "Bad gal, bad gal," or "Sad gal," or "Caw, caw, caught." It wus all tearin' me apart. Here I wus, a married woman with a good husband that I love. An' my baby dead that he never know I expectin'. An' there be Ma, Pa, Mar, Kate, an' Hannah—none of them know nothin' neither. All this make me crazy.

An' David—remember what he say before he leave? I suppose to wait in Baltimore, an' he get word to me 'bout whar' he be, when he comin'. But already goin' on a year an' not one word.

So this my plan. I goin' out one night when everyone asleep. Gonna wears all black an' tells anyone I meet that I a grief-stricken mother, out to mourn by the grave of the baby I lost. Gotta be at night, 'cause I too busy workin' days. I gonna sneak back to whar' I last sees Johnny. Don't knows if he remember me, but I plans to identify myself an' tells him what happen to me when he run away. We from the same place, an' I know, in my heart, he a good man.

So crazy as it is, I concoct this plan. First, I gonna find Johnny an' gets him to forgives me—though there ain't nothin' to forgive. An' even if he thinkin' I the gal that turn him in, he gonna listen to me when I tells him the truth. Then the second part of the plan be that Johnny gonna agree to returns with me to Fayett'ville. I know he got kin there, an' he prob'ly still in love with his gal.

Plan sound far-fetched now, but I get myself convinced that Johnny gonna be at the woodpile I last see'd him at, an' he gonna wanna go along. *[There is a scraping sound, and the machine is clicked off, then on again, and Ms. Augustus resumes.]*

It July again. Before I knowed it, we right at the Fourth of July, an' that the time last year all this begin. I knows there gonna be commotion this whole week in Baltimore, an' folks be preoccupy with the holiday, what it stir up.

It wus a warm night—a week night before the fourth—an' L. B. come home early. We all ets supper outside the kitchen. Too hot in the house. We etin' cook meat—pork, day-ol' bread, an' bean salad, an' we settin' together on a choppin' log an' a bench we sets up. That when L. B. say that with the holiday comin', folks gettin' riled. Stir up sentiments on both sides.

"Folks getting more steamed than the weather," L. B. say. "No end I can see." He take a bite of pork. "Men love their wars, even if they have to die for them." L. B. let out a chuckle.

We go on etin'. Big tray with cold foods on the tree stump we use for choppin'. Nobody say nothin'. We in the back alley. No one else around. Most folks out in the front. There be a smell of garbage from nearby pile, an' we havin' to swat flies. The air thick an' humid. We all pickin' at the food, but only L. B. etin'.

"Eliza," L. B. say. Ma Eve an' Ellie sometime call me Sarah Louise when we home alone, which we usually is. But L. B., he always call me Eliza. "Eliza," he say now. "I tell you what. This winter Hell is going to freeze over, an' black folks still won't be free." L. B. take the ham bone he workin' on an' throw it across the street. It skip once or twice in the dirt.

"Think I go inside," Ma Eve get up, lift her skirts. "Ain't hungry but for some fruit. Anyone want a peach? Got a couple left."

"No, ma'am," I say. Ellie shake her head. L. B. rise, excuse hisself, an' go in.

Ellie an' me, we sit a minute. Then she say she got a bad headache an' go inside too.

My eyes cast 'bout till I find that pork bone. It gonna attract rats if some stray dog don't find it first.

I sit in the heat, an' I be thinkin' of Ma, Hannah, Kate, Mar—an' Pa again. How Pa home to us on a Saturday night, how we a family. An' yet here I is in a alley with a dirty bone attractin' flies. Then, I think back to remember Johnny when I see'd him first, how I knowed right off that he don't mean no harm—even with his hand over my mouth, an' how scared I be. Ma shocked when I tells her what happen, after all the trouble I cause. Then I thinkin' Ma gonna be surprise to see us walk on home together to Fayett'ville. Run'way Johnny an' me. She gonna be overcome with joy—nothin' else gonna matter.

By the time I stands up, I knowed that I gonna finds Johnny that same night. I thinkin' 'bout the route we tooks that night: down this alley, turn right, come to the church, turn left. Then we movin' toward the docks. Only has to follow the street. Maybe a mile, maybe less.

It gettin' dark already. The air turn gray, deep as a river. I thinkin' everyone inside, lost in their thoughts—all taken up with the same bad, lonely mood. Nobody gonna take no notice of me tonight. It too hot.

Probably L. B. gonna read his papers an' fall 'sleep. He gonna fold up the *Baltimore Sun*, an' it gonna slip into his lap. Seem lak he do that when he feelin' sick of the world. His family gonna just let him be.

Far as I concerned, it be settled. Tonight be the night I gonna find Johnny. So I picks up the tray an' carries it to the kitchen. Nothin' really to cleans up, so I go in to the parlor, an' tells Ma an' L. B. I gots myself a headache lak Ellie do, an' I gots to lay down.

"Must be the air," Ma Eve say. Ellie in her room with a wet rag over her eyes. "Yo' want yourself a compress, Sarah Louise? I'll make yo' up one good." Ma Eve darnin' by the window. Don't even look up.

L. B.—just lak I knowed—has his paper out, folded, an' he relaxin' in his chair, ready to falls asleep.

"No. No, ma'am. Thank yo' all the same," I say, puttin' the back of my hand over my forehead. Think I get undress an' go to bed."

"It too hot up there, Sarah Louise. Why don't you sleep down here? I'll get you the linen I launder last Wednesday. Bet it still smells good from the line."

"No, ma'am," I say. "I be fine with the window open. Really." I head upstairs.

"Suit yourself. See yo' in the morning." Ma Eve look up an' smile. L. B. almost sleep.

Upstairs, I lay down. Fully dressed. The window open, but it stifflin' hot up here, lak Ma Eve say. So I unfasten my dress lacin', undo a few buttons, an' pick up the Bible on the bed table. I reads a few minute, an' I falls asleep.

For some hours, I sleep. Deep. Then, I wakes up in a sweat. Ruffled up a bit, but still dressed. It be the middle of the night. I look out the window. A moon out, so I know it late.

I go to the hall, whar' there be a big wardrobe, finds my black mournin' dress, an' change. Then I tip-toe down the stairs, skippin' them that squeaky an' make noise. In the parlor, nobody there. Kitchen, nobody. Only moonlight streamin' through the windows.

I can feel my heart poundin'. I go through the rear hallway door, 'bout to turn the lock key, when I thinks to check the time. The mantle clock in the parlor read two in the mornin'. Take me a hour if it all go right. Any later an' the baker an' dock men be risin' to work.

I leaves the door unlock. Don't ever take the key out. No robber gonna come. An' nobody gonna miss me.

I wearin' my soft slippers, not my boots. An' just lak I been thinkin', there ain't nobody out. Streets deserted.

I walk by the cemetery, but I don't take the time to see my baby. *Oh, Eliza,* I think, *I be leavin' yo' soon, but I be back. Gonna see yo' gran'mammy an' gran'pappy, an' all yo' aunts. I gonna visit the place I lived as a gal. Forgive me, sweet baby that ain't never live an' I ain't never see'd.*

It take me awhile to find the place whar' I last see'd Johnny. An' of course, Johnny ain't there. It all deserted as the streets I be comin' from. Boats anchor in the bay, but ain't no folks around. I take one look, an' I heads back. Put some thought into what to do next.

Still nobody see me—which wus good, so I walk home, let myself inside, don't even check the clock, an' up I go, takin' care not to step on the creaky stairs. When I reach my room—hot as a glue pot—I undress an' lay down.

It were a stupid mistake: In winter, make sense that Johnny mind the wood pile. It summer now. *Stupid gal,* I think. *Summer, summer, summer.* An' I falls asleep. *[There is a long sigh, and the tape runs for a few moments before Ms. Augustus resumes.]*

I try a few mo' times to finds Johnny, slippin' out after dark. Once, I axe L. B. if he remember the guard by the wood pile that time we go out. "No," he say. He ain't got no special recollection of that man. Only see'd him in darkness that once time to bribe him to pretend to sleep.

But nothin' put me off the idea of findin' Johnny. No. The harder it get, the mo' I determined.

One night, upstairs in bed, another plan come to me: I decides to conjure Johnny. It be my only choice. Can't find him, gonna make him come to me. Ain't never done no conjure before. But maybe I call on my angels for help.

Next day, while I be cleanin' Mrs. Johnson house, straightenin' up the parlor, I get to thinkin' 'bout them angels. I standin' by the fireplace mantel, clock tickin', an' I close my eyes, try to conjure them that way. But instead of my angels, who does I see? Mammy Rae, clear as if she be right front of me. Her dark gray muslin dress stretch tight across her big bosom. She got on her dye apron, stained with ochre an' indigo. But she don't say nothin', just turn to me to nod her head.

Maybe it be some day dream I has, but there she is. An' I rememberin' again how she'd take her apron from the rusty shed hook when she ready to begin her day. How that shed be the place Mister Crow first find me. How even now I still the gal I wus back then. For a few minutes, I can't tells if I be already back home at the Smith place with Mammy Rae, or if she be visitin' me here in Baltimore.

"I tell yo' what," Mammy Rae whisper. "Shut yo' eyes, an' yo' angels gonna flurry lak snow flakes in yo' mind. If yo' relax, yo' gonna see them real clear. Gotta relax. That right, gal."

Maybe it all a dream, but *someone* sure tell me how to conjure my angels. Mammy Rae step towards me, take my hand, an' squeeze. We stand there, an' I close my eyes lak she say, an' sure enough, in a flurry, my faceless angels come.

"I see them, Mammy Rae. There they be."

"Yo' concentrate, Sarah Louise. Relax, but concentrate. Yo' a gal that know what yo' wants. Yo' the strongest gal on Earth." Mammy Rae squeeze my hand again, let it go, stand back; an' disappear. Poof. Gone. Lak candle light. I close my eyes tight again, relax, but concentrate on Johnny. In my mind, I think 'bout my angels too—I command them angels to bring Run'way Johnny to me.

Maybe this whole conjure take fifteen minutes. Standin' there, I could feel the power, an' sure as I here today, I certain that Johnny get the message. It work, just lak Mammy Rae say.

Johnny turn out to work dock labor—an' he ain't shy 'bout pickin' up other odds an' ends to sell when ships come in an' there be some goods that ain't accounted for. Otherwise, he at the dock, loadin', unloadin'.

Fact is, I rouse them angels so good that Johnny appear at our door— very next day. He come knockin' at our kitchen. Ellie answer. Johnny sellin' tomatoes—over-ripe, ain't good for nothin' but cannin'. An' he got a mess of them, crates that need to be sold. He been carryin' two big wood crates on his shoulders, an' they dripped juice down his shirt. He put them down to knock.

L. B. ain't in, but Ellie call Ma Eve to come. It late mornin', an' I be home from Mrs. Johnson house to pick up some clean rags stored in the cellar.

I jump up when I hears his voice. Before I gets to the landin' at the top of the stair, I stop an' gives God an' my angels thanks. *Dear God, dear faceless family of angels that follow me an' takes such good care, I offer yo' my thanks for this here Johnny, that come to take me home. Amen.*

I walk to the door, wearin' my house apron, an' got a bucket of rags in my hand. Then I sees Johnny, an' he see me. Right away he recognize me. Right 'way. He in the midst of sayin' somethin' to Ma, Aunt Eve—an' Ellie, who behind her—an' he just stop dead. Dead. He look at me, an' eyes bug out lak he see'd a haint.

"If they ain't no worse than those on top, I buy me both them crates," Ma Eve say. "An' I'll take them now." Ma Eve wipin' her wet hands on her apron. She stand by Ellie. Ellie, back a bit, lookin' lak she smitten. She got her head covered by a ol' piece of red cloth, but she a pretty gal, an' she know it; she give Johnny a big grin. She noddin' to agree with her Ma, "Both crates," she say.

Ellie lookin' at Johnny, an' Ma Eve lookin' at me. "Yo' knows each other? Yo' two meets?" Ma Eve turn to Johnny. He got his mouth slightly slack. We all stand there. This all takin' maybe ten seconds.

"Yas, ma'am, we meet long time ago. I think this gal remember." Johnny look at me with a challenge, a warnin', tellin' me that I ain't to say nothin' 'bout the circumstance.

"I knows this fella from Fayett'ville. Live the next farm over," I say, then realize that' I already sayin' too much.

Ma Eve shake her head as if all of a sudden she ain't take no interest in my past relations. "Comes to think of it, I only wants one crate now," she say. "An' I ain't got no money yet. Yo' leaves the one crate an' come back tonight with this second one, an' I'll pay for both. Mister L. B. be home, pay yo' then."

"Yas, ma'am." Johnny nod at Ma Eve. "I gonna trust yo' ma'am. I knows the gal. Gonna be back this evenin', lak yo' says." An' Johnny go.

Rag bucket in hand, I move to the parlor. My heart be racin' lak them soldiers comin' after me again. I can't catch my breath.

An' my mind goin' a mile a minute: *He your freedom, Sarah Louise. Yo' gots to explain him the truth. He be the man gonna take yo' home.*

When I returns to the kitchen, Ma Eve gone, an' Ellie got the wet mop an' tin wash bucket out.

"He comin' again later, Sarah Louise—*Eliza*. Then she grin. He awful handsome," she say an' grin again. "Whar' yo' know him from? How yo' know him?"

"What time he comin'?" I axe.

"How I know? Before sunset. Ma gonna pay him a quarter. Lot of money for two crates of half-rotten 'matoes." Ellie dunk her mop in the soapy bucket water, bend to wring it out.

"See yo' later, Ellie. Tell Ma that Mrs. Johnson done give me some collard green for supper. They in the tub outside. Be home later."

"What he lak, Sarah? He nice? Seem nice." Ellie swipin' the floor, but she neglect to put the chairs up.

"He from Fayett'ville, lak I say. Get them chairs up, Ellie." An' out I go.

My heart wus restless all that afternoon. Mrs. Johnson axe what get into me. I brung her tea in the porcelain pot, but forgot the cup an' saucer. I got the mail, but then couldn't think whar' I lay it.

I be thinkin' what I gonna say to Johnny, how to set the record straight. How maybe he won't believes me. Then I gots to convince him to run again—this time south. It all too much.

Early evenin', I returns home, help out with supper, cookin' them greens with the tomatoes, when the knock come at the kitchen door. I wait a minute, then follow to the hallway.

Johnny, he sure enough brung that second crate, an' he already talkin' 'bout how he day labor at the wharf. Say that folks sell him goods there, an' now he sell them again. He tell Ellie this, just as L. B. come in from somewhar'.

"Here yo' go, boy," L. B. say. An' he get two dime an' a nickel out from his pants. Missus says the first crate you bring us was nice an' full."

"Thank yo', sir," Johnny say. An' then he spot me behind Ellie. When I sees him look at me, I tick my head. Lak I gettin' a gnat off my face. *Another time*, the tick say. Then I motion up with my head. It mean *I live upstairs. Yo' come on back when we can talks alone.*

Johnny finish up with L. B., an' say goodbye to Ellie. Then he gone, an' we all return to fixin' supper.

Later that same night, I wakes to a pebble throwed up against my window. It wake me quick, an' I knows who it is. I puts my head out, an' there Johnny be. I gives him another tick, *around the back*, it say. I slip on my muslin dress on over the nightshirt gown. Down them creaky stair I go, avoidin' the worst.

"First off," Johnny begin as we standin' at the rear doorway. I don't invite him in, but we stand close, whisperin' real low. "I knows yo' ain't what one that turn me in." He say this outright. "I finds the gal that done it. I know yo' thinkin' I think it be yo'. But I always knowed it weren't." Johnny look at me real intense. It a look that could open a iron door rusted shut. Quick, I see that Ellie right. He be a real handsome man, with a strong frame an' clean, honest face.

"I wouldn't do it. Wouldn't turn yo' in." I meet his eyes. So different than David eyes. Mo' hurt, powerful. Johnny got eyes that know.

"The gal what tell, she turn against me. Long story. But I heard talk 'bout yo' problems at the Smith farm. How J. B. Smith punish all the Negroes till someone done confess. Word get around." Johnny talk all in a rush. He look over his shoulder lak someone comin' after him.

"Yo' in trouble?" I axe.

"No. But I gots to leave. I come back 'cause yo' look so scared this mornin'. Johnny take my hand. "We friends," he say, an' he squeeze.

I nod my head. Tears well up in my eyes, an' I start to cryin' right then an' there by the rear door. I mufflin' my sobs, but they comin' strong. "I wants to go home," I say.

"Home?" Johnny say. "What home?"

But it lak a faucet turn on. I just sob an' sob into his shoulder till I soak his shirt. Sob till there just gasps, no tears left.

"Sometimes I wanna go back too, gal," he say. "But not now. Maybe after the war end. Folks be sayin' South 'bout to lose, in it death throes. When it over, I go back to get my gal. She be waitin' for me to takes her to Baltimore."

I don't say nothin' right away, an' I ain't sure what Johnny mean. I ain't sobbin' no mo', but I can't speak to answer neither. I nod. Johnny stroke my head. Real gentle.

"We finds us a way to go, gal. But we gotta wait. Yo' with me? Johnny axe. "Can yo' wait?"

Again, I nod. Then, I looks up. "I trust yo'," I say. "I trust yo' before an' gonna trust yo' now."

It months before I sees Johnny again. But when I do, he got a plan. It the winter of 1864. I wait all that fall. Johnny show up just when I 'bout to lose hope. [Ms. *Augustus says to turn off the tape machine, and with a click, it is off. When she resumes speaking, it is another day.]*

October 12, 1937

Won't say much 'bout that last week. We wus plannin' to leaves on a Friday, the 30th day of December, 1864. Union Army wus fixin' to march south in the new year, an' Johnny an' me wus plannin' to follow. It been a year or so since Mr. Lincoln freed the colored, an' we all thinkin' the war be over soon. Then the weather turn mild for December—but that weren't gonna last.

Johnny done finds his way back to our kitchen door the week previous, before Christmas. He tell me to be ready. An' when I tell L. B., Ma Eve, an' Ellie I wus goin', they tell me it ain't a good idea. I should stay whar' it safe. But nothin' they say gonna convince me.

We has us a sad Christmas. Each has us some small gifts—I embroidered a flower for Ma Eve new dress an' got L. B. a ol' magazines I find. L. B., Ma and Ellie give me some money for the trip. Also, a knit hat an' a cape made'a wool. Everyone preoccupied with my leavin'.

I should of been sadder than I wus. That final week, I couldn't feel much of anythin'. Ma Eve end up slippin' me a few extra coins, an' she sew them into my clothes. I tells them thanks, over an' over, for all they done for me. But my heart weren't in it—the thanks.

Lookin' back, I think they knew—*they sensed I knew* the wrong they done me. A guilty cloud hangin' in the air before I leaves.

But for days, we say our good-byes. *Goodbye an' good luck* wus what we said mostly. There wus still talk that I be comin' back—that David might send word, an' they gonna see us reunited in Baltimore. But I wus thinkin' David wus dead.

It cost me plenty of sorrow, but I'd done much growin' up at L. B. house. I thought back to my weddin' night with David. An' the secret I kept from him.

An' before I leaves, I made one last trip to see Eliza Louise grave—her cold dirt cradle.

I tell Mrs. Johnson that I goin' up to visit relatives in New York, that they call for me 'cause I needed. She in a bad way the last time I see'd her. In her bedroom whar' she mostly stay. Lyin' there with a big, white bed bonnet on. It nearly cover her face, an' all she did wus turn to me an' say, "So long, Eliza. Yo' take care yo'self." Then she close her eyes—the goodbye take all her strength.

Ma Eve an' Ellie help me get two dresses ready—one new, the other not. One I fixin' to wears—it wus dark linen—an' one extra, the new one, I pack in my bag. Ellie give me her boots too. Tell me to wear them for the journey, which I do. We wear the same size, an' she want me to have them. Also, Ellie sew a cape for me—black wool—that wear well an' won't show dirt. I take my rags an' some underclothes. Don't wants to carry much. Mostly I prayin' hard them last few days.

I pray to my faceless angels, an' I pray to Jesus Christ—axe him for safe passage. Feel lak my requests modest enough, givin' what I been through. But I pray for others too—my family in Baltimore—Ma Eve, Ellie, L. B.—my kin in Fayett'ville—Ma, Pa, Mar, Kate, Hannah, an' I pray for my own li'l Eliza Louise Payne, that sure be up in heaven with Mar dead baby, Wednesday. They be cousins an' sure to find each other.

When Friday arrive, I all a'jitter, nervous, yet the whole day move slow, an' everythin' seem purposeful. Maybe it just me. Thinkin' 'bout myself, every small thing I do. *Sarah Louise, this be yo' last time yo' gonna cut cold chicken on this wood board. This the last time yo' sleep in yo' warm, comfortable bed. Last time yo' goin' out to the market place to haggle with Mrs. Tom, the thief that want you pay double for everythin'. Baltimore—ain't gonna be home no mo'. Yo' ain't gonna be settin' in this chair, ain't gonna light this lamp.*

Johnny come for me right at midnight—this the plan. Ma Eve have food prepare to takes with us: salt pork, corn bread, sweet an' hard biscuits—they in sacks, ready to go. Water in soldier canteens. Two of them. With long straps.

Plan is that we be mostly walkin' out'ta Baltimore. First, Johnny has a cart he gonna drive, then leave for a friend to pick up tomorrow. Then we gonna walk—follow the Union Army as they head south. But not too close. Maybe a half day behind.

I suppose to rouse L. B. before we leaves, so I goes to his bedroom. He already up. Ma Eve awake too. L. B. need to put on his boots, so I go over to the other side of the bed, an' Ma Eve hug an' kiss me lak I kin. Ma Eve remind me, "Yo' come back, 'cause that what yo' tell David. That yo' gonna be here for him. Yo' hear me gal?"

L. B. join us in the hall, an' he had drawn us a map that Johnny take an' fold up in his boot. I hug Ma Eve an' L. B. one las' time—thankin' an' thankin' them for all they done. We picks up our stuff an' leaves. *[Ms. Augustus sighs, pauses, then resumes.]*

At the outskirts of Baltimore we finds the Union Army trail. We nearly a mile behind the column. It stay by the coast, along the east. We dartin' one way, then another. There plenty of rivers, salt water. An' we follow dirt paths along to ferry points. They marked if yo' know whar' to look. Most has rafts carry folk across. That what we be searchin' for. We travel at night, sleep day. Army lead the way.

We finds ourselfs sheds, barns to we stay in. It gonna take us weeks, three weeks, we figure. The soldiers marchin' toward Fort Monroe, an' it a long way off. The month slip well into January. It rain an' snow, an' we stay in one place over a week. Army waitin' for rations shipped south by rail. We finds ourselfs a small stone cellar carved into a hillside, an' we camp there. Ain't nobody around. Johnny fish in a half frozen pond—use some salt pork on a hook, catched a bunch of catfish. But it a safe place, an' quiet—no battles, no cannon fire nearby. Johnny an' I do fine together. We rest, an' we a good team. Then the Army march again, so we follows.

The hardest part we travel wus the Potomac River. It a wide, deep water, an' we almost couldn't find someone to do the ferryin'. Union Army done cross on a pontoon bridge what they take up again when the soldiers wus all across.

Finally, a young Negro field worker agree to take us across. This man, a slave, but his marster gone to war, an' he 'bout left on his own. He could run, but he don't wanna leave—got a wife, couple'a children. He live off the river, do some farmin', an' got hisself a raft he keep by the reeds. He ferry us across at night.

Food wus scarce. Mostly we be livin' off the land—an' ain't much after the Amy come through. One time we finds us some 'taters hid under a chicken house. Farm deserted. It a kind'a lawless land now. Some farms with just ladies around—the men gone or dead. Some place still has their slaves, an' in others, they all just left.

No one trust no one. One lady raise her rifle to us, so we puts our arms in the air. Then she see we just Negroes an' that I a gal, an' she end up takin' us in an' feedin' us turnip stew. She wus completely alone.

There wus a lot of water to cross—rivers, creek, brackish streams flowin' on to the sea. This be mostly swampland. But we only fill our canteens with well water. The streams, they lak cemeteries. *[There is some scratchiness in the tape, but Ms. Augustus continues to speak.]*

I has one shawl I brings—heavy dark wool, lak my cape—an' big as a bed blanket—an' we make small fires when we be sleepin' out. But it wus hard to find dry wood. An' Johnny say we better stay back, that we followin' now too close behind the infantry. It make him uneasy. There lots of bad, rough men, rag-tag drifters latchin' on. We wus tryin' to pick up the very rear. I has my good boots on—the ones Ellie give to me. Johnny has him a long wool coat that still in fair shape an' some soldier boots he take off a dead soldier.

As we follow the coast, all jagged, so turn inland after a while. Travelin' south an' east—ain't dare come close to Washington. We lose the main regiment—gets ourselfs down to the place whar' Chesapeake River join the Potomac, tryin' to avoid skirmishes. Our route one that slave follow north, but we headed opposite. The big river, Potomac, wide at the sea, an' it got strong currents.

At one point, we has to pay a dollar apiece to a white man what runs a ferry. He take us at night. Live alone in a shack, claim to be war veteran—fight for both sides. Got nothin' good to say 'bout neither.

By February, we always hungry. An' Ellie new boots ain't broke in to my feet, so I gettin' blisters from all the walkin'. Skin rubbed raw, an' I bathe them in the cold, cold salt water, what suppose to help heal them. One foot especially—the pain so bad that I has to take off one boot, walk that way.

It slow goin'. I can't remember all them rivers, steams, creeks we cross. I hobblin' along. Johnny whistlin' to keep my spirits up. Sometime, he carry my bag. We just tryin' to keep from bein' noticed, singled out. We has to make small fires a few times a day, an' then a small fire at night on dry ground. Johnny has two pair boots that he trade off to keeps his feet dry. One point, I try to walk in his extra pair, but they too big, even with plenty'a rags stuff into the toe box. This my downfall—wet, blistered feet. Two week become three. We keepin' on.

One night, when we almost to Fort Monroe, we come across a camp of slaves, run'ways in the swamp. Men an' gals there, group 'bout six or seven. One gal has a baby. Woman name wus Zeno, Zena, Zensor…a strange name. Her baby, a boy-child, wus born in the swamp. She ain't never name the baby… just call it "baby." Seem unlucky to me.

Also, we meets up with a Quaker family live near the swamp camp. They has a winter kitchen garden, an' they take us in, feed us. But we can't stay the night. They puts us in the cow barn to tend to us. They got a bunch of li'l ones, three boys an' two gals. Family say they against fightin', against all wars. Against their religion to fight—an' to keep slaves. So they outlaws. Livin' on their own, by the edge of the swamp. The men conscripted, but they ain't gone to serve. Folks mainly leaves them alone, but deserters come all the time to this place. Some Union, but most Confederate. Some wounded, an' some hard, desperate men.

Never know who gonna show up at the Quaker house, so we advise to go back to the Negro swamp camp for the night, whar' it safer. Quaker woman bandage my hurt foot before we leaves. She has some herb salve she rub on it. Then put a fresh bandage around. I keep the one boot off, one boot on—gonna try hobblin' back. They gives us cob corn to roast in the fire an' cheese, soft cheese, an' bread. Fresh well water.

It ain't too far a distance to the Negro camp, maybe half a mile, but sure enough, we meets a group of raggedy white men on the path. It all swamp, an' the ground spongy. My bandaged foot already be soaked, same as my good foot in the boot

These white men, they be deserters an' bummers. But they ain't outlaws, lak the Quakers, religious folks that against the war; they simply be scroungers. Mostly start out Confed'rates, but now they ain't be on neither side.

They follow us to the camp. They don't care 'bout run'ways or rewards or nothin'. An' at least they ain't drunk. Dirty, but not drunk. They leave the next mornin'.

Zena—the gal I tells yo' about—she has her infant, an' she one of two gals there. The other is a ol' woman, keep by herself on the side. She ain't got no teeth, an' she sad an' shriveled. We stay with them for a couple days. They catch fish an' turtle, an' they keeps a fire goin' all the time.

I had come down with a fever an' wus sick. That why we stay on for a third day. Also, the weather turn cold, an' there be a light snow. Johnny sleep near me, on the ground. I weren't too sick, an' the fever break soon.

I remember Zena come in to the tent whar I at, an' she bring her infant boy. He a pretty thing. An' I has myself some dreamless, heavy sleep when I sick in that camp. An' I ain't thinkin' 'bout Eliza, David, nothin'. I just numb. Think that I gotta get myself well, keep movin', pray to my angels for my fever to break, foot to heal.

That second day, when I comin' out'ta my fever, Johnny an' me go to the creek to wash up some. I got my dress loose, my boots off, an' Johnny help me walk with my hurt foot.

There by the bank wus a old walkin' bridge, a foot bridge half broke, but safe enough to carry my weight. It low to the creek, so we set on it to wash. I bendin' down to splash water on my face, an' when I looks up, I see that Johnny got his shirt off. An' there be his naked back—with snakes crawlin' beneath his dark skin. He near me, so I shift a bit to touch his scars—run my hand over them.

"Oh," Johnny say. An' he stop his washin', an' sit down near me, his back to me, but we real close.

"Always want to do that. From the first time I saw them scars." I leaves my hand on his warm back for a moment.

Still Johnny don't move or turn hisself around so I can see him. But I knows he got a grin on his face—come right through his body.

The sun be settin' in the east, over the swamp, an' changin' the blue sky into a deep orange, yella'-orange. There that winter chill, an' Johnny bump hisself closer, so his back now be touchin' me.

"I know what yo' been through, gal." Then silence. "L. B. tell me before we leaves. I wants yo' to knows yo' has nothin' to worry about with me." His voice get calm an' smooth lak it blend right into the sky.

"I knows," I say, though I didn't. But somehow I feel safer once Johnny say these things. I leaves my hand on his back an' rub it in the middle, near his heart. Mammy Rae uset'ta say that yo' could soothe the heart through the back of a person, if yo' found the right spot.

When we gets up, neither us say nothin'. I knowed Johnny a good man—from the very beginning. That what I try to tell my Ma. But she just think I a foolish gal. An' I hear Ma voice come to me through the swamp. *Tisk, tisk, tisk,* it say. Then she say, *Gal, yo' don't know nothin' about nothin'.*

Stop for a moment. Gotta stop. *[There is a scuffle of voices, and the tape machine is turned off for a minute. Then, when it is turned back on, Ms. Augustus starts to speak, and it is obviously later in the day.]*

…Better now. Feels better. Gonna picks up…now Johnny an' me leaves the swamp camp. We there for few days. My foot heal so I can gets my boot back on an' my fever leave, so I feelin' all right again. We both got our strength back, ready to push on to Fort Monroe.

Lak I say, we travel back roads, stay well behind the Army. Then, when we come close to the Fort, we stop to catch our bearings, come up with a plan. We figure that if we get too close to the sea, we gonna catch some Navy fightin', an' that ain't what we want. This Fort a big place—dangerous—with plenty of soldiers an' guards. It even got a big ditch dug all around—a moat.

We told by the Negroes in the swamp, there Confed'rates all by the Fort. Make sense—Confed'rate state under Federal flag.

We camp outside the Fort, by a dumpin' ground for the army trash, garbage an' broken things. There be chicken bones, cow bones, husks, bloody rags, broken up cots, rotten food, an' rats—plenty rats. First, it wus a dug-out pit whar' they bury the trash, but it get so big that it pile up, an' the men can't dig no mo' pits in winter. The soldiers don't expect to be there come next summer. But it stink real bad, even in the cold. The colored at the swamp camp say that this dump pile be whar' runways wait to gets themselfs inside the Fort. They needs for a Union soldier to come. The Union men patrol there. It just a matter of time.

Also, we hears stories of Confed'rates come to the dump, lookin' for run'way slaves to shoot, so we gotta be extra careful. Plenty taste their freedom before they gets it. Make it almost to the Fort, but then get sloppy—get caught or killed. Some Confed'rates puts on Union coats so the run'ways come to them. Then they fire.

We gets some thawin' weather now—a warm spell—so the garbage mess stinky an' rats swarmin'. But this the place we gonna wait.

Johnny gettin' nervous by then. Me too. Sometime in the night I think I sees Mister Crow spreadin' his feathery wings. But I just tired. Mister Crow ain't makin' no appearance at the dump.

"What that yo' lookin' at, gal?" Johnny axe me one evenin'. We settin' by some brush, back a ways from the pile, but we can see.

"Nothin'," I tells him. "Ain't seein' nothin'," but the truth is I think I spot Mister Crow, a black shape. Then I hear somethin' rustle. But as I look, I see a rat. A fat rat in shadow.

So, we sits there, Johnny gnawin' some hard tack. I still got my pack, my carpet bag, an' my foot still in the boot, though it achin' again.

Johnny hand me a piece of tack, an' I takes it, tries to et. But it taste lak the dump, an' puts it in my bag.

Johnny finish his piece, an' we hears some voices. We stand up to see better. They comin' from outside the Fort. From the path, we think. Quiet, we sneak over till we nearly out in the open whar' they can sees us.

Johnny cock his head, listen close. But we can't make out them voices good. Can't tell if we should come on out or keep ourself hid.

Voices come closer. My heart poundin' inside my chest, 'bout to pop out. I can hears Johnny breathin' hard, lak he just run all the way from Baltimore.

"Mail going out tomorrow," we hear one man say. Union soldiers there—two of them.

"That what I hear too," the other man say.

"Got some half dozen letters writ," a voice chuckle.

"I got one, six-page long to Abby. She still there in Boston with that widow aunt. She sure going to be pleased that I remember to post to her aunt. Last time I post it wrong, take twice long to reach."

Johnny look at me, an' stand up, nod. I nod, stand too. Johnny take my hand, an' we step out to show ourselfs.

"We come for sanctuary," Johnny say. An' I startled for a moment, thinkin' 'bout the word he use.

The men got weapons. Older soldier got a sword, an' he put his hand on it. The other got a pistol.

"No, no, no," Johnny speak to them, an' he nudge me to put my hands up too. "We come from Baltimore. We headed back to North Car'lina to find kin."

"Keep yo' hands up. Yo' keeps them way up, fella. Got papers? Identification? Stand aside," the one younger soldier take my arm an' pull me from Johnny. He must be fifteen year ol'. He in a Union uniform, but his jacket got a rip an' there some buttons off. He look mo' scared of us then we is of him.

"I'll get the Lieutenant. Yo' keeps them here." The older one trot off for the Fort. Can't tell how he gettin' in, just vanish.

Johnny an' me still gots our arms raised. The night be lit by moon now, full that shine down. Hadn't notice it before, maybe the clouds part.

"Quiet now, nothing tricky," the boy with the pistol say.

Finally, the other soldier show up, the lieutenant.

"Search him," the lieutenant order. An' the older solider pat down Johnny.

"What you got in the pocket?" Older soldier axe. "Get it out."

Out come a piece of crumbly hard tack. "That it," Johnny say. "An' sister here got a bag. Yo' wants us to gets that?" It on my shoulder.

The young soldier pull off my bag, an' he paw through it. "What are all these filthy rags for?" he axe.

"I is a woman, sir," I say an' lower my eyes. *[There is a brief pause in the tape. Then, Ms. Augustus resumes.]*

So they takes us into the Fort. Night now, an' they finds us a place to sleep on stretched canvas cots in a couple of hallways. It wus good to be off the ground an' under a roof again. There wus a fire in the fort plaza keep goin' all night. Men take turns stokin' it with what wood they has—mostly pine. Ain't a hot fire, but the embers keep it warm. Sometimes men huddle up in front of it, get the chill out their bones, go back to bed. An' there be other Negroes in the Fort. Mostly run'ways, even this late in the war, but what wants to fight for the Union.

Run'ways all thinks we crazy, headin' south. Wrong direction.

"Wait till the end of the war," we told by one mulatto that cleans the bunks. "Yo' fools to go back now." We sittin' by the embers that first night—an' I thinkin' 'bout that. He pokin', stirrin' the fire with a metal rod.

"We come this far," I say. An' he stab at some mo' coals, which spark up lak stars in the night.

"War be over by time we gets into Car'lina," Johnny say.

"Them Confed'rates ain't gonna surrender till they all dead. Every last one. An' first they gonna try to kill us colored—an' even thems that mulato. Ain't got nothin' to lose by it. That we gonna takes what left, an' maybe they be right. Yo' fools to go south." The man get up. I sees he got a bad leg, an' a crooked stick he use for a crutch. He hobble off. We hears from others that come up from Car'lina, Georgia, Alabama. Fort Fisher be under attack. Wilmington, whar' we goin', the Army next be goin'. If Wilmington fall, the war be over. There go the food, cloth, whole Confed'rate supply line.

We decides to stay a week longer when we hears that. First, we thinkin' a day or two, but it take to the middle'a February for the Union to get hold.

Still, when I speaks to anyone—tell 'em we plannin' our return to North Car'lina, folks just shakes their head.

An' all the time we there, I half expectin' to see Swell. But nobody even heared of him. Maybe he go by different name, or he ain't never make it to Monroe. Maybe we never gets in touch with the right folks that knowed him. Monroe a big place, but I axed around.

One captain, he tryin' get Johnny to stay. Roads needs to be built. Victory near, an' captain want strong bodies lak Johnny. Got a colored unit he could joins. Wants me to stay too—cook. I tells him I ain't good at that, but then he axe what can I do. When I tell him 'bout Doc Goldstein, an' he say he need nurses. "We short of good Negroes the likes of yo'," he tell me.

I knows he right—they needs us. But this powerful feeling be pullin' me back to Fayett'ville. Truth is, South gonna lose, an' we encouraged. [*Ms. Augustus clears her throat, and there is a brief pause before she continues.*]

Don't knows how many soldiers wus at Monroe. Fort spread out, huge, an' mostly they is white troops, but some Negro soldiers too. Run'ways, rag-tag men—an' thems that come to fight. There be the regiment from Baltimore. But others too. Mens join right here. Run'ways an' free, all able-body men.

Families lived there too—officers, wifes, a few chil'ren—that wus in quarters mostly. The commander, General Butler, in charge of the colored soldiers. He regiment commander, an' I see'd him from a distance. Once, he conductin' maneuvers with white troops in full new uniforms. Then I see'd him with colored, but they weren't never in proper dress.

Soon after we gets to the Fort that first week—temperature drop, an' it rain' hard every day—cold, but no snow. Stay wet for a whole week too. Winter rain. There be a new group of colored come inside that week, an' we all crowd in that hall, but we has us pallets or canvas cots, an' stay dry. Toward the end of that week, I come down with women trouble, a bad monthly, an' I take to my cot for a couple'a days.

Johnny keep busy. Gettin' hisself a map, information 'bout roads, an' he talkin' to everyone so we can make a plan. He gotta know everything.

One colored man at the Fort, from Fayett'ville. A free black man that work downtown before the war. Blacksmith. Had a forge on Ramsey Street by Green. Come to Monroe to fight. Can't recalls his name. Williams… or somethin'. He tell us how things change. Fewer folks to work the land. An' the munitions plant, the arsenal that the Confed'rates take, on Hay Street, it makin' the whole town nervous. Folks think it gonna get attack, just a matter of time. He warn us not to go. Say white folks gettin' strange 'bout their property.

While we wus at Monroe, a terrible thing occur. Soldiers, Federals, they wus on a boat at Cherrystone—Cherrystone the inlet nearby. Rebels come in durin' the dark of night an' captures the boat.

Federal post wus near, an' it have horses, cavalry horses, an' the Rebels shot 'em all. That's right. Shot every horse they has. Federals soldiers git scared, think they next. Also, there be fugitive colored men at that post, an' they so scared, they runs off into the woods. Rebels don't follow though, has enough to do with the white soldiers they capture. This news we get at Monroe.

By early mornin', the Rebels done unload the boat they take, steal everythin' from it, but leaves the boat. Could of blowed it up, but they didn't. An' they freed the prisoners, 'cause they ain't has the means to keep them. No one hurt, an' by the mornin' when we learns 'bout it, the incident over. But we all concern 'bout the colored men—a handful ain't accounted for.

That evenin', after dark, couple'a these fugitive Negroes sneak back to Cherrystone post, an' see they safe. Federal soldiers there take three of 'em to Fort Monroe, whar' Johnny an' me meets them. They be braggin' now 'bout how escaped the Rebels, an' the Federals gonna win the war.

Also, Union has a telegraph station at that post, send communication to Fort Monroe. In the skirmish, the Rebels cut the line. But we has two skilled Negro men know how to repair it. These fellas—another two that runs that night—they recruited to repair the wire. About to be taked into safety at Fort Monroe, but they then ordered to do the repair. An' so in peril, they undertake the mission, an' by the time we see them at Monroe, they both heroes.

This all happen over two or so weeks. Johnny an' me anxious to get goin', but we etin' good. We has meat, corn bread, biscuits. There a regular cook an' a army doc that tend my hurt foot. Got some powder he sprinkle, tell me to keep the boot off a day, so it dry. Heal up fine. We keep thinkin' we only gonna stay a few mo' days, but them Rebels at Cherrystone make us reconsider.

Johnny talkin' meanwhile with all the men, an' he try to get us a plan. Folks still callin' us fools, but we thinkin' we gonna try to travel down the coast'a Virg'nia, North Car'lina, to Wilmington. Then we gonna comes inland by steamboat, up the Cape Fear to our home.

In miles, it the longes' way, an' we tired just thinkin' 'bout it. So much goin' on that we on edge. An' sick of the war—exhausted just thinkin' 'bout the journey.

Fact is, after that first ten days or so, even me, I think 'bout stayin' put right there at Monroe. A fortress. Safe. Got a moat. Guards. Blacks free. An' we has good work that be offered.

After my foot heal, Johnny axe me one night, "Gal," he say. "What if we stay put whar' we is? War over soon. Might not have to wait long." We settin' outside a barrack room, in the stone hallway. Out in the courtyard, there a big fire goin'. Negroes talkin', laughin'. It cold, but the fire nice, warm. I has my boot back on my foot. An' I feelin' both ways. Want to go an' wants to stay.

"I ready to go now, Johnny," I say. I had myself a apple what wus give to me by a white woman, officer wife. I bite into it.

"Home plenty far away, gal. Take us a long time. No guarantee we make it to Wilmington neither." Johnny watchin' me take bites. "If we gets caught, ain't no tellin' what happen. Probably shot. Men in Cherrystone wus lucky." Johnny turn to me, an' I see the white part of his eyes in the firelight.

"I wanna go, Johnny," I say, but I ain't sure. "If we hug the coast till Wilmington, we be fine. Ain't no fightin' in the swamp between here an' there." When I finishes my apple, I gets up, walk to the fire, throws it in. Sparks flare, core sizzlin' in the flame.

Johnny standin' up when I returns. "I wants to go too, gal. But I guess I thinkin' we should wait. Not long. Maybe through February, March—no later. They offerin' us work here—an' safety." He touch my shoulder. "What yo' think?" Johnny motion with his chin, an' we walk over to the next hallway, whar my cot be. Johnny, he sleep with the men in another place. I gots six other women with cots here, Negro gals, one with a young child. So when we get to the cots, the mother with her li'l gal there, so Johnny an' me walk back a bit.

"But Johnny, we got a plan an' a map. My foot heal so good that I can keeps it in the boot now...." I raise my hurt foot so Johnny can sees I got the laces tied tight.

"If we didn't hears so much 'bout Fort Fisher, might be different. But we got to be sure. I knows you want to go now, but I ain't ready for no kind of stupid chance." Johnny stop, turn to me.

"Yo' wants me to go on alone? That it?" I say. Ain't even sure why I arguin' 'cause I ain't convinced myself. Now, we at the fire again—some men huddle by it, so we keep our voices down.

"Yo' ain't goin' nowhar' alone. Uh-uh. Ain't gonna happen." Johnny shake his head. His voice take on a low tone, a deep whisper. "Don't see why we can't be useful here a while." Johnny look at me, an' his face soften. Then he hug me. "I wants the best for yo'. I do. We come far, gal. Too far for somethin' stupid."

Johnny hug me to him, an' we rock slightly together, lak we family, on the same side.

It feel good, but I pull away, make my point.

"Yo' is one stubborn gal, Sarah Louise." Johnny grab me tight again, whisper in my ear so I smell his whiskey. "No, fuss now," he say. "Life too short." Then he let me go, them dark, dark lovely eyes lookin' at me, face lit up by fire glow.

"No," I say. "That ain't the plan. Yo' can't change the plan." I keep my voice low, but I angry. We be walkin' again.

Back to my cot. Standin' in the shadow, Johnny turn to me, squeeze my hand. We both done talkin'. We too tired.

"Talk mo' tomorrow, gal. Get some sleep now." Johnny squeeze my hand once mo', an' then he go.

Next day, I see Johnny first thing in the mornin'. The weather turn bad again—bitter cold an' gray. Captain empty out a extra storehouse to make room for colored folks still sleepin' in the courtyard. Big winter storm comin', everyone be sayin'.

Johnny an' me sits down to eat breakfast together in the big hall. "Weather breakin' further south, yo' think?" I axe. Johnny glare at me. I grin. "Be stupid to travel south in a winter storm," I say. Johnny grin back.

"Yas, would be," Johnny say. He bend, lak he gonna kiss my forehead but can't reach. So he wink at me. "Yo' one good gal, Sarah Louise. Stubborn, but good."

So that wus that. We gonna stay put a while longer. Plenty of work to do here. An' I do end up helpin' out the doc, but it ain't the kind of nursin' what I do with Doc Goldstein. Mostly, it wus emptyin' buckets, changin' bandages. Ain't a big hospital they gots, but plenty sick men there. Johnny sent out to work on the lines. Telegraph. So he gone for days at a time. He lak the work. But it wear on him.

One day—must be 'bout a month—when winter finally start to shake loose. A sweet smell come over the Fort, an' outside, the smallest buds form on the trees—a deep, damp, musty smell, an' temperature warm enough not to need a shawl in the afternoon. Johnny an' me both know it time to leave.

Spring on it way, an' there mo' talk around the Fort that the Army done broke the back of the Confed'racy. Wilmington under Union control now, an' folks what live there told to evacuate. This wus the third week in February, 1865.

An' we got ourself a better map drawn by a soldier what know the way. He come up recent from Wilmington. Up the coast.

Some folks from the Fort rise early to say goodbye to me an' Johnny, but ain't no one in particular we gonna miss. Shake hands at the gate, an' soldiers let us pass. We leavin' before first light.

We follow a footpath to a li'l swamp creek. At the bank, there a rowboat we told to use, leave downstream for them that be travelin' back up. Johnny lift the oars as we drift quiet through the winter reeds.

Soon, we floats to whar' the creek become a tidal river. There a wood wharf there, an' a bigger skiff tied up—a ol' oyster boat own by white men, an' they hides us under sacks. Men wus Southerners, but workin' with the Union Army.

Much of the shoreline, Johnny an' me travel on boats lak this—small, flat-bottom, ol' ferry rafts. Through inlets, swamps, with plenty'a folks livin' in-between. Some lawless, in trouble before the war begin.

When we get to North Car'lina, we meets another Quaker family on the coast—north of Wilmington. It a family—prob'ly still live there. Quakers. There Quakers everywhar'— Raleigh, Greensboro, on the coast. They good folks, willin' to helps us at peril to their own lifes.

For two nights durin' that journey, we stay in a Quaker house. We below Virg'nia now, in North Car'lina—lak I say.

Oh—an' once we come on a Rebel farm, almost get shot for stealin' chicken. We ain't had no choice. This right before we meet the Quakers that hide us on their farm.

We took us a big ol' brown hen, right from the farmer chicken house. Farmer set his hounds on us, but we gets away. Least we thinkin' that. We run till we don't hears no mo' dogs. So we sit down, hungry. Snap the chicken neck, pluck the feathers clean, an' start a small fire. That the mistake we make, should of knowed better.

The hounds track us from the smoke. We takes off, leavin' the chicken still raw on the spit, an' travel through swamp water till the dogs can't scent. That how we end up at the Quaker farmstead. Them dogs never did get too close; lak I say, they lose the scent.

Missus of the house come to the porch, an' show us back to the kitchen. First, we set. There a bench on the side wall, an' the Missus keep the kitchen dark. We don't talk, just set. Close to a hour pass before it be safe, Missus reckon, an' she bring us a water basin to clean ourselfs. Then Missus get food, an' she offer us some too. We sit an' et. Hungry 'cause we left the chicken.

She fix us a place to sleep in the barn. A nice barn, well-kept, with fresh straw an' one milk cow in a stall. That first night after we gets cleaned up, et some supper, an' gets settled, the Missus bring us extra food—into the barn, late. She got cold ham an' biscuits, an' the dish wus covered by a fresh white cloth. Before she set it down for us on a ol' shippin' trunk, she say she want to axe us just one question. So she stand there in the dim light of the candle she brung us an' say: "Is either of yo' without sin?"

We silent a moment. Then Johnny pipe up an' tell her, "No, ma'am. We just steals a chicken."

The woman smile at us an' nod. She put the covered dish down on the hay, an' she suggest we hold hands. Then she say grace. "Amen," we say together. She say simply, "God bless you and goodnight."

That the first night; we stay two. Rest up in the barn mostly. The second evenin' for supper, Missus call us in to et with the family. Father gone off, don't know whar', 'cause them Quakers against fightin'. There three gals, one almost full-grown, an' a young boy, maybe seven. We at the table, settin' with the white folks, joinin' them. This my first time to et with white folk at a table.

We has our grace for sinners again, an' then we pass around plates for helpings. Everyone quiet, an' afterwards, we ready to goes back to the barn. But as we excuse ourself, Missus tell us to come an' set a while with the family, in the parlor, main room of the house.

I wide awake, havin' been asleep most of the day, but Johnny, with his full belly, he near to noddin' off. He make hisself comfortable, at the Missus urgin', on a rug. There a blanket quilt from a basket she get for him. I sit on a window bench with a cushion on it, an' there be a chill air come through the panes.

A big ol' clock tick off the minutes. An' we each with our own thoughts. The boy, on a chair, he in the shadow, readin' by a single candle. The younger gals darnin' or doin' needlework some kind. They got two lamps lit, an' the light be soft. The room peaceful.

Then Missus axe, "Are you a bornthrall?" She look at me. I look at Johnny, but he fast asleep. She got ten children, she tell us—some married. "This here is my Mary," she say, an' motion at the one gal by me on a stuff chair, do some knittin'. The Missus settin' on a rocker, creak back an' forth.

"Ma'am," I say. "I don't know the word." Missus busy with her small needles, knittin' socks from home-spun.

She take a minute, rockin', knittin', then say: "I'm asking if you were born into bondage. If you were born into *thrall*dom. *Thrall* meaning slavery."

I quiet for a bit. Thinkin' 'bout the word. That there be such a word for me, my condition.

The fire crackle, an' when I don't say nothin', the Missus return to her home-spun. I raise my face up, ready to speak, but nothin' come out.

Then I say, "I is a bornthrall, but now I free."

The place fall silent again but for the sound of the rocker an' the clock tickin' steady an' slow. I settin' on my window bench.

Then the Missus, the young missus, along with the younger gals, an' the li'l boy-child readin' in the corner, begin to pray.

The Missus begin: "We come together this night, dear Lord, to welcome these two bornthralls into our home, our house of freedom and equality. May all who are born into bondage be released. May our home be their home. Our freedom theirs. For this we pray, dear Lord. Amen."

The woman say this, an' we just say the amen. Then the boy go back to his book, an' the gals continue with sewin', darnin', what they doin' before. Johnny sleep through the whole thing. *[There is a long pause, and then Ms. Augustus sighs and continues.]*

It weren't till later—much later—that I come to understand that night, why it sting me so. What that word *bornthrall* rouse in me. I get a feelin' up from the grave. I thinkin' about my li'l Eliza Louise Payne. I feel her with me. She the gal child I set free by givin' her life without no master, no missus. I feel that somewhar' she alive—an' free. Yas, I thinks, *she free. [There is an abrupt stop, and the tape is silent. After a few scratchy moments, Ms. Augustus says that she wants to take a break. The tape machine is clicked off.]*

October 13, 1937

How yo' lak all this rain? Put a chill in yo' bones. Winter comin' sure as a dog got fleas. I has mo' tea brewed. Whole pot on the wood stove.

Missus give us some food an' clothin' before we leaves the next day. Outfit us from a ol' trunk chest she got. Plenty of sizes—lak she always be prepare. She a soft spoke, kind woman. Got her own angels—inside.

When we leaves, we go at night. Walk our way to Wilmington. There still be a couple of days we got to travel in swampland, 'cause we can't risk the beach. There be folks fishin' on the waterway, an' outlaws—black an' white—scrapin' by. Nobody take much interest in us. Only care that we keep movin', don't cause no trouble. Poor folks got problems of their own.

One house we come to, a shack, look deserted. There a couple of pigs inside, an' the front door left wide open—them two pigs wus lyin' beneath the kitchen table. Two tea cups on the table. Look to me lak ma an' pa pig gonna has themselfs a party.

"Howdy do?" Johnny say when we step in. One pig lyin' on the wood floor, the other stand up when we comes in. He grunt, look at us, then mosey on outside. Johnny think we ought'ta slaughter one, but I say no. Ain't enough time, an' somebody gonna miss a pig. Bad enough to steal chickens.

We check the empty cupboard, an' there a ol' dresser by a broke down frame bed—nothin' of any use. When we leave, both pigs outside now, rootin' around, gruntin'.

Sudden, a wind blow, up, startle us as the front door hinges squeak an' the door bang against the house a couple times.

"Better go," I say.

Johnny nod, an' we make out the back of the property, through a swampy area, whar' there be Cyprus trees in a shallow pond. We edge our way around it, but we get plenty wet.

At the other side, I needs to go. So Johnny turn his back to me, an' I go off behind a bush.

It almost dusk now. Sky gettin' crisp, the way it do on clear, cool spring evenin's. There a sharpness in the air, somethin' firm yo' can almost touch. Slight breeze rustlin' the milkweed an' tall grasses. There young leaves with heavy buds, some openin' already on the trees.

"Up, gal!" I hear. An' Johnny suddenly beside me, yankin' on my arm as I squat. An' the second Johnny pull on me, I hear men voices, an' know we gotta run.

Wet an' with my drawers half up, I lopin' along. Johnny still got my arm, an' we ain't lookin' back.

The men—we never even see'd them, only heared their voices—must of not seen us. We thinkin' they be Confed'rates but can't be sure.

Everywhar' Union troops go, colored suppose to be free. But Rebels gonna shoot anyways.

We out'ta breath when we stop. By now, we on dry pasture land, fenced in with split rail. Ain't no animals, no folks around. Nothin'. The grass ankle high, an' we alone. [*Ms. Augustus lets out a sigh, pauses for a few seconds, then resumes.*]

Late evenin' next day, we get to Wilmington. Strange to come on a city after all that swamp. We come in by a stage road, whar there Union troops posted.

There shacks set back along the road, an' I see'd a Negra gal hangin' wash, so I axe her which way to the wharf. Johnny know somebody we suppose to find there. Captain somebody. If we finds him an' pay him, he gonna get us passage on a steamer up the Cape Fear. [*There is a pause in the tape, and the tape is turned off and on. The interviewer and Ms. Augustus exchange some muffled words, and the tape is clicked off and on again before Ms. Augustus resumes.*]

Wilmington wus suppose to be evacuated. But there be plenty of folks around. There a odd hush to the city, but folks wus out an' doin' business. The streets wus full of soldiers, mostly Union, but some Rebels out of uniform. An' there be colored if yo' knowed whar' to look. We walk through the city, natural as we can—to attract no attention. Just two colored, goin' 'bout our way.

We get ourselfs to the wharf all right. Johnny have me stay back—ain't no women on the loadin' end. An he talk to this captain somethin' or other, who tell him that there steamer expected for the Cape Fear. He tell Johnny whar we need to go.

I strollin' by a small market, a few street sellers out. Many buildin's shut tight. When Johnny find me, he say we goin' upriver on the Hurt.

Same ship brung David.

An' for a minute I think *he* gonna be there—waitin' for me. Then I think maybe I has me a letter from him in Baltimore—a important message that I miss. Or maybe he gonna just show up at the dock.

Johnny an' me get off the street. We near a magnolia by a grassy spot. We walks to a alley behind a closed shop. Johnny say that he caution to take care, that the Hurt carry Rebel soldiers, an' there a chance we recognized.

I has a bonnet on, an' Johnny say I needs to keep wearin' it. An' we gots ourselfs a ways to walk yet. Steamship dock ain't here. The man Johnny speak to, he ain't sure when the Hurt scheduled. Ain't gonna be today, but he say there a lots we gots to do. An' the man say we needs to get to the dock quick to check the schedule.

So we walk. Entire streets is deserted, storefronts closed up. An' after Baltimore, Wilmington look small. My foot begin achin' a bit, an' I has to move slow. Johnny hold my elbow, help me over some busted cobblestone. One time, I bump into a man comin' out a gate. He tip his hat at first, but then he see my face, an' he turn an' spit on the ground. "Excuse me, sir," I say, an' walk on. But when I looks at Johnny, he upset.

When we gets to the dock, we learns that the A. P. Hurt ain't arrive for a few mo' days. So we needs to make plans to stay. Johnny has to arrange for papers too. An' gonna talks to some men 'bout us goin' as passengers. We need papers an' a story. Especially as we travel inland.

But good papers cost money. Union money. Ain't nobody take Rebel paper now. They take gold an' silver too. But Johnny got some dollars from Baltimore—an' we each gots some silver coins.

There a print shop in town, employ free blacks, an' they counterfeit our papers. Mostly they print advertisements, notices, handbills, but they take care of the papers we need.

There be ladies peddlin' on the streets. Soldiers carousin', drunk. Rebels in a hotel once, I hear them say they gonna shoot Yankees lak dogs before they gives themselfs up.

Wilmington—it full of black men in ragged country clothes, walkin' the streets. Women an' children left behind, poor, beggin'. Federal soldiers patrollin'.

Union ships out in the port, keepin' out Rebel runners. Blockade or no blockade, there be commerce, ships from England—come after the cotton we pick.

We stay in Wilmington with free Negroes. Free before the war. They be a bricklayin' family, two growed sons an' the pa. They build for the Confed'rates durin' the war, whatever needed. But now, there ain't work to be done no mo'. [*There is a brief pause. The tape machine is snapped off and then on. Ms. Augustus continues.*]

Wilmington be a inland port, with two ways up the Cape Fear. Fort Fisher sit at the big mouth. But there plenty of small forts there too. I remember that there be two channels. Smith Island sit between. New Inlet an' Ol' Inlet. An' Smith Island—that 'bout ten mile long. Then, there be the "Fryin' Pan Shoals"—named for their shapes. On the island, Smith Island, there some of the smaller forts: Holmes, Johnston, Anderson. But the big fort wus Fisher. An' that still there.

It snow late into the season that year. Spring plantin' start late. We wus cold comin' down. A couple of warm days, but they a false promise.

The colored bricklayer family named Brown. Neither Johnny nor me tell him nothin' 'bout ourselfs—only the names we take. Mr. Brown don't care. Make no difference to him. We all mind our own business. Safer that way.

Brown say his family—his ma and pa—wus slaves that work on a big rice plantation above Charleston. I heared stories before 'bout them rice fields. How they use dams an' locks to flood 'em. How slaves standin' in them wet swampy fields get snake bit. Come down with the Yellow Fever, die. Yellow Fever bad in '63.

But Mr. Brown give us good food—fry fish, corn mush, taters, an' dried apples.

We spend a couple night there. Gets ourselfs clean again. Neighbor woman sell me lady shoes. Johnny get himself a clean jacket. I takes a bath in a tin tub, wash my hair. So we all right.

Our papers say that we trusted slaves lent out to our marster relatives, name of McDonald. We gonna travel by boat up the Cape Fear to Fayett'ville, then walk the road north, up Ramsey Street to Bunn Level, by the stage route. Our papers say my name Rebecca, an' Johnny my cousin Thomas. We knows the stage route good, an' we ain't suppose to talk to no one. *[There is a brief pause, and Ms. Augustus sighs, then continues.]*

The day we go, there be confusion by the river. Union blockader have a skirmish with a runner what ain't seem to know Wilmington already surrender. Folks on the street tryin' to figure out what goin' on. Our boat, the Hurt, almost get shot up. There some cannon fire off the coast. An' there be folks again that say this here signify the war end.

All this commotion happen right on the Cape Fear, down whar' the river meet the ocean. Couldn't see much, but could smell the thick smoke, watch the large black cloud hangin' in the distance, settle. Union attack the blockade runner, an' they fire their guns back. A. P. Hurt suppose to load whar' we wait. But after this skirmish, it gonna load now off another dock, a mile upriver.

So we go up land, hitch a ride on a wagon. It be a ol'-fashion buckboard with a rough front seat. Driver want two silver dime each to take us, which wus robbery, but we have the coins, so we agree. The driver ain't got all his teeth, an' he smell of whiskey. He has his young daughter settin' up beside him on the seat. Only got one horse pullin', but the wagon empty. He been to market, an' now he returnin' home. He ain't the trustworthy sort.

We load on the back. Ain't too dirty. The cart lean a bit to the left side, an' off we go. Gonna be a hour trip.

The li'l gal keep turnin' around to look at us. Don't say nothin'. Her daddy slap her thigh when she stare. She a cute thing. Maybe four, five year ol'.

As Johnny an' I ride, I remember the hangin' on Ramsey Street—'cause the wagon so similar. Same bumpy ride as the one before, but this cart ain't pull by a mule.

The day warmin' up, sun high as we turn right on a small dirt road. Johnny glance at me, an' me at him. We worryin' bout this man, what he might do, if he be honest to his word. But the li'l gal is with him, an' that make us feel better.

We travel for a time, road mostly go through lowlands, empty swamp. There a few buildin's, a creek, an' the river dock at the end. There a brick market house too, with doors wide open. A slab marble countertop run the length of the room, with scales on the floor beside. Heavy iron thing used to weigh freight.

Both the Hurt an' another boat be roped up to the wood dock, whar men be loadin' an' unloadin'.

We hop out'ta the wagon. The man that bring us nod. Then he lift the li'l gal off the bench an' put her down. Off they walk to a saloon by the swamp side. There be a few men drinkin' whiskey there. The horse get hitch to a post by a colored man.

A few empty wagons, without horses or mules, wus settin' by the road. Some broken. Flies wus swarmin' by a dung heap mixed with ol' hay, dumped near. I wus feelin' uncertain, thinkin' bout Rebel soldiers. But we don't see none. Johnny look nervous too.

We has to go into the brick custom house whar' they sell tickets for upriver an' make up bills of ladin'. Ol' white man behind the marble counter got a younger white boy to weigh goods. Freight go by weight. Colored go by size an' age.

We comes to the counter. The ol' man in some uniform but too ol' for soldierin'. He take our travel papers, look them over real slow an' say to Johnny, "Boy, cans yo' read or write?"

"No, sir. No, sir, never learned."

"How about yo', gal? Man turn to me. "Yo' look smart. Write yo' name." Ol' man push the papers to me.

"I ain't know nothin' 'bout no readin' or writin', Captain." I keep my eyes turn down. "I sorry, sir."

There one man an' a lady behind us. Ol' man notice them. "I be right with yo' folks. These Niggers give me a hard time." An' he smile.

We don't do nothin', don't say nothin'. We look forlorn, keep starin' at the ground. It rough brick, but clean.

"Yo' Niggers stand aside. Let these white folk purchase tickets. Yo' ought'ta know better than to jump ahead."

We move aside. Now, there other white folk lookin' at us. Stop, stare. My heart be wild, about to leap from my chest. I breathe slow. *Breathe,* thinkin' this the same air I breathin' a moment ago. Nothin' change. *Breathe,* I tell myself.

Johnny, still starin' down at the brick floor, actin' lak he ain't worthy of meetin' no one eyes. Feel lak we stand there for hours. Time stop, the air so hot an' thick, it feel lak the season done turn to summer.

"Yo' two! Get movin'!" The ol' man shout.

Hurt about to leave, an' they ready'. What yo' waitin' for? Whar' yo' bags, Niggers? Ain't yo' carry nothin'?"

"We been robbed, sir," I say. We gots our bag stolen in Wilmington by them Yankees—ain't no good."

"Can't even takes care of yo' own bags? The li'l yo' trusted with? Worthless. Yo' Niggers needs a leash." The man—I lookin' up at him—barely—see he got a big grin on his face. An' I notice another ol' man sittin' off to the side on a stool—ain't see'd him before. This talk for *his* benefit, 'cause there ain't no one else listenin'. Them other white folk unconcerned, do their business, an' leave.

"Now yo' 'bout to miss yo' boat. Stupid. Yo' the cause of this war. Get on with yo'." Can't yo' hear good neither?"

Ol' man—the one on the stool, look lak the other man twin—he get up from that stool, an' as we walk out, he be standin' up with a rusty chain in his hands. He jingle it, sound like iron. Thick enough to anchor a ferry.

"Yo' say they needs a leash, Henry? That what yo' say. Niggers like leashes. Just lak dogs. Least they loyal, dogs is."

But we out the door, the side door between the two. An' there a plank an' a man standin' on top the plank onboard. "Hurry yo' up, yo' two!" he yell, wavin' his arms.

Next thing, we on the Hurt. We hears the horn blow. An' the steam engine vibratin' beneath the floor. Cloud of smoke over us.

We told to stay on the rear deck, an' there a large wooden trunk there for the anchor rope. We sit down together, close. Johnny in a sweat. It a cool day, but we both a mess. My heart slow down some but still poundin. "Yo' all right, gal?" Johnny axe me.

We off to the rear side. Folks around, but the boat is loud, an' there ain't nobody can hear us. I take a deep breath, end in a long sigh. "Fine," I say.

Johnny take his hand an' put it over mine. Pat it gently. Then he take it away an' lean back against the wood ship rail. We don't say nothin' for a while. I close my eyes, an' I drift off, so very tired.

That trip a blur. The Hurt make a few stops, whar' folks load an' unload. There a large pig that get roped near us. He drop his manure, an' it mix with the smell of the steam. [*Ms. Augustus lets out a long sigh, then continues.*]

Never did learn what A. P. before the Hurt stand for. [*The machine is snapped off.*]

October 14, 1937

Now… we… we on the Cape Fear, up the river, almost to Fayett'ville. Boat take time to come north. We arrives at night. Real late or real early. Gonna stay docked till mornin', but they start to unload now.

They gets a heavy plank out—must be a hour or so before sun-up. Plenty moon still. Mo' goods comin', they say, by mornin', so the boat gots to be ready.

Two men set the plank in place. We groggy from the long trip. They unloadin' crates of somethin'. Also some sacks. An' they lets off passengers that wanna leave. Good. We thinkin' that we can travel by night again, the dark work in our favor.

Then a local man unloadin' at the dock stop us, axe, "Whar' yo' goin', Niggas?" He a large man in overalls. Yo' can see he drunk, smell the liquor.

"We headed up near Bunn Level. Gonna walk the stage road." We standin' in the small moonlight out, just off the plank, when I catch sight of the big oak. It has it new, tiny leaves, buds, an' I seein' it wide branches spread. But I drops my eyes an' ain't say nothin'.

"Whar' yo' papers? Who let yo' Niggas on this ship?" The large man turn to a small, older man sittin' on a wagon buckboard that must'ta arrive early. "Hey James, James, yo' know these Niggas?

The small, ol' man that get spoke to, stand up at his seat. "I ain't got no time for Niggas, Sam. Just get them sacks throwed on. Get that Nigga boy do it."

Johnny already have his papers out, an' Sam grab them. "What's this?" he say when he get them open. "Someone waste his scratchin' on this paper an' on yo' Niggas." Sam look at the documents, move his lips, then fold them, shove 'em back at Johnny.

Johnny nod, tuck the papers away into his trousers.

"Can yo' read, Nigga? What those papers say?" Sam axe.

"No, sir. Can't." Thems our travel papers that let us pass, I told." Johnny shift his eyes down.

"Who this here?" The fat man point his stubby chin to me.

"Cousin. She my cousin, Rebecca. My ma sister gal."

"Fine," Sam say. "She fine." The fat man look straight at me, but I keep my face turn to the ground. Then he make some smackin' noise from his lips, lak he about to eat a hot cooked meal, an' he plenty hungry. Can't wait to get started.

"Ain't got all day, Sam. Get that damn Nigga throw them sacks onboard. We gotta go," say the ol' buckboard man—sittin' back down.

"Yo' hears what that gentleman tell yo', boy? Yo' see them sacks. What yo' waitin' for? Need a whuppin' get yo' movin'?" Sam raise his voice.

"No, sir. I glad to help," Johnny say.

"I don't like no surly Niggas." The fat man lift his chin lak he pointin' with it. Lead to a pile of two big sacks off to the side of the dock. Johnny nod, quick go over an' he heave one up to his shoulder an' make his way to the wagon.

"Rebecca, go over yonder by that big tree, rest awhile. Long way home." Johnny say. His tone rough.

"Rebecca, Rebecca." The fat man say. Make that smackin' noise again.

"Excuse me, sir. I gonna set 'cause I pretty tired." I never looks him in the face. But I nods, make a curtsy, an' walk to the tree.

Johnny heave the first sack onto the wagon, an' the James fella on the wagon shout out, "Tell him to load from the bottom, Sam. That rice sack tearin'."

I almost half way to the tree, an' Johnny get the second sack. Has to take the split one on the bottom, hold it up. "Careful, Nigga. Yo' gonna pay for what yo' lose."

Johnny say nothin'. He just wanna get the wagon loaded an' leaves quick as he can. Me too. I feel that jack rabbit heart of mine start up again.

Over at the tree, I set on the same big root that David an' me sets on when we meets so long ago. Roots knotted an' rough. I see David walk to me. A lank boy, shy but sure of hisself too. My eyes fill up now, thinkin' how things move so fast. All of life part of the spirit world. David walk with a certain bounce in his step. An' there he is, grinnin' at me, them green eyes sparkle lak they jewels. I wants to reach out an' touch his face, that young face again.

Johnny must'ta be loadin' mo' than twenty sacks. Take him forty minute. No one bother me. I sittin' at a distance. The tree got tight, new buds—bright green fists 'bout to spring.

Mornin' now—day beginnin', with cool fresh air, an' growin' sunlight. It be promisin' a fine day ahead. As the sky lighten, there ain't a cloud above us—blue sky stretchin' out. So blue an' different than the sky in Baltimore that always got some gray to it, lak the smoke from guns an' chimneys stain it even on the clearest days.

Road we soon takin' be clay an' sand. An' I set there thinkin' how it gonna cover my new lady shoes in dust, even this time of year, I see Johnny in the distance, luggin' his last sack to the wagon. He ain't gonna get nothin' for his trouble.

Finally, Johnny walkin' up the hill to whar' I is. The land slope down to the river, so he walk up the bank, throw hisself down on the roots by me. We ain't got nothin' to drinks, but I knows Johnny thirsty. Hot an' tired.

"Gots to rest a minute," Johnny say. He wipe his brow an' face with his sleeve. Then he sit down, lean against the tree trunk, close his eyes.

"What yo' thinkin' about, Johnny?" I touch his hot, sweaty shoulder.

"I thinkin' we got our luck with us today, gal. Lucky to make it this far. Them men, they ain't nothin' but a reminder of home." Johnny open his eyes, look at me.

"For me too, Johnny." But inside, I wonderin' 'bout the luck we have.

Johnny tap my knee. "Ready?"

I up an' dustin' off my bottom, smoothin' my skirt—ain't so fresh as when we start. Johnny nod. Then we walkin' up the bank to the road I knows so well. It gonna lead us home if we stay on it.

It still early mornin', an' without sayin' much, we start walkin' north. We pretty much alone, an' nobody botherin' us. Walkin' the road, keepin' by the side of it.

Then, I say, "Yo' hear that?" We must'ta walk less than quarter mile when I hear somethin'.

Johnny stop an' listen. "No," he answer. We stand there.

"That?" I say. "Yo' hear it now?" Johnny raise his head up. A couple of mockin' birds call out. Then there be dead silence.

"Don't lak it." Johnny take my hand, an' we go off the road into the bushes. Scrub an' weeds. Ain't too thick in the season yet, but it cover.

Inside the brush, goin' down to the river, there a foot path. It red clay, an' slippery in patches, but we decide to take it for a time. Suddenly, the day don't feel so bright.

"Johnny, I gotta sits down. Feel shaky."

Johnny an' me go on to a small clear place besides the path, whar' we sees a ol' campfire, stones around some half burnt logs. We look at each other.

"Gotta think out this last part," Johnny say, keepin' his voice low. "We close."

"Sure is," I whisper back.

Then voices come from up north the road we just left. Loud, boisterous boys an' men voices. Soldiers, bummers, or deserters, we think, 'bout four or five of them. Johnny press me to the ground. His eyes wide, tellin' me *hush*. An' on top of them voices, I can hear that rabbity heart of mine, leapin' around my chest lak it got a rifle pointed to it already.

Them men must be walkin' down to the river dock to catch the Hurt on her trip back to Wilmington. They maybe twenty feet away, but there enough undergrowth, an' we keep still. One boy say that nature call, an' he go into the weeds just above whar' we is. Johnny stare at me. I stare at him as we hear the boy, the thin trickle, his boots rustlin' in the underbrush.

"Yo' daddy give yo' that watch, Jud?" The voice so clear, an' it got North Car'lina all over it. Almost hurt to hear. These the boys local, though I can't recognize them.

"He say he would, an' he good to his word."

"Whar' he get it? From some dead Yank?" Another voice. Someone chuckle.

"Finish up. Or we gonna miss the boat," one yell.

"My sister say it don't leave till noon. Noon!"

"What time yo' got, Jud? On that watch—what time?"

We hears as the boy finish up, but he don't say the time. He return to the dirt road whar' the others is. "I gonna shoot my rifle," one say. "Let them know I comin'!"

"Put that thing away, fool."

"Save yo' powder for killin' Yanks," another yell. Silence.

"Come on, Calvin. Ain't no time for this. Gotta go!" Then we hears them boots shufflin' along the road. One start whistlin' a song 'bout Jesus.

Voices fadin' as they leaves. [*Ms. Augustus sighs. She says to stop the tape because she wants tea. The tape machine is stopped, and when Ms. Augustus resumes, it is later that same day.*]

I lak rain. October rain different than September, even November. If yo' stuck me down in Raleigh an' give me different kinds of rains, I be able to tells them apart—which month they from. Ain't just the rain itself. It the air that come with it. This one ain't got a chill exactly. Somethin' else—sharp—ought'ta be a word for it.

After them soldier boys pass, Johnny an' me stay put for a few minutes. Now we listenin' real good. We still got our travel papers to Bunn Level, but we ain't goin' there, an' anyone that knowed these parts gonna figure that.

So we gonna takes it slow, we decides. We goin' by the road, listenin', an' then goin' some along the river path. It dangerous either way. [*Ms. Augustus clears her throat, pauses, and then resumes.*]

Lookin' back, I glad them soldiers scare us. We been takin' foolish chances. An' it real good we ain't by the dock when they show up. They is only local boys, but sometime it's the young'uns what throws their weight around.

This road—this part of the road—I knowed good. We come down it on the wagon when we sees the man hanged an' come on the river path to see David. We sure is close now.

Johnny, he need to go further up to the Ellicott place. North. He gonna do that part alone. First, we needs to get to the Smith farm.

We stick to the river path after them soldiers go. But now we take it slower—listen an' look. We so dog tired that each step be a chore.

We travel 'bout a hour mo'. The air get warm, sun rise high till it full overhead through the trees. Don't get lak that in Baltimore. Sun here so direct, so heavy, even in early spring. Make yo' feel lazy. Thickness to the air. Mo' so in Fayett'ville even than here in Raleigh. Hard to describe—but talkin' 'bout it make me homesick.

We try not to make much noise. We trudgin'. Slow but sure. Lak mules, weigh down.

An' we ain't meetin' no one. Couple of wagons travel on the road south down Ramsey—prob'ly some headed for the Hurt—with goods goin' out or comin' in. Them folks never see'd us. We hidden, an' we stop when we hear the wagon wheels turnin', an' horses cloppin' on the hard-pack dirt. Harness creakin', chains janglin', voices.

But we come upon two chil'ren—young gal an' her brother, fishin' on a ol' river platform that uset'ta be a ford. Wood platform broke down, near in the river, with some footings slipped. They got river cane fishin' poles, an' the sun be settin' there.

They sees us before we can gets back toward the road or hide, so we keeps to the path an' walk on by them. They turn to us, an' Johnny take up my arm—real natural, just folks.

"Howdy, sir, young sir, missus," Johnny bow, tip the hat he don't have.

"Howdy, yo'self, Nigga. Yo' ever catch fish here?" the boy axe.

"Can't say I have…" Johnny begin, but the boy continue. "We ain't caught none yet. Usually go up the river by the swell. Pa say try this spot an' don't comes home till we catch somethin." The boy must be nine. Gal younger—six maybe. She wear a gingham dress lak I wore the day I seen David. She pretty as a picture, she is—long brown hair tied half back. A li'l rough, but a sweet thing.

"Yas, sir. I bet yo' gonna catch yo'self some nice catfish here. I uset'ta try up the river a bit, but this spot looks good an' fishy. Yo' pa right. I bet they bitin' soon. Just got to wait."

"Ain't got a nibble all mornin'." Got a dead garden snake we find, chop for bait. Pa say catfish lak the stink. This here ain't quite right. But my pa say find somethin' better than worms, though catfish ain't particular."

"Yo' pa right again. That snake good bait. Bet yo' 'bout to catch somethin'—any minute now."

Johnny an' me start to go. These children turn their attention to the river, that muddy ol' river. "Good luck to yo' sir," Johnny say. "Yo' keep that line down there with that snake. They gonna bite today. Pa sure gonna be proud of yo'."

We pass right by them on the trail. All the while the li'l gal say nothin', nothin'. She only watchin' the spot whar' her line sink beneath the water—that muddy swirlin' water. Only thing got her attention.

We keeps on walkin' north. The air gettin' heavier, sky begin to cloud over. Rain maybe. Birds callin' every now then. An' every once in while my heart get that jack rabbit jumpin' inside. Then it calm down. We close. Johnny out in front, look back at me on the narrow path, an' we just walk.

We follow a stretch beside the bank. At this part, the river path a long way from Ramsey Street, the road. We recognize a short-cut back to home, but it so over-growed that we don't takes it. Also, we dead tired—bent over now as we pickin' our way

We stops for a minute before the ford at Carver Falls. The path narrower, mo' windy than I recalls. We finds us a pine tree down, an' we sit on it, side by side.

"We needs to split up soon, go our separate ways," Johnny say.

"I be thinkin' yo' come to the Smith place, spend the night." I say.

"No," he say. "I better keep on."

"We can hides yo' good, Johnny. There a mule barn, far from the big house. An' a tool shed stay half fill. That way yo' get cleaned up an' rest before yo' travel home. Look good for yo' gal."

"Up ahead is whar' we part. Here yo' papers." Johnny stretch his leg to get the paper from his trousers, whar' it lie flat.

"But, Johnny. Why won't yo' come? It all workin'. All workin' out."

"Better if I go, an' yo' don't mention me. Keep it a secret how yo' come back."

I take the paper, unfold but don't reads it, then folds it up again, an' puts it in my dress. "Long way we come together, " I say, an' looks at Johnny. But his eyes be fixed on a black beetle strugglin' to cross the path. Sunlight hit it shiny, black shell, turn it green, blue, then black again.

We sits there a minute, in the afternoon, both watch the beetle. The day turn beautiful, sky clear—air fresh, warm. If a stranger come on us, might think we lazy Negroes with all the time in the world.

Then, without sayin' nothin', Johnny stand up, nod. He take my hand, help me up, an' he fold me into his strong arms. "My soul tied to yo' soul, Sarah Louise. I hopes yo' finds what yo' wants" An' we hug tight. I know Johnny cryin'. Ain't big sobs, but I feel his hot tears on my face.

I be sobbin' too now, with deep, heavy sobs—must weigh a hundred pound each. "Johnny, thank yo'." I say.

Johnny got a few silver coins left, an' he take from his front trouser pocket to give to me. His face look tired. He wipe it with his sleeve. "We gonna meet again, gal. Maybe back in Baltimore. Yas, Baltimore—sure to see yo' there. Gonna meet at L. B. house, see that Ellie gal gonna flirt with me lak I some big lady man. Ma Eve there too. We all gonna sits by the fire. Get me some of that fine pie—Ellie make—hot from the oven."

I take the coins. Johnny nod with his chin. It tell me to get goin'. Which I do. Down the path that lead to the Smith place. *[There is a long pause. Then Ms. Augustus tells the interviewer to turn the tape machine off. The machine gets clicked off. When it is turned on again, it is the next day.]*

October 14, 1937

Well, it late afternoon—that day we part. I can remember startin' down that last length of trail come in the back way to the Smith place. Johnny watch me go until I too far down to see. Just stand there as I walk away.

I alone again. Feelin' scared. Been a long time. The trail—as many times I walk it—look strange. I slow down a bit to get my wits 'bout me.

Maybe it all a mistake. What happen if Ma ain't there? What if somethin' happen that I don't know.

Memories start pourin' in. Mostly good. I thinkin' to when Missus takes me to Virginny, what she call it. I just a child. Then all that happen. Too quick. *But now ain't then*, I think. Years has pass. I been with child, make my way up through war to Baltimore. Has a baby, lose a baby. *Eliza Louise Payne that I never knowed.* I recalls Mar an' her li'l Wednesday. How we both has gals we lose.

I be so close to home, an' I been thinkin' 'bout this moment for so long. Now it just 'bout upon me, an' I can't face it.

I think 'bout Hannah. Sweet Hannah. She be older. Wonder if I recognize her. An' there's Ma, pinnin' clothes to the line or hangin' them over the bushes. Maybe hummin' her *Sweet Jesus*. But the thing I keep recallin' for some reason is our oath. It come back after all these years:

We Smith sisters do solemnly swears…on the holy Bible, on the lives of our Ma, Pa, an' sister Hannah…an' on our own lifes…that from this day forward…to eternity…we, the Smith sisters, will abide by our own secrets…

to keeps our secrets secret. Somethin' lak that. Well, them secrets is told. This oath broken. *[There is a pause in the tape again, and then Ms. Augustus resumes.]*

Nearly dusk now, an' that prob'ly best. Goin' home in the cover of darkness. The path look shadowy an' mo' overgrown than I remembers. But still the same—I recalls all the times I walk this path down to the creek—river so trickily here, branch off the Cape Fear. Dirt path, white sand. An' I walkin' so slow, can't believe I home. Maybe Missus be there or maybe in Virg'nia with her gals.

Then, the path open up to the lower field. It shinin' in the settin' sun, sky becomin' deep blue. I travel by the fence—split rail, alongside the pasture. I see my cabin. No one about. A picture in the distance. I stop, catch my breath. Heart poundin' lak it wild.

I comin' to the cabin by the rear, but I just walk around to the front. An' there they is, standin' out in the cool air, fire goin'. Hannah see me first. She talkin' 'bout somethin', but when she spy me, she stop an' stare. Ma there, Mar, Kate....

"Sarah Louise," Ma look at me, a wood bowl in her hand. She let it drop. I nod, an' step toward them. They just finish a early supper. Cleanin' up. Tin plates in the big wash pot, scraps for the pigs in a pail. Kate, she settin' on the step with something in her hand, an' she rise, push a last bite of her pone into her mouth. Mar walk to me. Everythin' happen slow.

"I come a long way," I say.

"It's yo'," Mar say. Then they all over me—Ma, Hannah, Kate, Mar—with hugs an' kisses.

"Baby gal, my baby gal!" Ma keep cryin' out. "My own Sarah Louise. An' yo' all growed up. A woman." We lock in embrace—rockin' back an' forth lak we a small ship on a big sea.

"Inside," Ma mutter. An' they whisk me away. I some kind of treasure, an' they ain't gonna let go. It don't feel real. I away so long, an' now I home—the home I dream 'bout, wants so much....

Ma the first to pull herself from us. She gonna get some pone for me an' a cup of water. "Set here, gal, et. Yo' too thin." She pull me from my sisters, put me on a ladder-back chair I ain't never see'd. I look, an' there a new wood table, an' five matchin' chairs.

"We thought yo' dead. Dead." Ma look at me, settin' on a chair, an' someone find a candle, light it. Kate come with a slab of ham. An' I gobblin' it up, so hungry now.

Mar put a pine log on the hearth, an' it bright enough now for me to see Hannah—growed so big—but still my baby sister, though she turn into a pretty gal. She put a basket of darnin' on a shelf—that new too, hung with wire—an' she come sit by my chair. On the floor.

"Yo' remembers me?" I axe her. "Yo' so small when I leaves. Such a big gal now, so tall, so fine."

"I miss yo' so—Sarah Louise." She rise to hug me. "I never forgets yo'."

"Missus come home few summers ago, tell us yo' dead," Ma say, dryin' her hands on her ol' apron. Then she pull up a chair, set by me. "Say yo' got attacked by Yankees, go missin'. They finds pieces of yo' dress by the bushes at a creek. Say yo' gets carried away by the waters. But yo' body ain't never found. Only traces of yo' dress. When she arrive home from Virginny, she tell me herself. Say how sorry she be."

I look down at Hannah. I can't get over how she a regular gal. Ain't no baby no mo'. She change the most.

"We holds a funeral service for yo', Sarah Louise," Kate say. "We ain't has no body to bury, an' we ain't even mark the ground proper. But we has the service, in memory…"

"I ain't dead…" I say. But we all quiet. The fire flickerin'. Turn us into ghosts. *[There is a long pause again. The tape continues, and Ms. Augustus begins to speak.]*

Mar take out a few pallets, an' we pull them together. But before we gets to bed, I take me a bath in the ol' tin tub, set by the fire. Ma tell Mar to gets water at the pump, an' heat it, lak we do in the ol' days.

Mar has a ol' dress that clean. Good enough. It a loose thing, comfortable. An' when we on the pallets, with quilts pulled up, we settle. A moonlit, clear night, an' I flooded with memory.

Once Hannah fall sleep, I tells the story of what befall me. It somethin' I ain't plan on speak 'bout so quick—somehow spill right out. All them years in Baltimore, I been preparin' to tell this, but I wanted to wait till the time be right. Now, it just pour from me. Even tells them things now that I ain't ever tells myself. About how I feels, the anger I has inside.

So all that night we keep awakes, me talkin'. They listenin'. I tells them how I be a married woman now—married to David. How I lives in Baltimore with L. B., his folks. How I meets them. An' then, the hardest part, I tells them what happen to me on the riverbank. How I conceive a baby, runs for my freedom, an' how my baby die.

When I comes to this part, I weepin', an' soon we all weepin'. Baby born of sin but don't deserve the punishment it get.

The only part of my story what surprise them be 'bout Run'way Johnny from the Ellicott place, how we meets up in Baltimore an' how we comes home together to Fayett'ville.

So much livin'—an' the tellin' so strange—lak a book Mister Charles Dickens hisself write.

We decides that night—long before it turn mornin'—I gonna hides myself for a few days, then we gonna hatch a plan.

That night, I also learns that Dirty Bones get sold by his master to a speculator at the beginnin' of the war. "Bram," Kate say, "he the best thing ever happen to me. An' he sold off same as a mule. I ain't love nobody since." Kate still tore up about it.

"What 'bout James Henry?" I axe Mar.

Mar sigh. "He around," she say. "We still married, but he don't come by much. I become a ol' maid, Sarah." She sigh again. "An' Doc McNair say I can't have no babies no mo'."

"What 'bout Pa," I axe, though I sorry I did when I see Ma face.

"I know yo' want to know, Sarah." Ma rise to puts a log into the fire. Then she pull up a chair an' sit down on it. "Pa run off. To Canada. He write one time, say he write again when he git hisself settle. Gonna make money, send for us after the war." By firelight, Ma face seem ol' an' worn. "He say he find railroad work, layin' track. Want a better life—for him, us all." Ma rise an' pace the floor. Ain't quite as smooth when she walk now. *[There is a short scratchy pause in the tape, and then Ms. Augustus continues.]*

Ma stand beside me, take my hand. Mar an' Kate in thems ol' pallet beds, look on. "Ain't no one fault, Sarah Louise. But he gone."

"How?" I axe. Though I ain't all that interested. The sad news don't want to sink in.

"Got a letter from a rail company, an' they sent his things."

By dawn, we in our pallet, lyin' down. Gray, dreary beginnin'. Ma already start her chores.

Later that mornin', the rain burst from the sky. Drenchin' rain, an' it last the next few days. Which make stayin' in the cabin seem right. Ain't many folks 'bout.

So I stays inside, an' no one but kin know I there.

Two night later though, when we get a break an' the sky clear—I go out. Can't stand stayin' in no mo'. But it late. Everyone sleep.

I sneaks—walk over to the big house—pale in moonlight. The white picket fence knocked down. An' the summer kitchen look small, shabby. I take the path past the privy whar' I meets Johnny that first time, an' sets on a rock by it. But I ain't feelin' my memories here, not lak I thought. Ain't quite part of the Smiths no mo', an' I ain't quite Sarah Louise Augustus, neither. Ain't a mother—'cause my child buried in the ground, an' I don't feel lak a daughter to Ma anymo'. Ain't a good sister neither. I sorry for myself an' for all the dead.

That same night somethin' pull me to Mammy Rae dye shack. Her ghost be callin'. Ol' stain apron on its hook—maybe Mammy Rae 'bout to appear an' snatch it up, fix it around her big, solid middle, start stirrin' her pot.

I coulds almost hears Mammy Rae voice scoldin', that she ain't gonna help me see no beau by no Cape Fear river dock. That it wrong, an' I gonna catch it if Ma find out. Then she show up with that gingham dress. I feel her strong arms around me, her soothin' hand on my back. *[There is a long pause in the tape, and then Ms. Augustus continues.]*

Always strike me that Augustus a good name. Go by the library in Raleigh once, look it up in a big name book. It mean "great an' inspirin'." So it right that David have this name, an' I wanna take it.

What happen at the dye shack is I decides to comes forward an' tell Missus an' the others that I alive. Maybe it Mammy Rae spirit that come give me strength. It a risky thing to do 'cause Missus still own me—accordin' to Rebel law. But I knows that the Union troops comin', an' there ain't no market for slaves.

When I be settin' there on the dye shack bench, my mind turn to Mister Crow—the first he come. Then the rain start back up. Big, thick drops.

"Whar' yo' be, Mister Crow?" I axe aloud.

Only answer, my heart. Beat steady, an' I feel Mammy Rae inside; I gonna be just fine.

"Mammy Rae," I say aloud. "I marry him. "That boy with the green eyes yo' help me meets by the Cape Fear. It long, long ago, but I knows yo' remembers him."

I settin' with on the bench, eyes closed. Tears begin to well up, sting. Air smell of Mammy Rae, an' I breathe deep. It the musty, rain smell that she gets after workin' a day. She always gonna be there.

"Yo' one fine gal, Sarah Louise," she say, in a husky whisper.

"Mammy, I ain't finish yet," I tell her. "There a lot of bad happen."

"Yo' angels done tell me what occur, child," I hear Mammy say.

The air get cool, an' the big drops turn to needle rain. Then whoosh… Mammy gone. An' I half-expectin' Mister Crow make his appearance next—for ol' time sake. But he don't.

After a while, I picks myself up an' walks slow back to the cabin. I tired an' wanna sleep. *[Ms. Augustus lets out a long sigh.]*

Next day, I still determined that I ain't hidin' no mo'. I gonna walks myself over to the big house, finds Missus an' show her I alive. Ma like this idea, 'cause she say no good come from lyin'. An' Missus, she so preoccupy with her own losses that she ain't gonna do nothin'. Marster, Marse George dead, an' only handful of slaves left on the place. *[Ms. Augustus clears her throat. Then, she insists that the machine be turned off until tomorrow, and there is a click. Ms. Augustus resumes the next day.]*

October 15, 1937

Next day, sun shine, an' the place be green. Mar, Kate, Hannah, an' Ma at their mornin' chores by the time I be climbin' the veranda steps to find Missus. I use the front door—a lady visitor from Baltimore.

The big house have a shabby, wore-down look. Need paint. Railing loose. Wood boards on the steps broke.

I don' knock, just squeak open the door. Hallway empty. I stands there a minute. The furniture is dusty. Ain't a soul around. "Hello," I calls out. "Hello."

No one answer, so I walks right through the house to the side door, go down the veranda steps, an' off to summer kitchen. The summer kitchen door wus closed. Flowerbed dug up. Then I hears some stirrin' back in the big house kitchen, so I goes up the rear steps there.

Luna, a woman that uset'ta work the fields, wus inside. She got her back to me as I come in. She stirrin' a big bowl on the wood kitchen table. She older than me, an' I ain't never had nothin' much to do with her—she bein' a field worker—but as she turn around, we recognize each other.

"Sarah Louise…" she say an' put her hand over her mouth. "Yo' suppose'ta be dead."

"I ain't," I say.

Luna put down a big spoon, wipe her hand on her dirty apron an' come towards me. "Child," she say, an' give me a big hug. She smell of blood, lak she already out killin' chickens this mornin'.

"Whar' everybody at?" I axe. We standin' close in the cool kitchen. Chill of night ain't gone from it. Luna return to spoon again, git to stirrin', some dough in it.

"Missus say yo' wus dead. Found yo' dress by a riverbank…. How yo' get here? When yo' come back?"

"Long story, Luna. Long story. Whar' Missus?"

"Yo' mamma, she done grieve, child. She grieve a long time. Grievin' for yo', yo' pa, Miss Ida… lots folks gone, Sarah Louise. Yo' don't know the half of it." Luna stir the bowl, seem taken up by it. "What yo' ma say? She know yo' here?"

"Family know. Ma know. Need Missus. Whar' she at?" I axe.

"She et her breakfast an' out in the back garden. Sarah Louise. Li'l ol' Sarah Louise… yo' ain't dead." Luna waddle back close to me, with that wooden spoon in her hand. "Yo' one of our own. Yo' just all right" An' she give me another hug.

"Everybody else? Whar' they?" I axe.

"There only be 'bout ten colored left. That it. An' that countin' yo' ma an' sisters. Most folks, they run aways. Pick up an' go."

I sees some ol' biscuits under a flour cloth, an' looks at Luna.

"Go on, take one. Take two."

I stuff a biscuit in my mouth. "Thanks," I say. "Sees yo' later." Luna watch me go; she still lookin' lak she see the dead.

Outside, the day be warmin'. I walk past the closed summer kitchen again an' down the stone path to the garden. Missus be standin' by a iron table an' a couple'a chairs. She seem to be watchin' somethin' down the path. We look at each other, but she seem to stare right past me. She wear a white dress, too fancy for the house. Hair pinned up, but no bonnet.

Then…"Sarah?" I hears. "Sarah Louise? That you?"

Her voice strike me hard. I knowed it but had forgotten the sound. "It me," I say. An' I approach, look Missus square in the eye.

"I never…. I never…." Missus begin, an' she take a step backward. We alone there. My rabbit heart start up, wild. My head seem clear, but there a cushion of spongy air between us.

"I ain't dead, Missus," I say. An' then, all a sudden, I feel dead. Almost lak my angels be floatin' down from the sky, an' they 'bout to take me with them.

"I thought… thought…" she begin again. An' she pull a handkerchief from her sleeve, wipe her forehead.

I take a step toward her, an' she toward me, an' then we close. She lift her arms an' I make another step till she fold them around me, hug me lak I a long-lost friend. She commence to weepin'. Low sobs, but I can feels her short breaths against my body. I has my arms around her too. "It all right," I say. "All right."

Then, Missus break away from me, her face distraught. She take me by my wrist, point with her chin lak she uset'ta, motion that we goin' into the big house through the kitchen. I nod. Missus too broken up to speak.

We go in the kitchen door. Luna at the big bowl, stirrin' away, singin' some hymn. But she stop when she hear us an' watch us go by.

We in the small parlor, not the big one, but the library room. Missus set down on a upholstered chair. I still standin', an' she don't say for me to join her.

"What happened? You've got to tell me," Missus don't look up at my face; she starin' straight ahead, into my dress. "I thought you were dead. *I knew you were dead.* Those soldiers…"

"It a long story," I say again, my voice a whisper that take on a raspiness. "I is dead," I say. "The *gal* yo' knowed is dead."

Missus gasp, put her hand over her mouth. She understand what I sayin'. [*There is a pause and a muffled sobbing sound. Then there is an abrupt clicking as the tape machine is turned off. When Ms. Augustus resumes, it is later the same day. Ms. Augustus's voice begins mid-sentence.*]

… all right now… I ready.

After the first shock, Missus say she wanna hear my entire story, an' she beseech me not to leave nothin' out. So I tells her the whole thing. An' I tells her that it wus her job to protects me. I find myself angry at her. Angry lak she be one the soldiers. I take it upon myself to set down on the fancy chair by the side table.

I brings her back to the day I go to feed the lame horse in the pasture. She remember that just fine, listenin', noddin' at points, but she not sayin' nothin' till the very end. That when I tells her I married, an' my name Augustus, an' I free by my own reckonin'. She stiffen a bit when I say that. Sun comin' through the window, makin' the dust visible.

"Mine too," is what she say. "By my reckoning too." She look at me in the silent room. "You've earned your freedom, Sarah Louise. I'm not your owner. Far as I'm concerned, you're a free woman." An' with them words, she stand up, I stands up, an' she come to embrace me again. This, a joinin' of equals, ain't no fine woman lookin' down on a lesser one. [*There is a short pause and some scratchiness in the tape before Ms. Augustus continues.*]

We sits back down an' continue. Whole conversation take about thirty minutes. When I gets to the Baltimore part, I find myself just tellin' the bare bones. Right before we walk out, Missus axe if I got plans—for me, Ma, sisters. It be lak she tellin' me that we all free to go. Lak my freedom done earned my family freedom too.

"No, ma'am. No plans yet."

Missus nod her head. "You know we're all in for a hard time. Mr. Lincoln just took his oath again. Our Davis… well, it doesn't look good. This war is coming to an end, Sarah. But not without… some more suffering. They say Sherman's troops are headed here."

"We ain't be goin' nowhar' soon," I say.

Missus nod. "Thanks," she say.

Then we done. Missus give me a squeeze, an' pull back. She nod with her chin, an' she walk me out to the front door. Two fine ladies an' we just has us a nice visit. Missus dress rustlin', with all them petticoats she wear. I remember that sound—down the steps we go—each of us in her own way. Fact is, the splendor Missus uset'ta carry done gone. She past her prime, an' the war rip her to pieces, bit by bit—take her husband, son, property.

"It all right, Missus. We all—gonna be fine," I say.

Missus nod her head. "We've taken the silver and buried it. Sent the livestock into a corral I had built in the woods. And we've hidden some hams and canned vegetables from last year—locked them in the summer kitchen, below, in the cold cellar, hidden. If your family needs food…."

"No, ma'am. We has flour, provisions… ham too, I believe."

"Hide it good, Sarah Louise. Your ma knows."

We stand a moment. The plantation, already a thing of the past. The future be hard upon us. In fact, it here.

As I walk back to our cabin, I gets a strong sense that Marster gonna appear. Any moment, he grab me by my arm, take me to the back veranda whar' all the slaves be lined up. Gonna announce that I done wrong, that he hate to do it, but he have to get the whip. Mister Marvin then come from behind the shed with his rope an' whip, an' hand them to Marster, who be wearin' a clean linen suit with a fresh black jacket. I sees him strut up an' down front us, nod his head. I ready to put my hands out to get them ropes fasten. It a blue North Car'lina sky, chill spring air, a robin bird chirpin' her song—an' Marster walkin' back an' forth in front of the big house, ready to pass his judgment, strike at me with his whip. The weight of this story I tellin' myself stop me right there. "Lawd," I say. "No need to be too merciful on his soul."

By noon, all at the Smith place knowed I back. Not that anybody celebratin'. Too busy talkin' 'bout Sherman—that he comin' through North Car'lina soon, maybe not here, but the next county west. Folks say he be marchin' from the south an' west. But ain't nobody know exactly whar'.

Sherman burn Atlanta last fall. Then Savannah. An' now his army be marchin' on us—stealin' lootin', burnin' down 'bout everythin'. Sherman got Mister Crow inside him, an' Mister Crow done eaten away his heart.

Well, I comes back to our cabin that day, an' Ma still doin' chores. Now she hangin' up clothes across a big holly bush. I see her there, an' it come over me again, new—that I back in Fayett'ville. I goes over to her from behind, an' I turns her around.

"I loves yo', Ma," I say. "I miss yo' so, an' I loves yo'." Ain't take much. Ma hugs me to her an' cries.

"Ain't nothin' never gonna be the same," Ma say.

"Gonna be better," I say.

"Folks gone. Men dead. An' now Yankees comin'. Burnin' houses an' thievin'… an' we ain't even got enough crops in."

"Gonna be all right, Ma," I say. "They fightin' on our side. Freedom, Ma. That what it mean." I pull back, look at her.

"We ain't free, ain't never gonna be free." Ma walk away to the cabin rear. I see she hobble a bit.

"Yo' all right, Ma? Wanna sits down?"

We sit on the stoop, door open. House dark. "Whar' Mar, Kate, an' Hannah?" I axe, lookin' around.

"I think Hannah at the big house garden, help Missus." Mar gone to the fields—ain't workin' there regular, but she go when she needed. Kate… well, she out doin' somethin'. She can't just sets around."

"Ma, has we hid the good food?" I axe.

"Atlanta burn," Ma say. "South Car'lina in ruin."

"I knows, Ma. I knows. We has anythin' of value here? Whar' yo' keep the corn meal?"

Ma just knittin' her brow. "Ain't no good. Folks should'a leave things how they wus. That way, yo' Pa still be here." Ma hold her head in her hands.

"Headache, Ma?" I axe. "Missus might got some powder you can takes."
I rub her shoulders between the blades.

"Lincoln done get hisself sworn in again, an' the world ain't ready."
Ma eyes is wet.

"We gonna be all right, Ma," I say.

"My baby. My Sarah Louise…" Ma say. She put her arms 'bout my
neck an' start to sob. Hard. I hold her to me an' feels somethin' heavy,
a big ol' wounded animal caught inside her breast. "They comin' for us,
Sarah. Missus say them Yankee soldiers gonna takes what li'l we gots.
Even Missus take to bury the silver in the barn." *[There is a brief pause in
the tape, and some clicks are heard; then Ms. Augustus begins again, obviously
the same day, just a few moments later.]*

Then he come—up near Cheraw—west of here. Sherman.

After Lincoln swore in, everyone on edge—all the colored an' all the
white folks. It a mess. Sherman do mo' damage in South Car'lina than
in Georgia. Folks say he show his hatred for South Car'lina 'cause they
start the war. They uppity, got mo' money, mo' slaves, big plantations.
So Sherman hate them. But I tell yo'…they suffer plenty for what they
do."

That week—right before the soldiers come—the sky cloud over an'
it rain an' rain. We ain't gots ourselfs no valuables to bury, but Ma have
a pit dug in the woods an' hide our meal sacks beneath some boards.
Everybody hidin' somethin'. *[The tape stops abruptly. When Ms. Augustus
begins, it is the next day.]*

October 18, 1937

Hardee troops come through first. Confed'rates. They rag-tag men,
barely soldiers. Bedraggled. Foragers—we gets two groups. One come on
horseback; the other come walkin'. They all gots rifles, an' they come the
tenth day of March. Lak I say, we been havin' rain—rain, then sun, rain,
sun. That what we gets in March. But the tenth—that day wus sun.

We wakes up early—how we always do. That mornin' Hannah wus
suppose to sow the ground with lettuce for the kitchen garden.

She wus out there maybe a hour, maybe less, when we hear her holler. "They comin'!" she scream, an' she be off runnin'. She stop at the front of the big house, hollerin' "They comin', Missus. They here!"

We look up, see Hannah run by; then she nowhar'. What we do see is men on horseback, stopped by the upper field. They conferrin'. First, only two men—then maybe six. They gets off their horses, drop the reins, an' walk right through the nearby field. That field wus always muddy after a rain. Red clay hold the water. Then they trompin' up to the big house. Mar, Kate, an' me—we make our way down to watch.

The one man what first speak ain't sound so bad—an' he look lak a officer, not a rogue. "Anyone home?" he call out.

Missus out in a flash. On the veranda in a simple dress, one I ain't never seen—plainer than most. "I am," she say. "I own this house."

Officer take off his cap, nod at Missus. "We all are Confederate troops here, ma'am, sent to defend Fayetteville and the honor of its people."

"Sir," Missus say. "I heard you might be coming, and now you're here." She go down a few steps.

We too far away to hear what they say next. But our Hannah wus right there, shot out the front door. Flyin' lak she on fire. But when she get down to Missus, she come to her senses, 'cause then she see'd them soldiers. She back right up an' try to hide behind Missus skirts.

Hannah later tell us that she so scared she shiverin'. Misses put out her arms an' hold Hannah just lak she be one her own daughters.

"More slaves here?" one of the soldiers axe.

We all lookin' on, but ain't no one payin' attention to us.

"We only have ten left," Missus tell him.

"Heifers? Livestock? We ain't see no goats or sheep. The General aims to feed a hundred hungry men. An' we under his direct order to take what we need. Which we are going to do with as little disturbance to your place as possible. You have any men folk here? White men, Confederate wounded or feeble?"

"No," Missus say. "We have a few Niggas but can't spare none. Our fields have to be planted…"

"Ain't see no cows in the field. You stable the heifers? I knows you got some. And your chicken? Where they be?"

Missus direct the men to the barn but Belle, our milk cow, wus staked out deep in the pine woods. We has one small bull occupyin' the big stall.

We all knowed those soldiers gonna takes the bull, but our last two pigs got butcher in the fall. Missus don't tell them 'bout the ham or the salt pork. An' the men seem satisfied with the bull. We got them chickens in the tool shed, but they ain't so interested after they finds the bull. They in a hurry to get back.

The men go into the barn an' come out leadin our bull away by his nose ring. He our breeder bull, but we gets off easy. They takes the bull, leads him through the muddy field to the others an' their horses, that they mount. Then they rides away, one of them with the bull on his nose lead trailin' behind.

Probably butchered that bull over the next hour, 'cause they seem half starved. But from that moment—till Sherman come an' leave—we felt the full brunt of the war.

When the men go, Hannah see me an' Ma, an' she run to us. Ma scold her that she ought'ta knowed better than run through Missus house with soldiers around.

"What yo' thinkin', gal? Ain't yo' got no sense. No, yo' ain't!" Ma say. But Hannah say she so scared an' didn't knowed what she wus doin'.

We all in a uproar. Luna be in the big house kitchen, an' Missus tell her to cut up the last of the salt pork, give us each some, tell us to keep it safe—hides it with whatever else got hid. Ain't no tellin' if or when them men be back.

Right then, we all knows the war is over—not yet the fightin' an' sufferin, but by the looks of them bedraggled men, the South done lost.

By late that night, the sky turn red, an' the air become heavy with black smoke weighin' it down. All of Fayett'ville wus burnin'. Town up in flames through Hay Street. We has our own li'l Atlanta.

After that first Rebel group come, that same night, Smith Negroes around joins up at the barn. We holds us a prayer meetin', but without no preacher, exceptin' for Jaspers—a ol' man from another farm—who lead us in a hymn.

We all join hands an' pray. Hannah, Mar, Kate there. Ma too. Luna, some others. The sky lit up with fire, an' we hears big guns or cannons—I can't tells which. The smoke so thick it hurt to breathe it in. We form a circle, ten of us, an' Uncle Jasper, he lead us in a song. I remembers it good, an' I gonna sing the part what I recalls. Go by "Not Weary Yet"—sometime "Me Ain't Weary Yet." [*Ms. Augustus clears her throat, and her thin, high, but tuneful voice is heard.*]

> *Oh, me not weary yet. Oh, me not weary yet.*
> *I have a witness in my heart, oh, me not weary yet.*
> *Since I been to the field to fight, oh, me not weary yet.*
> *I have a heaven to maintain, oh, me not weary yet.*
> *The bonds of faith is in my soul, oh, me not weary yet.*
> *Ol' Satan toss a ball at me, oh, me not weary yet.*
> *Him think the ball would hit my soul, oh me not weary yet.*
> *The ball for hell, and I for heaven, oh me not weary yet.*

Song bring me back. Voice ain't so good now. That night when we be singin', we could hear the gun fire, an' some of the women start to cry. We all swayin', clappin', prayin' lak this be the end of the world.

The Smith farm ain't never be the same.

We prayin', but the world ain't taken up with the same prayer. Jaspers axe us to be silent for a moment an' imagine we be free. Think whar' we gonna go, what we gonna do. I beam thinkin' 'bout David an' havin' enough money to put a stone on Eliza grave.

Next day, it be the worst. We wakes up to see some horsemen chargin' through. Twenty or thirty bluecoats. Scouts. Kilpatrick or Sherman men. General Hardee done make off with' our bull, but he sure ain't protectin' us.

It begin at daybreak, chill, still dark. The air got that burnt smell. We hear some whoops an' hollers—the ground shakin' as they ride up.

Them thunderin' hooves rouse us from our pallets. We wus awake, just wusn't rose up. But that hollerin' an' shakin' get our attention.

"…What you waiting for? Niggas, rise up! The end is coming!" One soldier ride up to the cabin, knock open the door with his rifle butt.

We fly out'ta bed, pullin' on anythin' handy. We see the men converge on the big house. Light now, but so dim they seem lak shadows.

All the Negroes wus bunched in the muddy yard. We wus afeared the men wus gonna torch the big house lak they done the town. They breaks all the windows an' the kitchen an' front doors. We can't sees what goin' on inside, but we see Marster desk get throwed out the front. It topple down the stairs. Two legs broke off, a drawer full of papers come out, scatterin'. Tables an' chairs get tossed too. Make a big rude pile. Marster an' Missus furniture that pass through generations. Wood furniture we cleaned an' polished for years.

I figure they wus gettin' ready to set it on fire. Mar whisper that maybe we should do somethin'. No one answer her. No one move.

Some men finds the few chicken we gots left. They be carryin' them out by their feet, lash them to saddles.

Somehow the soldiers find our milk cow, Belle, in the woods. I heared her moo before they shoots her. Mar don't say nothin' now, just shake her head. Others mutterin', "Jesus… Lawd."

Missus come out to the veranda—she ain't dress proper. One man come toward her, but she raise her hands, cower, sink almost to the ground. I never see'd nothin' lak that—never see'd Missus so afeared. He leave her alone, but he smash a last window whar' she be. An' Missus cower again.

Out the back, pans an' pots wus bein' throwed out, clangin', bangin' as they roll. Summer house get broke into, an' the flour, corn meal—what li'l we has left—get taken. We all be thinkin' how wise Missus wus to give the meat away.

The ground wus muddy, an' them horses trample our garden. It a awful sight. But these men, horrid, lawless as they is, they still leavin' folks alone. They didn't touch Missus…. *Could be worse*, I tell myself. *Much worse*. An' I wus right.

All that day they come lak locusts. In big, dirty swarms. Bummers, stragglers, irregulars. Soon it don't make no difference to us or Missus, what they wus or wusn't. After that day, she never the same.

After the first group that day leave, us Negroes try to clean up some. Ma, Luna. Other women put Missus to bed; she shaky, ain't doin' too good. Remind me of Mrs. Johnston back in Baltimore.

Mar go to Missus—stay with her, sit by her bed, fix her some food. Me an' Uncle Jasper, others—Kate too—go up to the furniture pile an' begin to sort out what might be fixed. The pots an' pans that get scattered all through the yard an' in the flowerbeds—most too dented or broken up to use, but others could get banged out.

We still thinkin' we wus lucky, thinkin' the furniture pile would get lit up an' the house get burned to the ground, lak so many in town. They make a pile lak they gonna set it afire, but then they go. Don't axe me why.

But then the others come… an' later, at the cabin, I see Hannah with a basket of soiled clothin' she collect from the muddy yard whar' soldiers throwed it. She go past as I comin' in. She look strange.

"Hannah," I say, touchin' her shoulder. "Yo' all right, gal? Yo' ain't hurt, is yo'?"

"No," she tell me. "I fine."

I look at her again. She 'bout to burst into tears. So I nod, urgin' her on.

"It just them bummers," Hannah begin, an' she look down at the hard-pack dirt beneath her feet. "One… tried… pull off my new flour-apron Ma just sew for me, hadn't wore but once… I pull, get away."

"Hannah, anythin' happen? Yo' tell me." An' I touch her shoulder, keep my hand there.

"I swear I didn't go near the house again… I promise I didn't. But he find me in the field… sneak up from behind…I swear…." Hannah shake her head lak she back in the field. "No," she say. "No."

"It be all right. Yo' be all right, gal." I say an' give Hannah arm a squeeze.

"I gonna wash the laundry now, Sarah Louise. Ma be angry if I don't." An' before she gone, I notice there blood stains on her pretty apron.

I stands there for a moment. Ain't got no mo' words for Hannah. She gettin' to be a woman, an' she gonna has to learn. Ain't nothin' I can do. Ain't nothin' to say. I see her by the basin, bendin' over the tub, though it way too late to be washin'. She got her apron off, an' she scrubbin'.

Ma, when I sees her next, she nod over in Hannah direction, then say to me, "Sarah Louise, if this be Yankee freedom, I don't want none of it."

Sherman an' his men don't stay in Fayett'ville but a few days. An' later I hears Sherman didn't want no burnin' here. He want to burn up South Car'lina, but plan to pass through Fayett'ville, take what he need, then go. But the Rebels burn the bridge behind them, an' the Yankees get angry. Start burnin' too. Yankee soldiers left a lot of bad blood, an' I don't think Fayett'ville ever get over it.

Day after day, bummers straggle through, but we ain't see'd no mo' real soldiers on our place—Yankees or Rebels. By Wednesday, fifteenth March, all of Fayett'ville wus in ashes. Folks tryin' to pick up the mess they has. At the Smith farm, we all tired, spirits numb. But we got work to do—repairin' what we can an' findin' food.

Luna lash Marster desk back together with some rope—best she could. Nails wus scarce. Other broken things got mended too. Furniture an' pots. Missus come down with the dysentery an' keep to herself.

All this go on, but we begin to has nice weather, spring. Fields dry out but look trampled—an' we ain't got no horse or mule to plow them. Ma an' Mar hoe up a acre on the lower field. Greens mostly.

Miss Ellen come back to visit at the end of March. To comfort her Ma. I see Miss Ellen, but we don't speak. She arrive one day, leave the next. Horses barely gits to rest before they hitch up again.

That time before the official Surrender but after Sherman come through were a time lak no other. We wus all driftin' along lak leafs downstream. Whispers all around—but no one knowed what exactly next.

An' the general drift turn to sadness. Slavery wus over, but there nothin' come to replace it. The big house windows stay broke—an' some colored be makin' plans. To stay or to go north, not knowin' what that mean. Some too afraid to leave. Nobody gots no money. Jeff Davis dollars ain't worth the paper they printed on. We use them in the privy.

Official Surrender come short time after Sherman march through Fayett'ville. Month or so. Just long enough to clean up his mess.

One April evenin', Missus call us ten Smith Negroes to the front of the big house. It were a weekday. She didn't have no bell—the big bell we uset'ta ring got taken—bummers carry it off. Missus bang a dented pot with a long-handle spoon. Last light wus behind the house, an' the orange sky promise a clear day tomorrow.

"You darkies give me good service. I don't have any complaints," Missus begin. She look frail, lost her weight, an' she wear a ol' house dress, head bare, gray hair pulled back but straggly. She stand alone on the veranda.

"We free, Missus. That what we hear." It be Luna speak up. This tone surprise us, 'cause she usually so quiet.

"Yes. And the war is over," Missus say. "Y'all can do whatever you like. Stay or leave." She turn behind her lak she expectin' someone. No one there.

Folks in the small crowd murmur, nod.

"If you leave… you're on your own. If you stay, I'll have some land for you to crop— eventually. Master Harry says he going to draw up papers." Then Missus look up, sort of out an' over us, an then she say, "Dismissed." An' she head back through the heavy front door.

We mill 'bout for a few minutes, but we all get the message. No fireworks, fanfare. No celebration. We just wander off to finish up evenin' chores.

Soon, Negroes—alone an' in groups—began to pass through. We put them up as they head north. Most talk 'bout whar' they goin', what they gonna do. Some say their masters be comin' home soon. Farms an' plantations ain't got enough men folks to work them, what with so many dead, sick, an' injured. White men come hobblin' home a mess.

I wus out one afternoon by the creek, gatherin' wood—twigs for kindlin'. Sky cloudy 'cause it rain that mornin', an' the ground be muddy so I wus concentratin' on keepin' my boots dry. My foot, by the way, never heal completely. The bone get inflamed when it rain, swell the foot. This prob'ly the cause my arthritis.

So I careful steppin', favorin' my bad foot, findin' wood that weren't too wet. We plan to cook supper outside this evenin' with the big stewpot don't fit good in the house.

I hears rustlin'… looks up. Deer, I be thinkin'? So I stays still, watching a patch of green briars.

"Who there?" I call. "Who walkin'?" I finds me a sharp stick, an' I gonna use it as a weapon.

Silence. Then I hear a man voice behind me. I turn, an' it be Johnny.

"Sarah Louise," he say. I feel his strong arms around me, an' I throw mine around him.

"Why yo' scare me so… what yo' doin' here?"

"I gots news, Sarah—a letter that come to me at the Ellicotts. It concern yo'." We standin' by in the thicket near the path.

"Come here." Johnny lead me back on the path, whar' the light better. Then Johnny take out a folded paper from his trouser pocket. "It all here. Yo' ready?"

"David?" I axe. "It from David?"

"No. From Ellie, Sarah. It from Ellie, but it got stuff in it 'bout David. He come lookin' for yo'. Better yo' reads it." He hand me the folded paper. It worn, an' the ink done bleed so bad, I can barely make it out.

Dear Johnny… it begin. *I wants yo' to find Sarah Louise an' tells her easy 'cause what she need to hear is hard.* Then the ink get blurry or maybe my eyes gone bad 'cause suddenly I afeared again.

"Can't make this part out, Johnny. What it say here?" I pointin' to the page. All this happen fast.

"It say that yo' is a mother, Sarah Louise. Yo' baby ain't dead."

My heart stop. My head getting' pounded with waves of sound lak I drownin', bein' sucked out to sea.

"Yo' hears me, Sarah? Yo' can reads it yo'self? Go on." I feels Johnny strong hand on my shoulder lak some big boulder be placed on me, keep the deep ocean from draggin' me away.

I looks at the letter again. "I can't reads it, Johnny. The print too far gone. It been wet."

"It come the day after them last bummers straggle through. Ain't even sure how the stage make it. Mail set a while at Jumper Store. An' Ellie ain't date the letter neither. Can't read the ink on the front real good. So no tellin' how long it set."

"Eliza? Alive? I know she ain't…" but even as I say this, I knowed it wus true. True as anythin'.

"Don't yo' wants to hears 'bout David? David, Sarah Louise, he livin' up in New York. Gonna pass through Baltimore late March."

"Almost the end of April now," I say.

"True," Johnny say. "True."

I folds the letter, all the blurry, bleedin' ink the color of the Car'lina sky. Then I hike up my ol' muslin dress, tuck the letter in my boot.

"I makin' plans to leaves soon," Johnny say. "There work on the railroad in Canada. That whar' I bound. Gonna take a inland route. Through Ohio. I got kin already there now—from Ellicott place, gonna helps me out."

I almost mention Pa, but I don't. "Goodbye, Johnny," I say, an' looks at him, his face caught in some urgency, lak there be a young child pullin' at his coat-tails.

I feel unhooked from my body, lak I broken in two, an' part of me already dead, driftin' up to Heaven. I breathe deep, look around, try to get my bearin'.

"Yo' all right, Sarah?" Johnny axe. I nod, but the trees, the thicket, the path—I can't get them into focus. They all part of some big distant picture that I ain't a part of. Can't seem to step into. The best I can do is nod. So I nod. Then nod again.

Johnny grab hold of my shoulder. "Ain't no place sit down," he say.

"I gotta go now, Johnny," I whisper. "Don't needs to sit down, needs to get home."

"Me too, gal. Me too." Johnny kiss my forehead. I feel his warm lips against my skin.

"Take care," he whisper. Our eyes meet one last time; then he gone— his quick footsteps rustlin' in the brush, then nothin' as I lose sight of him. I ain't never see'd Johnny again.

To this day, ain't knowed what happen to him or his gal, if he take her to Canada or not. Somehow I don't think so.

I stand there—don't know how long—but long enough for the sky to darken an' large cold drops of rain come ploppin' down. *[Ms. Augustus stops here. There are some muffled sounds, and the tape is stopped. When it resumes, it is the next day.]*

October 19, 1937

After we gets done talkin' yesterday, I has me some supper. Sweet potatoes an' greens. Then, when the rain start, I get a notion to out into the street, feel them first drops.

If any neighbors see'd me, they think I a crazy, ol' lady hobblin' out the street in the rain. But when them drops come, I wants to feel them—same cold drops that come down when I stands on that path in Fayett'ville.

Houses lit up inside by stoves or candles, gaslight or electric, but the street be empty, an' I be lookin' at the sky.

The tears come, an' I want them. I think, *Ol' lady, yo' gonna catch yo' death of cold, but here yo' is.* An' then I think, *I ain't ready for my reckonin' yet.* It be my Eliza, my baby gal, Eliza Louise Payne, that keep me here. She alive then, an' she alive now. *[Ms. Augustus pauses, but the tape continues. After about ten seconds, she begins again.]*

I think Eliza tap me on the shoulder last night. Or maybe it be God come down from the sky. Or that Jesus stand with me in the rain an' give me my Eliza.

Maybe I just a ol' feeble woman, believin' what I wants. An' maybe that be all fittin'. *[Ms. Augustus pauses here, clears her throat. Then, she begins to speak.]*

I ain't never see'd Eliza. Never. I tell yo' that straight out. She come to me in my dreams, an' after I gets this letter, her face—the one I imagine for her—an' I puts her face on all them faceless angels I been seein' my whole life.

That the truth. Few times them angels come visit me, they all gots the same face, an' I knows that it be the face of my Eliza. *[The tape goes silent and is turned off. Then a few clicks are heard, and Ms. Augustus sighs and continues.]*

This the end of my story. Time after Surrender, there be many colored what be wantin' to head north. Pass by the Smith place. I travel that summer to Baltimore, to see L. B. Ma Eve, Ellie. But David never did show.

This here story I ain't goin' to tell yo'. I make it to Baltimore, to Ma Eve, Ellie, L. B., but I can't stay with them 'cause I have too much hate in my heart. Ain't proud of that. These wus peoples I trusted, but they betray me an' take away my baby gal.

I finds work at a white family on the edge of Baltimore city. Works for them for years. But I could never live around the streets I did at wartime. I once walked by Mrs. Johnston house, whar' she knowed me as Eliza, but I never knocked on that door. I heared she die near the end of the war, but I didn't have the heart to know.

I the only gal in the family that travel north. Ma, Hannah, Kate, Mar, they stays near the Smith place—whole lifes they stay south. They gets a piece of land to crop on. The cabin we lived in still standin' in Fayett'ville, but nobody there now.

Yo' wonderin' why David never come back? He die as he comin' to see me. Steamboat accident, ain't got nothin' to with the war. After all that danger an' bloodshed. He wus the only man I ever love.

L. B. come to me with the news. He get a notice from the steamboat company. An' he got a watch, David broken watch he brung me. That the last time I sees L. B.

When I heared David wus dead, I retreat inside myself. Part of me die too. Again.

I walkin' around those days in a haze. I bury the watch. There a Federal cemetery right close to whar' I work, an' I find a portion of earth by a big willow tree—a willow oak, almost lak the one in Fayett'ville—an' I bury it. [*There is a silence. Then the tape is shut off. When the tape machine is turned on the next day, Ms. Augustus begins mid-sentence.*]

October 20, 1937

… remember that love letter David write to me? The one Kate grab an' tease me with? I look for that last night again an' still couldn't finds it. So I ready to give up. Must be lost.

Tea? I got some steepin' on the stove. [*There are some shuffling sounds. Then the tape machine is clicked on and off a few times. Then some mumbling is heard in the background, but there are no discernable words.*]

When L. B. brung me the news from the steamboat company, I finally find it in me to axe 'bout Eliza. But he claim he don't know nothin'. Only that my baby gal get taken by a white family live in Canada. He say the family had just lost a baby gal, an' when they hear of Eliza they thinkin' she heaven-sent. The family happy to take her 'cause I wusn't in a position to raise a child. Especially one that look so white an' wus conceived in sin.

L. B. say it wus God will. Ellie—she might just have been a jealous creature—when I looks back—but Ellie an' Ma Eve meets the friends of this family when they in church. They passin' through, goin' back to Canada, an' I never gets the whole story. L. B. never come out an' say this, but he say that David knowed I wus pregnant all along, an' he tell Ma Eve he didn't want the baby if it born too light. So when Eliza born white, they pass it to this family to take north. So it be David idea that my baby be given away. *[There is some scratchiness and about fifteen seconds of dead time before Ms. Augustus resumes.]*

I done forgive them all the best I can. I a ninety-two-year-ol' woman now. It in the Lawd hands, I tell myself.

I never knowed my baby gal. Never knowed whar' to find her. I only knowed that some white family in Canada take her up as their own. *[There is a short pause of only a few seconds.]*

When we begins—yo' an' me, talkin'—I tell yo' that my story is a love story—between a man an' a woman, David an' me. But, really, it the story of mother love—for her baby, the one she never got to raise. *[There is another silence lasting a few seconds; then the tape machine is turned off.]*

J. B. Smith, believed to be Sarah Louise Augustus's owner. Etching found in the the Southern Historical Collection at the Wilson Library, University of North Carolina, Chapel Hill.

Addendum

I completed my lengthy transcription of the Sarah Louise Augustus tapes late one December night, after midnight. I knew I was close to the end and should finish—I had twenty-six freshman English papers coming in the following day.

I sat in my home office with Jake, our golden retriever mix, asleep on the small wool rug at my feet. I kept looking at the computer screen, scrolling back and forth through the lengthy manuscript, reading bits and pieces at random.

I had lived with this woman, Sarah Louise Augustus, for over four years. Her words had come to life under my fingertips as I listened to her voice, often working alone—except for Jake's loyal company—during many hours. Some nights I had far too much grading or committee work to spend time on my project, but on other nights, Sarah Louise's story became enmeshed with my own.

I write now at the end of a decade. We've recently elected and put into office our first African American president, so finishing Sarah Louise's story seems to have a greater urgency for me. Although I'm not sure exactly why.

I'd like to tell readers now the rest of Sarah Louise's story, but once again I have to ask for their understanding and forgiveness because I have no artful way to tell it. I simply wish to convey, as plainly as possible, how Sarah Louise's story and my own are related.

For a few weeks after I completed the transcription, I found myself, as I did on that first late night, scrolling back and forth through the computer file, which was over five hundred pages long. As I had on many nights, I read over bits and pieces, sort of amazed—stunned really because I was struck by the way in which I had become Sarah Louise, inhabiting her words, her language, her life. So much so that I was reluctant to let go.

I was changed. I mention this change in the book's introduction, where I promise to explain it more fully, in an addendum. True to my word, I will do it here.

Toward the end of spring semester 2009, after reviewing the manuscript for a few weeks, I was ready to print and share it—not with a general readership, but with Mrs. Henderson. Samantha had graduated a semester early and had left for a job in Seattle, where she is, to my knowledge, currently living. Samantha had come in and out of my life through the four years I transcribed, and she was the person through whom Mrs. Henderson and I stayed in contact. I had it in my head that I didn't want to speak to Mrs. Henderson again until I finished the entire project—although this requirement was certainly only in my head, and perhaps Mrs. Henderson felt slighted that I had not checked in with her directly.

I have no good excuse, only an apology to Mrs. Henderson, an apology I made to her in person when I saw her for a final time—with a printed copy of the manuscript in a box, and the big reel-to-reel tapes returned in the child's coffin.

Sam wasn't there, but our conversation began with my speaking about her. And Sam again became our intermediary.

Over the years, I had had a casual relationship with Sam. It was a relationship between professor and student, never especially close but seemingly warm. Whenever she was in the General Classroom Building, where I taught my classes and had my office, Sam would stop in to say hello and catch me up on courses she was taking, papers she was writing, professors she liked and disliked. Before she left for Seattle, I saw her at graduation and we gave each other a hug. "Stay in touch," she told me. "And let me know when you're done." She pulled away and looked at me. It was a look that said I'd already taken too long with the transcription and perhaps implied that I might never finish. "Here," she then said and pulled out a piece of paper from a pocket beneath her graduation robe. On it were her Seattle address, her cell phone number (which I already had), and her grandmother's phone number, street, and mailing address—a P.O. box in Harnett County.

Then she was gone. It was December, and I had to come to terms with the notion that Samantha's suspicion might be justified—perhaps I would never finish the transcription.

But after the academic year had ended, on a July afternoon, I found myself once again in Mrs. Henderson's living room. She hadn't changed much—or at least I couldn't see any changes. She still had her cane, and she was still slow but lithe as she greeted me. Before we sat down in her living room, however, she asked *me* to bring the tea tray—complete with fresh-brewed tea and homemade cookies—out to the living room for her.

"I never mind asking for help," she said as she sat down on the sofa. And she smiled her soft smile, a smile I had almost forgotten—radiating tolerance and generosity—and for which I felt immediately grateful.

I had placed the small coffin with the tapes neatly arranged inside on the floor in the foyer and had carried the manuscript box and placed it on the coffee table. It looked very official—I had ordered the box online from a company that made such boxes, and it was of brown, recycled cardboard, very clean and strong looking—a worthy container for a four-year project, I thought.

We could both feel Sam's presence. I asked Mrs. Henderson if she had heard from Sam recently.

"She writes me a letter once a month," Mrs. Henderson said. "Like clockwork. And I write her—once a month. Don't talk on the phone, but I do enjoy her letters." Mrs. Henderson lifted the ceramic teapot. "More, Professor?"

"Yes," I said. "Thank you." The tea was red and tasted naturally sweet. "This is good, very good," I remarked as I sipped. "What kind of tea is this?" I asked.

"Sassafras," Mrs. Henderson replied. "Homemade sassafras. Gathered here, dried, and treated. Good for what ails you, my mother used to say. She taught me about herbs, medicinal herbs, healthy herbs, especially teas."

"If you don't mind me asking," I interjected, and as I looked up, our eyes met, and I saw a secret in them. Something that Mrs. Henderson, who seemed without guile, was withholding. "Was your family, your mother from here? Is she still living?"

"No," Mrs. Henderson said. "I don't mind your asking, and no, my mother lived in New York and then Maryland, where the family had roots."

I put down my teacup, which rattled in my hand. "What part of Maryland? Baltimore?"

Mrs. Henderson nodded as she sipped her tea. She wore a woven, close-fitting dress, one that had a 60s style, although it seemed newer. It was linen-colored, with a lovely texture to it. Mrs. Henderson, a trim woman, sat with her knees together as if she were out visiting for the day, perhaps in some elegant place…. My thoughts were getting away from me.

We sat silently, but not awkwardly, for a few moments. July sunshine poured in from the big bay window, which was bowed and had a shelf not quite deep enough for a seat. A few houseplants were neatly displayed there—a rather large aloe and a snake plant. Beyond the window was the paved road in the distance, but there were absolutely no cars passing.

"What brought you to Fayetteville?" I asked.

"We have family land here, family land and ties. Another cookie?" Mrs. Henderson picked up the plate on which there were a dozen homemade sugar cookies neatly arranged. "It's been a long time," Mrs. Henderson added, and she glanced down the hall to the coffin in the foyer. Of course, Samantha kept me informed about your progress, but I didn't hear from *you*."

"Actually," I said, "the transcription took about four times longer to complete than I expected. I apologize, Mrs. Henderson. I do." I finished my cookie and took another off the plate. "They're very good. Excellent."

"I think it's me who must apologize, Professor Greene."

I nearly insisted that she call me Robin, as I had done during our first meeting, but then didn't. I sipped my tea.

Mrs. Henderson sat back, and again we found ourselves silent. Our conversation seemed to be happening in slow motion, and somehow I felt confused. The sunlight remained strong, and the room had an odd aura bathed in bright light, and then I smelled something starting to burn. Something from the kitchen—toast, I thought. I said nothing.

"Samantha didn't tell you," Mrs. Henderson said. "And you never asked." As I looked at Mrs. Henderson, I noticed that she appeared different, younger, stronger. "Samantha's middle name is Eliza."

The smell became strong, and suddenly I felt the need to stand up. So I did. And as I stood, I noticed there were shadows in the room, and they were moving. I looked out the large window and saw—or thought I saw—cloud-like figures dancing in a circle on the lawn. I stared.

"Pretty time of day," Mrs. Henderson said. "I love late afternoon when I can see the light dissipate. It's lovely, really, isn't it?

The angels danced in a circle. About eight of them. Young girls they were, with skin the color of ash. They wore bonnets, old-fashioned bonnets. And as they turned in their dance, I could see they were faceless.

Mrs. Henderson looked out the window. "There's never any traffic, and I'm grateful for that. The State nearly constructed a secondary highway through here in the 70s, but then the project was cancelled." I didn't look at Mrs. Henderson; her voice was soothing and unremarkable.

The angels danced and danced. Then the sun plunged a little lower across the flat sky, and the angels disappeared in the diminished light.

"Are you telling me something, Mrs. Henderson? Something I should have known?" I turned back to her and saw a face I hadn't seen before. A younger face, less African American, more…how shall I say this? More European.

"I want you to sit down," Mrs. Henderson insisted. "Because I do have something to tell you."

I felt tired, as if I had just completed a long journey and was now being asked to walk yet another mile. A mile that seemed impossible because it was the last.

Mrs. Henderson turned on the lamp on the end table by the sofa. It was a three-way bulb, and she turned it on to its brightest, then clicked it back to its lowest light. "There now. We can talk." Mrs. Henderson leaned back and made herself comfortable, as if she were about to watch a favorite television show or hear particularly good news, news for which she had waited a long time.

"The woman who interviewed Sarah Louise," she began, "was my aunt." Yellow light hung in the late afternoon air, and as the sun set, a halo shadow formed on the carpet. I thought about the dancing angels I'd just seen.

"Did Sam know that?" I sat deep in a wing-back arm chair with gold upholstery.

"Yes and no," Mrs. Henderson said. "Samantha isn't going to have any children, so we've never told her directly. She had surgery as a little girl, and she's… not able to bear children."

"I'm sorry to hear that," I said. I felt both confused and oddly confirmed by the news. I rubbed my head and felt a headache begin behind my left eye. This sort of pain, especially accompanied by light auras, sometimes signaled the coming of a migraine.

Meanwhile, I was having a sort of déjà vu. With eyes closed, I remembered running barefoot along the beach at Rockaway, New York. I could feel the hot sand against my feet. Then, I remembered Sarah Louise Augustus describing the little girl who took off her shoes by the Atlantic Ocean and how she shared in the girl's sense of freedom. The image merged with the words *thralldom* and *freedom*.

"So your mother was Eliza Payne's daughter," I said.

"That's right."

"Did Sarah Louise Augustus ever know?"

"She wrote her grandmother a note. I have it here. I have the whole story here." Mrs. Henderson patted the sofa, but there was nothing there.

"Where's here?" I asked. And then I no longer cared. I saw the connections. I'd been a reader my whole life. I'd read good and bad novels—read them tirelessly because I loved stories, loved mysteries, loved romances. But frankly these kinds of books, dependant on a series of unlikely connections, had always struck me as far-fetched. Yet here I was now, involved in the same kind of labyrinthine, far-fetched plot. Before I could say anything more, Mrs. Henderson interrupted.

"I have to ask you, Professor Greene, how has your time been? These last four years, I mean. The time you've been transcribing our story."

"Difficult," I said. "Difficult." My headache began to throb, and now it was a full-fledged migraine, a deep pounding behind the left eye. It made me unfocused, almost as confused as Sarah Louise had been, rising up after being chloroformed and gang-raped. "Why withhold all this information?" I asked.

"Because the story was already there, and I wanted you to find it. A white, educated woman, a reader."

"The interviewer," I began, still rubbing my forehead above my left eye. "When…"

"That part, who the interviewer was, I didn't learn until her death in 1975. Her daughter, who is also now dead, sent me a packet—the story—in a series of handwritten letters, notes, other correspondences. I've never completely sorted through them. But when I do, I want you to write a book."

Then, Mrs. Henderson excused herself and disappeared into the kitchen. I couldn't think. My head pounded, and the Atlantic Ocean roared in my brain. It was as if I were unwillingly meditating—trying to conjure thoughts, rather than to be satisfied without them.

"A minute," Mrs. Henderson's voice called from the kitchen. "I thought I'd make us a new pot of tea. Special, for headaches. And get a little something to eat." I closed my eyes and found myself almost weeping.

When Mrs. Henderson returned, she served her special tea, and soon my headache, while not gone, was much improved. She drew the living room curtains closed and, along with the tea, she had put out some white bread sandwiches, cut, without crusts, on a platter.

"Pimento?" I asked, lifting one.

"And tuna salad," Mrs. Henderson looked at me, her chin lifting slightly as if she wanted to ask me a question but had just changed her mind.

"Good," I said, and bit into one. "Tuna." And I then thought for a moment I would tell Mrs. Henderson about my own difficulties, about which she had almost inquired. I thought I would tell her how Sarah Louise's description of her rape had triggered memories of my own rape during adolescence. I had been attacked outside my dorm, during my sophomore year in college. I was living in New York City and never reported the incident because I had been out very late and felt partly responsible. When I found myself pregnant, I had a legal abortion. I never told my parents, and only years later did I confess—first, to my best friend and then to my husband—what had happened. But confession of trauma and dealing with trauma are two different things. I had done the former but not the latter. And now, during my late night transcription sessions, Sarah Louise's story had brought me back, head-on to these powerful memories, which flooded out and created an intense generalized anxiety and a prolonged period of insomnia.

I didn't seek out formal therapy—perhaps I was too afraid. And as I recovered some specific memories concerning my rape, I relived them and went through a period during which I couldn't allow my husband to touch me. I began staying in my study, and not going to bed—working at night, often through the night, cat-napping, then resuming work in the morning before school.

After about three months, my husband moved out. He explained he couldn't live with the stranger I had become.

When I finally found the strength, toward the end of my project, to invite my husband back into the house, it was too late. He had been seeing another woman, for we had been separated almost a year.

Meanwhile, our younger son, Ben, had gone away to college, and my role as mother had changed. He was our second and last child, and I grieved for him and for the mother I could no longer be.

My husband did return, and after seeing a professional counselor, we decided to try to make our marriage work.

The process of mending what was broken was a long and difficult one. But I had become a stronger and more psychologically-integrated person. I had learned a lot about loss, and I believe it was Sarah's story—page after page, month after month, year after year—that finally allowed me to forgive my husband and reconcile the pieces of my life.

I said none of this to Mrs. Henderson, and I regret that I did not speak my heart. Instead I asked about her herb garden, then told her that I had a set of papers to grade, which was true, and needed to get home.

As I stood up to leave, Mrs. Henderson and I hugged—a small yet important gesture. She promised to call me when she finished reading the manuscript and assured me that she would soon mail the packet of documents she had discussed. She wanted some more time with them and wasn't quite prepared to let them go.

CODA

The bad news—and I hate to end my book on this sad note—but Mrs. Henderson is dead. And the tapes and all the correspondence Mrs. Henderson promised to share with me are also gone. A couple of months after our visit that day, a house fire of suspicious origin burned the structure to the ground. They think it was electrical. Mrs. Henderson was asleep inside, and she burned to death, along with all the correspondence, the tapes, and all other records of Sarah Louise Augustus's story. Nothing remained.

Nothing but the relationships and my manuscript survive. So there's nothing to prove anymore. No mystery to solve, no tapes to authenticate, though after completing the transcription, I had planned to revisit the

Library of Congress. In this final period, I had contacted a young African American historian there who seemed interested. I had hope that with the correspondence Mrs. Henderson promised me, I could make a stronger case.

But after Mrs. Henderson's death, I decided to find a publisher for the manuscript and move on to other projects. For now I believe that Sarah Louise Augustus's story—told in 1937, recorded on wax cylinders and later re-recorded on magnetic tape, delivered first to a relative in Harnett County, North Carolina, where it survived in a child's coffin, and then transcribed by the hands of a white English professor—has come full circle to find its final resting place.

Discussion Questions

The following are suggested discussion questions, appropriate for book clubs and educational groups. Robin is available to custom-design additional questions for your club or group.

1. Discuss how Sarah Louise is at once the victim of circumstance and the heroine who triumphs over circumstance. Are there moments when she is clearly a victim? Moments when she is clearly a heroine? Discuss.

2. When Sarah Louise gets gang-raped, she unconsciously wanders off. Yet her unconscious action leads to her escape and freedom. Discuss moments in your own lives when a seemingly unconscious action led to a significantly positive outcome. Some might say that Sarah Louise's action is indicative of "women's way of knowing," which is different than the ways that men "know." Discuss.

3. Upon her trip home to Fayetteville, Sarah Louise encounters Southern white men who verbally suggest that they might take sexual advantage of her. What prevents them? Is it Johnny's presence? Are the men held back by their own ethics? Is the situation too public for them to act upon their sexual insinuations? Or is there something about Sarah Louise's new persona that demands respect?

4. What "allows" men to act on their sexual aggressions and what holds them back? Discuss.

5. Although there is sexual attraction between Johnny and Sarah, neither of them acts on that attraction. Why? Discuss.

6. In Augustus, readers get a close look at chattel slavery. Discuss the slave system in terms of the information presented in Augustus.

7. Most Americans agree that slavery's legacy is profound. Discuss that legacy in terms of your personal experience and as member of your community.

8. Every plantation or slave-owning farm had its own culture based on the culture of the community, of the slave owners, and on the home culture of the particular group of enslaved people. Discuss the culture of the Smith Plantation.

9. There is much about Sarah Louise's faceless angels and Mr. Crow. Weigh in on how these "magical" figures might—or might not—cast doubt on Sarah Louise's "reliability" as a narrator.

About the Author

Robin Greene is professor of English and Writing, director of the Writing Center, and editor of Longleaf Press at Methodist University in Fayetteville, North Carolina. Greene has published two collections of poetry, *Memories of Light* and *Lateral Drift*, and a collection of women's birthing narratives, *Real Birth*. She regularly publishes her poetry and nonfiction in journals. Greene is married and has two grown sons, Daniel and Benjamin.

Robin Greene is available for workshops and discussion groups. She can be reached by email (info@robingreene-writer.com) or through her website at http://www.robingreene-writer.com/

Photo by Radu Andriescu